# The One You Can't Forget

## RONI LOREN

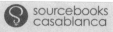
sourcebooks
casablanca

Copyright © 2018 by Roni Loren
Cover and internal design © 2018 by Sourcebooks, Inc.
Cover design by Dawn Adams/Sourcebooks, Inc.
Cover image © PeopleImages/Getty Images

Published by Sourcebooks Casablanca, an imprint of Sourcebooks, Inc.
P.O. Box 4410, Naperville, Illinois 60567-4410
(630) 961-3900
Fax: (630) 961-2168
sourcebooks.com

Printed and bound in Canada.
MBP 10 9 8 7 6 5 4 3 2 1

*To the Possum Posse, because writing would
be a lonely job (even for this introvert)
without great friends like you in my life.*

# chapter
# ONE

THERE'S A REASON WHY ROMANTIC MOVIES ONLY SHOW the beginning of people's love stories. That's the exciting part: the thrill, the magic. There is something undeniably enticing about the ripe sense of possibility. What will their life become now that they've found each other?

Well, Rebecca Lindt could tell them. They had about a one-third chance of maintaining their happily-ever-after, a one-third chance of staying married but being miserable about it, and a one-third likelihood of ending up in front of someone like her, battling it out over who gets to keep the Le Creuset pot collection or the riding lawn mower, even though neither of them cooks or cuts their own grass.

Today's battle of the exes was over a crotch-sniffing standard poodle that somehow had made it into the office and the divorce mediation session. The wife was claiming the dog was her Official Emotional Companion (the words always spoken with utter reverence and implied capitalization by her lawyer) and therefore had to remain with her. Rebecca's client, Anthony, was vibrating with barely leashed anger as he tried to explain through clenched teeth to the mediator that his wife had always hated the dog and that the poodle should remain with him.

Prince Hairy, the fluffy beast in question, didn't seem to care either way. He just wanted to hunt beneath the table and give a filthy how-do-you-do with a wet nose to the private parts of every person in the meeting. Rebecca sent up a silent thank-you that she was wearing a pantsuit, but that hadn't stopped her from feeling slightly assaulted every time the dog moved her way.

A wet tongue licked her ankle, sending a shudder through her, and she gently shooed the dog away, trying to keep her expression unhorrified and professional. But Raul, the other attorney, lifted a knowing brow at her. She had no doubt he'd be telling her later that she owed the dog a drink for all the action.

"Prince Hairy has been with us since he was a puppy," the wife said, her tone curt, as if she was biting the words in half. "I named him. I take him to the groomer. He's home with me when you're at work. My therapist says that he's part of my recovery. He is my Official Emotional Companion."

"*Emotional companion*," Anthony sneered, his calm breaking. "Come on, Daphne. Your emotional companion was the goddamned contractor you screwed in my bed!"

"Mr. Ames," the mediator said, a schoolteacher-style warning in her voice. "You both chose mediation to avoid court, but in order for that to work, I need you to keep the accusations—"

Anthony scoffed. "Accusations? They're not accusations if they're true."

Rebecca placed a staying hand on Anthony's arm, silencing him and sending her own warning message. *I've got this. Calm down.*

Anthony deflated beside her, and Rebecca took over. "I think what Mr. Ames is trying to say is that there is no paperwork designating Prince Hairy as an emotional companion. He may, perhaps, be a comfort to Mrs. Ames, but he is not an official therapy dog." He was just Daphne's best bargaining chip because Anthony was ridiculously in love with the canine menace. "Therefore, that should not factor into the decision of where Prince Hairy will live. The dog was adopted under Anthony's name. He is the one to take him for walks and to vet visits. Since Mr. Ames plans to remain in the home, he'll have adequate space for him."

"*What?*" Daphne demanded, her words ripping through the veneer of her pretend calm. "Are you effing kidding me right now? You *are not* getting the house."

*Effing.* Rebecca smirked. They'd all agreed to no foul language during mediation. Daphne was apparently willing to fudge on the rules like she'd fudged on her marriage vows.

The mediator gave a deep sigh, clearly questioning why she'd chosen such a career path in the first place. Fridays made one do that anyway, but this one was going for the gold medal of Fridayness. "Mrs. Ames, we all agreed to keep our voices at a normal level."

But Daphne was having none of it. Her lips were puckered as if she'd sucked a lemon, and there was fire brewing in her blue eyes. A fuse ready to blow.

"I'm getting the house," Anthony said simply.

Rebecca smiled inwardly. *And three, two, one…*

Daphne stood, her manicured hands pressed flat against the table and a dark lock of hair slipping out of her French knot. "You will *not* take my house from me, you worthless piece of shit. I just spent two years remodeling it."

"And screwing the contractor."

"Mr. and Mrs.—"

"It's mine!" Her palm slapped the table, which earned a bark from Prince Hairy. "And I slept with Eric because you neglected me and were never home, and you... you..." Her gaze zeroed in on Anthony as she found her weapon. "You were *bad in bed*!"

Anthony bristled, but Rebecca gripped his arm tighter, praying he'd weather the low blow. When well prepped, people could deal with a lot of insults in mediation or court, but she'd learned men had a figurative and literal soft spot when their manhood was called into question.

"Mrs. Ames," the mediator admonished.

"Excuse me," Rebecca said, her tone utterly calm, which would only make Daphne look more out of order. "Can we have a minute? I'd like a private word with my client, and I think everyone could use a break."

The mediator's shoulders sagged with resignation, and she adjusted her glasses. "Five-minute break. Everyone needs to come back ready to be civil, or we're going to have to end the mediation and let this go to court."

Daphne huffed, and Raul soothed her with gentle words as he offered her a bottle of sparkling water. She took a long sip, her gaze still shooting daggers at Anthony. Raul nodded at Rebecca. "We're going to take a little walk and bring Prince Hairy out for a bathroom break. We'll be back in five."

"Thanks," Rebecca said, knowing that taking the dog with him was their version of posturing—acting like the dog was Daphne's already—but Rebecca wasn't worried. This was all going exactly as she'd planned.

Once the door to the conference room shut, Anthony turned to her, his perfectly styled brown hair a mess from him raking his fingers through it. "I'm not bad in bed. She's lying."

"Anthony."

"Women always, you know, have a good time, and Daphne always, you know…" A hurt look filled his eyes as he let the sentence trail off.

A pang of sympathy went through Rebecca even though her patience for hand-holding was low on a good day and nearly nonexistent after a court battle this morning and mediation this afternoon. Anthony's head was no doubt whirling. Was he bad in bed? Had his wife faked her enjoyment? Was that why she'd strayed?

Rebecca reached out and gave his shoulder a gentle squeeze. "Anthony, you know she's just throwing out words to rile you up. I told you she'd say the ugliest things to get you off your game. This is a standard emasculation tactic."

He blinked. "What?"

"The easiest way to knock a guy off his game is to insult his penis size or his ability in bed. Men seem to have some inborn need to defend against that type of insult." In her head she called it the Dick Kick, but she couldn't bring herself to say that to a client. "On the other side, men insult the woman by saying she's frigid or ugly, getting fat or old. When cornered, people strike right at the clichéd insecurities. It's completely unoriginal and the tactic of someone who knows she's losing the fight. It means we're winning."

Anthony gave her a you've-got-to-be-kidding-me look. "Winning? She's going to get her therapist to label Prince a therapy dog. She has that guy wrapped around her finger because she's paying way more than he's worth. Watch. Then I'll lose Prince, too."

His voice caught and he glanced away, hiding the tears that jumped to his eyes at the thought of losing his dog.

Rebecca frowned. She'd never had a pet because her father had deemed them unsanitary and high maintenance, but she was regularly amazed at how people would throw away everything to keep a pet or some sentimental item. She always preferred to have the client who was less attached to those things. Sentimentality made people irrational. *You can take the eighty-thousand-dollar car as long as I can keep my mother's china*.

She didn't get it. But, of course, when the mother you worship leaves your family without warning when you're in fourth grade to go start a new family, you learn not to get attached to much. Nothing was permanently yours.

But Anthony was her client, and he'd told her in no uncertain terms that the dog was the number one priority. He was paying Rebecca to get what he wanted, so she would accomplish that because she was good at her job and not there to judge whether a crotch-sniffer trumped a million-dollar home.

Rebecca patted his arm. "I promise. This is going exactly how we want it to. As long as they don't have any curveballs we didn't prepare for, what we discussed will work."

He looked up. "Curveballs?"

"Yes, any treasured items you didn't tell me about that could make you fold." Rebecca glanced at the door, making sure they were still alone, and casually rose from her chair and leaned over the table to flip open Raul's folder. She read the neat handwriting upside down. There was a jotted list of notes and talking points. She recognized and expected most of them. *House. 401(k). Cars. Time-share. Antique furniture. Jewelry.* All things she'd gone over with Anthony. But one buried near the bottom caught her eye.

She quickly flipped the folder closed and settled back into her seat. She pinned Anthony with a look. "Tell me about the record collection."

His eyes widened. "What?"

"They have it on their list to discuss."

"They have *what*?" A bright flush of anger filled Anthony's face. "Those are *my* goddamned records. I've been collecting them since I was fourteen."

*Uh-oh.* "Have you added to the collection since you were married?"

"Yes, but—"

*Great.* "Is it worth a significant amount of money, or would it be hard to replace?"

His face paled. "I have original editions. Some signed. Some would be near impossible to replace. She can't have it. That collection is… It's my childhood."

A sinking feeling settled in Rebecca's stomach. "The dog or the records, Anthony? If you have to die on one hill, which one is it?"

"You want me to pick between my dog and a collection I've spent twenty years putting together? That's impossible."

"We could take this to court. You know we'll have

the upper hand." She'd suggested this from the start. They'd both make more money if they went to court and showed fault. They had evidence. Daphne wouldn't come across well. A big win would further Rebecca's chances for making partner and would most likely get Anthony everything he wanted. Win-win.

Anthony shook his head and pressed his fingers to his brow. "I don't think I can handle dragging this out. But my dog or my records?"

Rebecca shook her head, her tone no-nonsense. "I will work to get both, but if I have to cut one in order to get the other, I need to know which one to drop."

But the door opened before he could answer, and everyone filed back in. Raul and Daphne looked smug as they walked the dog back into the office. Prince Hairy proceeded to duck beneath the table and plop down on Anthony's feet.

Anthony gave Rebecca a forlorn look.

She lifted a brow, and he nodded.

*The dog wins.*

The mediator took her seat. "Okay, why don't we start again now that everyone has cooled down."

Rebecca folded her hands on the table and straightened her back. *Poker time.* "I've talked with my client, and I believe we have a workable compromise. Mr. Ames will give Mrs. Ames the dog, his old records, the Mercedes, and her antique doll collection in exchange for the house and the SUV."

Anthony went tense in his chair, and Rebecca could feel the what-the-hell-are-you-doing vibe coming from him, but she didn't look his way.

Daphne's eyes went comically wide. "My doll collection? That's mine anyway."

"It was acquired during the marriage." Rebecca kept her tone professionally bored.

"The doll collection is off the table," Raul said smoothly.

Rebecca made a note on her legal pad. "Then the record collection is, too."

"Fine." Daphne nodded. "Take your crappy records."

Raul frowned, his sentimental bargaining chip slipping out of reach.

Rebecca fought a smirk. One down. "Okay, Ms. Ames, so you get Prince Hairy and will be solely responsible for his care and vet bills. Mr. Ames will get the house and will buy you out of your half. Agreed?"

"No," Daphne said, glancing at her lawyer with a do-something look. "I'm not leaving here without the house. I picked every paint color, every tile, chose every piece of furniture. It's *mine*."

"You could move in with your parents, Daph," Anthony said casually, playing his part again. "Until you find another place."

She blanched. "I'd rather kill myself than live with them. I'm not leaving my house."

Anthony propped his chin on his fist as if settling in for a really good movie.

Rebecca tried not to grimace at Daphne's comment. She'd never gotten used to how easily people tossed around those dramatic words. Threats of suicide and murder rolled off people's tongues all the time, especially in divorce mediation. She knew it was just hyperbole, but in high school, two people had made those threats and then carried them through. No one had listened. They'd thought it was an exaggeration. *She'd* thought it was an exaggeration. They'd all been wrong. So very wrong.

Her stomach flipped over and she took a sip of water, trying to shake off the memories that were like the off-key elevator music of her life, never far in the background and always ready to turn up louder. She clenched her jaw, forcing her expression to remain neutral. "It seems we're at an impasse."

"Mr. and Mrs. Ames," the mediator said, "if we don't resolve this here, it will have to go to court. Try to remember that compromise isn't losing. Seeking things just for revenge feels satisfying in the short term but will drag this process out, cost you more money with your lawyers, and create more stress for you. You will be dealing with each other for a long time. If we can resolve this here, you can walk away and not have to see each other again."

"Well, there's a bonus," Anthony muttered.

"I'm not afraid to go to court to get my house," Daphne said, her tone frosty.

Rebecca set her pen down and focused her attention on Daphne. "Mrs. Ames, I'm sure your counsel has warned you that if this goes to court, you're going to risk losing more than you will if we can come to an agreement here. Texas allows fault to be shown in divorce. We have proof of your affair. These details will be fair game in court."

Daphne wet her lips, and her throat worked.

Rebecca cocked a brow in a way that she hoped conveyed, *Yes, all those dirty details you're replaying in your head right now? They will be exposed in court. And no one is going to side with you after that because no one likes a cheater.*

She had watched the incriminating video at Anthony's

side since he'd wanted to see the whole thing but didn't want to do it alone. Daphne had forgotten about the security cameras her husband had installed outside by their pool, and she'd put on quite an X-rated show with the contractor one night when Anthony had been out of town. The explicitness of the video had made Rebecca feel equal parts uncomfortable and fascinated. She'd definitely never had that kind of intense sex. She'd never had the urge to literally rip someone's clothes off to get to them. Frankly, she hadn't realized people actually did that outside of movies. She couldn't fathom being that... feral with anyone.

But seeing it had made Anthony vomit, and that was when Rebecca had understood the real story.

The man had truly loved his wife, and his world had just been ripped in half. He'd thought he was in one kind of movie and had ended up in another. He wasn't the hero. He was the fool. He'd wound up in the wrong third of the statistics.

So Rebecca had no qualms about taking Daphne down. Cheaters deserved what they got. And, too bad for Daphne, they were Rebecca's specialty.

"You're trying to scare me," Daphne said finally.

Rebecca leaned back in her chair and crossed her legs, relishing that calm, cool control that filled her veins in these moments. "I'm simply stating the facts, Mrs. Ames. Ask your lawyer if he thinks I'm exaggerating. If we go to court, you will be deemed at fault and the settlement will most definitely reflect that."

Raul folded his hands and rested them on the table, his own poker face in place. "We're prepared to go to court if necessary. My client will not bend on the house."

"Mr. Ames, what would it take to compromise on the house?" the mediator asked. "If there's nothing, then we should just move this to court."

Anthony settled back in his chair, arms crossed casually, expression smugly confident. Rebecca wanted to cheer. The game had finally clicked for him. He was playing his part. He shrugged. "Sounds like I'd be better off going to court. That way I'll get the house, the ridiculous dolls, the better car, and my dog. You'll end up back home with your parents. You can call Eric and have him remodel your parents' crappy seventies ranch to make your room real nice."

Daphne's jaw flexed, and Raul put a hand on her wrist as if sensing what was about to happen, but it was too late. She was already talking. "Fine. Take the stupid dog! I know that's what you're after. He's a filthy, dumb waste of space anyway."

Prince Hairy lifted his head beneath the table and whimpered, as if he recognized the description and took offense.

Daphne waved a dismissive hand. "Take him and whatever else of your junk you want. Just give me the house, my furniture, and my car. Then, you never have to see me again. I'm done with this crap."

Rebecca gave a Mona Lisa smile.

Anthony's chair squeaked as he sat forward, victory all over his face. "You've got a deal."

Raul closed his eyes and shook his head.

But the mediator pressed her hands together in a silent clap. "Fantastic. Well done. I'm so glad you two could make this work. The agreement will be drafted up, and we'll be finished with all of this."

Another love story ended with a signature on a dotted line.

Daphne grabbed her purse and stood, her chair rolling behind her and banging against the wall. "You're such a smug asshole, thinking you're so much better than me. If you wouldn't have treated me—"

"That's enough, Mrs. Ames," Rebecca said. "You've said your piece."

Her attention swung Rebecca's way. "And I don't care that you're some famous survivor or whatever. You're a stuck-up, know-it-all bitch!"

"Daphne..." Raul warned.

But Rebecca held on to her polite smile, the words rolling off her like water on a windshield. Let Daphne have her tantrum. People had all kinds of preconceived notions about Rebecca when they figured out she was *the* Rebecca Lindt who'd survived the Long Acre High School prom shooting—that crying redheaded girl who was rolled out bleeding on a stretcher on the nightly news twelve years ago. These notions often involved shining light and singing angels, or that she had some secret sauce recipe on how to live a meaningful life. But she had news for them. Surviving a tragedy didn't make you magical. It made you tough. Not special. Just lucky. "Have a nice day, Mrs. Ames."

Daphne made a disgusted noise and flounced out the door without a goodbye. Her "emotional companion" didn't even lift his head. Raul gave Rebecca a vaguely apologetic look. "Sorry about that. She's just...processing all this."

Rebecca smirked. "That's one term for it. But no worries, I've been called worse. Probably by you on some days."

He chuckled as he slipped his things into his brief-case. "Only when I lose. And only respectfully."

She rolled her eyes but didn't feel any malice toward Raul. She called him a smarmy bastard on the regular. Rebecca lifted her hand in thanks to the mediator as the woman escaped the room and probably headed to the nearest bar.

"I heard your dad's running for state senate," Raul said as Rebecca walked him to the door. "You gonna take his place when he's elected?"

Rebecca shrugged. "Who knows? I've got to earn my way to partner here like anyone else, so it's not up to me. But my last name's already on the building, so it'd be economical not to have to change it."

He laughed. "Right? You'd be doing them a favor. But I bet you have it in the bag anyway, no nepotism needed. Tell your dad I said good luck with the election."

"Thanks, will do. Have a good weekend."

They shook hands, and Raul followed the mediator out.

When Rebecca closed the door and turned around to face her client, Anthony pushed his chair back, let out a whoop of victory, and patted his thigh. "Come here, boy."

The dog scrambled to his feet and leapt into Anthony's lap with glee. The giant poodle was way too big to be a lapdog, but Anthony didn't seem to mind. He buried his face in the dog's copper-colored fur, which really did look like the color of Prince Harry's hair, and let go a litany of mushy endearments.

Prince licked his owner's face and made happy, huffing dog noises. Rebecca crossed her arms and shook her head as she stepped closer, amused. "I could've won you a lot more money *and* the house."

Anthony looked up, absently rubbing the dog's neck. "I know."

"But the dog is worth it?"

"Of course he is. Look at him." Anthony cupped Prince's snout.

Rebecca eyed the ball of fur skeptically. "Well, if you're happy, I'm happy."

"Well, 'happy' isn't the word, but relieved," Anthony said. "Going to court would be too hard." He looked down at the dog as if eye contact with Rebecca was too much. "Every time I look at Daph, even with all the anger, I can't help but see the girl I fell in love with."

Rebecca tilted her head. "Even when she's calling you an asshole?"

"Yeah. I know that version of her I loved is not in there anymore, but I can still remember that feeling of when we first got together, that high. Love ends, but it leaves… I don't know, *imprints* on you. Like the person I used to be still loves the person *she* used to be. I don't want to have to see her in court and drag this out. I can't watch that video again. It'd feel like having my guts ripped out fresh all over again. Like I've failed at something I thought couldn't fail."

Rebecca frowned. "I'm sorry."

"Me too." He leaned back in the chair with a tired look, stroking Prince's neck. "You ever have a moment you wish you could just go back and change? I wonder what my life would look like right now if I hadn't offered Daphne my umbrella the day we met, if I had just kept walking."

*A moment she could change?* Rebecca tucked her hair behind her ears, her ribs cinching tight and her composure trying to falter. "No amount of wondering can change the past."

Prince jumped from Anthony's lap and settled at his feet, obviously exhausted by divorce mediation and philosophical conversation. Anthony absently brushed the dog hair from his slacks. "I know, and they say we shouldn't want to change anything. The butterfly effect and fading photos in *Back to the Future* and all that. But would you change one moment if you could?"

Even though she tried to stop it, memories flashed through Rebecca's mind like a gory movie. Thoughtless words. A boy seething with something sharp and danger-ous. Because of her. Blood. Screams. The sound of gunshots. She swallowed past the dryness in her throat and ignored the phantom pain in her leg. "In a heartbeat."

Anthony nodded solemnly like he was a comrade-in-arms. "Me too. I'd walk right by Daphne and let the rain soak her to the bone."

Rebecca smoothed the wrinkles in her pants, trying to re-center herself, to push away the ugliness. "If you'd passed her by, maybe you wouldn't have Prince."

Anthony's staid face broke into a slow smile. "You're right. And he's the best."

"He better be," she said with a tight laugh.

He rubbed the dog's head. "To be honest, this is all I need. I'd rather be broke than go home to an empty house. The past week that Prince has stayed with Daphne has been rough. There's nothing more depressing than knowing no one is waiting for you at home. That no one cares if you show up or not."

The words pinged through Rebecca, hitting places she'd rather not examine. She forced a smile. "Right."

She stepped over to pet the dog, who immediately buried his nose between her legs. She took a big step back. "Well, I think this guy will definitely be happy to see you at the end of the day."

"Yes. I don't like to brag, but I *am* his favorite crotch."

Rebecca chuckled. "High honor."

"Indeed." Anthony tapped Prince to get him to his feet and stood to shake Rebecca's hand. "Thanks for everything. I won't say it's been fun, but at least it was quick."

*Sounds like most of the dates I've had in my life.*

"You're welcome. Sorry we had to meet under these circumstances," she said and then walked Anthony out. Those were her standard parting words, but she meant them. People hoped to never need someone like her, and she found it a little depressing to know that this seemingly decent guy who'd loved his wife had ended up here, too.

But it was a story she saw every day. Anthony had bought into the infatuation model that was sold to everyone as "true love." *Trust that rush of endorphins and attraction at the beginning, and all will be okay. It won't matter that the person is a completely impractical and incompatible choice. Believe the feelings. There's magic at work.*

But feelings lied, and magic wasn't real.

Rebecca had spent her high school years as a hopeless romantic, in love with her best friend, thinking they were fated to be together, believing she was one of those special girls who'd get her happy ending. She'd even written a time capsule letter with her friends senior year, painting her perfect movie-like romance that she was going to have with her crush. She was going to be

Sally to his Harry, Joey to his Pacey, Rachel to his Ross. Turns out she was Duckie. Or Dawson. Or worse, the geek with an underwear fetish from *Sixteen Candles*. Finn, the guy she'd hung all her hope on, had been in love with someone else the whole time. Still was.

She'd closed that chapter and wished him well, but she hadn't forgotten the lesson. She also got a refresher every day at work. Love wasn't just a risk. It was a bad bet. If she had to argue the case for it in court, the evidence would be stacked so high against it that she wouldn't have a shot at winning. A lasting, loving marriage was a unicorn. And the person who loved the deepest in a relationship—the romantic, the idealist—was the one whose guts got ripped out in the end. No, thanks.

Rebecca paused in the hallway after Anthony left and looked at the clock, which was ticking closer to six. She considered calling it a day, but Anthony's words about going home to an empty house were pulsing at the back of her brain like a bad headache. Maybe she should go out tonight. Have a drink at a bar. Maybe call one of her friends to go with her. Shake off that antsy feeling his words had stirred up.

She headed back to her office to give her email one last check and to make sure she had everything buttoned up before she called anyone. The most recent email was flagged and in bold to mark it as urgent. All emails from her dad were urgent. She clicked to open it.

Rebecca,

The firm's charity fund hasn't been assigned for this fiscal year. I'm putting you in charge of it. Choose a charity by the end of next week that will match up well with my campaign platform. Something everyone can get behind. Nothing animal-related. Nothing controversial. Needs to be people and community focused. We did the Long Acre Fund last year, so we can't do that again. Bethany can get you on the account once you've selected something.

Best,
W. L.

His initials, not *Dad*, because at work they were not father and daughter.

Rebecca groaned. She didn't mind helping her dad, but the last thing she needed was another project on her plate, especially something that was all about the PR and not the actual charity. There was no pushing back on this kind of stuff, though. Lawyers who wanted to be partners took on extra things. And the daughter of William Lindt did not complain about added responsibility. She'd been taught that early on.

With a sigh, she got up and poured herself a cup of coffee and let go of any plans to go out tonight. If she had to make time to research charities next week, she needed to wrap up all her normal work tonight or it'd be hanging over her all weekend.

She started by making notes in the Ames file. Twice she caught her eyes drifting to the screenshots from the videos. She couldn't see much of Daphne besides the rapt look on her face, but the tense, flexing muscles of the mostly naked contractor were hard to look away from.

Rebecca usually found herself more attracted to men in suits, men who had a certain amount of polish, but maybe there was something to be said for a guy who was a little rougher around the edges and worked with his hands.

Love was a bad bet, but sex with a hot guy… That didn't sound so bad.

She rolled her eyes at her R-rated thoughts and forced herself to finish her work. Before long, the sunset cast swaths of burnt-orange light over her desk, reminding her that she should be getting home.

To her empty apartment.

Where no one was waiting.

And no one would be getting naked with her.

She grunted and leaned back in her chair, rubbing the bridge of her nose. What was with her tonight? She couldn't let Anthony's words or these photos get to her.

She lived a busy life, was good at her job, had friends. She was comfortable being alone. If she felt pent-up sexual frustration sometimes, she knew how to handle things on her own. Frankly, taking care of things solo was more satisfying than the few awkward encounters with men she'd had along the way, and it saved her from having to explain the ugly, pitted scars on her leg—always a fun conversation. Her life worked.

Anthony hadn't wanted to be alone, and look where that had landed him—in a messy divorce, crying over his dog. She wanted no part of that kind of drama.

With renewed resolve, she closed the file she'd been working on and shut everything down. This had been a good week. She'd won two cases. She'd gotten a few things in place for her father's campaign. She deserved to be celebrating, not ruminating in her office.

A new plan formed quickly in her head. She'd pick up her favorite wine from the store down the street, get takeout and dessert from that fancy Italian restaurant that had just opened, and rent a new movie with a pretty guy to look at.

She wasn't craving a date. She was just craving a break and a little indulgence. She didn't need anyone else to give her that. She could handle it on her own.

She'd been doing it all her life.

Why stop now?

# chapter
# TWO

WES GARRETT PEEKED THROUGH THE CRACK IN THE door to the apartment inside, eyeing the small group of women laughing and drinking champagne. One was wearing a party hat with a big light-up dick on it. He shut the door and leaned against the wall in the hallway. "I can't believe I'm considering this."

Suzie grinned wickedly at him, her lip ring glinting in the hallway light. "Don't be such a prude, Garrett. What happened to that wild, try-anything-once guy I used to know?"

His jaw clenched. "Are you really asking me that?"

She waved a dismissive hand. "You know that's not what I mean. I don't want post-apocalyptic you. That sucked."

"Ya think?"

She rolled her eyes. "I'm talking about the you before everything went to shit. You've swung too far in the other direction." She shrugged. "Walking the straight and narrow doesn't mean not having any fun or, you know, a sense of humor."

"Suze…"

"This is a *good* gig." She pinned him with her gaze. "Three hundred bucks for two hours of your time. All you're going to be doing is teaching drunk chicks how to cook simple things. You teach cooking every day. This is no different."

He gave her a droll look. "I teach cooking to teenagers. I get to wear my chef's whites. I don't have to cook naked."

"Ugh. You're not going to be *naked*. That would be a major kitchen hazard. Just…shirtless. And hey, with all your tattoos, you have some added coverage."

*Christ*. This was what his life had come to? From four-star restaurants to this? He'd thought teaching at an after-school program was a giant tumble down the staircase from his chef dreams, but this was a new level. The basement. At least with the kids, he could convince himself he was training future chefs. Here he would be the special of the day. "I don't know."

She reached out and grabbed his hands, her face earnest beneath the fringe of bright-pink hair. "Come on, Wes. My other guy called in. Shirtless Chefs is just getting off the ground. If I have chefs no-showing for parties, I'm going to catch hell in the online reviews, and the business will tank before I really get rolling. You've got the skills. You've got the blond bad-boy thing going, which is going to rock their socks off. And once upon a time, you could charm the ladies, so I know you're capable. Plus, you said you needed the extra money. This is easy cash. Win-win."

Wes grimaced. He hated *needing* the money. Hated that he was anywhere near that place he'd been so long ago, where he'd had to scrape together every damn dime. He'd thought he was far past that, and then *boom*, life had exploded. But *need* wasn't even the right word. He had enough to live on right now with his teaching gig. He knew how to stretch his dollars. What he wanted the money for was a stupid idea. Something he shouldn't be messing with. His family would kick his ass if they even knew he was thinking about it.

Still, he couldn't help closing his eyes and picturing the beat-up school bus his friend Devin had shown him last week. The old bus had looked like it'd been rolled off the side of a rocky cliff and set on fire, but Wes had been able to see the bones beneath, the potential to be converted into a food truck. He'd gotten that itch he'd tried to ignore since he'd lost everything. The what-ifs.

He'd found himself inquiring about a loan at the bank. He'd known the answer before asking, but he'd asked anyway. And he'd put out feelers with his friends, telling them to give him a call if they had any extra catering or temporary cooking gigs.

Of course, Suzie had been the one to call, and she hadn't told him exactly how her new private chef business worked or the name she'd chosen for it until he'd arrived. She was smart enough to know he would've run in the other direction.

But now he was here and she needed his help. And dammit, he wanted the money. He tilted his head back against the wall and closed his eyes. "What am I teaching them to make?"

When she didn't answer immediately, he lifted his head, finding her biting her lip.

"Suze," he said, warning in his voice.

She held up her palms. "Don't hate me, okay? There's a bruschetta recipe and a bourbon nut brittle that you're going to love. But some of the other stuff is…themed."

His shoulders sagged in acceptance. "I'm making dick-shaped things, aren't I?"

"Um…" Her nose wrinkled. "There may be recipes for Big, Meaty Balls and Eat My Taco Dip."

"I fucking hate you."

She grinned and stepped up to pat him on the cheek. "You're the best, Garrett. If I didn't want to put lipstick on the merchandise, I'd kiss you."

"You say the sweetest things, Suze. I just feel showered by your sweetness and affection."

"Right?" She pinched his hip. "Now go in there, be nice, and look pretty."

He gave her a look. "You treat all your employees like cattle?"

She stuck out her tongue. "Only my friends who won't sue me."

He let out a tired breath. "I won't sue you, but if you tell anyone about this…"

"I won't."

"I could lose my job." Not to mention whatever shreds of dignity he had left.

She mimed sealing her lips and tossing the key. "Your secret's safe. I swear."

"Fine. I'll go in."

She did a little celebratory clap, but then her smile sagged a bit. "And you sure you're cool with alcohol being at the party? I mean, I know I'm pushing you to do this, but for real, if that part's a problem—"

"I told you it's not an issue," he said, cutting her off, anger trying to surface. "Tonight, that's the least of my worries."

She pressed her lips together and nodded. "Okay. Good."

He ran a hand through his hair, resigned. "Let's get this over with."

"Right." She swept an arm out toward the door. "Godspeed, my friend."

With one last steeling breath, he stepped past her and pushed open the door. All eyes turned his way, and the blond woman with the penis hat grinned widely and clapped her hands together. "Ooh, y'all got me a stripper?"

Wes almost reversed his steps right there. *Three. Two. One. Right back out the door.* But he gritted his teeth and kept moving forward.

"Even better," said a tall, dark-eyed woman at her side. "He doesn't just strip. He cooks for us!"

"Yum!" another of the group said, and Wes couldn't tell if that was about him or his food.

"Hello, ladies." Wes forced a charming smile and then unbuttoned his black chef's coat as a little part of him died inside. "Who's ready to get some hands-on lessons?"

All the women eagerly raised their hands, laughing as they made their way over to the long bar in the kitchen. His ingredients were neatly arranged, his *mise en place* set up by Suzie ahead of time, and the recipe cards were stacked in front of each chair at the bar along with colorful Jell-O shots and flutes of champagne.

Wes inhaled a deep breath as he took in the festive atmosphere, trying to center himself.

This was a party. Someone was getting married, and this was their fun night with their friends. Maybe the *last* fun night if this chick's marriage went anything like Wes's had. They didn't need some grumpy-ass dude ruining their evening.

He tried to keep that in his head as he laid his chef's coat over a chair and reached back to tug his T-shirt off.

The ladies made appreciative sounds and comments as the cool air hit his bare skin. Their reactions should've stroked his ego. If he'd been his younger self, he would've rolled around in that kind of attention, would've egged them on and played it up. If he'd been that guy, he would've sidled up to the bar with them and knocked down some of those shots, found a hot single woman in the bunch and charmed her into his bed for the night.

But right now, looking at all the pretty faces and roving gazes, he couldn't find an ounce of interest in anything but the booze. Since his divorce, that part of him had died as well. All he saw when he looked at women now were trouble, drama, and disaster waiting to happen.

*No, thanks.*

One of the ladies leaned over and poured him a tall glass of champagne. "What's your name, handsome?"

*My name is Chef Wesley Garrett. I trained under renowned Chef Amelia St. John, and for a half a second, I owned the restaurant of my dreams and was going to be the next big thing in the city.* "Roman."

"Ooh, nice name. You speak Italian?"

"No. Spanish." Because that was what his adoptive mother spoke and was the language of half his former kitchen staff. But he'd be damned if he was going to perform it like some circus trick. "I'm rusty, though."

"That's okay, darling," said an older lady from the far end of the bar. "We didn't hire you to talk."

A few of them laughed, and the muscles in the back of his neck tightened. The light scent of the champagne drifted his way, and though he'd never been a champagne drinker, his throat became parched. He closed his eyes for a second, breathed through the urge, and focused on why he was here.

*Money in the bank. Money in the bank.*

He picked up a knife, pasted on a smile, and grabbed a bowl of ground beef. "All right, who's ready to handle some balls?"

# chapter
# THREE

THE GARLIC SCENT WAFTING UP FROM THE BAG OF takeout made Rebecca's stomach rumble as her heels clicked along the broken pavement. She shouldn't have worked so late without eating something. Her bad knee was aching because she'd forgotten to tuck her flats in her bag today, but she tried to keep up the pace. Her limp would be visible tomorrow after pushing herself like this, but at least on a Saturday she wouldn't have to hobble around the office. Plus, she only had a few more blocks before she got to her house, and she was so starved that she was strongly considering finding a bench and digging in.

She resisted the urge, knowing this part of Austin wasn't bad but it was late and quiet, the businesses on the street closed for the evening. She'd taken a different path home than normal so she could swing by the restaurant, but now she missed the bustling street of bars and quirky shops she normally took on her way home. She switched the sack with the bottle of wine to her other hand and fished a piece of bread out of the takeout bag. She took a big bite, groaning at the buttery taste, but didn't stop walking. The sooner she got home, the sooner the chicken marsala was all hers.

But as she crossed another street, she heard something behind her. Not footsteps exactly but something light and quick. She tensed and turned her head, ready to crash the bottle of wine over someone's head, but instead, a scruffy black dog the size of a Lab but with fluffier hair stared back at her.

She let out a breath in relief but took a step back anyway in case the dog wasn't friendly. "You scared me, pooch."

The dog eyed her bread, and his tongue lolled out in a pant. If his expression could talk, it would say, *How you doin'?*

"Oh, no you don't," she warned. "This isn't for you."

He trotted closer, looking more goofy than aggressive, but she wasn't going to trust that. He wasn't wearing a collar, and though he wasn't skinny, he looked like he'd been living the hard life for a while. He dipped his head and bumped the takeout bag.

"No," she said, moving the bag away from him. "This is expensive Italian food. It'd probably make you sick."

He moved closer, his nose angling for her ankles. He sniffed her like he was searching for gold up her pant leg.

"Ugh, not you too. I've been canine assaulted enough today." He probably smelled Prince Hairy on her. She gently nudged him away with her shin. "Come on, Scruffy. I've got to get home."

He barked, a soft woof that seemed to come from deep in his chest, and then stared up at her with big, black eyes.

She let out a heavy sigh. "Well, damn. You've

got that look down pat, don't you? You've charmed someone out of their dinner before."

He plopped his butt on the ground and panted, some dog version of a smile on his face.

She groaned. "Fine. You win."

Rebecca tossed him the bread. He opened his mouth to catch it in the air, but it bopped him on the snout and then fell to the sidewalk. He didn't seem to mind a little dirt. He wolfed it down in two bites and then sat again and looked up.

"That's all I've got for you, buddy. The chicken's for me."

He woofed.

"This is not a negotiation. I'm hungry. I need to eat, too, and I have nothing in the fridge at home." She looked to the stars above and shook her head. "I'm arguing with a dog." She peered down at him. "You shouldn't try this with me. I'm a very good lawyer. I'll win."

He dog-smiled again.

"Fine." She grabbed the last roll from the bag. "You're right. You win. Now go." She tossed the bread far down the sidewalk and watched as he chased after it. She turned and headed the other way before he could waylay her with those puppy eyes again. She needed to get home. She couldn't do anything else for him. But a pang of guilt went through her, and she grunted in frustration. When she got home, she'd call the animal shelter and let them know his description and where he was so they could pick him up.

"Look for the dog with buttery garlic breath," she muttered to herself.

The dog didn't follow her, and she walked for a few

more minutes, listening to the sounds of a car playing music in the distance and enjoying the cooling night air. She was only a few blocks from home when she heard something shuffle behind her. The back of her neck prickled. She paused, planning to turn around and have words with the dog again, but before she could, an arm banded around her from behind.

Her body went rigid, and everything dropped from her hands, the wine bottle shattering on the sidewalk, the bag muffling the sound. She opened her mouth to scream, but something cold and hard pressed against her temple. All her words evaporated.

"Make one noise, and I pull the trigger," someone said against her ear, his voice shaking but his hold firm.

The gun cocked, and the distinct sound flipped a switch inside her, sending a cascade of cold dread through her. Familiar dread. *Click. Boom. Click. Boom.* The sound loop was one she recognized. One she still heard in her nightmares. Only this time, the bullet wouldn't lodge in her leg. This time, there was no Finn to throw his body in front of the bullets. It'd land where it was meant to.

*Click. Boom.*

She'd be on the news again. This time with a sheet over her face.

The mugger said something in her ear. Something angry. Demanding. She heard nothing but a few disconnected words. "Kill… Now… Bitch."

But his voice morphed in her head. Became someone else's voice. Other words.

*You think you're so much better than me. You're so fucking pathetic. I can't believe I actually let myself give a shit about you. You're just like the rest of them. An empty-headed sheep.*

*Click. Boom.* Her ears started to ring like the gun had already gone off.

She closed her eyes, everything going still inside her. Not fear. Not terror. But…inevitability. *Of course* this was how it would go. She'd escaped when she wasn't supposed to. Now it was time to pay off that debt.

"Are you listening to me?" The guy shook her and pressed the barrel of the gun harder against her temple.

But she hadn't been listening. She couldn't. All she could hear were screams and bullets pinging into lockers, shots hitting flesh, calls to *get down, get down, get down.*

"What the hell is wrong with her?" a second voice asked.

*Oh.* There were two.

Of course there were. How could it be any other way?

A hand yanked at her purse strap, ripping it off her shoulder. "Give me your watch or you're dead, bitch."

She didn't move. Couldn't. Her muscles had forgotten how. One of the attackers shoved her to the ground. She hit the concrete hard, and pain shot through her reconstructed knee, the shock of it briefly breaking through her sticky thoughts. She needed to react, to give them what they wanted, but she couldn't make her limbs work. The gun jabbed into her back.

They were going to do it. Shoot her right here on this street to get her anniversary gift from the firm, a TAG Heuer watch she rarely wore, and she couldn't make herself move.

*Click. Boom. Click. Boom.*

She closed her eyes, bracing for it, but a different sound came instead.

A vicious snarling ripped through the air, and the press of the gun disappeared. Her attackers shouted at each other, cursing, and Rebecca rolled over in time to see a big, black ball of fur leaping at a tall, thin assailant. The docile dog from earlier was gone. In his place was a wild animal with bared teeth and wolf hunger in its eyes. He knocked the guy with the gun to the ground.

The other took off down the street, his baseball cap falling off behind him, but the one with the gun was flat on his back and blocked from her view, wrestling to get the dog off him and crying out when the animal sank his teeth into his arm.

Rebecca tried to push herself to a stand, wanting to help the dog, but pain stung her as glass from the wine bottle cut her elbows.

"Hey!" A deep male voice shouted from a distance. Footsteps pounded against the street.

"Gun!" Rebecca yelled, the word coming out in one big gasp. She needed to warn whoever was coming closer. She couldn't have another death on her hands.

She crawled forward, but before she could reach the fray, the gunshot went off like a firecracker. The sound echoed in Rebecca's ears, reverberating down to her bones and hurtling her deep into terrifying memories. But the high-pitched yelp of the dog snapped her back into the moment. Her stomach lurched. "No!"

Her attacker—a thin, white guy in a hoodie—got free and took off in a stumbling run. The dog collapsed, blood already pooling beneath him. Rebecca crawled to his side, frantic.

Whoever had yelled finally reached them. She heard him skid to a halt next to her. "Jesus Christ."

Rebecca pressed her hand to the dog's head, and he whimpered. Tears jumped to her eyes, and everything that had been moving in slow motion in her head jolted into full speed and bright colors. "Oh God. No, no, no."

"Shit." The man stepped closer, the soles of his black Vans touching the edge of the blood and his breathing labored from his run. "You're bleeding. We need to get you—"

She shook her head, trying to get words out.

"Ma'am, I think you've been shot. I'm going to call for help. Just—"

"No. Not me," Rebecca said, finally managing to make her mouth work. "The dog."

"The dog?"

"He's *dying*." She didn't recognize her voice. She sounded hysterical. She never got hysterical. "Do something!"

"We need to call the police. Those guys—"

She grabbed the leg of his jeans. "No!"

"But—"

"He saved me." She looked up at that, finding light hazel eyes staring down at her, worry etched into a serious face. "We need to help him. *Now*."

The guy crouched down next to them and braced his arms on his thighs, revealing colorful tattoos beneath his rolled-up sleeves. He let out a breath. "Okay. Right. The dog first. My brother's a vet. I'll try him. Then I'm calling the cops."

"Okay."

He shifted to his knees and tugged off the black button-down shirt he had on over his T-shirt and handed it to her. "If you can find the wound, put some pressure on it."

"Thank you." She balled up the shirt and peered back down at the dog, watching his flank flutter with rapid breaths. She couldn't tell exactly where he was shot, but she pressed it near his backside where the blood seemed to be the thickest.

The man stood, pulled a phone out of his back pocket, and stepped away to make the call.

Rebecca shifted closer to the dog, gently petting his head as tears rolled down her face. "It's okay, sweetheart," she said softly. "We're going to take care of you. Thank you for saving me. If you can just hold on, you can have all of my chicken."

Fifteen minutes later, a work van sped down the street, and her Good Samaritan flagged it down. The van parked at the curb, and a guy hopped out. He was dark-haired and built like a linebacker, but the burnt-orange Texas Longhorns pajama pants made him look much less intimidating than he would've otherwise. She didn't see any familial resemblance to her rescuer—who was taller, leaner, and blonder—but the brother, obviously used to handling emergencies, was calm and efficient as he assessed the situation and the dog. That took the edge off some of her panic.

After setting up a few things to make the dog as comfortable as possible, the three of them gingerly got the injured animal into the back of the van. Rebecca sat with the dog on the way to the clinic, watching every ragged rise and fall of his breath. She probably should've considered that getting into a van with two strangers wasn't the wisest idea, but no alarm bells had gone off in her head. All she could focus on was getting help for her canine hero. As long as she focused on that, she would be okay. She wouldn't have to think about how close she'd come to dying.

Or how she hadn't fought back—or even tried.

She closed her eyes.

She wouldn't have to think about the small sense of relief she'd felt at the thought that it was finally done. Debt paid.

———◦◦◦———

"What the hell happened?" Marco asked as he stood next to the exam table, applying pressure to the dog's wound with one gloved hand and pointing to the things he needed Wes to grab with the other.

Wes had left the woman in the lobby of the animal clinic with the cops and paramedics. Meanwhile, he'd become his brother's makeshift assistant. He handed Marco the items and tried not to look at the injured animal. He could deal with blood, but ever since his birth father had demonstrated his vicious method of getting rid of a neighbor's nosy cat when Wes was eight, animals in pain made his stomach twist. How Marco dealt with this stuff every day, he'd never know. Of course, Marco would probably say the same thing about Wes dealing with delinquent teenagers.

"I didn't see all of it," Wes said. "I was too far away, and it was dark. At first, I thought it was people horsing around after leaving a bar because she wasn't screaming or struggling or anything. But then the dog came out of nowhere and attacked. I ran over there to help and didn't realize it was a robbery until I heard the shot and saw one of the guys running off with her purse. I thought she was the one who'd been shot. Scared the hell out of me."

Marco glanced up, concern flickering through his eyes. "You both got lucky then. You could've gotten shot running up blind on that kind of situation."

Wes crossed his arms, daring his brother to say he should've stayed out of it and just called the police. That was probably what Marco would've done. *Think first. Act second.* Wes had heard that particular lecture enough times. Screw that. Not in this case. "She needed help."

Marco glanced toward the lobby door, even though they couldn't see what was happening on the other side. "Well, I'm glad she's okay and that you didn't get yourself killed. Someone who's willing to shoot a dog probably wouldn't hesitate to shoot a person."

"I don't know," Wes said with a frown. "I didn't get a good look at the guys, but she thinks they were pretty young. Maybe they didn't plan to use the gun, but the guy reacted to being bitten. The dog was like Cujo."

Marco lifted a brow. "So you're defending the attackers now?"

Wes didn't bother answering that. Mr. Do-the-Right-Thing wouldn't understand. Once upon a time, Wes had been one of those kids. Now he taught those kids.

Wes peeked at what Marco was doing but then grimaced at the sight of the matted fur. "Is he going to be okay?"

Marco's brown eyes narrowed, focused on the intricate work. "They got him in the hind leg and he's lost a lot of blood, but I think he'll be all right. At least for now."

"What do you mean?"

A line appeared between his brows. "This guy's got to be a stray, so I don't know exactly what we're dealing with. If he's rabid or violent, he's not going to last long anyway. The shelter will have to put him down. He attacked someone."

Wes frowned. "He was defending someone. They should give him a damn medal and some steak."

Marco gave him that wary, big brother look that said he was about to deliver news Wes wouldn't like. "She's not his owner. It'd be odd for a normally docile dog to defend a stranger. Chances are high that he's got issues."

"Because he's a stray."

"Yes."

Wes scoffed. He knew what being a stray was like and couldn't deny the charge. Marco's parents—technically Wes's aunt and uncle—had taken Wes in at age fifteen when his parents had gone to prison. Carolina and Ed had treated Wes like their own, but he'd brought a truckload of drama with him. "Well, I hope this dog isn't really Cujo. The woman out there has had enough bad news tonight. She was more upset about the dog than the fact that she'd just been attacked and robbed."

"She was probably in shock. And you don't have to say anything yet. Let her finish talking to the cops and getting patched up by the paramedics. Then, you can give her my number if she wants to check on the dog tomorrow. No need to upset her more right now. Our friend here is going to be staying for a while and will be asleep for hours anyway." Marco concentrated on the dog, preparing him for whatever it was going to take to get a bullet out and sew him back up. "We'll figure out what we're dealing with when he wakes up."

Wes's stomach turned as his brother went to work. He looked away and concentrated on a poster about the life cycle of a heartworm. "I think I should probably go out—"

"What were you doing out that late in that part of town anyway?" his brother asked. "You're not picking up kitchen shifts, are you? Because I told you if you need money—"

Wes's jaw flexed. He knew it was because Marco cared and worried, but feeling babysat all the time drove him up the fucking wall.

"I don't need money," he said, not mentioning the loan he'd inquired about. The one that had earned him that patient, condescending look from the banker. *Mr. Garrett, with your credit and history, I'm sure you understand our position...* "I was just helping Suzie with a private catering gig she was doing. She had someone no-show and was in a bind."

"Suzie? The one with the crazy hair?" Marco looked up, deep lines appearing around his mouth. "Wes, you know that environment and the people in it are no good for your sobriety. That whole scene is—"

"It wasn't a big thing, all right? Nothing bad happened."

Except that he'd left feeling humiliated and frustrated as hell. He'd been more than a little tempted to step into one of the bars that he'd passed on his way home. He couldn't stop thinking about how many gigs like that one he'd have to pull off to get anywhere close to buying a food truck. He'd ended up taking a turn onto a quiet street, one block away from the hopping nightlife and the neighborhood where he'd once owned a restaurant, trying to talk himself out of having a drink and saying fuck it all. He'd been losing the argument.

Then he'd heard the dog.

"Wesley, you need—"

"How is he?" The worried feminine voice came from behind Wes, saving him from another lecture he didn't need or want to hear. He'd heard more than enough about *setting yourself up for success* (Ed) and *not returning to enabling or high-stress environments* (Marco) and *staying away from temptation* (Carolina) to last him a damn lifetime.

He'd like to shout that he wasn't that weak and could handle it. But tonight, he'd be lying because he'd felt that thirsting beast pushing at the door of his willpower. Maybe the dog had saved more than one person tonight.

Wes turned. The redhead, whose name he hadn't managed to get yet, had pushed through the swinging door that led to the front office. This was the first time he'd seen her in the full light. Her clothes were stained with dried blood, her gray pants were ripped at one knee, and her elbows were bandaged. But she'd washed her face clean of her streaked makeup and had pulled her hair back. Her blue eyes looked wide, concerned…and vaguely familiar.

Wes frowned.

"The bullet hit his leg," Marco said from behind him. "I think he'll be okay. I'm going to patch him up and keep him here for observation."

"The leg." A strange look crossed the woman's face. "That's…good news."

Wes couldn't stop staring at her. She was easy to look at, pretty in a girl-next-door way with faint freckles across her nose, but he couldn't shake the feeling that he knew her from somewhere, which didn't make sense. The circles he ran in now were small and limited to teachers and restaurant people. This woman had high-powered executive written all over her.

"Wes," Marco said. "Why don't you show…"

"Rebecca," the woman filled in.

"Rebecca to the back room. I have extra sets of staff scrubs in there. She can change into some clean clothes."

*Rebecca. Rebecca. Rebecca.* The name wasn't ringing any bells.

Finally, she turned, as if just noticing Wes was there, too. She stepped forward and put her hand out formally. "Thank you for intervening. A lot of people wouldn't have jumped in and tried to help like that."

He took her hand, surprised by the firm shake but liking the up-close view of her. Pale lashes, a full bottom lip, and bright-blue, serious eyes. "Not a problem."

Her gaze skimmed over him, and then she met his stare, holding the eye contact for longer than was polite. Awareness filtered through him as the hint of a blush appeared beneath her fair skin. *Well, then*. She was checking him out right back.

And unlike the women ogling him earlier in the night, this attention hit him square and twisted something old and rusty inside him. He *liked* her looking at him that way, which was an odd, almost outside-himself feeling. But there was something stripped down and honest about the way she stared, like it'd caught her off guard and she wasn't sure how to act.

"If you want to get changed, I can drive you home," he said, his voice coming out gruffer than he'd intended. "Unless you have someone picking you up?"

She let go of his hand quickly, like she realized she'd held on to it a fraction too long. "I haven't called anyone yet. They stole my phone, and I don't have the numbers memorized."

"I don't mind giving you a ride." He glanced at his brother. "I'm sure Marco will work quicker without us in here staring at him."

"The van keys are on the desk," Marco offered. "I'm all good here. Rebecca, you can call tomorrow and check on our patient if you'd like. We're under Garrett Veterinary online if you need the number, or you can grab a card from the front counter."

Her attention jerked to Marco. "Garrett?"

"Yep."

She stepped back, her gaze darting to Wes. All interest that had been there was gone, as if he'd only imagined it. It was like a bucket of ice water dumping over his head. "I appreciate the offer, but if you let me know where the scrubs are, I can change and call a cab. It's late. There's no need to have to double back to return the van." She glanced at Marco. "And thank you so much for doing this. I'll definitely call tomorrow to check on him. Whatever the treatment costs, I'll pay."

Marco waved her off. "No payment needed. I work a few charity cases into the budget every year."

She gave Marco a smile with genuine warmth, and Wes found himself disappointed that she was no longer directing that kind of energy his way. Had something happened? He'd barely talked, so he couldn't have offended her. He wasn't quite *that* skilled at chasing people off.

He cleared his throat, trying to shake the feeling. What did it matter what she thought of him? It wasn't like he was in the market to ask someone out. He didn't do that anymore. "It's really not a problem to drive you.

You'll be waiting forever for a cab in this part of town. Plus, they took your purse. How are you going to pay for the cab?"

"I…" She glanced at the clock above the exam room door, and her shoulders sagged. "Yeah, okay. Thanks."

Marco told her where to find the scrubs, and she pushed her way through the swinging doors again to find them, leaving the two men behind.

Wes watched her go, frowning, some weird, creeping sense of unease filling him.

"Did she look familiar to you?" Wes asked his brother.

"No. Why?"

Wes shook his head. "I've got the strangest sense that I've met her before."

"Is that why you were staring at her like she held the answers to the universe?"

He turned to Marco. "What?"

His brother smirked. "You were about to go into full Wes Garrett charm-the-lady mode. I'd almost forgotten what that looked like." He switched out whatever tool he was using for something else. "Good to see that side of you still exists, but I'm glad you didn't go there. Not the time or place. She doesn't need some guy hitting on her tonight."

Wes scowled. "I wasn't going to hit on her. I just thought I recognized her."

"Uh-huh," his brother said. "You were trying to *recognize* her really hard. She's probably just someone you've served in a restaurant once upon a time or something."

Wes blew out a breath. "Yeah, probably."

Marco frowned down at the dog like he didn't like what he saw. "Just get her home safely. She's had one hell of a night."

"Right."

"And Wes?" his brother said, looking up.

Wes ran a hand over the back of his head, knowing what was coming. "Get it off your chest, man. I can feel the lecture coming."

A sympathetic look crossed Marco's face. "No lecture. Just...don't torture yourself."

"I—"

"Walking in the neighborhood where your restaurant used to be will never lead to anything good. You have to let it go, man. All of that old life. Looking back is a trap. You'll fall into a manhole or crash into a wall you never saw coming. Enjoy what you have now."

Wes ground his teeth as cold, sick grief clawed at his insides.

*Enjoy what he had now.*

A life he didn't ask for.

A job he'd fallen into.

A destroyed marriage.

And not a drop to drink forever and ever, amen.

"Yep, Marco. You're right. I'm living the dream."

Marco frowned, but Wes was done. He didn't want to hear it. *Don't look back. Move forward.* But what if every stride felt like one on an endless treadmill where one misstep would send him flying backward onto his ass?

His legs were getting damn tired.

# chapter
# FOUR

REBECCA SAT STIFFLY IN THE FRONT SEAT, KEEPING HER
eyes forward and counting the street signs as they passed,
trying to keep her mind focused on numbers instead of…
everything else. It was an old trick she'd picked up in a
therapy group she attended in high school. When she got
too overwhelmed or anxious, she counted, or conjugated
verbs, or recited the capitals of all the states. *Seven street
signs. Three stoplights. Ten trash cans.*

She didn't want to think about what had happened
tonight.

*Three taco restaurants.*

Or how she'd reacted. How the fight had gone out
of her.

*Two drugstores.*

She didn't want to think about injured dogs and
blood—or how for a moment she hadn't been able to
tell the present from the past, reality from the ghosts.

*Two men.*

*One gun.*

She closed her eyes.

To top it off, she really didn't want to think about the man sitting next to her. When he'd first taken her hand in the clinic, she'd had a spark of *Hello, sailor* that was one hundred percent inappropriate considering the circumstances. Her body had flushed, her gaze had drifted where it shouldn't, and her belly had gone tight at the view. She'd blamed the feeling on the high-stress night and him coming to her rescue—well, and the guy was exceptionally easy to look at. But then she'd heard his last name, and all those sparks had been snuffed out with one swift gust.

*Wesley Garrett.*

He didn't recognize her yet. Last time he'd seen her, she'd been going through an unfortunate phase where she had thought a Michelle Williams pixie haircut and bleach job were good ideas. But when he did put the pieces together, he wasn't going to be happy about it. He'd been part of one of her cases from a few years ago, one of her first victories at the firm. And he'd been on the other side of the table: the cheating husband. One with a fiery temper and a bad attitude, based on his antics in court.

Now she was alone in a van with him. She didn't think he was a threat to her. He had come to her rescue tonight and helped her save the dog, but she needed him not to remember her or the fact that she'd helped his ex-wife get a hefty settlement. She didn't have the energy for anything else tonight.

"You sure you're okay?" Wes asked, his voice low and carrying a hint of what sounded like a West Texas drawl to her Austin ear. "You took a hard fall."

She glanced over at him but in the darkness could only see his profile and the colorful tattoos on the arm he had draped over the steering wheel. She tried to remember what he did for a living. Maybe owned a business? Probably not an office job, with that kind of ink and hair long enough to touch his collar, but the details wouldn't come to her. "I'm fine. The glass from the wine bottle cut me up a little, but the paramedics took care of it."

"That adds insult to injury. You get mugged and have no wine to drink afterward."

She smirked. "Or dinner."

He frowned and peeked over at her. "Damn, I didn't realize. You must be starving. I can run by a drive-through, or I know a guy who runs a food truck that serves great Indian food not far from here. He stays open late."

She shifted in her seat, her body aching in more places than she'd expected. "It's fine. I'm really not that hungry anymore."

But as soon as she said it, her stomach growled loudly.

He laughed under his breath. "Your body betrays you. Come on, I really don't mind. I didn't get a chance to grab dinner either, so I'd need to stop for something anyway."

Another *no* was poised on her lips, but then a terrifying thought hit her. "*Shit*."

Wes pulled up to a stoplight and glanced over, brow furrowed. "What's wrong?"

She pressed her fingers to the spot between her eyes where a headache was suddenly brewing. A headache and scary-ass images. "I don't know what's wrong with me. It just hit me that those jerks took my purse, which has my house key."

"You don't have your keys?"

*Shit. Shit. Shit.* "I have a spare hidden that I can get to, but I wasn't thinking. They have my key and my—"

"Your license with your address," Wes said grimly.

Anxiety crept through her chest like thorny vines. "I have a house alarm, but I'm not sure if I set it this morning. I don't always remember to do that."

"You need to call a twenty-four-hour locksmith. Get everything changed tonight," he said, already pulling his phone from the cup holder and passing it her way. "I doubt those guys are going to show up at your place, especially with one injured, but you can't risk it."

Goose bumps broke out on her arms, images of dangerous men lurking around her home making her throat close. She took the phone. "Goddammit, I just wanted to take a hot shower, go to bed, and forget tonight happened."

Wes sent her a sympathetic look. "Get a locksmith headed out there, and we'll pick up some food. The locksmith can work. We can eat. And I'll stick around until you can do a thorough search of your place to make sure nothing is out of order."

She frowned his way. "You don't need to do that. I'm sure you need to get home. And—"

"I'm not going to leave you until I know you're all right. That's not going to happen." He said resolutely. "So...McDonald's or Indian?"

She stared at him. His hazel eyes held calm determination, and under different circumstances—if she didn't know the type of guy he really was—she would've let herself enjoy the chivalry for a moment. Guys didn't take that road with her often because she wore her toughness like a cape. *Stand back, boys. I can handle it.* And she could.

But right now she wished she could fold up that cape and put it in a drawer for a few hours. Let the man with the pretty eyes and the sexy smile take the lead for a little while and allow her to just take a breath, shake off the night, and find her footing again. To feel safe and not so alone, despite all her worst anxieties pushing at the back of her brain like an angry crowd ready to riot. But she couldn't trust this man. Whoever this version of him was, it was a facade. Somewhere in there was the angry guy she'd seen in court. The man who'd stepped out on his wife. He was showing her his good side.

However, knowing he wasn't that great of a guy beneath the surface wasn't going to stop her from accepting his offer. She was woman enough to admit that she was way too freaked out to go home alone. She'd have a panic attack before she made it through the front door. Plus, she spent her days dealing with liars, and she didn't get the sense that Wes had some agenda. He didn't have anything to gain. And he wasn't trying to hit on her—not shocking news.

Beside the fact that she looked like hell right now, guys like him didn't pursue women like her. She didn't attract edgy or rebellious. She tended to draw businessmen who wanted to impress their mother with "a smart girl from a good family." She had a feeling Wes couldn't give a shit about impressing anyone, but for whatever reason, he was genuinely concerned and trying to be helpful.

Tonight, she'd take it.

Rebecca wet her lips. "Indian."

She'd never actually had Indian food before, but she got the sense that was what Wes wanted, and a greasy hamburger just didn't sound all that appealing at the moment. Indian food had rice. She knew, at the very least, she could get that.

A genuine smile broke out on Wes's face. "Excellent choice. You call the locksmith, and I'll take care of the grub."

Fifteen minutes later, they were in one of the many food-truck parks in Austin, and a guy with a mischievous smile and thick, dark hair was chatting with Wes from the window of a shiny, converted Airstream trailer called Mad Masala. He peered down at Wes's stained jeans. "I thought you were helping Suzie out tonight. You come back looking like you've been through war. What the hell happened?"

"Long story. But it involved police, a hurt dog, and both of us missing dinner." Wes cocked a thumb toward Rebecca. "Dev, meet Rebecca. Rebecca, this is Devin Madan, head chef of this fine establishment."

Devin leaned out through the window and shook her hand. "Lovely to meet you. And no dinner? Well, we need to fix that. What do you like? Curry? Biryani? Dal?"

She lifted her shoulders and gave him an apologetic look. "So, if I've never actually tried Indian food…"

He put a hand to his heart and grimaced. "Wesley, you are letting me down. Your friend has never had Indian food. What kind of person are you not to have introduced her to—"

Wes lifted a hand. "We just met tonight, Dev. Give me a break. I got her here as quickly as I could to indoctrinate her." He turned to Rebecca. "All right. You tell me some basics, and we'll hook you up. Spicy or mild?"

"Somewhere in the middle."

"Vegetarian or carnivore?"

"Omnivore."

"Do you feel like potatoes or rice?"

"Rice."

Wes looked up at Devin, and at the same time they both said, "Butter chicken."

Rebecca didn't protest. Anything called *butter chicken* couldn't be bad. "I'll trust you guys."

Wesley's lips lifted at one corner. "It's not the most adventurous choice, but I'll go easy on you since this is your first time."

Rebecca's face heated like she was thirteen again and everything a boy said was a double entendre. *Very mature, Bec.*

"That's what she said," Devin supplied.

Wes groaned and gave him a look. "Really, man?"

Devin shrugged. "You walked right into that one. It was my duty."

Wes shook his head. "Get us some food, chef. Vegetable korma for me. Throw in some garlic naan, too, for that comment."

Devin laughed. "Lucky for you, I have a stack of naan that won't be any good tomorrow. I experimented with a jalapeño-and-cheese version tonight. You can tell me what you think."

"Nothing sounds bad about bread, cheese, and chili peppers," Wes said as he grabbed one of the bottles lining the counter and squirted a green sauce into a little takeout cup. He repeated the action with two more colorful sauces, his movements efficient and sure, like he'd done that routine millions of times.

"You come here a lot?" Rebecca asked as Devin got their food ready.

Wes looked over as he put covers on the sauce containers and then stacked them on the ledge for Devin to put in the bag. "You can find some of the best food in the city in these kinds of places. Lots of experimental stuff. New chefs finding their groove. Gourmet stuff at reasonable prices." He sidled up next to her and glanced out at the U-shaped park, something wistful crossing his face. "I mean, it's kind of amazing. Who wouldn't want to come here?"

She studied his profile for a moment before following his gaze to see what he was seeing. Not many trucks were left at this hour, but there were twinkle lights strung above the well-worn picnic tables and colorful potted flowers dotting the ground. A lone couple was sharing a tray of three colorful cupcakes as crickets serenaded them from off in the dark. The park did have a bit of a magical quality to it, especially at this hour when it felt like some kind of secret. "It is really lovely. I don't live that far from here, but I didn't know this existed."

"Well, after you try Dev's food, I bet you'll put it on regular rotation," Wes said, tucking his hands in his back pockets, which made his biceps bulge, temporarily distracting her from her vow not to check him out anymore. "You should also try the street taco truck, the Korean-Texas BBQ fusion, and Reel Cupcakes. The chef there names her cupcakes after horror movies. I recommend The Shining—it's a red velvet cupcake covered with coconut snow."

She lifted a brow. "You seem like quite the connoisseur of the food park. I guess you're into eating?"

Not that anyone would be able to tell. His T-shirt was snug enough to show a body that didn't look like it'd ever had a cupcake. Not that she was still looking. Nope. Not her.

Wes shrugged. "I teach culinary arts at an after-school program."

"What he means to say," Devin said, his back still to them, "is that he is a chef. Not as good as me, of course, but passable." He turned and placed two takeout containers and a foil-wrapped package on the ledge. "Who is currently wasting his talent teaching children how to fry an egg and denying the rest of the world his skills."

Wes's expression darkened at Devin's words. He grabbed the bag and tucked the food inside. "How much do I owe you?"

"On the house." Devin smiled. "When you make that purchase I told you about, you can return the favor."

Wes frowned and pulled out his wallet. He dropped a twenty on the counter, apparently making some point. Rebecca didn't know what was going on between the two friends, but she sensed the tension, the air of challenge.

Wes turned to her, his expression softening into something friendly again. He pulled out a steaming piece of flatbread dotted with jalapeños and handed it to her. "Best to eat these warm. You ready to go?"

She took the bread, inhaling the enticing scents of garlic and hot peppers, and looked up at the truck. "Yeah. Thanks, Devin."

"Anytime." He lifted a hand in goodbye. "You come back and tell me what you think."

"Will do," she said and then bit into the bread as they took a few steps away from the truck. The soft dough was filled with melty cheese, and she moaned at the rush of flavor—garlic, spices, heat. Her empty stomach rumbled in victory as she stopped in her tracks. "Holy hell, that's good."

Stretchy cheese tried to escape, but she caught it with her finger and then licked it off the tip. Wes turned to face her, his lips curling at her obvious pleasure and the mess she was making.

He leaned close, next to her ear. "Don't say that too loud. Dev's ego is big enough."

She shivered at the tickle of Wes's breath along her neck and shook her head. "I can't help it. You've got to try this."

Without thinking, she held out the naan, the cheese oozing. Wes smiled at the invitation and bit into the bread while holding her gaze. The move should've been nothing more than a man taking a bite of food, but the way he watched her, the way he lingered in her space, made her heartbeat pick up speed.

He pulled back, a string of cheese stretching until it broke, and wiped the corner of his mouth, his eyes still on her. "That's pretty damn good."

"Yeah," she said quietly, her body staging some kind of protest while her mind tried to remind her that this man was a cheater. And that she'd been mugged tonight, so she was in some weird vulnerable state that made her think inappropriate thoughts. And that she had way bigger things to worry about than how long it'd been since she'd felt attraction on such a visceral level.

*Focus, Bec.*

"This is fantastic, Devin," she called out, breaking the eye contact and forcing herself to look somewhere else besides at Wes.

Devin's face broke into a wide smile, and he lifted a hand in thanks. "Enjoy!"

Wesley handed her an extra napkin. "Let's get you home."

She didn't trust herself to say anything appropriate, so she took another big bite of naan and followed Wes to the van.

She needed to get home.

She was tired. And traumatized. And based on her reactions to Wes, clearly out of her mind at the moment.

New locks and a good night's rest were what she needed.

Only another hour or so, and she'd never have to see Wesley Garrett again.

And he'd never have to know that he'd just bought a delicious dinner for the woman who'd taken him down in court.

# chapter
# FIVE

Wes and Rebecca beat the locksmith to her house, which was a small but pristine Craftsman bungalow near Zilker Park. The prime location must've cost her a fortune, but the place looked homey and unassuming. The porch light was on, illuminating a bright-red door and pale-gray siding. Her shiny, black BMW was parked under the carport, and nothing looked disturbed.

Wes parked the van in front of the house and cut the engine. "Well, I'll take it as a good sign that your car is still here. If those guys showed up with your keys, they would've taken your ride."

Rebecca frowned. "No. I didn't have my car keys with me since I walked today, but at least everything looks the same as how I left it. Plus, my car keys are hanging on a peg in the kitchen. They wouldn't be hard to find."

Wesley eyed her. Her voice was confident, but she kept smoothing the leg of her scrubs, her hands like nervous birds not knowing where to settle. He had the weirdest urge to hug her and tell her it was going to be all right, to take that fear from her. But a sure way to freak her out even further would be for some strange dude she'd just met to hug her. He was freaked out enough for both of them that he even *had* that urge. "Hey, why don't you tell me where your spare key is hidden, and I'll go in and check the house for you first?"

There. That was a reasonable, not weird way to help.

She glanced his way, frowning. "If the alarm's on, I need to turn it off, and I don't want to sit out here. That'll stress me out more than going in with you. I'm the only one who will be able to tell if anything's been moved anyway."

"Fair enough. Whatever makes you feel most comfortable is fine. But the minute something seems off or out of place, we bail and call the cops. Pinch my arm or something to signal me."

Her frown deepened, a little line appearing between her brows, as if she couldn't quite figure him out.

He couldn't stop his smile. "What's wrong? You look like you're trying to figure out a really hard math problem."

"I wouldn't make this face for math. I'm good at math." She let out a breath. "I guess I'm just trying to figure out why you're being so nice to me. You don't... know me."

"Does that matter? If I knew you, would I not want to help you out?"

She stiffened. "What?"

He tilted his head. "I mean, are you secretly some evil comic-book villain who's about to take over the city? Or do you have plans to kill me and store my body in your basement when we get inside?"

Her pinched expression flattened into something droll. "Austin houses don't have basements."

"Whew." He wiped his brow. "I'm safe."

She snorted and then covered her nose and mouth like she was surprised the sound had escaped. "You're kind of strange, Wesley Garrett."

He shrugged. "I get that a lot." And that was a helluva lot better than what most people probably called him these days. "Now, are we going to bravely search your house like two TV detectives? Because I am so down for that right now. I need to bang open doors and yell, 'Clear!'"

She laughed, the soft, husky sound filling the space between them and sending a pleasant ripple through him. The feeling was so unfamiliar that it stalled his breath for a second. How long had it been since he'd been around someone he could simply joke with and relax around? Someone who wasn't looking at him like he was damaged goods? Or who wasn't checking him for signs of a backslide?

He didn't get clean-slate conversations like this anymore. Not with his family. Not with friends. Not even with himself. Rebecca felt like a gulp of clean, fresh air. He wanted to close his eyes and inhale. In this moment, he could be a man with no past. He could be whoever he wanted to be. And right now, he wanted to be the guy who was making this woman laugh.

She cocked her head. "You say that like you've been planning to do this TV detective routine for a while."

"It's a life goal," he said solemnly. "I mean, I've done it at home alone, but that really isn't as fun. Plus, it pisses off the neighbors. All those banging doors."

She laughed again, and he felt like he'd won some

kind of prize. She seemed like someone who didn't give those laughs away easily.

"Now all we need are weapons," he declared.

She reached into the bag of takeout and pulled out the eco-friendly cornstarch forks Dev used in place of plastic cutlery. "How's this?"

"Perfect. We can go for the eyes." He took his fork and grabbed the keys. "Let's do this."

"I'm ready." Some of their playing around must've distracted her from her nerves because when Rebecca got out of the van, her shoulders seemed looser and there was a tentative smile on her face. She nodded toward the house and set her fork on the hood. He followed suit, since if he really had to take action, he'd need his hands free. "My extra key is by the back door."

They headed around the house and into the small backyard. She hunched near an overgrown herb garden and fished around, finally coming up with one of those fake rocks. She flipped it over and keyed in a three-digit code on a spinner combination lock.

Wes snapped a leaf off one of her plants and inhaled the scent. "Mmm, lemon thyme. You've got quite a collection out here. Cilantro. Oregano. Italian parsley. I'm a little jealous."

She glanced over her shoulder at him. "I honestly have no idea what most of them are or what to do with all of them. I had the house landscaped when I moved in, and I guess the gardeners picked the perfect spot because they grow like crazy. Except the basil, which was the one I actually knew how to use. That one was a goner during the first hundred-degree day of summer."

"Basil is a sensitive soul." It was on the tip of his

tongue to tell her he could show her how to use the herbs, but he held the offer back. His brother had been right. Making her laugh was like some weird sort of drug to his starved system, but she didn't need a guy flirting with her right now. It couldn't go anywhere anyway. He didn't date, for one. And even if he was doing the casual hookup thing these days, she didn't strike him as the type who'd be down for that, especially with someone like him. So he had nothing to offer her besides garden-care tips.

She stuck the key in the lock and opened the back door. There was no beeping alarm to greet them. Rebecca made a frustrated sound. "Goddammit. I didn't set it."

That information sobered him quickly and got his mind back to where it should be. Though it was unlikely, someone could legitimately be in the house. He tossed the thyme aside and stepped in front of her, his gaze scanning the small, white kitchen. He kept his voice low. "Anything look off?"

She peeked over his shoulder. "No."

"Okay." He took another step inside, taking in all the dark corners and possible hiding spots in the kitchen. "Do you keep a gun in the house?"

She sucked in a breath, and he turned his head to find her with a stricken look. "No. I can't—I hate guns."

Something in the way she said it gave him pause. He could sense true fear there. Probably because she'd had a gun pointed at her tonight. He reached out and squeezed her shoulder. "Okay. I wasn't asking because I wanted to use it. I just wanted to know if someone else could get to one."

She rolled her lips inward and pointed at the kitchen counter. "I have a big knife if we want something to walk around with."

He went over to the wooden knife block and grabbed one of the smaller knives. He was good with a chef's knife in the kitchen, but in a fight, he'd want something closer to a switchblade. He'd carried one when he was younger, living in a watch-your-back neighborhood, and still knew how to protect himself that way. He pressed his phone into her hand. "You're on phone duty. If you hear or see anything, don't wait."

She nodded and took the phone, but she also grabbed a large, steel pepper mill in her other hand.

He smirked. "Is this where you bash me in the head and drag me to the basement?"

Her smile was brief, but her eyes sparked with humor. "Yeah. You scared?"

"I could think of worse fates than being held captive by a pretty redhead."

The second the words were out, he wanted to snatch them back. They'd slipped out automatically, some old version of himself flickering to the surface, but the way her expression went flat told him how bad a move it'd been. *No flirting while searching her house for bad guys, you dumb-ass.*

He winced. "I'm sorry. I didn't mean it like—"

She shook her head. "I know. It's fine. Let's just do this search. Nothing seems out of place, so we're probably fine. The sooner we get this done, the sooner we can eat."

"Right." He cleared his throat and motioned for her to follow him. "We have Indian food waiting."

He stepped into her living room, which looked like a photo from a home magazine. Refinished hardwood floors, oatmeal-colored couch, nature photography on the walls. The only thing that revealed that a person actually lived here was the stack of books on the floor by the comfortable-looking red armchair and an abandoned glass of wine on a side table.

"Everything look all right?" he asked.

Her gaze scanned the room. "Yeah."

There were no closets or hidden alcoves, so he moved toward the hallway. If anyone was here, they'd probably know it by now, but he stayed alert just in case. The hallway was narrow. There was one small bathroom off to the left and an office to the right. Both were empty and in order. Last was the master bedroom at the end of the hallway.

He eased the door open and peeked inside. This was the only room that didn't look photo perfect. A pale-green comforter was pushed halfway down the bed, a pillow still held the indent of the head that had rested upon it, and a few clothing items were on the floor next to the bed. His gaze traced over them. A striped pajama top, thick woolen socks, and a lacy pair of blue panties.

His mind tried to go there—as if it were a reflex to picture the woman behind him getting ready this morning, sliding those sexy panties off and tossing them aside. Had she strode into the bathroom after that without a stitch on?

He swallowed hard and tried to ignore the fantasy images popping up in his head. He was a grown man. A pair of women's panties shouldn't get him that distracted. But apparently, his libido was starved enough to revert to teenager mode when activated. *Panties...oooh.* He took a deep breath, forcing his focus elsewhere, and headed toward the open closet door. "Uh, anything out of the ordinary in here?"

She moved into the doorway, and he heard her under-the-breath curse from behind him. He turned her way and found a look of mild horror on her face. She glanced at him, and then her gaze shifted away. "I, um, was in a hurry this morning."

He cleared his throat. "Closet looks fine." He moved to the next door and peeked into the attached bathroom. A stand-up shower and a claw-foot tub surrounded by a sea of white subway tile. *Totally not picturing her naked in either one of those. Nope. Not at all.* "Clear!"

"Great!" she said, her voice pitching high.

He turned to step out of the bathroom and almost ran into her. She had ditched the pepper mill and phone and had her dirty clothes clutched to her chest.

A tight smile jumped to her lips. "Guess we're all good then. Why don't you grab the food from the car, and I'll meet you in the kitchen?"

*Don't look at the panties. Don't look at the panties.* He ran a hand over the back of his neck. "Right. Food. I'll go get that."

He cringed inwardly. Now he was turning into Tarzan. *Me. Asshole. You. Hot.*

A loud banging rattled the window, and Rebecca screamed. She dropped the clothes and leapt forward. Instinctively, he grabbed her, pulled her against him, and dragged her into the bathroom, his heartbeat thumping in his ears and the knife clutched in his hand.

But before he could figure out how to get them out of

the room or to the phone, the banging came again. Not gunshots. A fist. "Hey, someone need a lock changed?"

The sound of the deep smoker's voice had him releasing a breath. The locksmith.

"Yeah, be right there," Wes called out.

There was grumbling from the other side of the window as the guy trudged back to the front, and Wes could feel Rebecca shift against him.

Against him. *Oh, hell.* She was pressed along the wall, and they were body to body. Good parts to good parts.

And his good part was quickly taking notice.

He hurried to move away from her, give her some breathing room, but she clung to him, her face pressed to his shoulder. Only then did he realize she was trembling all over.

*Uh-oh.*

# chapter
# SIX

REBECCA DID NOT WANT TO BE FREAKING OUT, BUT HER whole body was shaking without her permission. When she'd heard the banging, she'd thought for sure those boys with the gun had come back. She'd braced for the shots she'd expected to shatter the window. Could already feel the glass cutting her skin, the bullet hitting. Wes had dragged her into the bathroom, blanketing her body with his, which had given her a sense of protection, but it'd also brought back horrid memories of feeling the weight of Finn on her and the pain in her leg when she'd been shot at the school.

Another hard tremor went through her.

"You okay?" Wes asked, his voice soft and urgent against her ear. "Talk to me."

Only then did she realize that she was still huddled up against him, her fingers gripping the front of his shirt and her face pressed to his shoulder. Clinging. *Oh, shit.* She quickly released her hold on him, and he stepped back. She scrambled for words, trying to get her nerves in check. "I'm—I'm really sorry. That was…"

"A totally reasonable reaction," he finished for her.

She looked up and curled her quivering fingers into her palms.

He scowled. "Who the hell goes banging on windows like that this late at night? Damn. Call my cell, man."

She swallowed hard, trying to keep the tremble out of her voice. "Right. But I'm sorry anyway. I'm not usually this…" Her hands fluttered helplessly. "I don't know what I am tonight."

"You're someone recovering from a terrifying night. Seriously, give yourself a break. Even my brain went to gunshots first." He walked back into the bedroom and set the knife down on the dresser. "Nothing to be sorry about."

She followed him out, her legs feeling a little steadier beneath her but her muscles still tingling with adrenaline. "I know. I just hate acting like some damsel in distress. I'm usually more together than this and—"

"Hey, stop, all right?" he said, breaking into her rambling. "You damsel however you damn well please. No one's grading you on how to react after being robbed. You've had a hell of a night. You didn't expect to be attacked. You didn't expect to be saving a dog. And I'm sure you didn't expect to have some strange dude traipsing through your bedroom at midnight."

"With my underwear wrapped around his shoe," she said, forcing the joke out to push back the fear, to bring this back to something she could deal with.

"What?" He glanced down at the scrap of lace hooked over his boot. "Aw, hell."

She couldn't help but smile at his obvious chagrin. He crouched down, but she put a hand on his shoulder, stopping him. "I should probably get those."

He coughed, trying to cover a laugh. "Right. Yes. Good life lesson. No touching other people's underwear without permission."

She bent and snagged the lace from the floor, balling it in her hand, and then tossed it into the bathroom. "How about we pretend I didn't panic and you didn't see my underwear, and we can let the locksmith in?"

He gave a quick nod. "I've already forgotten everything. What's your name again?"

She rolled her eyes. "Come on. All this freaking out has made me hungry."

—∿—

A little while later, the locksmith had changed the lock on the back door and was hard at work out front while Rebecca and Wes dug into their food at the kitchen counter. She tried to make small talk, asking Wes questions because she didn't want to talk about herself. She was under no illusion that once he figured out who she was, things wouldn't turn awkward and ugly. She didn't have the energy for that tonight, and right now they had an easy rapport. She wanted to keep it that way. Wesley Garrett could eat his food and leave before he ever realized that they'd met before.

"So you work at a school?" she asked between bites of butter chicken. "This is delicious, by the way."

"Devin knows what he's doing. And not a school. I teach culinary arts at an after-school program for teens who've gotten in some kind of trouble—with the law, with school." He smirked. "You know, giving kids with anger problems knives and access to fire."

"Ah, living on the edge," she said with a nod. "You like it?"

He was looking at his food again, but she caught his hesitation, his frown. "It wasn't my plan to do this, and the cooking itself is pretty basic. But I like the kids, and I'm not teaching them one of the standard subjects, so they don't mind coming to my class. It's not too bad."

She considered him. She didn't think that was the job he'd had when he'd been married. He'd been some type of chef. When Devin had mentioned Wes cooked, the memory had clicked into place. But she'd won Wesley's ex-wife a big settlement, from what she could remember. More than what a teacher could afford. "And Devin thinks you shouldn't be doing that?"

"Devin has a vested interest in me doing something else. He's trying to get me to buy a food truck from his uncle so that I can open up my own."

She looked up at that, remembering the wistful look on his face when he'd stared out at the food park. "Is that something you want to do?"

His expression clouded. "'Want' or 'don't want' isn't really the question. I'd love to fly a fighter jet, doesn't mean I should. I had big plans in my twenties to open my own place and I got close, but it…didn't work out." His jaw flexed and he looked up. "There are lots of pluses to where I work now. Regular paycheck. Predictable schedule. All that good, stable adulting stuff. But I do miss cooking my food and the creativity involved. Dev thinks a food truck would be a good compromise. Something smaller scale and, at least in theory, more manageable."

"They seem to be all the rage now."

"They are, which also means heavy competition. It'd still be a high-risk bet, and the truck's in rough shape. I'd have to build the thing up from scratch on my own and do all the remodeling in between my teaching hours. I'd also have to get an investor or two to help with the up-front costs. So if it doesn't work, I've lost a ton of my money, other's people's money, and my job."

"There's that." She broke off a piece of naan and dipped it in the green sauce. "I'd say no risk, no reward, but I'm not one to talk. I'm not a gambler."

He considered her. "Sure thing kind of girl?"

*Understatement of the year.* "Failure isn't fun. Plus, I work all the time. There's not a lot of opportunity for risks or chasing some passion project anyway."

He ignored the wine she'd poured him from a bottle she'd found in the back of her pantry and took a sip of water instead. "All work and no play carries its own risks. You may end up seeing ghosts and chasing people in a snowy hedge maze with an ax."

"True. I'll make a note to avoid all creepy hotels and mazes." Though it was a joke, she couldn't help but think how the parallel to *The Shining* wasn't all that far off. She *had* heard and seen some ghosts tonight. She took another long sip of her wine. "Maybe if I had a hobby I wouldn't have been walking home so late from work tonight."

He frowned. "That's not what I mean. What happened tonight could've happened at any time, so don't put that on yourself. But too much of anything can turn bad. If you did have the time, what kind of project would you want to do?"

She shrugged. "No idea."

"Really? What are you into?"

She laughed under her breath, no humor to it. "That's the problem. I've spent so much time working on school or career stuff that I wouldn't even know where to start." She shook her head. "And damn, that makes me sound boring."

She glanced up to find him staring at her, and she realized she'd said too much, that the wine and the stress of the night had messed with her normal guards. She was being overly chatty and philosophical. God help them both.

She waved a dismissive hand. "Sorry. Ignore me. Tonight has put me in a weird mood, and I talk too much when I drink."

"Don't apologize, and I don't think that makes you boring, just focused. Plus, figuring out where to start may be the fun part. You could try different things and see what clicks. Take a class on something or volunteer somewhere. I could show you how to cook. I've heard I'm a pretty good teacher of egg frying."

A choked laugh escaped her. "You *do not* want to take on that train wreck. I once set my dad's kitchen on fire making popcorn."

He grinned. "Oh, but I love a hopeless case. I have a student who couldn't make toast when we started this year. This past week, she made crepes that I could've served in a white-tablecloth restaurant. I have faith."

Rebecca bit her lip, realizing that maybe he was being serious, that he wanted to see her again and teach her to cook. Images of that flitted through her head. Wes next to her, sleeves rolled up, his hands on her, guiding her through the steps, feeding her bites of food. And...

*What. The. Hell.*

She needed to end this conversation before it went off the rails along with her good sense. She'd let herself forget she wasn't supposed to be talking about herself or enjoying his company too much. She could not see Wesley after tonight. Could. Not. "I don't think I have a hidden passion to cook."

"Fair enough," he said, his eyes meeting hers. "But there's something in there. You don't strike me as a woman without passion."

Her belly dipped, and she tried to ignore the shimmer of awareness that went through her at the way he was looking at her, like he was seeing right through her unaffected facade and reading her thoughts. "How do you figure?"

"You were passionate about saving that dog tonight, and you have stacks of books by your couch, which I'm guessing are about topics you're into. And when you first tasted Dev's food tonight, you got this look on your face like it'd taken you to another place. Not everyone savors food like that. Believe me," he said softly. "That's like chef crack. It makes us want to feed you all the things."

She'd just taken another bite of the chicken, and she became hyperaware of the way he was watching her lick the remnants of sauce off her lips. *All the things.* What would he feed her? Would *he* taste as spicy as the chicken? She forced the bite down. "Eating for a hobby would be dangerous."

"Also"—he gave her a serious look—"you wear blue lace underwear, which I'm thinking isn't worn by passionless women. I mean, if they were green or that weird nylon material, then all hope would've been lost. But blue. Blue is the color of the sky and the ocean. It means hidden depths and endless possibilities."

"We were supposed to forget you saw that."

He lifted his palms. "We're talking about hypothetical blue underwear, of course."

She arched a brow. "You normally talk to strangers about their hypothetical underwear?"

"Don't you?" His smile was playful. "You can learn a lot about a person that way."

"Oh really? What do yours say about you?" The question was out before she could stop herself.

"Hmm." He peeked down and apparently reached for the waistband of his jeans to check. "That I'm irresponsible because I forgot to do laundry again and had to go without."

Her gaze automatically slid down, even though his lower half was beneath the counter, and she quickly jerked her attention back up, but not before she felt her face heat. "And the TMI is complete."

He laughed. "Fine. Enough about underwear. All I'm saying is that there are sparks already. You just have to try new things and figure out what's going to set you on fire."

She rubbed her lips together, her skin too hot. He wasn't talking about the two of them, but her mind kept wanting to go there. Trying things with him and seeing what set her on fire. She pushed the thought away, shoving it into an increasingly stuffed mental closet labeled *Shit You Should Never Think About*. "And cooking lights that fire for you?"

He rested on his forearms, bringing him closer, his gaze intent, honest. "It does. Among other things."

If she closed the space, leaned in, she could kiss him. Some reckless part of her wanted to, wanted to pretend that he wasn't a guy who'd cheated on his wife and that she was a woman who could hook up with a hot stranger without a care. She could already see the scene playing out in her head. Wes's lips on hers, the spicy taste of the food and wine lingering between them. Him stepping around the island and pushing her up against a wall, making her forget the horrible night. His mouth moving down her neck, her fingers in his hair, his hands sliding beneath her shirt. He wouldn't be shy or halting. He'd take over. She could almost feel the heat of him against her, his palms sliding along her bare skin.

"Rebecca…"

Her pulse quickened at the rough sound of his voice, and she swallowed past the dryness in her throat. "Huh?"

"I think the locksmith called out for you."

"Oh, right." She quickly shoved her chair back with a loud scraping sound, breaking the strange, quiet spell between them. "Sorry. Excuse me a second."

Wes leaned back and nodded. "Sure."

Rebecca hurried to the front of the house, sweat gathering between her breasts and her body too hot in the best places. What the hell was wrong with her? She was not allowed to fantasize about Wesley Garrett. She was not that stupid.

*Trauma.* People reacted to it in all kinds of weird ways. This had to be some strange response to what she'd been through tonight.

Her brain was seeking a distraction. A super hot, tattooed, hazel-eyed distraction. Something all consuming that would shut down the scary thoughts and let her get swallowed up by pure physical sensation. Sensation she had no doubt someone like Wes could dish out banquet style.

*Great.* She was now making chef metaphors about sex. She needed to get Wes out of her house, pronto.

When she walked into the living room, the locksmith was packing up his gear. He gave her a brief humorless smile and handed her keys. "Ms. Lindt, I've got both the front and back door done. Top-quality dead bolts. You should be good to go. Do you want to pay now or have us bill you?"

She frowned. "Go ahead and bill me. My purse was stolen, so I have to get new credit cards and I don't have any cash on me."

"No problem, and I'm sorry to hear that."

"Thanks."

He tipped his ball cap at her and grabbed his gear. "Call us if you have any trouble with anything."

She walked him out and then shut the door behind him. She tested the keys and locked the door, anything to delay going back into the kitchen. But eventually, she had to face Wes.

When she walked in, he was cleaning up the remnants of their dinner, bicep flexing as he wiped down the counter. "All is well?"

She cleared her dry throat and nodded, resenting the fact that the man even looked hot cleaning. "Seems to be."

"That's good." He set down the rag and tossed the takeout boxes in the trash. "Do you want any more wine?"

She lifted her palm. "Nope. Please cut me off."

*Because I'm this close to doing something stupid.*

"Do you have a mason jar?"

"Um, probably. Why?"

"Best way to keep the wine fresh. Recorking it is a waste. But if you put it in an airtight mason jar in the fridge, you can get a few more days out of it."

She smirked and went to a cabinet to get an empty jar. "Helpful tips from Chef Wes?"

"I don't like to waste things, especially good wine."

"You didn't drink any of yours."

Something tightened in his expression, but it was gone as fast as it was there. "It's late, and I'm driving. Don't want to fall asleep on the way home."

She handed him the jar, his fingers brushing hers, and she quickly stepped back. "Thanks again for everything tonight."

He smiled as he poured the wine into the jar. "No problem. I'm glad I could help, and though I hate the reason why we ended up here, I enjoyed the company."

"Me too," she said, the honesty falling out of her before she could think better of it.

He screwed the lid tight and tucked the wine into the fridge. When he turned back around, he stepped a little closer. Still a friendly distance, but she felt the shift in his demeanor. "And I know you nixed the cooking lessons, but if you like to try new foods, I could show you around the rest of the park sometime. Give you a tour of all the best stuff. I know Dev has more things you should taste."

The offer took the air out of her for a moment. "You're asking me out?"

He blinked at her blurted question and then gave her a chagrined smile as he tucked his hands in his back pockets. "No, of course not. Because that would be a completely dick move after the night you had."

She blinked, still trying to process everything.

"But I like talking to you," he went on. "So maybe we can call it a request for tonight not to be the last time I ever talk to you. How about that?"

"A request for further conversation."

He nodded resolutely, eyes sparkling with humor. "Yes. Totally. Should I send a formal invitation through your secretary? Because that sounds pretty official."

She shook her head, unable to fight a smile. Why did this guy have to be so damn charming? The insane part of her wanted to say yes. But charm was probably what had gotten him in trouble in his marriage. He could talk his way into any woman's bed.

*Ugh.*

She'd finally met a guy who made her laugh and got her thinking dirty thoughts, and he was a cheater and a former adversary who would eventually figure out who she was. Once he knew her last name, it'd probably all click into place. Disaster was imminent, which meant there was only one logical answer. And she was a logical person. She met his eyes. "I'm sorry, but I can't."

His smile sagged. "Have further conversation?"

"Right. Sorry. It's just, I'm always busy and you're… not my type." She winced inwardly at the choice of words.

His wince wasn't so inward. "Ouch. Not even the type for further conversation. Okay, fair enough."

"It's not… I mean, you're…" *Beautiful. Ridiculously charming. Freaking dangerous.*

He lifted his hands in surrender. "No need to explain. Seriously. I asked. You said no. We're cool. But I'm going to head out and let you get to bed. Do you have a house phone if you need anything tonight?"

She shifted on her feet. "Yeah, I'm covered."

"All right. Well…take care."

In that moment, she saw snapshots from the night. Of a man fearlessly running toward her to help and cradling a hurt dog on the way to the vet and blanketing her body in her bathroom to protect her. Of making her laugh when she felt like she was going to lose it.

On impulse, she stepped forward and wrapped her arms around him for a quick hug. He may be a jerk in other parts of his life, but tonight he'd been anything but to her. She wanted him to know that what he had done meant something to her. "Thanks again for everything. It was way above and beyond the call of duty."

He stiffened in surprise, but then he wrapped his arms around her, his warmth and scent surrounding her. "You're welcome. Glad I could help."

She held on for longer than was appropriate, the comfort of his embrace like a cozy blanket after the hellish night. But when she finally relented and eased back, Wes didn't release her fully, his big palm staying pressed to her back. Her hands remained on his waist.

He stared down at her, his gaze searching like she'd confused him, and she had no idea what kind of look she was giving him back.

Then, she felt herself lifting up on her toes, and before her brain caught up, she cupped his stubbled jaw and pressed her lips against his. He made a choked noise, but he didn't back away. Instead, his fingers curled into the back of her shirt, the grip tight, like he was afraid she'd bolt.

Her logical self was screaming in her ears. *What the hell are you doing? Abort! Abort!* But she couldn't stop a horse that was already out of the gate. His lips softened against hers, and he kissed her back gently, an exploration. He tasted of spicy food and maleness and every delicious fantasy she had conjured. The basic, needy parts of her revved with anticipation, readying for more. Maybe she could have this. Just for a minute.

But as her muscles went soft and pliant and his tongue grazed hers, logical thought shoved its way to the front of the line, demanding to be heard. *Cheater. Cheater. Cheater.*

*Shit.* She dropped her hands from his face and leapt back, her heart beating too hard and her body feverish.

Wes blinked down at her, desire clearing and confusion replacing it. "I, uh... What was that?"

She winced and wanted to fold in on herself. "Um, a thank-you and goodbye?"

He ran a hand through his hair like he was a little scattered himself. "Goodbye? That...felt like the opposite of a goodbye, Rebecca. That felt like a whole lot of hello."

"I know. I'm sorry. I don't know what that was." She crossed her arms and shifted on her feet. "I may be a little drunk."

*Such. A. Lie.* Tipsy, maybe. Drunk, not so much.

He let out a breath and nodded. "Drunk. Okay, well, *that* is definitely my cue to leave."

He stepped forward, and her heart nearly came to a stop in her chest. He was going to kiss her again. But

Wes's hand came up to cup the back of her skull, and he kissed the top of her head instead. "Get some rest and have a nice life, Rebecca. Hope you find something that sets you on fire."

He stepped back and she deflated, a pang of embarrassment heating her face. Good Lord, what was wrong with her? She was acting like a hard-up fool with a man she definitely didn't need to get involved with.

She gave him a tight smile. "Thanks. Sorry for the… weirdness. Hope you figure out the food-truck thing."

"Right. Weirdness." A rueful expression passed over his face, and then he turned and headed out without looking back.

She stared at the place he'd vacated for a long moment, his presence still lingering like a quiet mist. Her shoulders sagged, and she trudged to the back door to lock the new lock. She tapped her head against the doorjamb a few times.

Well, she'd wanted him to leave. She'd accomplished that with epic awkwardness. No more worrying about getting wrapped up in something or someone she shouldn't.

She leaned against the door and pressed her fingers to her tingling lips, a hard kick of longing going through her. *Longing?* No. Wesley Garrett was not someone to long for. Not only did he have a checkered history, but if he'd known who she was, he never would've requested more conversation or…kissed her back.

This was for the best. Obviously.

So why did she suddenly feel like she'd lost something?

# chapter
# SEVEN

REBECCA SLID INTO THE BOOTH IN THE BUSTLING Broken Yolk restaurant, earning the surprised gazes of her three friends. "Sorry I'm late. It's been a morning. And I couldn't call because I had to get a new phone. Long story."

Kincaid shifted over along the bench seat to make room, her blond ponytail swinging. "Rebecca Lindt is fifteen minutes late for Bitching Brunch. I was starting to worry the apocalypse was nigh." She flagged the waiter down. "Sugar, can you get my friend a mimosa? I'm guessing she needs one. Or two."

The young guy smiled a smile that Kincaid seemed to inspire in every male with her Southern belle accent and long-lashed beauty-queen looks. "Right away, ma'am."

"Thanks," Rebecca said, tucking her purse between her and Kincaid and sending a smile to her other two friends, Liv and Taryn, who were sitting on the other side. "I may need three. And lots of pancakes."

And these women. Which was a new concept for

Rebecca. Up until a few months ago, she'd lost touch with these three ladies, former classmates from Long Acre High. Rebecca had thought moving on from the tragedy in high school meant leaving everything and everyone having to do with it behind, but when they'd all come back together for a documentary about the school shooting, they'd reconnected.

Based on what they were in high school, they would've been an unlikely crew. Olivia the artsy, goth Latina who was too cool to care what anyone thought. Kincaid, the dance team captain who was on top of the popularity food chain. Taryn, the quiet but dedicated student and athlete. And then Rebecca, obsessed with grades and student government and anything that earned her a gold star and made her look good to her dad and colleges.

They hadn't been friends until after the shooting, when they'd ended up together in a support group, and then they'd lost touch for over a decade. But now Rebecca realized how much she needed these women and was thankful to have them back in her life. Women who knew her before. Women who understood exactly how hard it was to move on when something that traumatic defined your past. Now, even though they were all busy with their own careers, they'd made a promise to get together regularly and to be there for each other. The Bitching Brunch was one version of that.

Liv, whose black hair was pulled into a messy bun atop her head, glanced at the bandages on Rebecca's arms and frowned. "Whoa. What happened, Bec?"

It was on the tip of Rebecca's tongue to say she'd fallen and leave it at that. After years of saying she was all right after the shooting, putting on a brave face and pretending she wasn't a complete disaster inside, she had a tendency to default to that response. *Move along. Nothing to see here.* But she took a breath and dragged the automatic response back. She didn't have to fake it with her friends. "I was mugged Friday night on the way home from work. I got knocked down onto the pavement."

Taryn's brown eyes went wide behind her plastic pink-rimmed glasses. "Oh my God, girl. Are you okay?"

Liv and Kincaid had matching expressions of horror on their faces.

"I'm all right," Rebecca said tiredly. "It could've been a lot worse. They got away with my purse and phone. But they…had a gun."

Her voice caught on the last part, and Kincaid pressed her hand to her chest, her bangle bracelets jangling. "Oh, honey."

"Jesus," Liv said, reaching across the table and giving Rebecca's hand a squeeze. "I would've freaking lost it."

She and Liv shared that phobia. Liv hadn't been shot on prom night like Rebecca had, but she'd had a gun pointed at her face. She'd had that moment where she knew she would die. That imprinted on a psyche. Rebecca would know.

She squeezed Liv's hand back and sighed. "It all sucked, but I'm okay beyond a few scrapes. This big dog came to my rescue and went after the one who had the gun. But the guy shot the dog in the leg."

"They shot the *dog*?" Taryn asked, horrified.

"There's a special place in hell for people like that," Kincaid said before taking a long sip of her mimosa, her eyes full of concern.

The waiter brought Rebecca two drinks, and she quickly ordered a plate of banana pancakes.

"So is the dog okay?" Liv asked, sitting back in the booth and sweeping her bangs away from her eyes. "Did the guys get caught?"

Rebecca took a gulp of her drink, letting the sweet fizziness soothe her, and nodded. "I think the dog is going to be okay. This guy came to help me, and we took the dog to a vet. I called to check on him yesterday, and I'm going to stop by the clinic this afternoon. But the guys who robbed me got away—one with a pretty nasty dog bite."

"Well, I hope the wound festers and goes septic, the sick sonofabitch," Kincaid said before tucking a big bite of pancakes in her mouth, the thought of septic wounds and revenge clearly not impacting her appetite.

"Amen," Taryn agreed. "I'm just glad you're okay, Bec."

"*Are* you okay?" Liv asked, her gaze meeting Rebecca's. "That sounds traumatizing in its own right, but…"

*For us, it's more. It's always more.* Liv didn't have to finish that sentence for Rebecca to know what she meant. Rebecca rubbed the spot between her brows. "I think I'm okay. I haven't slept much. Friday night, I had to call all my credit card companies and the bank to get my cards canceled. And even though I had a locksmith come out that same night, I haven't been able to stop picturing people lurking outside my house. Then I go from scared to pissed, and that keeps me awake, too."

"You know you can always stay with me and Finn for a few days if you don't want to be at your house," Liv said. "I know it's a bit of a commute, but you wouldn't be alone. And Finn wouldn't mind."

"Thanks. But I think I'll be okay." Rebecca appreciated the offer and knew it was coming from a genuine place. Finn was an FBI agent, so she'd definitely feel safe there. Plus, Liv and Finn's place by the lake was in Wilder, far outside the city and away from any potential attackers. But the option didn't hold much appeal.

Even though she was happy Liv and Finn had found each other again, being around them still held some awkwardness. Finn had been the one Rebecca had loved in high school, her best friend, the one her hopelessly romantic self had been convinced was for her. But all along, Finn had secretly loved Liv. And since all the ladies at the table had opened their high-school time capsule letters about their hopes and dreams a few months ago after the documentary filming, *everyone* knew how ridiculously head over heels Rebecca's crush on Finn had been. She was still trying to figure out how to be around Liv and Finn without feeling like the uncomfortable teen she used to be.

"Were you able to get all of your credit cards squared away?" Taryn asked, kindly steering the conversation back to a safer topic.

The waiter dropped off Rebecca's pancakes and provided refills all around before leaving them to it again. Rebecca poured syrup over her stack. "Yeah. I got a new debit card yesterday and a phone this morning. So I think I've got everything taken care of. All I have left to do is go check on my rescuer."

"Did the dog belong to the guy who intervened?" Kincaid asked.

"No, he's a stray," Rebecca said between bites. "I'd fed him some of my dinner earlier on my walk, and he must've followed me. He was really sweet when he first came up to me, but he turned into a beast with the muggers. I'm not sure what would've happened if he hadn't attacked the one with the gun. I completely froze."

*And accepted my fate.*

She shook off the chilling thought.

"Damn, sounds like a badass stray dog," Taryn said, adjusting the colorful headband she was using to keep her halo of black curly hair away from her face.

"Right?" Rebecca's lips curved at the memory of the dog's fluffy face while he tried to con her out of her bread. "He really was kind of amazing. The vet said he has to heal, and they have to make sure he's not aggressive or rabid or something. But if he's okay, I might… give him a place to stay."

The words came out before she could evaluate them, but she realized they were true. A dog was not part of her plans. She worked too much, and her house wasn't set up for one. But there was no damn way she was letting that dog go to the pound.

"You're going to adopt him?" Liv asked.

"Maybe…foster him," Rebecca said carefully. "Like, until he has a family to go to."

Kincaid gasped and then did a fast clap with her hands like a happy child. "Yay, she's doing the thing!"

"The thing?" Liv asked, her flat tone channeling her former emo self.

"The letter," Kincaid declared like it was the most obvious conclusion in the world.

"Oh Lordy." Taryn rolled her eyes. She held up a piece of bacon and swirled it in the air like a wand.

"Here we go. She's going to break out the spirit fingers. You've been warned."

"Kincaid—" Rebecca began.

"No, it's Bartholomew," Kincaid declared. "Your time capsule letter said you would get a dog and name him Bartholomew."

"My time capsule also said I would stay a virgin and marry Finn in Paris," Rebecca said. "I don't think we should take these things literally."

"No, 'cause then we'd have to fight," Liv teased. "The boy's mine."

Rebecca laughed and raised her palms. "He's all yours. And as for the dog, he's definitely not a Bartholomew."

"That doesn't mean it doesn't fulfill something in your letter," Kincaid insisted. "A few months ago, you said you didn't have time for a dog. Now you might adopt one. Progress, Bec."

"I still don't have the time. Work is crazy, and I'm helping my dad with his campaign and this charity thing he needs me to do. All I said was *foster* the dog until he has a home. I'm not on some mission to fulfill something I declared when I was seventeen. I'm just not going to walk away from a dog who saved me if he doesn't have a home to go to."

That was all it was because she could remember that letter word for word, and it was *not* her life plan.

> On this day, August first, I, Rebecca Lindt,
> promise the Class of 2005 that I will not waste
> the second chance that I have been given, that
> I will honor all the people we lost by living my
> life to the fullest. Professional goals: I will get

*a law degree and graduate at the top of my class. After practicing law for a few years, I will run for political office and will fight for better gun-control laws and more mental-health interventions for teens. I will make a difference in the world. Personal goals: I will stay a virgin until I'm married. And I will marry Finn Dorsey in a Paris wedding. We'll have two kids, preferably one boy and one girl, and a dog named Bartholomew, after my grandpa. I will be a good friend, wife, and mom. I will be happy.*

The words had been the ramblings of a girl who was terrified, hurting, and racked with guilt. A girl who thought she could maybe repay her debt to the universe by living a life dedicated to important causes and who could will herself into happiness through some good-girl, TV-sitcom life.

Seventeen-year-old Rebecca had thought if she tried hard enough, she could go on with her life like she hadn't been damaged by what had happened. As if she hadn't been irreparably altered by it. Thirty-one-year-old Rebecca knew better.

"So some Good Samaritan helped you and the dog?" Liv asked, pulling Rebecca from her ruminating.

Rebecca shifted her attention to her food, trying to beat back the embarrassment that automatically appeared with thoughts of Wes. "Yeah. He ran over to help when he saw the dog attack. Turns out his brother's a vet, so he was able to call him for help. I rode to the clinic with them."

"Wow, that was really nice of them," Taryn said.

Rebecca shrugged. "It was. Unfortunately, the guy who helped happened to be a former client's ex-husband—one who I took down pretty hard in court. He didn't realize who I was, but it was kind of awkward."

"Ouch," Taryn replied. "That's bad luck."

"Yeah. Luckily, he left my house none the wiser."

"Your house?" Kincaid asked. "What was he doing at your house?"

*Making me laugh. Driving me insane with want. Kissing me back.* Rebecca waved her fork dismissively but didn't look her friends in the eye. "He gave me a ride, and I was kind of freaked out that the guys who robbed me could be in my house, so he came inside with me to check it out. And we'd picked up food, so I figured I should let him eat it there. But then he kind of asked me out, and I obviously couldn't say yes and—"

"Hold up," Kincaid said. "Honey, you knew who this guy was, but you got dinner with him and let him into your house?"

Rebecca pursed her lips. "It wasn't… He offered, and I didn't have a way home otherwise."

"You could've called one of us," Liv said. "You know you always can."

"Y'all live an hour outside the city, and it was late. It just made sense, and he was being genuinely helpful. He was actually really nice and funny and…charming, if I didn't think about the fact that he was a cheater. I kind of got swept up in it and then didn't know how to get out of it gracefully. I ended up telling him he wasn't my type."

"Harsh," Liv said, laughing.

"I didn't know what to say. It just…came out." *And then I kissed him.*

"Would you have said yes if you hadn't known who he was?" Taryn asked, head cocked, eyes curious.

Rebecca shrugged and poked at her food. "I don't know. I'm not sure how much we'd have in common. He's kind of got that tattooed bad-boy thing going."

Kincaid's eyebrows arched high. "Oh. So he was cute."

Rebecca straightened, her face warming. "I… That's not what I said."

"But he was," Kincaid pushed.

Dammit, she was blushing. Indignation filled her. "Which is totally irrelevant because he was a cheater and that means he's a jerk. And if he'd realized who I was, I'm sure he would've shown that lovely side of himself."

Kincaid eyed her and sipped her mimosa. "Hmm."

"Don't *hmm* me, lady," Rebecca said. "There's no intrigue here. Yes, he's hot. Fine. I can admit that."

"Ooh, not cute but *hot*. Better." Kincaid grinned wickedly.

Rebecca groaned. "I also know he stepped out on his wife and had anger issues in court. So, I'm thankful he helped me out last night, but I'll never see him again so none of this matters anyway."

Kincaid shrugged. "Probably not, but all I'm saying is that not everything has to be so black and white all the time. I've never seen you get all red-faced and evasive talking about a guy before. You should take those opportunities when they present themselves."

"Opportunities?" Rebecca said sardonically. "You mean when strange men who cheat are at my house?"

Kincaid gave her a patient look. "Honey, I know you're always working and are probably more of a date-with-an-eye-to-the-future kind of girl. I get it. We're in our thirties now, clock's ticking, all that bullshit the world likes to remind us of. But sometimes it's fun to just, you know, find a hot guy to hook up with, especially one who's outside your normal dating zone."

Rebecca stared at her. "He's. A. Cheater."

"Which doesn't really matter if you're just going to take him to bed once or twice," Kincaid said. "That doesn't mean he's not going to be any fun. A guy can be terrible relationship material but a fantastic lay."

Liv laughed. "I hate to say it, but she speaks the truth."

Rebecca turned to Liv, lips parted. "*Et tu, Brute?*"

Liv's mouth curved wryly. "Hey, I'm all about the committed relationship now, but before Finn… Well, you know. I wasn't out to put a ring on anybody."

Taryn shook her head and dabbed her lips with a napkin. "Clearly, I'm doing this single thing all wrong. I can report that these random hot men are not hanging out in Long Acre or at the university research library."

"No, apparently, they're hanging out on the streets of downtown Austin waiting to save a damsel in distress and her trusty doggy companion," Kincaid said.

"I am no damsel," Rebecca announced. "And believe it or not, I'm not holding out for The One. I don't believe in that concept. I'm not even looking for long-term."

"Really?" Liv asked, surprise in her voice. "But your letter…"

"Was written by a lonely, infatuated teenage girl who didn't know any better. I'm a divorce attorney. What I see at work every day doesn't exactly boost my confidence in the institution of marriage. I don't want any part of that, but hookups are complicated."

"Complicated?" Kincaid cocked her head. "Then

you're doing it wrong. By their very definition, they're supposed to be the opposite."

"Not for me," Rebecca said. "The last true hookup I had was in college. The guy was someone I met at a bar my friends dragged me out to. I went with him to his place, and the minute things got R-rated and he took off my pants, I had to deal with all the questions."

"Your scars?" Taryn asked.

"Yeah. There's no way to hide them in that situation, and there's no way someone's not going to ask questions. So if the scars don't turn them off at first sight, the answers to those questions are just about the number one mood-killer for a hot night." She stabbed her fork into her pancakes. "The guy couldn't…perform after that. I had no idea if it was because of my story or the scars themselves. So, yeah, fun night. I'd like to avoid a repeat. I'm better just casually seeing someone who's already a friend or colleague and knows my background. The friends-with-benefits kind of thing."

Though she didn't have that many friends, and it'd been far too long since she'd had any benefits.

Liv frowned. "I'm sorry, Bec. That sucks."

"But that was one guy," Kincaid said gently. "Not all guys are going to react that way. If you don't want to get into the whole story, just make up something."

"You want me to *lie* to a guy to get him in bed?"

"You're not doing it to *get* him into bed," Kincaid clarified. "He's already in your bed at this point. Just tell him you were in a car accident. Something simple that doesn't bring up all those questions. You shouldn't have to relive that night every damn time you just want to get laid. That's not fair."

Rebecca chewed her pancakes, absorbing Kincaid's words but shaking her head. "I don't know. I think I'm incapable of something that spontaneous anyway. I overthink everything."

Kincaid shrugged. "All I'm saying is that not every guy has to get all A's on your report card. For a long-term partner, sure. Make someone meet all the standards. But for a good time, it's okay to find a hot C student."

Rebecca sniffed and tipped her chin up in mock haughtiness. "Valedictorians *do not* date C students."

Kincaid grinned. "I didn't say date one, sugar. Just screw one."

Rebecca burst into a laugh, her friends joining in, and people at other tables turned their way to send them dirty looks. Rebecca pressed her hand over her mouth, trying to staunch the guffaw, but she didn't really care if she was being obnoxious at the moment.

She needed this.

She didn't know if her friends gave good advice, but they certainly knew how to get her mind off her horrible night and its awkward ending.

She leaned back in her seat, trying to catch her breath. "I heart you people."

Liv and Taryn grinned back at her, and Kincaid patted her leg. "Back at ya, Becs. Now let's finish up these pancakes and drag your ass to the pet store because we know Bartholomew is going home with you soon, and Aunt Kincaid needs to buy him a sparkly collar."

"He's a boy."

"This matters how?"

Rebecca shook her head and ate her pancakes.

# chapter
# EIGHT

WES CARRIED ARMFULS OF GROCERY BAGS UP MARCO'S stairs and was about to bang on his brother's door with his elbow when he saw the sticky note with Marco's atrocious doctor's handwriting over the peephole. *Downstairs at clinic.*

Wes grunted. "Things you could've texted me before I went up two flights of stairs."

He shifted the bags in his arms—not wanting to leave them on the doorstep since some of the stuff needed to be refrigerated—and traipsed back down to the clinic. The place wasn't open on Sundays, but Marco was probably checking on patients who'd stayed the night. Marco paid techs to do that, but his brother had a hard time not poking his head in since he lived right upstairs.

Wes pushed his way through the back door, where he was assaulted by animal smells and barking. He poked his head into the kennel area. "Marco, you in here?"

The only answer was a chorus of yapping, yipping, woofing canines and intermittent meowing from the cats.

"Dammit." Wes glanced toward the front, seeing the lights on in the lobby, and headed that way. At least there he'd have somewhere clean to finally set down the groceries. He pushed through the door. "Dude, you could've fucking told me that you were going to be—"

But as soon as Wes looked up, his words cut off. His brother was at the front desk with raised brows, and he wasn't alone. Two sets of female eyes turned Wes's way. One of which belonged to the woman he'd never expected to see again. A woman who'd promptly shut him down after he'd stupidly made things awkward and then had given him the hottest goodbye kiss he'd ever had, leaving him reeling and half-hard by the time he'd gotten home that night.

Rebecca had done the right thing, sending him away. He'd been ready to continue that kiss, preferably in the horizontal position. It'd been so damn long since he'd felt that blinding, full-bodied urge to be with someone that it'd been like the rush of a drug. But Rebecca had been drinking, and she'd already told him he wasn't her type. Plus, he'd been playing a role, acting like someone he wasn't capable of being. Some light-hearted guy who made jokes and flirted and had no rattling skeletons in his closet. The whole thing had been a mistake, but he also wasn't immune to the dent in his ego her comment had left. Mainly because it hadn't just been "not my type" for dating, but for friendship in general. Even his best, fake version of himself wasn't up to par for her.

Now she was here, looking at him like she wanted to turn tail and run. *Great*. Now awkward would escalate to full-out uncomfortable. "Sorry, I thought you were closed."

"Sorry, ladies. My younger brother apologizes for his language." Marco sent him a look.

"Your brother?" the blond woman said. She turned a beaming smile on Wes. "The one who helped Bec out the other night?"

"That'd be me," Wes said flatly.

"Well, hi there." The woman gave him an evaluating look. "And don't worry about us. We're not that easily scandalized."

Rebecca gave him a grim smile.

"Rebecca wanted to stop in and check on our patient," Marco added.

"Hi again," Wes said, hoping he sounded casual. "Marco, I need your key so I can put some of this stuff in the fridge."

Marco jabbed a finger at a table that had handouts about pet care on it. "Just set them there for now. I'm heading up right after I finish this. Rebecca's going to foster our canine rescuer once he's healed up enough. Isn't that great?"

"Fan-frigging-tastic," Wes muttered as he set the bags down.

Marco frowned his way, letting him know that his mutter wasn't so quiet. "Why don't you take her back to visit him while I process this paperwork?"

Wes straightened. "What?"

Marco cocked his head. "He's in the big kennel on the far end. Walk her back."

"Oh, he doesn't have to—" Rebecca started.

But her friend cut her off. "Oh, you should go, Bec. This is bonding time…with Bartholomew."

Rebecca closed her eyes as if she was counting to three to keep her cool. "That's not his name, Kincaid."

Her friend smiled and shooed her. "Go on. Go visit. I'll keep the good doctor company."

Marco glanced up at the woman, Kincaid, and smiled this goofy-ass smile. Wes had to swallow back a snort. Was his big brother *blushing*? God help him. That chick talked like she was made of honey and sweet Southern sunshine, but those were the type who could take you down before you knew what had hit you.

Rebecca, on the other hand, sent Wes an apologetic look as she walked over.

*Great*. Pity. How fun.

He tried not to notice how good Rebecca looked in her fitted white pants and pale-blue sleeveless top. She still had a few Band-Aids covering some of the damage from the other night, but he hadn't seen this polished version of her yet. Makeup subtle but covering her freckles, long auburn hair twisted into some kind of knot. All class and sophistication.

No wonder he wasn't her type. She looked like a woman who threw garden parties in the Austin hills and hired men like him to cater them and bring her wine.

And blue. Of course she was wearing blue.

She didn't speak until she was close enough for only him to hear her. "So we meet again."

"Fate has a sense of humor."

She glanced back at her friend. "So it seems."

"Come on. Your doggy friend awaits." He motioned for her to come with him and walked quickly down the hallway, ready to get this over with, but he had to pause at the door to the kennels when he realized she hadn't kept up with him. He turned to see what the deal was, but he didn't have to ask. There was a hitch in Rebecca's gait. She gave him a tight smile. "I'll catch up. Just lead the way."

But he didn't move. "Did you hurt your leg in the attack?"

Her gaze flicked away. "No."

"But…"

"Not this attack. An old injury got aggravated."

"Not this att—"

"Don't worry about it. I'm fine. Where's the dog?"

Her tone snapped him back to reality. "Right. This way."

The cacophony of dog noises increased as they stepped into the kennel area and the residents discovered there were people present. Most of the animals in the front part were pets staying while their owners were out of town. So they were all eager to get out and play or go home. But as Wes led Rebecca to the other side, the noises became quieter, more whimpers than barks. The infirmary area.

Rebecca glanced around, frowning.

The big, black dog that had saved her was in one of the larger kennels in the corner. Wes walked over there and squatted down. "Hey there, big guy."

Sad eyes looked up at Wes, and the dog let out a little whine. The pup's leg was bandaged, and he had one of those cones on his head to keep him from aggravating his injury.

Rebecca stepped up behind Wes, her breath whooshing out of her and tickling the back of his arm. "Oh God, he looks so pitiful."

She crouched down next to him, and the vanilla scent of her shampoo or perfume cut through the dog smells for a moment, making Wes want to lean closer and inhale. He gritted his teeth, mentally berating his body's natural reaction to this woman.

She reached into the cage and brushed her fingers over the dog's muzzle. "How you doing, sweetheart?"

The dog's tail thumped hard against the floor as he wagged it, and he whined.

"I know, baby. Shots in the leg are a bitch. Are they treating you well in here?" she asked. The dog licked her fingers.

"Of course they are," Wes said. "He's got the best doctor." He reached out to scratch behind the pup's ear. "But don't tell him I said that, big guy, or I won't sneak you treats."

Rebecca sent Wes a half smile. "You have any pets?"

He sat back on his heels. "Nah. I can't even remember to do laundry. I definitely can't be trusted with living things."

"I hear you. You know what I did to the basil."

Wes chuckled and put his hand over his heart. "May it rest in peace."

Rebecca continued to pet the dog but glanced over at Wes. "Look, I know this is weird. I'm really sorry about how I acted Friday night. I think the combo of wine and the stress of the night made me…I don't know, react strangely. I was out of line with that goodbye kiss situation."

Wes swallowed hard, fighting to keep his expression neutral. "I didn't exactly push you away. I should've realized you'd had too much to drink. I used to be a pro at spotting that with customers in restaurants, but I'm out of practice."

Her gaze darted away. "No, the whole thing was on me. So I just wanted to say sorry."

He forced a shrug. "No worries. No permanent damage."

She gave him a tense smile. "Good. And hey, don't feel like you need to stay back here if you have stuff to do. I can find my way back to the front. I know you had groceries to deal with."

"It's not a problem. Plus, Marco wouldn't want me to leave a client back here alone. Hell, I'm surprised he let me back here. He's very particular about rules. But I don't know, maybe I should go up front and keep him safe from your friend. My brother looked ready to propose."

Rebecca smirked. "Don't worry about Kincaid. She flirts with every good-looking guy she comes across. It's her way. She's harmless. Mostly."

Wes stood, unsure why hearing that Rebecca considered his brother good-looking annoyed him. Was Marco more her type? Mr. Responsible Doctor. He shoved his hands in his pockets, pushing the old jealous instinct down with them. That was dangerous territory.

"So I'm assuming those guys never showed up at your house?" he asked, changing the subject.

She looked back to the dog, stroking his scruffy head. "No. Not that I've been able to sleep, thinking about it, but I'm guessing if they haven't shown up yet, they're not going to. And the cops called and said they have a few leads."

He frowned. "That sucks that you're not sleeping, but I'm glad the police might be close to catching whoever it was."

"Me too."

"Well, if you adopt Scruffy the Wonder Dog, you'll have an added layer of protection. That guy who attacked you has probably developed a fear of dogs."

"He should. Bastard," she said, her tone hardening. "And I'm not adopting at this point. Just fostering."

Wes watched how gently she stroked the dog, how attached she already seemed. "How come?"

She shrugged. "Like I told you Friday night, I'm always working. I wouldn't be able to give him all the attention he deserves. He should have, like…a bustling household with a family and kids and stuff. Not a single woman who doesn't get home until seven or eight each night."

"Maybe he can be what inspires you to end your day a little earlier," Wes suggested. "Give you something to come home to. A mini passion project."

"We'll see," she said with a resigned tone, as if she didn't believe that was a possibility at all.

Wes shifted and crossed his arms, fighting hard not to take his fill of the view. The slope of her bared neck, the hint of lace beneath her thin blouse, the narrow strip of skin exposed at her lower back. *Look away, Garrett.* "I never did get to ask you what keeps you so busy."

Her shoulders drooped at that, and she let out a breath. "No, you didn't."

Something about the way she said it gave him pause. She gave the dog one last rub and then grabbed the cage to hoist herself up. When she turned to face him, her expression reminded him of the way the banker had looked when Wes had gotten turned down for the loan. "I'm an attorney."

"Oh." The words registered but also nudged something in the back of his brain. He frowned. "What kind?"

She cleared her throat. "Divorce."

*Divorce.*

His stomach sank, flashes of an image coming back

to him. A woman with short blond hair preaching to a judge about all of his flaws. A woman with sharp words and biting accusations. *Mr. Garrett broke the vows of his marriage. Mr. Garrett can't control his temper. Mr. Garrett drinks too much and scares his wife. My client deserves half of anything the restaurant's worth.*

Awareness dawned, pinpricks of cold fury breaking over his skin. He stared at Rebecca, switching out the hair color and cut. All his breath left him, and he stepped back. "You've got to be fucking kidding me."

Her throat bobbed. "Wes…"

"You represented my ex," he said, voice flat. "Your last name is something with an *L*…"

"Lindt."

*Fuck.* "You know who I am."

And who he used to be. All those ugly things. Things he wished he could forget. Things he'd been so happy to be free of for a few hours Friday night.

"I—"

A chilling thought hit him. "When did you realize who I was?"

She winced.

"*When?*"

She sighed. "When I heard your last name at the clinic."

He stared at her in disbelief. "So the *whole time*? And you just let the night go on like it did and didn't say anything? You were… You *kissed* me, Rebecca. What *the fuck*?"

She turned her head with a cringe. "At first, I didn't think it was relevant. The night had been stressful enough. I didn't want to add to it."

"But what about after that? All that talk about

restaurants and passions and shit? You *knew* that I used to have a restaurant, how I lost it. You knew the whole time." He scoffed. "No, you didn't just know. You helped *make that happen*. Were you just laughing at me in your head? Was that kiss some sort of game?"

She frowned. "Of course not. I wouldn't do that. I just didn't know how to undo the situation once it started rolling, and then wine happened and I got caught up in a moment. I thought by saying no to seeing you again, that it would be the end of it, but…here we are."

He ran a hand over his face. "I can't believe I bought dinner for the woman who helped take my restaurant from me."

She stiffened at that. "Are you really going to hold it against me that I did my job?"

He gave her a hard look. "Why wouldn't I? Brittany didn't deserve a damn dime of my restaurant. I lost everything in that courtroom because her parents could afford a high-priced lawyer and Brittany could put on a show."

Rebecca's cheeks colored. "You cheated on your wife. You flipped out in court. I didn't do those things. I just represented your wife to the best of my ability."

His jaw clenched. "So that means you can rest easy at night, right? You did your job. That's all that counts. It doesn't matter if your client was lying or not. Or if you helped destroy someone else in the process. Just do your job and collect your nice paycheck. Got it."

The dog barked at them as if sensing the tension.

"I don't have to worry about if she was lying if there were pictures."

A bitter taste filled his mouth. "And that tells the whole story, right?"

She crossed her arms.

His neck felt hot, all the old anger trying to bust through the surface. He wanted to yell, to tell her the whole damn story, to flip tables like he had in the courtroom. But then he'd just prove what she already thought of him. That he was out of control.

And what did it matter anyway? What was done was done, and after today, he would never see her again. She'd already decided who he was. *Not her type*. Yeah, no shit. He rubbed a hand over the back of his neck. "Whatever. Come on. I'm sure Marco is done with the paperwork, and I'm done with this."

He turned to head back to the front.

"So you're telling me that wasn't you in the pictures?"

His fingers curled into his palms but he didn't say a word. What was there to say? He couldn't say no.

He needed to get the hell away from this woman. She was stirring up old shit he didn't want to have to think about again, old versions of himself that he wanted buried. He could feel that treadmill speeding up, trying to knock him back. Thinking about all this was making venom rise up in his throat. Venom and destructive urges.

"Right," she said, taking his non-answer for affirmation.

That did it. He whirled around, making her pull up short. "No, not right. You of all people should know that there are gray areas, different angles to see things from. Isn't that what lawyers are supposed to find?"

"I'm not investigating a crime."

"No, just convicting me."

She let out a sound of frustration. "No, *you're* convicting *me*. Look, I don't care what you do in your personal life. That's not my business. I know you're not a completely awful person because you helped me the other night, and you seemed like a nice enough guy. But your ex hired me. I used the facts and evidence I had, and I did my job. If you're going to hate me for that, then fine. But I didn't do anything wrong."

He made a sound of contempt. "Right."

Her eyes held fire, but he turned on his heel and strode away. He didn't need this crap right now. He just wanted to go upstairs to Marco's place and get lost in prepping potential appetizers for the charity event. Not think about his Dumpster fire of a marriage. Or everything that had happened after the fall of a gavel in that courtroom.

Or why it bothered him so much that this woman had slapped a label on him and filed him away in the bastard category. So they'd shared a hot kiss. So what?

Rebecca Lindt's opinion shouldn't matter to him. But for some reason, the look on her face, that one that deemed him a cheater, a scumbag, an asshole who would step out on his wife got to him.

He couldn't deny what was in those photos, though, and the truth would put that curl of disgust in her lip anyway. He didn't know much about Rebecca Lindt, but he'd bet everything he had in the bank that she'd never experienced the kind of reckless dysfunction and drama he'd had in his marriage. In his life.

She was the woman whose house was neat as a catalog, one who'd wait to cross the street until the sign said *go* even if no cars were coming, and one who would definitely not understand how he'd ended up in X-rated photos with his wife's best friend.

*chapter*
# NINE

REBECCA FOLLOWED WES, ANGER SIMMERING, AND found Kincaid in the lobby beaming at Marco, her trademark smile at full sparkle. The doc looked totally and completely charmed. If he were a cartoon, he would have little hearts swimming around his head. Rebecca couldn't blame him. Kincaid was a force of nature.

Rebecca had no idea what that would be like, to have guys fall over themselves to hold her attention. Kincaid had been that way since high school. She was *that* girl. And Rebecca couldn't even hate her for it because Kincaid was a genuinely nice person. Rebecca had never seen her stoop to the mean-girl level.

No, Rebecca had been more likely to do that. Rebecca *had* done that. In the worst possible way. Her stomach twisted, but she tamped the feeling down before it could take over. She had enough to deal with right now. Like getting away from Wesley Garrett.

"All squared away?" Rebecca asked.

Marco glanced at her as he typed something into the

computer. "We're good to go. As long as our friend keeps progressing like he is and keeps showing us his docile personality, you'll be able to foster him once he's healed."

"Great," Rebecca said, feeling equal parts nervous and excited about the possibility of having a pet for a little while.

"Marco, I need to get these groceries upstairs," Wes said from her right, the words sharp with impatience.

Rebecca tried to ignore the ire she could still feel wafting off Wes. How dare he blame her for what happened in the divorce? She didn't make him cheat.

"All right, almost done." Marco peered back at Wes with a smile. "And I found us some extra taste testers so we don't have to rely on my steak-and-potatoes palate."

Wes froze in her periphery. "What?"

"Kincaid here runs a food blog on the side," Marco said happily. "She said she and Rebecca would volunteer to give you some feedback on your dishes today."

"Wait, what?" Rebecca shot Kincaid a look.

Kincaid smiled and shrugged in an oops-style apology. "Well, we just got to talking. You know how that goes. And it came up that Wes is going to be catering Marco's charity event. Marco said he didn't know what good he'd be at picking out the menu because Wes is cooking fancy vegetarian stuff, and that's not his thing. So I told him about my blog, and well, you said you were free this afternoon, right?"

Rebecca didn't know if she was successfully concealing the what-the-hell look on her face, but she definitely couldn't keep it out of her tone. "I said I was free *to go to a movie with you.*"

"Well, now we can have some food before and help out a good cause," Kincaid said happily.

"This charity's the one that helps pay for the care of strays like our friend in there," Marco added.

*Oh, great.* Rebecca grimaced inwardly. So a guilt trip on top of it. All because Marco probably wanted more time to flirt with Kincaid.

Wes's horrified expression was not well concealed. "Marco, I really wasn't planning to cook for a crowd and—"

"Oh, come on. It's not a crowd. Two more people isn't a big deal."

Wes glanced at Rebecca and, for the first time, they were on the same side of the courtroom. She was about to list all the reasons why she could not spend the afternoon there and was hoping Wes would have more reasons of his own to add to the argument. But Marco cleared his throat, and Wes looked back to his brother. Something silent but effective must've passed between them. Because after a moment, Wes closed his eyes and shook his head. "Fine. The more the merrier."

*What?* Rebecca's mouth opened to protest, but she couldn't get the words out before everyone else chimed in.

"Great," Marco said.

Kincaid clapped her hands together. "Yay."

Wes simply sighed. "Food needs to go up and into the fridge, or no one's going to have anything to eat."

Rebecca walked over to Kincaid while Marco helped Wes with the groceries, and she leaned close to her friend's ear. "I'm going to kill you in your sleep. Slowly."

Kincaid smirked. "No, you should be thanking me. I'm doing this as much for you as for me. You weren't lying when you said your Good Samaritan was hot. Woo, boy."

"Which completely doesn't matter because he figured out *who I am*, and now he hates me." Rebecca huffed. "I'm not feeling so fond of him either."

"Oh, I doubt he hates you. Who could hate you?" Kincaid patted Rebecca's arm. "Come on. It'll only be an hour or so. Maybe y'all can talk it out. And it's for a good cause."

"What? Your love life?"

Kincaid bit her lip. "Well, the doc *is* super adorable. And smart. I love buttoned-up, brainy guys. They are usually full of surprises behind closed doors."

Rebecca grunted.

"But if you need me to figure a way out…"

Rebecca glanced at Kincaid's hopeful face and couldn't bring herself to tell her to cancel. "You are going to owe me so big for this. Like, huge."

"You're the best." She grinned and grabbed Rebecca's hand. "Come on. Let's go and let hot, angry guy cook for us."

---

Fifteen minutes. That was how long it took for Marco and Kincaid to abandon Rebecca and Wes in the kitchen under the auspices of *Let me show you the view* from Marco and *Does this building have original details?* from Kincaid.

Kincaid had motioned at Rebecca as she slipped out of the kitchen, some invented sign language that probably meant *Talk it out with the hot chef* but looked more like a drunken game of naughty charades.

Rebecca had promptly flipped her off.

But now here she was. Alone with Wes again.

Wes stood behind the large island, black bandanna keeping his hair back, gray T-shirt putting all that colorful arm ink on display, and forearms flexing as he sliced and diced an onion with practiced precision. If not for the simmering annoyance, it would've been a nice show to watch from her spot sitting on a stool on the other side of the counter. But he hadn't said a word to her since they'd gotten into the condo. Just *chop, chop, chop* and irritated grunts.

"Do you need any help?" she asked for lack of anything else to say.

"Can you help me murder my brother?"

"I was thinking we could get rid of them both in one go. How far is the drop from the balcony?" Rebecca tapped her chin. "We could make it look like an accident. I know someone who could defend us."

Wes smirked.

The little break in the wall helped her relax some. "Why'd you give in anyway? I was about to get us out of it. I had a whole argument prepared. There were bullet points. Closing statements. We could've saved ourselves this lovely moment."

He frowned and dumped the onions into one of the prep bowls. "Yeah, but you didn't see the look on my brother's face." He pushed a basket of strawberries and a paring knife toward her. "Can lawyers hull strawberries?"

"Sure." She took the berries and stole one of his empty prep bowls. "So what kind of look was that?"

"The don't-ruin-this-for-me look. The remember-all-the-times-I've-helped-you-out look. That look."

"That's a lot for a look to say."

"Yeah, well, it wasn't hard to get the point. He's always working and doesn't get to go out and meet women. He likes your friend, and she seems to like him for whatever reason"—he shrugged and grabbed a bell pepper from the stack of vegetables—"so I'm hanging out with my ex-wife's lawyer and taking one for the team."

She wrinkled her nose.

"What?" he asked.

"Nothing. I'm just having a high school flashback." Thankfully not the kind she'd had Friday night, but one that was unpleasant enough in its own right.

"How's that?"

She concentrated on cutting the stem off a strawberry. "I had a friend whose parents would only let her go on group dates. So I always got dragged out with her and had to be the date of her boyfriend's best friend, who pretty much reminded me every ten minutes that he was there as a favor and was *taking one for the team* by hanging out with me. It was super awesome for my fifteen-year-old ego."

"Ouch. What an idiot."

"Yeah, I should've just told her to leave me out of it and sneak out like everyone else."

"No, I meant him. What a douche."

"Oh. Yeah. He was." But even as she said it, she felt a pang of guilt in her gut. Craig hadn't made it through prom night. So douche or not, she felt guilty talking bad about the dead. "We were just in a doomed-to-fail setup. Popular jock and high-strung goody-goody were not a wise combination. Two different planets and all that. He probably thought I was an insufferable Miss Priss."

His lip curled. "Were you?"

She lifted her hand and held her index finger and thumb an inch apart. "Maybe a little. I wasn't...not. When they brought weed to date night, I couldn't just say no and let them do their thing. I gave everyone a lecture about how long it stays in your system and how having something on your record could ruin your college chances."

He cringed. "Ahh, you were that girl. We had one of those at my school, too."

"Yeah?"

He nodded. "Laney Becker. And she thought I was a douche."

"Were you?"

He lifted his fingers, repeating her motion back to her but widening the gap further.

"Nice."

"I probably would've done better if I'd been friends with someone like her. I could've used a girl telling me not to blow off class and get high. Or doing a lot of other things I shouldn't have been doing back then." He tossed more chopped veggies into a bowl. "And I'm sorry about the 'taking one for the team' comment. I didn't mean it that way. This is just...a screwed-up situation. I'm willing to call a temporary let's-forget-we-have-history truce for today."

"I'm on board with that."

"Good." He frowned down at her chopped berries. "Hold up. That's not how to hull."

She looked down at the berry in her hand. She'd cut off the top. The stem was gone. She didn't see any problem. "What's wrong?"

He set down his knife and stepped around the island. "You're wasting a big part of the berry that way. Here." He held out his hand for the paring knife, and she handed it over. He shifted until he was right next to her and held the fruit in front of her. "The woody part is just under the leaves. That's what you're after."

He poked the tip of the knife right beneath the leaves and then made a circle around the stem. He popped out the stem and only a little piece of the berry, leaving much more of the fruit intact.

"See." He held the strawberry in his palm, the sweet scent of the ripe fruit wafting up to her. "Lots more berry, and you also don't lose the shape of the fruit that way."

"Oh." She tried to focus on what he was showing her and not on the fact that he was so close and she could feel his body heat against her arm. Her hormones apparently had no qualms about this man. They remembered what his lips tasted like and were ready to ignore everything she knew about him. *Stupid, misguided hormones.*

"Now, you try." He dropped a berry in her hands and gave her the knife again.

She rolled her lips together, concentrating, and poked the knife into the spot he'd shown her. She made a little circle, not quite as quick or precise as he'd been, which irritated the perfectionist in her, but she managed to get the stem out. "Like that?"

"Exactly," he said, flashing a brief smile. "See. Not a hopeless student."

"I'm sure your real students would run circles around me."

"Some would," he admitted. "But we haven't gotten

to hulling berries yet. The shoestring budget for the cooking program doesn't exactly allow for fresh berries. Even frozen would be a stretch."

She frowned. "Is it a state-funded program?"

"No, donor- and community-funded, and the cooking program is in a rebuilding phase. It was inactive for years, but they hired me to try to get it up and running again. There's not a lot of money to work with since it wasn't part of the original budget, and we're in a poorer neighborhood so the parents can't really help. But I'm working with the kids on some fund-raising ideas so we can get some new equipment and better ingredients, and maybe do a special project or trip during the summer."

"That's got to make it tough to teach how you want."

He shrugged. "I grew up on a shoestring budget, so I can make a meal out of almost anything. But the equipment thing is a pain. We're down to one oven that saw its best days in 1985." He set down his knife. "But enough work talk. Your reward for learning how to properly hull is that you can be the first to try this recipe."

He went to the fridge. Her gaze followed him, and she absolutely *did not* notice how his T-shirt rode up at the back waistband of his jeans when he leaned inside to get something. Nope, didn't see the strip of tanned skin either. Not at all.

*Ugh*. Next she'd be humming the song "Hot for Teacher." She shifted her focus back to the berry in her hand. "So what are you making with them?"

He spun around, a small container in his hands. "This."

He walked back to her and plucked the strawberry out of her fingers. "I made the filling ahead of time so it'd be good and cold. For the party, I'll pipe it in with a pastry bag and make it look fancy, but you'll still get the flavor this way." He dipped a spoon into the fluffy mixture inside the container and then stuffed it into the strawberry. "Try that."

She took the strawberry from him, eyeing the creamy concoction, which looked to have tiny chocolate chips mixed in. She took a bite, the juice of the strawberry running down her hand, and then sighed when the flavors hit her mouth. Tart and sweet and creamy and rich. Decadent.

"Good God, that's good," she said, mouth still full.

He smirked, all confidence and sex appeal. "Right?"

The rest of the filling tried to escape the berry, but she quickly caught it with her other hand and licked it off her finger.

When she glanced up, finger still in her mouth, she found him watching her, something dangerous flickering in his gaze, something that made the back of her neck heat. She quickly lowered her hand to the counter. "That's amazing. What is it?"

"Chocolate-chip cheesecake filling."

"Ah, I should've known," she said, grabbing a napkin and cleaning her fingers. "All the naughty things."

He lifted a brow. "Naughty things?"

She cleared her throat. "You know. All the things people who want to fit into their pants aren't allowed to eat. No wonder it's good."

"Not true. It's vegan," he said, closing the container and popping it back in the fridge. "This event is animal-product-free. But the fact that you can't tell gives me the information I need."

"Wow, really?" she asked, genuinely surprised.

He went back to his cutting board. "Yep. It has cashew cream and dark chocolate, so no dairy. And there's a little lemon juice, which gives you that tartness you'd get from cream cheese. So really, not forbidden at all. Though I take issue with calling any food naughty."

She started working on the strawberries again. "Why's that?"

He glanced up at her. "There aren't that many things in life that are pure pleasure. Think about it. The list is short—food, sleep, sex. They're meant to be enjoyed. Why ruin it with all that guilt?"

The comment shoved her mind into a different place, back to what she knew about him. She pressed her lips together and forced herself to concentrate on the hulling. "Right. Guilt clearly isn't your thing."

He made a sound of contempt in the back of his throat.

She glanced up. "What?"

"Nothing." A smug smile touched his lips as he ran his knife through another pepper. "You can't help yourself. I can feel the judgment rolling off you in waves. You've got me all boxed up in the asshole category. It's as if high school me had just offered you weed and you're ready to lecture me."

She set down her knife. "Well, what do you expect, Wes? I was in that courtroom. I can't un-know that stuff. You did shitty things. And it…pisses me off."

"You're angry?" His eyes narrowed as he considered her. "I get judging me, but why get pissed? What I did got you a victory. You won. What's it matter to you now?"

She stared at him and then deflated. He was right. Why should she care? The case was done. Her client was satisfied. Yet anger simmered hot. "We're supposed to be pretending we don't know each other."

"It's not working, so we might as well get it all out there."

She stuck out her chin. "Fine. It irritates me because I *wanted* to like you. You came to my rescue Friday night. You were funny and nice. Someone that I could see—"

"Getting drunk and kissing?" he asked, not hiding the sarcasm.

"Being friends with," she said tartly. "But it's ruined because you're also someone who cheated on his wife and acted like a jerk in court. Someone whose word can't be trusted. And I'm mad that you had to be that person."

His expression darkened. "Because your friends have to be perfect?"

"I didn't say—"

*"I'm* the one who has the right to be angry. You helped someone steal things from me that I can never get back. I made you money. You should be thanking me. But no, you're mad at me because I don't fit into the image I'm supposed to. You can't neatly tuck me into the villain box because I helped you the other night. And you can't let yourself like me either because you're only allowed to like people who have a flawless record and who have always done the right thing, like you."

Her throat went tight at that. "Don't act like you know me because I told you one high school story."

He lifted a brow. "So you haven't always done the right thing?"

A fist of tension gathered in her chest, old panic pushing at her nerve endings. "No."

He leaned close, putting his lips right next to her ear.

"I don't believe you. I bet your dates have to bring a résumé and a background check with them before you let them hold your hand."

"Screw you. You know nothing about me."

He rose to full height again, his thighs almost close enough to bump her knees, and met her gaze. "You don't know me either, Rebecca. And you're too locked up in your fortress of self-righteousness to take the time to ask me the whole story or see the person in front of you. You have some photos and the word of a woman who hated me. How would you fare in court if all anyone got to hear about you was your worst mistake? How would you look if you were distilled down to that one thing?"

Her stomach plummeted at that.

"What would your sentence be?" he challenged. "Because I'm still paying for mine every damn day."

She closed her eyes, trying to breathe through the wash of anxiety that flooded her, the familiar cold dread of that *what-if*. What if people knew? What if the truth about what she'd done in high school came out? What if…

"My sentence would be worse," she said softly, the admission slipping out without her permission.

"Worse?" He scoffed. "The divorce *ruined* me. Restaurant I dreamed of all my life? Gone before I could open it. My credit? Blown. My credibility? Shattered. And as a bonus I picked up a fun drinking problem I had to deal with because getting wasted felt a whole lot better than realizing I had nothing left, that I'd climbed to the top of the mountain only to be pushed off the summit before I even got to snap a damn picture." His jaw flexed. "I'll be the first to admit that I was a shitty husband and had no business being married. But I didn't deserve to lose everything, and I don't deserve your judgment."

The back of her throat burned. The words hitting her like pellets of ice. She hadn't asked him the whole story, even when she knew better than most that there were at least three sides to every story. She'd just believed what she'd known from her client and what she'd seen in the photos. She lifted her head. "Was it you in those pictures?"

"Yes." His gaze met hers, steady and clear. "But my ex-wife was the one who took them because she was there, too."

She blinked, the words not lining up. "What?"

"Two years before the divorce, we had a big fight because she'd racked up all this debt on our credit card without telling me, so to make it up to me, she surprised me with a threesome."

"A…" Rebecca's words got jumbled in her mouth. "She… That's…"

"Screwed up?" he asked dryly. "Yeah, it was. That was the kind of fucked-up dysfunctional relationship we had. You get in a fight, so you surprise your husband with your best friend naked in your bed."

Rebecca's face heated, the topic far out of her comfort zone.

"And I was too young and too reckless to realize how epically messed up it was to use that kind of shit to try to fix something in a relationship," he continued. "But it happened, there was a camera involved, and she apparently saved the photos of me and her best friend for a rainy day."

Rebecca stared at him, the admission knocking around inside her and bumping assumptions off-kilter. "She set you up?"

He exhaled, a pained expression tightening the corners of his eyes. "I'd like to think that it wasn't the original plan. But when the marriage went to hell, the pictures were convenient. She wanted me to give up the restaurant because I was obsessed with it and ignoring her—which was one hundred percent accurate. I refused and told her I wanted a divorce. So she decided to make me pay for that decision and figured out how to make sure I lost the restaurant anyway. It worked."

"Shit."

He crossed his arms. "Yeah. And you helped her do that. When my lawyer brought up the truth, you tore that apart. You got a fabricated statement from Brittany's best friend. You painted my ex to be this fine, upstanding citizen who would never engage in that kind of lewd behavior. She was a good Baptist girl from a wealthy family who got swept up by this troublemaker with anger issues."

Rebecca wet her lips. The details of the case were coming back to her now. She vaguely remembered the other lawyer claiming the pictures were from a kinky night, but she'd gotten that dismissed so quickly that it hadn't gotten any traction. And of course, it could all be a lie, a convenient story from Wes, but something about the empty tone in his voice and look on his face told her otherwise.

"Wes, I—"

But he was already talking again. "So, now you know. And no, I don't blame you for doing your job and buying Brittany's bullshit, but don't sit here and act like you're somehow morally superior or a crusader making the world a better place because you take down the big, bad cheaters. You're just a lawyer who likes to win and feel better about taking people's money. But you winning means other people lose. And not all of them deserve to."

"I—"

"So, what's on the menu, brother? I'm starved," Marco said, walking into the kitchen and startling Rebecca.

The dark look on Wes's face disappeared behind a faux smirk as he took a step back. "Slow your roll, man. Art takes time. And I've been teaching Rebecca how to hull berries."

Kincaid glanced her way, questions in her eyes.

Wes went to the fridge and pulled a tray from it. "But you can start on these spring rolls if you want."

"Ooh," Kincaid said, leaning over the tray but sending Rebecca another questioning look and mouthing, *You okay?* from behind the two men.

Rebecca didn't have it in her to give her friend any kind of response. Her nerves were on a razor's edge, and she couldn't breathe in here. Wes's admission had set her off balance, and her mind was sifting through too much. And what could she say in her defense? Not much.

She *did* have a job that was focused on winning and making the most money possible. She believed in helping her clients, but knowing she'd possibly ruined someone who didn't deserve it made her gut churn. She wasn't supposed to worry about that. It wasn't her job to protect the other side. It was the opposing lawyer's job.

Even so, she couldn't get the image of Wes staring longingly at the food-truck park out of her head. She'd felt that yearning from him. She'd helped destroy that dream.

She pushed her chair away from counter and stood. "You know, I just forgot that I was supposed to pick up a prescription before the pharmacy closed today. I'm not going to be able to stay. I'm sorry."

Everyone turned her way and Kincaid frowned. "Honey, I can go with you."

Rebecca waved a hand, trying to appear nonchalant. "No, it's fine. We're in separate cars, anyway. You stay and enjoy the food. Guys, thanks for the invite. I'm sure everything will turn out delicious."

Wes's eyes met hers, a pointed look there, but he didn't say anything.

What else was there to say?

# chapter
# TEN

"YOU OKAY, CHEF G?"

Wes blinked, his hands cold under the running water at the sink, and turned toward the small group of students gathered next to him in the classroom kitchen. "Huh?"

Lola nodded at the stove behind him, pink lips pursed as if she were a seventy-year-old grandmother instead of a sixteen-year-old girl. "You're burning the soul out of that French toast."

"What?" Wes turned and saw the smoke, the scent finally registering. "Oh, dammit."

He turned the faucet off and grabbed a towel.

"Swear jar," Xavier called out, his head in the large fridge on the far side of the student kitchen. "One dollar."

Wes groaned and hurried to the stove to pull the pan off the burner, the stuff formerly known as toast now a charred triangle. He flipped the switch on the ancient vent hood, and it rattled on. "Someone open the window so we don't set off the fire alarms."

Keisha, one of his star students, hurried over to a

window on the far side of the room and opened it wide. "I'm not sure it smells any better outside. Why they gotta put the Dumpsters right next to this room? Smells like something died. Twice."

Xavier sauntered over with a fresh carton of eggs, his loping basketball-player walk making him look even more pleased with himself. He pointed to the mason jar they kept on Wes's desk. "Pay up, Chef G."

Wes pulled his wallet from his back pocket and tugged a dollar from it. He dropped the bill in, adding to the pile. When the kids cursed in class, he made them put in an IOU to do a chore in the classroom, but he held himself to that standard, too. Instead of chores, he put money into the jar to be used to get extras for the class.

Wes went back to the stove and scraped the mess out of the pan and into the trash. Everything smelled of burnt sugar, and the bread looked fossilized. "Okay, everyone. Today's lesson is how not to make French toast."

A few of them snickered.

"You nailed that lesson, dude," Steven said from his spot at one of the tables in the front of the room where he'd been flipping through an old copy of *The Joy of Cooking* to find some new recipes they could riff on. The class had decided that they should make something for a local fair to earn a little money and wanted to do something traditional with a twist, which was Steven's specialty.

But Steven flipping through the book was what had Wes distracted in the first place.

"Sorry, guys," Wes said, rinsing out the pan. "That's why it's important not to take your eyes off quick-cooking things. That was my fault." He nodded at Xavier. "Go ahead and crack a few more eggs and add some milk and the spices. We have enough time to try again. Maybe you should take over this time, Lola. Show us how it's done."

A beaming smile broke out on her round face. "On it. I've been making this for my little brothers for years. Watch how it's done, people."

Lola waved the kids over to the main counter while Xavier whisked the eggs. Wes headed over to Steven and grabbed a chair, spinning it backward to straddle it. Steven looked up from the cookbook and tugged down the sleeve of his oversized sweatshirt.

"Any luck?" Wes asked.

He shrugged. "Not yet. Who the hell eats snails?"

"I don't think escargot would be a big seller at the fair." Wes nodded at the arm Steven had covered up. He'd seen the bandage poking through at the wrist when he'd been flipping pages. "What happened to your arm?"

Steven's gaze slid away, and he shifted in his chair. "It's nothing."

*Nothing. Right.* Wes had heard that before—*said* that before. The kids that ended up at the Brant Street Youth Program came from all kinds of complicated situations. Injuries from fights weren't out of the ordinary. But Wes also had to be on the lookout for more serious things, things caused by the adults in their lives. Wes had met Steven's father, a local cop, a couple of times and had gotten that prickly feeling at the back of his neck at the way the man had looked at and spoken to his son. That survival instinct of Wes's had picked up a whiff of a certain type of malevolence.

Wes had been in that situation once upon a time. His father hadn't been around much because he was busy running his drug business, but when he was home, he was usually angry. He used to put out cigarettes on Wes's arm when he was pissed and knock him around even when he wasn't. Until Wes had gotten big enough to fight back, he'd become a master of hiding the marks so he wouldn't get looks from teachers or social workers. But now he knew the tricks and could spot them. Like the fact that Steven was wearing a thick, blue Texas Rangers sweatshirt on a warm spring day.

"That looks like a pretty big bandage to be nothing," Wes said.

Steven grimaced. "It was stupid. I'm fine."

"What was stupid?" Wes tried to keep his tone casual. "Did something happen at home?"

Steven closed the cookbook and fiddled with a ripped corner of the worn dust jacket. "My friend got a new dog, and the dumb-ass thing bit me."

Wes stiffened, the answer like a sucker punch. "A dog?"

"Yeah. Thing nearly ripped my arm off. Had to get a few stitches. Then I had to hear it from my old man about how expensive emergency room visits are. Fun weekend."

*A dog bite*. Wes didn't want his mind to go there, didn't want to think it. But he got a flash of someone running away. White kid. Dark hair under a ball cap.

A cold feeling crept through him. "When did it happen?"

"Friday. It's getting better, though. I'll live."

*Shit*.

"Chef G," Lola called out. "Come check this out. Xavier cut out shapes in the French toast. Looks fancy."

Wes glanced back at the eager faces of his students, thoughts running through his head too quickly. Just because Steven had a dog bite didn't mean anything. Wes couldn't—wouldn't—jump to conclusions. But as he headed to the front of the class to check on the students' work, a cloak of dread wrapped around him, turning his skin clammy.

Even if it turned out not to be Steven, Wes knew there was no getting out of the next thing.

And it was the very last thing he wanted to do.

―⁓―

Rebecca put her sticker name tag on her jacket and read the numbers above each door. The hallway was unnaturally quiet for a building filled with children, but she could see kids doing different activities through the narrow rectangular window on each closed door—an art class, some kind of martial arts, a computer room. The building was showing its age with its battered bulletin boards and scuffed-up floors, but there were colorful posters lining the walls and student artwork on display. The place was trying to be cheerful even though there was a police officer parked out front and metal detectors at the doors.

She knew most schools, not just these types of after-school programs, had higher security these days. Long Acre had helped launch that new era. Those measures saved lives. But part of her hated that these kids would never get to experience the blissful ignorance she'd had her first few years at Long Acre when the biggest threat at school was dealing with someone you didn't like or getting a mean teacher or having your heart broken by first love. The ugliness of the world encroached far too early now.

She rubbed the chill bumps from her arms and caught sight of the number she was looking for. She took a steadying breath and headed that way. She'd been more than a little shocked when she'd gotten a call from Wes late Monday afternoon. He'd been on her mind since leaving Marco's on Sunday. She hadn't been able to shake the things he'd told her or the thoughts he'd put in her head. She'd spent that night going through the file for his divorce, studiously ignoring copies of the illicit photos and reviewing how the case had shaken out.

Reading through the notes had brought a lot of it back. His ex, Brittany, had gotten a monster settlement. Wes had been a few months away from opening a farm-to-table restaurant in a hip area not far from Rebecca's house. There'd been write-ups about it, lots of buzz, slick photos of Wes looking edgy and gorgeous in his chef's coat. He'd been considered the hot new chef on the scene. But he'd built up too much debt getting the place ready and had apparently been counting on the grand opening to pay it back. Losing so much in the divorce had probably meant bankruptcy for him. Rebecca had looked it up, and the original property had been bought by another chef and was now a high-end barbecue joint.

While Wes worked here, teaching in an after-school program for at-risk youth, which probably paid less than a line cook's salary at one of those places.

He hadn't broken his marriage vows, but he'd lost everything anyway. Rebecca had helped crush his dream. Even though she knew she'd only been doing her job and working with the information she had from her client, the knowledge that she'd played any part in that had kept her tossing and turning the last two nights.

So when Wes had called her, she'd almost wondered if she was imagining it because she'd been considering calling him. She didn't need more debts on her conscience. That bill was already long enough. But he'd told her he needed to talk to her about something, so she was going to take the opportunity to say what she needed to say as well.

Before knocking, she caught sight of him through the window in the door. He was in a black chef's jacket, pen clenched between his teeth, and his attention was focused on a notepad in front of him. She let herself take a moment to stare. He really was unfairly good-looking. She usually veered away from that type. Sure, men like that were nice to look at, a glossy page in a magazine. But she'd learned that being too handsome often meant an entitled personality to match. She didn't get that vibe from Wes.

The man from the photos was still in there. If he looked up and smiled like the world was his, it'd be those newspaper photos in the flesh. But the world wasn't his anymore. That world had beaten him down, and she'd been in the attacking crowd. With a sigh, she raised her fist and knocked.

He glanced up, his gaze colliding with hers. Her heartbeat picked up speed, as if her body couldn't decide if there was danger present or if this was something to get excited about. The moment hovered between them for a long second. Friend or foe? She had no idea what awaited. All she knew was that it was suddenly warmer in the hallway.

Instead of calling for her to come in, Wes got up and walked to the door. When he swung it open, his somber expression looked anything but welcoming, answering her question. "Thanks for coming."

She hiked her purse up higher on her shoulder. "Yeah, sure. Sorry I couldn't get here until today. I've been in and out of court since Monday."

"I understand. I know you're busy. Come on in." He stepped back and let her inside. The office was small with cream-colored cinder-block walls and a window that looked out onto a scrubby patch of grass and a graffitied wall of another building. He had a bookshelf in one corner that was stuffed with cookbooks, old and new. And on the wall next to his desk were a certificate from a culinary academy and a photograph of him, Marco, and two older people she assumed were their parents.

She took the seat across from the desk and folded her hands in her lap. "I'm glad you called, actually. I'd planned to get your number from Marco so I could call you."

"Call me?" Wes lifted his brows as he settled behind the desk. "About what?"

"About what happened Sunday," she said, not wanting to dance around what needed to be addressed. "I'm sorry about the things I said to you. Regardless of what I knew about you from the case, you'd been nothing but kind to me up until that point. You helped me. You made a horrible night not so horrible. I had no right to judge you or make assumptions." She concentrated on plucking a piece of lint off her pants. "I have... strong feelings about cheaters, and I'm not so good at hiding that."

"You've been on the other end of it?"

She smirked despite herself. She'd never had anything serious enough with a guy for that to matter.

Friends with benefits arrangements didn't come with commitment clauses, just a *don't ask, don't tell* policy. "No. But my mom left my dad—and me—for someone else, for another family, when I was a kid and never looked back. And in my job, I get to see people tear apart their marriages all the time for a quick thrill." She looked up and met his gaze. "The whole idea of infidelity makes me seethe. I don't understand why people who want to keep their options open don't just stay single. Why destroy other people and families in the process? But it wasn't fair to make it personal, especially without hearing your side."

"Rebecca—"

"And for what it's worth, I won't apologize for doing my job, but I am sorry that I helped your ex get something she didn't deserve. If I'd known the whole story, I wouldn't have taken her money. Or helped her take yours."

Something softened in his expression and he nodded. "Thank you. I owe you an apology, too. I wasn't fair to you. My disaster of a marriage was on me and my ex—as is the aftermath. I think seeing you and realizing who you were just brought all that crap rushing back. I was an asshole about it. So I'm sorry."

She absorbed his words and nodded. "Thanks."

"But that's not why I called you."

She frowned. "No?"

"I wish it were." He leaned back in his chair and let out a breath. "One of my students came in Monday morning with an injury. A dog bite."

The words were like cold water in her face. "What?"

Wes rubbed his brow, his face weary. "I don't

know if it's related, but from what I remember of your attacker, it could've been him. And this kid…he's a smart kid. Talented in the kitchen. But he's gotten into trouble before, and I get the impression his home life is not great. It's not out of the realm of possibility that he could be involved."

She sat back, her fingers curling around the arms of the chair. "Jesus."

"I haven't called the cops yet because"—he shook his head—"well, one, his dad is a police officer, but also, I've built some trust with this kid and don't want to put him through that kind of accusation if there's no chance it's him. Having said that, I obviously can't ignore the possibility either. I wasn't close enough that night to rule him out. You may have been."

She let out a breath. "You want me to try to ID him?"

"Yeah. If he's the one, I'll call the cops. It needs to be reported. But if he's not, then I can save him another run-in with the law and protect some of that trust I've built with him." He glanced at the clock. "I know it's a lot to ask, but if you have a few minutes, my class with him is about to start. I can tell the kids you're there to learn about the program."

She chewed her lip, the thought of possibly seeing the person who'd put a gun to her head making her throat want to close. But if he was the one, she needed to know. "Um, yeah, okay. I can stay."

He nodded, face grim. "All right. I hate to ask you to do this, but I couldn't think of a better way."

"It's okay. I don't want anyone to be falsely accused."

"Right." He stood and stepped around the desk, putting a hand out to help her up from the chair. The warmth of his fingers seeped into hers as he gave her hand a quick squeeze. "Thanks for this."

She nodded and tried to ignore the tremor of pleasure the simple act of holding his hand inspired. "Of course."

Their gazes held for a moment, but then a bell sound came over the loudspeakers, announcing the end of a period and breaking the spell. He quickly let go of her hand and led her out into the hall.

The hallway filled with teens, and she and Wes were swept into the flow. The noise rose to a level that made conversation impossible, and Rebecca just let herself watch all the kids as they passed. Teenagers laughing and talking. Some quietly making their way through the crowd like mice in a maze. Others rushing to the two vending machines for a drink or snack. And a few bumping fists with Wes or greeting him as Chef G.

Rebecca's muscles tensed as the crowd thickened, any reminder of high school life setting off that hyperalert part of her, but Wes seemed completely comfortable in the chaos, making sure to respond to any kid who acknowledged him. Rebecca focused on that and the obvious affection he had for his students. Maybe he was just teaching them how to fry an egg and it wasn't his dream job, but anyone could see that it was more than just marking time for both him and the kids.

Wes cupped her elbow and ushered her through a stream of people into a room at the end of the hallway. A few kids were already in chairs behind one of the tables in the room, and a short Hispanic girl was behind the big counter in the front, loading ingredients from a cabinet onto the tabletop.

She raised a hand in greeting when they walked in.

"Hey, Chef G, can we try that oven-fried chicken recipe Steven found? The one that uses pancake batter? I have an idea for a maple syrup sauce that might go with it. It'll be like chicken and waffles without the waffle."

"Yeah, Lola, that's fine. I defrosted the chicken before I left yesterday. It should be good to go. But let everyone else get here before you start anything."

Rebecca followed Wes to the front, her attention skimming over the kitchen area. The white Formica counters were chipped and the stove was electric, which even she knew was not ideal. And Wes hadn't been kidding about the oven. It was legit avocado green—and not in a cool retro way, just an old, ugly way. But the girl, Lola, was humming to herself as she pulled ingredients out of the cabinets like she was about to cook at Le Cordon Bleu.

More kids filed in, about ten in total, and Rebecca nervously skimmed over the faces of all the boys. When a tall, skinny white kid wearing a beanie walked in and greeted Wes with *What up, Chef G?* her breath stuttered in her chest. His voice didn't sound familiar, but when Wes told the kid, Steven, to take off his hat and the guy removed his beanie, stringy dark hair fell into his face. Rebecca stilled, snapshots of memories flashing in her head. Snapshots she couldn't trust. Friday night, she'd been hearing Trevor Lockwood's voice, seeing his face. This kid resembled him, but had she seen *this* kid or was her memory just superimposing familiar features?

"Hey, Steven, Chef G said okay to the waffle chicken," Lola announced triumphantly.

Steven grinned. "Sweet. I was thinking we should add something spicy to the maple sauce. Straight-up sweet is just, uh, whaddya call it, Chef G?"

"One note," Wes supplied.

The kid snapped his fingers. "Yeah, that's it. I'm not doing no one-note chicken. This is going to be like a rock song." He mimicked moving his fingers along guitar frets. "All kinds of notes."

Wes laughed, but Rebecca could tell it was a little forced. His gaze slid to her, questions there. And she could see it in his eyes, that desperate hope that this wasn't the kid, that his student wasn't capable of putting a gun to a woman's head and shooting a dog.

She found herself shaking her head.

*No?* he mouthed.

She swallowed hard, glancing at Steven, who was now joking with another student and taking ingredients out of the fridge. From behind, he reminded her so much of Trevor that it made her insides cramp. But that was the problem. Her memory was screwing with her. Everything about that night was a mix of past and present, images blending.

She already knew the stats on eyewitness memory and how faulty it was. She'd learned that as far back as Long Acre when conflicting accounts from students on how many shooters and what had happened had been the norm in the days following. Friday night, she'd been in the middle of some traumatic flashback during the holdup. Her brain had barely been functional. There was no way she could positively identify this kid. Resemblance was a possibility, but it wasn't proof.

She stepped over to Wes and pulled him out of earshot of the group. "I can't say no for sure, but I don't...think so."

He frowned. "He was right next to you when the dog attacked."

She licked her lips. "I was panicking. My head was somewhere else, and my attention was on the dog. It was all happening too fast."

Wes crossed his arms and eyed the group, evaluating. "Okay, how about this? Why don't you stay for the class? I'm going to watch him when I introduce you. You may not recognize him, but if he was the one, he'll recognize you."

She frowned. "Not necessarily."

Wes glanced over at her, a come-on-now look on his face. "He would remember you, Rebecca. You're…"

She raised a brow. "A carrot top? Tall?"

"Pretty hard to forget," he said finally. "Believe me, I've been trying with little success."

The words hit her with a pleasant rush. "Oh."

His lips lifted at one corner. "So, will you stay for class?"

She nodded. "Yeah. Okay. I could do that."

"Good." He looked genuinely pleased that she wasn't going anywhere. "Hope you like spicy waffle chicken, lawyer girl, because we're about to rock your taste buds."

He took a step toward the front, but in a fit of bravery, she reached out and touched his shoulder. "Wes…"

He turned back to her. "Yeah?"

She shifted on her feet, a weird bout of shyness trying to overtake her. "I would like to issue a formal request for…further conversation. And possibly some Indian food on Friday night."

His smile went full sex appeal now, and the impact of

all that masculine charm hit her in her gut. No, not her gut. Lower. Definitely lower.

"I thought I wasn't your type of friend," he said.

"I'm"—she cleared her throat and straightened her suit jacket—"expanding my palate."

"A food metaphor. Nice." His gaze narrowed. "And did you just flirt with me in a room full of children?"

She crossed her arms and gave him her best haughty lawyer look. "Of course not. This is a request for a friendly meal."

He laughed, a deep, melodic sound. "I like it." He moved his hand around, indicating her general person. "I like this whole version of Rebecca who doesn't hate me."

"Keep picking on me about it, and the tide may shift again, chef."

His grin didn't abate. "Noted. I'll be on my best behavior…for now."

There was a dare in his eyes—*Ask me what it's like when I'm not*—and a hot shiver went through her, but she managed to keep her expression neutral.

He turned and clapped his hands. "All right, chefs. My friend Ms. Lindt is a very fancy lawyer, but she works too much and doesn't know how to cook a thing. Who's going to teach her how to make some spicy waffle chicken?"

The kids all turned to her with curious eyes. Steven glanced up from measuring out spices but didn't show any particular reaction. Just looked at her and then went back to what he was doing like he couldn't care less.

Rebecca let out a breath of relief and lifted her hands. "Oh, I just came to watch. I don't need to cook."

Lola, the girl who seemed to take charge of everything,

walked over and hooked her arm with Rebecca's. "Come on, Ms. Lindt. Watching is boring. Chef G says if you're not getting your hands dirty, you're not doing it right."

Wes smirked, the devil in his eyes.

Rebecca tried to ignore the ripple of heat that look sent through her. She slipped off her suit coat and laid it across the back of a chair.

Guess it was time to get dirty.

# chapter
# ELEVEN

THE SETTING SUN CAST SWATHS OF RUSTY-ORANGE light over the worn picnic table as Wes set a falafel sandwich in front of Rebecca, a fatoush salad in front of himself, and unloaded containers of hummus, baba ghanoush, and pita bread for them to share. "Dev parked the truck outside a concert tonight so no Indian food, but the Middle Eastern place is fantastic, too. I figured I'd get a little bit of everything for you to try."

She smiled. "This all looks great."

Rebecca had met him here at the food-truck park after work and had told him to order whatever he recommended. Her easy trust in his taste did more to him than it should. One of his greatest pleasures in life was cooking for people, but feeding them was a close second, and Rebecca was someone who was fun to feed. He'd learned on that first night that she savored each bite and didn't edit her visceral responses. Watching her enjoy that first meal had made his mind wander into dangerous territory, made him wonder if she luxuriated in other physical delights just as wholeheartedly.

The white twinkle lights blinked on in the trees above them as he finished arranging the food, and the Friday night crowd milled around nearby. He took his seat opposite her and pointed to each dish. "Hummus, eggplant dip, your sandwich has deep-fried chickpea patties. That's their specialty. My salad is marinated veggies with chunks of bread. Feel free to share mine if you want some of that, too. And then you have your various yogurt, tahini, and garlic sauces. We will have excellent breath after this. Flowers will wilt in our very presence."

She laughed and unwrapped her sandwich. "I'll take the risk. This smells amazing and looks about a hundred times better than that chicken I attempted to make in your class the other day."

He smirked. "Hey, that was a valiant attempt."

She gave him a surely-you-can't-be-serious look. "The batter fell off into a soggy mess, and the chicken was undercooked. It was not just inedible but potentially deadly."

"You got your wet-dry steps mixed up and battered your hand more than the chicken. It happens. But yeah, maybe don't quit your day job just yet."

"Don't worry," she said wryly. "I'm sticking with what I know. Your kids are great, though. They were sweet to try to make me feel better about my very sad chicken."

*His kids.* That sounded so odd but also…kind of nice. Which freaked him out. He wasn't supposed to get comfortable in his teaching job. It was supposed to be a temporary stop, a stable income while he figured out how to save enough to open his own business again.

His classmates at culinary school had always used the old joke *Those who can, do. Those who can't, teach* to make fun of their militant professors. And though he didn't necessarily buy into that sentiment, he'd known at least two chefs who'd gone to teaching after failed restaurants. He didn't want to be that guy. He wasn't even teaching at a respected culinary institute. He was at a shoestring-budget after-school program. That was like planning to be a rock star and ending up a wedding singer. Or taking your shirt off and cooking for a bachelorette party.

"They're a good group of kids." They weren't the star students at their schools, but in the kitchen, misfits almost always had a home. It was where he'd found his place once upon a time, too. "And if you want to feel better about the chicken, just blame the crappy oven. That's what we do when a recipe fails."

He spooned some of the hummus onto his plate.

"It wasn't the oven," she said after she swallowed a bite of her sandwich. "But you do need a new one. Two new ones, really."

"Believe me, I'm well aware. We don't have the funds for that yet. Any donations the school gets are usually earmarked for the technology program. Just give the kids a tablet, and that will fix everything, right?"

Rebecca shook her head. "You know, Silicon Valley tech executives send their kids to fancy schools that don't allow technology. They think it hampers creative thinking. I think what you're doing with the kids is great. They get to flex all those creative muscles plus learn some life skills."

"I hope so. I know cooking saved me. But we're on our

own to raise money. So the class will be selling some of their favorite dishes at a fair in a few weeks as a fund-raiser. I'm hoping that will raise enough money for the first oven."

Rebecca wiped her fingers on a napkin and rummaged in her navy-blue bag, which was next to her on the bench. She took out a square of folded paper and held it out to him. "Here."

"What's this?" He took the paper from her and unfolded it. His stomach bottomed out at the sight. "Uh…"

Rebecca took a sip of her lemonade. "Will that cover it?"

He stared at her. "Rebecca, this is a check for three grand."

"I know. I looked up prices on gas ranges after I left your class. That should be able to get you two decent ones. You also may be able to work a discount on installation if you go to a local place and tell them it's for a charitable organization."

A tight feeling crawled up the back of his neck, gripping him. "No way."

She glanced up. "On asking for a discount? I mean, I could talk to a store if you want—"

"I'm not letting you give me money. That's… No."

A line appeared between her brows. "I'm not giving *you* money. It's for the program, for those kids in your class. I have the money to give and believe in what you're doing. The school takes charitable donations. What's the problem?"

Wes stared at the neat handwriting on the check, some weird combination of irritation and embarrassment moving through him. "The problem is this feels like some sort of pity payment. Or guilt."

"Guilt?"

"Yes. Like now that you know about what happened in the court case, you're going to throw some money at me either because you feel sorry for me or because you want to make yourself feel better. Either reason sucks. I don't want a handout. The class can raise the money."

She pursed her lips. "That's not what this is. I know your kids can fund-raise, and they should. That will be a good experience for them. But your program needs a lot more than new ovens. This can be a start. I want to—"

"Well, hey there!" a loud voice said before Rebecca could get out her next words.

Wes scowled at the conversation and the shrill interruption, but automatically turned toward the intruder. A vaguely familiar blonde was a few steps away, smiling wide and making a beeline for him.

*What the hell?*

She sidled up next to the table, her hand pressed to her chest like she was just so surprised and delighted. "Oh my gosh, I cannot believe you're here. It's like fate!"

Wes tried to place her but couldn't land on anything. "Um…"

"I *just* put in a call with your boss to see if you were available for another party," she went on. "She said she'd have to check and gave me some song and dance, but I told her we weren't doing it unless it was Roman. We wouldn't settle for anyone else. And now, here you are!"

Rebecca sent him a questioning look as all of Wes's oh-fuck alarms went off.

It was Penis Hat.

He found his voice. "Excuse me, but I'm having dinner with—"

But the woman wasn't listening to him. "So I have a friend who just got engaged, and she would *love* you. I mean who wouldn't love a hot, shirtless guy cooking for them, right?" She did some sort of nudge-nudge, wink-wink pantomime. "But I was thinking a pool party. Could you do it poolside in a swimsuit? Maybe one of those Michael Phelps numbers. She would *adore* that."

Wes closed his eyes, the fuck-my-life thunderstorm raining down upon him and his dignity draining off toward the gutters.

"Excuse me," Rebecca said, her tone sharp as a meat cleaver. "I don't know who you are or what exactly you're going on about, but we're in a private conversation, and I don't remember you being invited. Do you mind?"

Penis Hat made a choked sound, and Wes's eyes popped open.

Rebecca had cocked an eyebrow at the woman and was giving her a look that would make just about anyone get to their knees and apologize.

The woman's lips puckered. "Well, I'm sorry. I didn't see you there."

"No, of course you didn't because you're too busy gawking at my friend and announcing his private business in a public place," Rebecca said, lawyer voice in full effect. "Would you like me to get a bullhorn so you can talk even louder, or are you done falling over yourself and interrupting our dinner?"

Wes bit back a laugh. *Well, damn, lawyer girl.*

The woman bowed up like she'd accidentally *sat* on a penis hat, and her face paled. "I didn't mean to—"

"I'm all booked up," Wes said, cutting her off and

peering at Rebecca. "For the next few months. You'll have to find someone else."

He could feel the woman looking at him, but Wes's attention was still on the lawyer.

"Well, pardon me then," the woman said tartly. "So sorry to bother you."

Rebecca nodded as if to say, *You should be. Now remove yourself from my line of sight.*

Wes looked back to the woman and she stared at him, her eyes pleading for intervention, but he shrugged. She was on her own.

Penis Hat huffed and stalked off, muttering a few choice words as she went, her high heels sinking into the soft grass.

Rebecca finally looked Wes's way, holding his gaze, ice and fire wrapped up in one prim package. She took a long sip of her drink, her expression as calm as could be. For some reason, that cool, above-it-all demeanor—along with her quick dismissal of the woman—made him a little hard.

She set her cup down. "I'm not sure I even want to know."

He adjusted the front of his jeans beneath the table, trying to will away that unexpected but potent reaction to Rebecca and her suffer-no-fools attitude. "Excellent. Because I definitely do not want to tell."

She tore off a piece of pita bread and dragged it through the hummus, her evaluating gaze still on him. He could almost hear the gears turning in her head, and the sound was deafening.

"Okay, I lied," she said between bites. "I won't be able to stop wondering what she was talking about, and that means you must tell me right now or you risk me going into full lawyerly interrogation mode. You have no shot against that. Spill, Michael Phelps."

He cringed, and his unwelcome hard-on died a quick death. "It's nothing. I did a private chef thing for a friend."

Rebecca looked unmoved. "Uh-huh. Which doesn't explain why that woman was talking to you like you were her own personal stripper. What kind of private chef-ing is this?"

He sighed and stabbed a bite of cucumber with more force than necessary. "My friend, Suzie, who is both brilliant and ridiculous, has a new business and asked me to fill in for someone who was sick. They work bachelorette parties and such. It's called Shirtless Chefs."

"Shirtless Chefs?"

"Yes."

"Shirtless. Chefs." Rebecca bit her lips together, her eyes sparking with trapped laughter.

He waved his fork around. "Go ahead. Do what you need to do. I don't want you to pull a muscle from all that restraint."

A snort escaped her, and then a laugh followed it. "I'm sorry." She dabbed her mouth with a napkin, not doing a good job of covering her obvious amusement. "But that's real? Women hire you to cook without your shirt on?"

"It'd be a really shitty business name otherwise."

She grinned. "And you cooked for that woman while half-naked?"

He shrugged. "It was a burn hazard and a little cold, but it paid well."

Her laughter was light and melodic. *Delighted* even. He wanted to rewind time.

"I hope it pays well. Based on how that woman was looking at you, I'd say it's a very high-risk work environment. You could've been mauled," she said with faux seriousness. "How much do you charge?"

He groaned and looked to the darkening sky. "Enough. Why?"

"Because maybe I'm in the market for cooking lessons after all."

He waved a hand in a bring-it-on motion. "Go ahead. Get it all out there."

"I mean, I'd certainly pay more attention if a hot shirtless guy was giving me the lesson. But no banana-hammock bathing suit. There are some things I don't want to see while I'm eating. Things could fall out."

He looked at her and cocked a brow, her words taking some of the sting out of the embarrassment running through him. "Oh, so you think I'm a hot guy, huh?"

"I didn't say *you*. I'm sure there's a whole menu of guys I could choose from." She set her chin in her hand and gave him a cheeky smile. "I would need to peruse. Weigh the options. Gauge my mood. Do I want dark and broody guy? Or surfer guy? Or—"

He tossed a cucumber chunk at her.

She dodged it, eyes bright. "So you're being serious. This is an actual thing."

"It is a thing. Though I hope to God there is no menu of men. But the last time I saw that woman, she was wearing a hat shaped like a penis, and I was teaching her and her friends how to make big, meaty balls."

"Big, meaty..." A full laugh burst out of Rebecca,

one that seemed to echo around the park and warm him from the inside out.

He couldn't help it. He laughed with her.

She dabbed at her teary eyes with a napkin once she got her composure again. "Oh my God. That sounds both hilarious and painful. And like something Kincaid would be all over. She may get engaged *just* to have a party like that."

"And you?"

"Me, what?"

"You said you'd hire a shirtless chef."

She shook her head and lifted a hand. "I was kidding. I would never."

"No?"

She made a sour face. "No. I have a high aversion to paying some guy to act interested in me. I don't want pity flirting."

"*Pity flirting?*"

"You know what I mean." She took a bite of her sandwich.

He frowned. "No, I don't."

She waited until she'd swallowed her food and sipped her drink. "Yes, you do. It's like the whole concept of a strip club. Or even something as simple as a bartender who's being flirty just to get a good tip. I feel like in their head, they're really making fun of you. *Oh, look how easily I can fool this clueless chick into thinking I'm interested*. They're playing you."

Wes stared at her, knowing he had to be giving her a what-the-hell look. "Rebecca, no one would need to be paid to flirt with you."

She gave him a skeptical look, the compliment

seeming to roll off her unheard. "Did you flirt with those women at the shirtless chef party?"

He let out a breath. "Yes."

"Were you interested in any of them?"

"No."

She tilted her head in a point-proven way. "There you go."

He grunted. "Does it help to know that I hated every minute of it? Playing them doesn't feel any better than being played."

"Really?" she asked, sounding surprised. "Pretty ladies fawning over you seems like it'd be quite the ego boost."

"That's not the kind of ego boost I want. I spent most of my adult life busting my ass and honing my skills to be a chef. I take pride in my food and running a kitchen. But there I was, having to do a job that depended more on my workout routine than what I can cook." He ran a hand over the back of his head. "I'm sure the guys who work for my friend have a good time with it and are there because they're into it. But for me, it was fucking humiliating."

Rebecca's eyes met his, sympathy there. "I'm sorry, Wes. I didn't think about it that way. I wouldn't have teased you about it."

"I know," he said with a shrug. "It's really not that big of a deal. Just not my scene."

"Why'd you do it at all if you hated it so much? Was it just to help out your friend?"

His jaw flexed, and he looked back down at his meal, prodding it with his fork. "I'm not that altruistic. She needed the help, but I did it for the extra money."

"The money." She braced her arms on the table, her

attention feeling like a spotlight on him. "For the food truck Devin wants you to buy?"

Wes rolled his shoulders, trying to shake off the frustration her question inspired. "For the idea of it. That thing will sell long before I save up enough to buy it. But next time an opportunity like that comes up, I at least want to have the ability to consider it. I don't want to get complacent and stuck where I am forever. A safe and stable job makes my family happy, but it doesn't feed that thing inside me that craves the adrenaline and risk of being in charge of my own business. I want to know that I can do it."

"I get that," she said, no jest in her voice. "I sometimes get this urge to break out on my own, start my own law practice, to know I could do it without my dad's help or influence."

"Why don't you?"

She smirked. "Because it'd be stupid. I have a gig that lawyers dream of and am close to making partner. People would think I was nuts. Not to mention, my dad would be livid. It's the family business. I'm supposed to take over a lot of his role if he gets elected. He's running for state senate."

"That sounds like a lot of damn pressure."

She shrugged. "I'm used to it. It's just part of the deal."

He watched her, taking in the tightness in the shrug, the not-quite-believable nonchalance. That pressure was more serious than she was letting on. Wes understood pressure. He put it on himself. But he was driven in the opposite way—how *not* to be like his birth parents, how *not* to end up broke like he'd been growing up, how *not* to end up in jail. But even with privilege and money and an involved father, Rebecca's pressure didn't sound much better.

"I think you'd kick ass at running your own business," he said.

She smiled. "Thanks. I think you would, too."

"I'm not so sure of that, based on how things went the last time, but that doesn't stop me from wanting to try again."

She drummed her fingers on the tabletop, her focus on him intent. "Will you show it to me?"

The question caught him off guard. "Show you what?"

"The truck. I'm curious to see it."

"Why?"

"I'd like to hear what you think you'd do to it."

"You want to—" A crazy thought hit him, and he pinned her with a look. "You're not going to try to buy me a food truck, are you? Because I don't care how much money you have or what kind of amends you're trying to make, that's not happening. I still haven't agreed to accept the ovens."

She rolled her eyes like he was the most ridiculous person in the world. "You're not going to turn down the ovens because you want the kids to have them. And no, I'm not going to buy you a food truck. I'm not feeling *that* guilty."

His shoulders sagged in relief. "Okay, good. Because you have a weird look in your eye."

She smiled. "Maybe I'm just weird."

He laughed, the heaviness of the earlier conversation lifting. "Well, you did threaten to tie me up and keep me in your imaginary basement the first night you met me."

"See." She picked up her sandwich. "Better be careful, Wesley Garrett."

He lifted his drink in a mock toast but kept his gaze on her. *Better be careful*. She had no idea how right she was. Because the more he was around this woman, the more he was beginning to question why he'd shut down the possibility of having someone in his bed.

*No, not someone*, the baser part of him whispered. *This one*.

He didn't want Rebecca's money. And he didn't need her apologies.

But he was starting to want something else.

He was starting to want it quite a lot.

chapter

# TWELVE

After finishing their dinner, Rebecca rode with Wes to the lot where the food truck was being sold. It was much like the first night when he'd driven her to Dev's restaurant, but the nervous energy running through her this time was there for a completely different reason. She was enjoying hanging out with Wes. Enjoying it *too* much, probably. But she'd asked him out to dinner tonight for more than good company, and she had a feeling that could blow up in her face. The bomb was ticking in her ears.

"It's right over here," Wes said, turning off the road and into a lot between buildings, orange sodium lights illuminating their way as they parked.

Wes came around to her side and helped Rebecca out of his pickup truck. She wasn't the type to get or seek out a lot of chivalrous treatment. Her male coworkers treated her like one of the guys, which she preferred. But it was nice to have Wes take her hand and help her out.

He led her through the alleyway—the broken black-top wet with unknown substances since it hadn't rained in a while—and stopped in front of a chain-link fence. He pointed to a small opening where they could peel back the fencing and squeeze in. "This is the only way in after hours."

She gave him a skeptical look. "So…an evening of trespassing?"

"Hey, you said you wanted to see the truck." He rolled the length of fence back for her and smiled. "Afraid to break the rules, lawyer girl?"

She put a hand on her hip. "More like afraid of being arrested, attacked by a guard dog, or shot on sight."

He chuckled. "Dev's uncle owns the lot. There's no dog. And he wouldn't press charges or shoot us. We're good."

"Comforting." She crouched down, thankful she was wearing jeans and flats, and stepped through the opening.

Wes followed behind and took her hand once they were both upright, giving it a gentle tug. "Come on, Adele is over here."

"Adele?" Rebecca asked, trying to ignore the tingling sensation that tracked up her arm at the feel of his big, warm hand around hers.

"Yes. I named her. Feel free to judge me." He guided her through an intricate maze of junk cars in the lot, like playing Frogger on pause. *Forward. Side step. Forward, forward. Side step.*

As they moved deeper into the lot, Rebecca glanced back over her shoulder, wondering if they'd ever find their way back. "Is this the part where joking about me being a demented killer turns out to have been just a diversionary tactic to hide your own murderous tendencies so that you could get me alone and hide my body in a rusted-out Chevy?"

He scoffed. "Give me more credit than that. This would be way too obvious a place to hide a body. I'd take you out camping in the hills."

"Comforting."

He laughed and finally stopped in front of a banged-up school bus that was parked near the back fence. It looked alone and unloved, yellow paint peeling and a black-and-orange FOR SALE sign stuck to the grimy front window. Wes swept a hand out. "Behold the mighty Adele."

He said it with a playful, dramatic tone, but Rebecca was watching his face, and there was no hiding the way his expression changed, the obvious pang of want hovering there. This was no joke to him. He was looking at the ugly school bus like it was the woman of his dreams. A woman who would never give him the time of day.

The impact of that stripped-down desire hit Rebecca right in the chest, made her feel hollow inside. Seeing that rapt, wistful expression, she understood exactly why Wesley's marriage had fallen apart. He already had a true love.

She couldn't help but be envious. Had she ever looked at anything like that? Had she ever felt that passionate?

She'd felt committed to goals. Determined. Obsessed, even. Maybe before today she would've said passionate. But no, she hadn't felt what he was showing on his face. This was something different. She could feel it rolling off him, that magic of wanting something so much.

Rebecca let go of his hand and faced the bus, needing to shake off the empty ache it'd opened up inside her. She stared at the hulking beast and tried to see what Wes saw, tried to taste a little of that magic. "So…a school bus."

"Yeah." Wes stepped closer and patted the hood with affection. "She was. Someone started the process of converting it to a food truck but abandoned the project when they ran out of money or energy. A few of the seats have been taken out and there are hookups for equipment, but that's about it. She needs a lot of love."

Rebecca sent him a look. "She? A name and a gender?"

He pointed to the school district name on the side of the bus, Del Valle. "Clearly Adele is a she."

Rebecca shook her head with a smile, charmed by how boyishly enthused he was. "You've got it bad, Wesley Garrett."

He gave her a rueful smile. "That obvious?"

"Quite. It's kind of adorable."

He pointed to his chest in mock shock. "Me? Adorable? I feel like we're making progress here, Lindt. From not your type to asshole to adorable."

She rolled her eyes. "The scale can shift back and forth, so don't get too cocky." She walked over to eye the price, which was written in bright-green greasepaint on the side window. "Tell me what you'd do to her."

He leaned against the side of the bus, and a slow smile lifted his lips. "Now that sounds dirty, lawyer girl."

"Are you flirting with me in front of Adele?" she teased, not recognizing the playful lilt in her voice.

"Depends," he said, eyes narrowing. "Is this a date or a further conversation?"

"I…" She gave him a tense smile. "Must we define it?"

"Okay, then how about this?" he said, his focused gaze not giving her any place to hide. "Did you kiss me because you were drunk?"

The left-field question wiped the smile from her lips, and her heart jumped into her throat. "What?"

He pushed off the bus and stepped closer, not touching her but not exactly keeping a friendly distance. His eyes held challenge and not an ounce of the earlier playfulness. "I've tried to pretend that it didn't happen. I've tried to ignore it, but it's not working. Not when we keep finding ourselves in close proximity to each other. And with you standing here under these lights, smiling at me like that and looking like you really do give a shit about what I'd do to remodel this hunk of metal, I can't concentrate on anything else. So I need to know. That first night...did you kiss me *because you were drunk?*"

Her blood roared in her ears as he repeated his question, his broad body blocking out anything but her view of him. She was suddenly very aware of their aloneness, of the quiet intimacy of the situation. She forced a response past the tightness in her throat. "Why?"

"Answer the question, Rebecca."

*Answer the question. Answer the question.* She wet her lips. "I wasn't drunk."

His jaw flexed, and she couldn't tell if he was happy about her answer or pissed. "You knew who I was. You thought I was a liar and a cheat. You told me I wasn't your type. Why did you kiss me?"

She swallowed hard. "I wish I had the answer to that."

"Try."

Her shoulders lowered in defeat. "I don't know. I guess because I stopped thinking and just...wanted to know what it would be like."

"To kiss me?"

"Yes."

"That's not what it would be like. That was me in shock." He took another step, backing her into the side of a van parked next to the bus. He braced a hand beside her shoulder, and his face lowered close to hers, making her breath quicken. "So if you really want to know, I could show you exactly what it would be like. When I'm trying. When I know it's okay to want you."

Heat rushed up her neck. "Wes..."

"Tell me not to kiss you, Rebecca. To fuck off. Tell me that tonight isn't a date and that you just wanted to give me money for the school. Or that you want a new friend. Tell me I'm not your type."

She closed her eyes, a tremor working its way through her body and hot, liquid want blooming low. "You're not my type."

Wes hissed out a breath.

But before he could push away, she opened her eyes and grabbed his shirt. "That wasn't a no."

Heat and something dangerous flared in his eyes, some resistance breaking. His big hand slipped behind her to cup her head, and his mouth came down on hers in a rush. Every cell in her body came alive at the touch of his lips. And this time there was no hesitation, no confusion. He held her where he wanted, and the tip of his tongue teased the seam of her mouth, making sensual promises she had no doubt he could keep. She parted her lips, needing it all, and melted when his tongue stroked against hers. He tasted like the baklava they'd had for dessert, of honey and pistachios and sin. She wanted to gorge on him.

Some needy sound slipped out of her, one that showed all her cards, and his other hand slid to her hip. He pulled her against him and let her feel exactly what this was doing to him, the utter maleness of him growing hard and heavy against her.

*Christ*. Her sex clenched, ready to throw a ticker tape parade welcoming him to the neighborhood. She gripped his shirt hard, afraid her bad knee would give out beneath her. This was Wesley Garrett, the confident chef in those magazine photos, the man who took risks and worried about the consequences later, the man who could undo her with one hot kiss.

And she didn't know who the hell she was right now. Because it certainly wasn't Rebecca Lindt, responsible professional who would never make out with a sexy tattooed chef in a used car lot, who would have more self-control than to be imagining routes to the nearest hotel.

"The one I was telling you about is right over here. It's... What in the world?"

The unfamiliar voice broke through the erotic fog in her mind, and Wes made a strangled sound. They quickly broke away from the kiss, both turning their heads toward the noise.

An older man with wrinkled brown skin—presumably Dev's uncle based on the last name on his shirt—was scowling at them while the two men behind him were holding hands and grinning at them.

"Um, Mr. Madan, I... How are you?" Wes said, smoothing down the front of his shirt where Rebecca had left it a crinkled mess.

"Wesley, what is going on?"

Wes crooked a thumb toward Adele. "Just...shopping."

The older man frowned, his thick, black brows lowering. "That is not what shopping looks like. This is not a place to..." He waved a hand. "Do these things."

One of the guys behind Dev's uncle, the hipster of the couple, laughed under his breath. "Didn't mean to interrupt."

Wes cleared his throat. "Sorry, Mr. Madan. I thought you were closed. We were shopping, and then we were…overcome. Your place is, uh, very romantic."

The man huffed. "Romantic. You are lucky you are Devin's friend." He pointed a bony finger at Wes. "But no more sneaking in. If you want to see something after hours, you make an appointment. This is my place of business, and I have customers who want to purchase this bus. Now, leave, please, so I can do my job."

Wes's face paled. "They want to buy Adele?"

One of the guys—the broader, more bearded one—smiled. "Mr. Madan has convinced us that a bus will be perfect for the gourmet barbecue truck we want to open. It will give us the space we need."

"But…" Wes didn't finish the sentence.

Rebecca stepped up next to Wes, putting a hand on his shoulder because he looked ready to pass out. Another lost opportunity. More freaking barbecue. "But Wes is interested in the bus."

Mr. Madan leveled Wes with a look. "Wesley, if you are ready to purchase, you need to make me an offer."

Wes inhaled a deep breath, a flat look descending over his features—a mask of hard indifference. "I can't make an offer." He glanced at the couple, his jaw tight. "Good luck with your new business."

Hipster guy smiled. "Thanks, man."

Wes glanced over at Rebecca. "Come on. Let's get out of their way."

He took a step to walk around them, shoulders

hunched, but she grabbed the sleeve of his shirt. "Wait."

He turned to face her, his look pleading. "Bec, come on."

She ignored Wes and looked at Mr. Madan. "Sir, I'm really sorry about what you walked up on, but Wes brought me here because he wanted me to see the bus." She took a deep breath. "I'm prepared to make an offer for a thousand over the asking price, which you know is at least two thousand more than it's worth. I can write you a check tonight, but you have to agree to it now. I don't want a bidding war with these two."

"*What?*" Wes said, his expression full of what-the-fuck.

But Mr. Madan grinned wide, flashing bright white teeth. "Fantastic, my dear. You have yourself a deal."

"Wait, hold up," the bearded guy said with a frown. "We should have a shot, too."

Mr. Madan patted the guy on the shoulder. "I have other things to show you. Perfect things. Wes is family. He gets privilege." Mr. Madan held his hand out to Rebecca to shake on it. "And I like a lady who knows what she wants and gets to the point."

Wesley looked on, horrified. "Rebecca, what the hell? You can't—"

"Thank you, Mr. Madan." She shook his hand, shooting Wesley a nervous glance. This wasn't exactly how she'd planned to do it. She'd planned to propose the idea to Wes, to give him the option. Not force things. But at the thought of the couple snatching the bus out from underneath Wes, her mouth had opened and out everything had come. Too late now. She'd deal with the consequences later. "Where do I sign the papers?"

Mr. Madan told her to head to his office on the other side of the lot and he'd meet her there after he showed the couple another option. Rebecca headed that way, Wesley in her wake. He caught up to her, her bad leg making it impossible to get too far ahead of him. "What the hell are you doing?"

She tipped up her chin. "Buying Adele."

"Buying? No. This is insane. You can't… You're not buying me a bus. I told you I don't even want to accept the ovens!"

"You're taking the ovens. And I'm not buying the bus *for you*…at least not exactly."

He stepped in front of her, blocking her way between two dinged-up Fords. "I'm not going to let you do this. Whatever you think you're doing, it's not going to happen."

"It's going to happen whether you want it to or not. This is why I had you bring me here tonight. I was going to talk to you about it, discuss options, but the plan just got a little…accelerated."

"*The plan?*"

"Yes." She crossed her arms. "And if you calm down for a second, you'll see that it's a good one."

"I doubt that. Because whatever it is, you just bought a bus *you don't need and I don't want*."

She ignored him. "I don't throw together plans lightly. I've given this a lot of thought the last few days. I'm in charge of a charity fund at work, and it's at my discretion what we use it on this year. I didn't know what I was going to do, but after I spent time with your class the other day, it hit me. I could buy Adele for the program."

He reared back. "What?"

"I know you don't want a handout for yourself or

them. I get it and respect the stance. This is not that. It's a project. One with real-world application. The kids could help you refurbish the bus, set up a business plan, a menu, all the things that go along with opening a business. It could be a project that rolls into the summer and could teach them great skills, give them job experience." She was talking fast now, trying to get it all out before Wesley blew another gasket.

"And then when you open it, a portion of the sales could go to the school to fund the program. The kids could even work the truck and earn some money once it gets going, if they want. It could be an ever-flowing source of support for the program. And you..." She swallowed past the knot in her throat. "I know it's not exactly what you envisioned, but you could have a restaurant to run again."

"I could have..." He stared at her, dumbfounded. "Holy shit, this *is* some sort of guilt thing, isn't it? You're trying to fix things. You're trying to give me a restaurant. Rebecca, that's nuts."

"It's not guilt, Wes, it's—"

"No. Listen to yourself," he said, squaring off with her. "People don't do this. People don't meet strangers and offer to dump a truckload of money on them. They don't offer to hand them a business on a platter for the hell of it."

"I swear it's not guilt." She pursed her lips, nerves trying to take over. "It's—"

He held his hands out, beseeching. "It's what? Please tell me because I sure as shit don't understand."

"I'm a Long Acre High survivor." The words tumbled out of her and fell into the tense space between them.

His combative expression went slack, his lips parting. "Long Acre. Like *the* Long Acre?"

"Yes. I'm assuming you didn't know," she said quickly. "That's why I limp sometimes. I was shot in the leg. And I'm only telling you now because visiting your class was the first time I've willingly been around teenagers or an active school setting since then. It brings up too much stuff."

A pained look crossed his face. "God, Rebecca, I would've never asked you—"

She lifted a hand to cut him off, needing to get the words out. "But I'm glad I got to see you teach that day because watching you with the kids… It was something special. Something *good*. It gave me ideas. I saw kids that I could've gone to high school with, ones who maybe have gotten off track but just need someone in their life to say, 'Hey, you've got potential,' or 'It gets better,' or 'You have a safe place or person to come to if you need it.' That program is a safe place, and you are that safe person." She held his gaze. "That is something worth fighting for. That is something worth investing in."

He laced his fingers behind his head, clearly anguished on her behalf. "Rebecca…"

"And you were right. I'm good at my job and it's a necessary profession, but I know I'm not doing anything that's going to change the world. But you…you are. Even if you don't think of it that way. And if this money can help you do that while you're there, then maybe I can go to bed at night knowing I helped a little bit, too. That I didn't escape all those years ago for no reason."

His brows knitted. "For no reason? You don't owe some debt to the world because you survived."

The back of her nose burned, but there was no way she was going to let herself cry. "I do." More than he or anyone else realized. "So maybe this is more self-serving than you realize. Maybe I'm doing it for me, too."

His hands dropped to his sides and he stepped closer, concern on his face. "Rebecca, I don't know what to say to all this."

She gripped her elbows and shrugged. "Maybe just say yes."

He cupped her shoulders, his eyes searching hers. "Promise me you're not trying to pay me back for something. I don't deserve that."

She shook her head. "I need to do something good. I want to help your kids. And I can't do that without you being on board with this. Tell me you'll do this."

He pushed her hair away from her face, his lips quirking into a small smile. "So this wasn't a date after all, huh? It was just some master plan to get me to agree to this project?"

A glimmer of pleasure went through her, cutting a path through her somber mood. "Well, getting kissed senseless wasn't part of the original agenda."

"Senseless, huh?"

She sniffed. "Don't look so pleased with yourself."

"Oh no, I'm going to look pleased. Knowing I kissed Rebecca Lindt senseless may need to go on my résumé. Right at the top."

She shoved him in the chest. "Shut up."

He gripped her wrist and pulled her close, touching his forehead to hers. She thought he was going to kiss her, but after a moment, he let out a long sigh. "What are we doing here, lawyer girl?"

"What?" she asked, a little breathless.

"I want to kiss you again. I'd like to keep doing that, actually, preferably not in a used car lot and without interruption. But it feels damn selfish."

Her heartbeat thumped in her ears. "Selfish?"

"Because that's all I've got to offer. I'm just barely getting my shit together and have steered clear of dating or anything resembling a relationship since my divorce for good reason. You've got to realize I'm a bad investment."

She lifted her head and met his tense gaze. "Are you worried I'm going to expect your class ring so we can go steady if I let you kiss me again?"

His expression turned chagrined. "Maybe? This isn't meant as an insult, but you strike me as the type of woman who'd want the traditional steps into a relationship."

She stared at him, not insulted, not even surprised. She held everything so tight and close—her feelings, her desires, her fears—that she was used to people layering their ideas about who she was on her like a costume. At work, she was the aggressive, confident lawyer. To her father's friends, she was the studious, obedient daughter. To her friends, she was the practical, unemotional one. She was all those things and none of them, but those masks gave her a comfortable place to settle, a role she knew how to play. With Wes, she couldn't find her footing or her lines, so blatant honesty slipped out instead. "I'll admit I'm not someone who does the hookup scene. But I'm also not looking for something serious from anyone. Ever, really."

He lifted a brow. "Ever?"

"I don't see the point. I witness what happens to marriages every day at work. If you want to talk about bad investments, there's a verifiable one. I have no desire to subject myself to that kind of ugliness and heartache. Things don't have to be that complicated. Me kissing you back doesn't mean anything more than it felt good and I like you."

He stared at her for a long moment as if trying to puzzle her out, but then he smiled, some of the light coming back into his eyes. "You like me, huh? Like, *like* me, like me?"

"Oh my God, you're twelve," she groused. "All I'm saying is that we can be friends…who maybe kiss sometimes."

He was still gripping her wrist, and he brought her hand up to his mouth, kissing her knuckles. "I've got a deal for you, Ms. Lindt."

She cocked a brow. "A deal?"

"Yes." He laced his fingers with hers. "I will allow you to buy this school bus for the program, and I promise I will throw everything I have into refurbishing and making it a great experience for the kids. We will also continue to practice this senseless kissing thing, and you can have rights to these talented lips."

She eyed him suspiciously. "What's the catch?"

"The kissing part is a guarantee, no fine print," he said. "But I'm only doing the first one if you agree to be part of the project, too."

She stilled. "What?"

"No writing a check and walking away," he declared. "I know you're busy and have obligations. We can work around that. But you told me that first night that you wanted a passion project. I know you don't think you have a passion, but you should've seen your face when you told me about your idea for the bus. This project means something to you, something that roots pretty deeply, from what I can tell. So, it needs you as much as it needs me."

"Wes, I can't just... Work is crazy. I'm up for partner, and I'm helping with my dad's campaign. I don't know anything about kids or food or restaurants and—"

He pressed his fingers over her lips. "I'm not negotiating this part, lawyer girl. Don't try to use your secret ninja attorney moves on me because they won't work." His hand slid to the back of her neck. "You need to do something that makes your eyes light up like that. I know because I need that, too. Plus, the kids liked you. They could use a strong, successful woman to look up to, one who isn't afraid to do the hard, messy work to make a difference."

All the breath sagged out of her. "Now who's the lawyer? You're laying *kid guilt* at my feet. Are you going to bring out sad-eyed puppies next?"

He smiled. "Kid guilt is *the worst*. But super effective. And if we need puppy eyes, we can stop by my brother's clinic and visit your rescuer."

She groaned and looked to the star-flecked sky overhead. How the hell could she commit to this? She was already stretched for time, and the partners and her father were watching her every move to determine if she was dedicated enough to become partner. She was not the girl who put aside work and responsibilities for a whim.

However, the thought of building something from scratch, of giving Wes's kids a project that could help shape their future, that could give them an outlet, made her blood pump harder and something bright and sharp bloom inside her chest. Did she really want to be the type of person who wrote a check and left others to do the real work? That was her dad's method. "One hour. I can probably find *one hour* in the afternoons that I'm not in court to help out."

His lips curved into a satisfied smile, and he pulled her fully against him, looping his arms around her waist. "I'll take it. One hour of work. Then maybe a little bit of this once the kids go home."

He bent his head and his lips captured hers again, soft and sweet, but enough to get her heart picking up speed and her mind emptying of all other worries.

Her cases. Her battle for partner. Her father's campaign. She'd figure out. She had to. Because right now, there was no way she was giving this up.

This feeling of exhilaration. Of being wanted. Of enjoying someone without any of the heavy stuff attached to it.

Good sexy fun. This was exactly what she needed.

No, *Wes Garrett* was exactly what she needed.

That was the scariest part of all.

*chapter*

# THIRTEEN

To: RLindt
From: ChefG
___

Dear Ms. Lindt,

It has come to my attention that after you gifted me with a very expensive bribe for my kissing skills and made promises to partake of those services on the regular, I have not heard from you in a few days. I am sending a formal request to share space with you in the near future. I can offer food temptations including pretentiously expensive cheese and cured meats. Dessert will be provided for good behavior.

Yours truly,
Mr. Wesley Garrett, chef and cheese aficionado

REBECCA HAD NEVER RESENTED HER JOB. WORK FUELED her. She liked being busy, capable, and successful. She

THE ONE YOU CAN'T FORGET

liked winning. But when she saw Wes's email come through on Tuesday morning, she had a moment where she wished she could toss her jam-packed day planner in a bonfire.

She'd returned to the office on Monday feeling hungover after the weekend with Wes. Friday night, she'd surprised him with the bus, which had been even more exhilarating than she'd expected because, well, kissing…and now the food truck was partly her project, too. Then they'd spent Saturday afternoon together at a coffee shop, plotting and planning how the business could work and make money for the program. Then there'd been more kissing. Not too much since they'd been in public. But enough that the crackle of possibility had sparked between her and Wes at every moment.

That sense of not knowing what was going to happen next, of not knowing how far they were going to take it, of teasing and flirting and feeling each other out was like a jolt of electricity to her system. Even the discussions about the bus and how they should set up the business had gotten her jazzed, the excitement a palpable thing. It was like she'd adjusted the setting on her life and now everything was plugged in and in high-definition color.

But when she'd strolled back into work on Monday with a spring in her step, the grayness of the office—something she'd never really noticed before—had hit her in the face like a cinder-block wall. And not just gray in color but in mood. The same people. The same clicking keyboards. The same burnt coffee smell.

A new stack of cases on her desk about the same old marriage problems.

A list of things her father needed her to do for the campaign.

The whole thing had made her feel deeply tired and… out of place.

Which made no sense since she'd worked there all her adult life and her name was on the goddamned building. If ever there was a place just for her, this was it. But it'd been like pulling on a sweater she'd owned for years and suddenly discovering it was itchy and that the tag irritated her neck.

She'd wanted to call Wes and make lunch plans, anything to remind her that the weekend hadn't been some weird dream, that there was another part of her life that wasn't this. But when she'd taken a look at her schedule, her heart had sunk.

Booked solid. Not just through the week but all the way through Sunday. Cases on the weekdays and campaign events on Saturday and Sunday. There was going to be no room for free time. No Wes. No Bitching Brunch with her friends. And no visiting the school this week. No color at all.

She sighed, her eyes gliding over Wes's words again. At least the bus wasn't going to get to the school until next week. They had a bunch of paperwork and red tape to go through to make sure everything was done correctly, that safety standards were met, signatures obtained. She could block off time next week to spend on the project. She wouldn't miss the reveal. She wouldn't have to break her promise to Wes that she would help. That was something. But this week was a wash, and she hadn't figured out how to tell Wes that yet.

Hell, she hadn't even known if Wes wanted to get together this week, but the email alleviated that fear. She put her fingers to her keyboard.

**To: ChefG**
**From: RLindt**

---

Greetings, Mr. Garrett,

I deeply regret to inform you that many people have decided to dissolve their marriages this week, and for some reason, they expect me to assist them with that. I am holding them personally responsible for denying me an opportunity to eat pretentious cheese. I am also blaming them for breaking my favorite fancy ink pen when one spouse decided to use it as a projectile. I'm also sorry to report that this weekend, my father's campaign has thwarted my attempts to actually have a day off. However, I will be available by phone late at night if you are so inclined as to speak with me at that time.

Warmest regards,
Lawyer Girl

**The response came a few minutes later and put a smile on her face.**

**To: RLindt**
**From: ChefG**

---

Dear Ms. Lindt,

Will you be wearing blue lacy panties during these phone calls? That may be a requirement for my participation.

Inappropriately,
Chef Dude

**To: ChefG**
**From: RLindt**

Dear Mr. Garrett,

Your request will be taken into consideration.
Perhaps it is better to wonder what I'll be wearing
than to actually know. Perhaps it's lace panties.
Perhaps it's footie pajamas and an ugly robe.
Perhaps nothing at all.

I assume a man of your creative nature has an
imagination.

Currently wearing a sensible pantsuit,
Lawyer Girl

**To: RLindt**
**From: ChefG**

Dear Ms. Lindt,

That is dangerous territory, but I am a man of great
bravery and will take on that risk. Imagination
engaged. I will call you tonight.

Currently wearing a smile,
Wes

**The quick exchange was simple and silly, but it made**

Rebecca's lips lift into a stupid grin and made the marathon day stretching out before her look a little more manageable.

She took a long sip of her coffee, stood, and headed out to the conference room to meet with the first client of the day.

When she got back to her office past lunchtime, there was a package on her desk. She leaned out of her doorway and got her assistant's attention. "Hey, Marian, what's with the package?"

Marian looked up from the pasta salad she was eating and turned Rebecca's way. "Oh, I'm not sure. It just arrived a few minutes ago. The man said not to disturb you, but that it was perishable so it shouldn't be stacked with the rest of your mail."

"Perishable?"

Marian shrugged, and Rebecca stepped back into her office. She picked up the maroon-colored box and examined the logo of a local gourmet store. Probably a client thank-you. She grabbed her letter opener to free the tape and opened the box. Inside, there was a small jar of fig jam and a sleeve of fancy crackers, but it was what sat in the center of the display that made her grin. Tucked inside was perfectly packaged, super-pretentious…cheese.

She picked up the folded note inside and opened it, finding scrawly handwriting.

> *If anyone throws another pen today, just toss this bottle of jam at them. No one should be denied the opportunity to eat their pretentious cheese in peace. Talk to you tonight. —W*

Rebecca held the note in her hands and sank into her chair, some weird combination of giddiness and fear going through her, like that feeling of plummeting down the tracks of a roller coaster.

"Everything okay?" Marian asked, poking her head inside Rebecca's office.

Rebecca looked up and offered a small smile. "Yes, it's just a gift."

"From a client?"

Rebecca shook her head. "No, from a…friend."

Marian's eyebrows went up. "Well, if it's the same friend who dropped it off, I know why you're smiling."

Rebecca laughed. "Marian."

"What? I'm old and married, but I'm not dead."

Marian left with a playful grin on her face, and Rebecca leaned back in her chair. *A friend*. She needed to remember that. This thing with Wes was a friendship with some added benefits. Just because the man had brought her a snack didn't mean anything more than that he was a nice guy who wanted to sleep with her. A guy who wanted to sleep with a woman did nice things for her. She couldn't let that hopeless romantic teen she used to be surface and pin meanings and feelings onto this thing with Wes that would only lead to her getting burned.

It was just a damn box of cheese.

# chapter
# FOURTEEN

Wes slipped on the generic black chef's hat and adjusted it, the hat feeling foreign even though he'd had to wear one often enough in his early years of cooking. This one was mainly for show, though, at the Sunday brunch event.

"Looking good, Garrett," Suzie said, walking around one of the big prep areas in the event space's kitchen and grinning his way.

"Even with my shirt on?" he teased.

She gave him an up-and-down look. "Well, we *could* scandalize all the nice ladies and gentlemen at the brunch if you want to flip omelets half-naked and piss off my boss. It would certainly liven things up."

Wes buttoned up his black jacket and gave her a wry look. "My Shirtless Chefs stint is done. In fact, this will be my last fill-in of any kind for a while."

"Oh yeah?" Suzie asked, perking up. "Did you hit the magic number you were saving for?"

He pinned a name tag to his jacket. "Not exactly. But

now I'm not going to need it. I found…an investor. She bought the bus I was looking at as a charitable donation for the after-school program where I work."

"*What?* When did this happen?"

"A little over a week ago, so the details are still coming together, but I'll be in charge of it. We're going to remodel it, and the kids are going to be a part of the whole thing."

He still couldn't believe the words, even as he said them. Nine days had passed since the night in the used car lot with Rebecca, and his head had been spinning ever since. Half the spinning had been panic. Agreeing to the project meant digging his roots deeper in his current job, something he hadn't planned on doing. This wasn't going to be *his* restaurant. Not in the financial ownership sense. And he knew by saying yes, he was committing to a longer stint as a teacher. That had freaked him out a little, but he'd calmed down by reminding himself that it wasn't forever. He'd set the goal of getting the food truck remodeled, launched, and running smoothly before he left. Then he could walk away with a clear conscience because he would have left the program in better shape than when he'd joined it.

But putting long-term career goals aside, the other half of him was filled with genuine excitement. He was going to build a restaurant. He was going to cook again. Be in charge of something again. All because of Rebecca.

Rebecca, who he hadn't seen since that night. He'd wanted to celebrate, to take her out again. But she'd been swamped at work and tied up with doing things for her father's campaign, so their conversations had been limited to emails and late-night phone calls where they spent part of the time flirting and the other part planning world domination with the food truck.

The week had been great, though. He'd gotten to know her better, and they'd discovered new things about each other. The phone brought out things that wouldn't have come out in person because late-night conversations tended to devolve into the random. Like how he read cookbooks like novels and how she had to watch *Shark Tank* before bed. Of course, then they'd had to debate which "shark" they'd want investing in the food truck.

The whole thing had been strangely easy, the rhythm of talking to her at night like they'd been doing it for years. The phone calls had given him something to look forward to after a long day of work, but they'd also made him realize how lonely his nights had become since getting sober. It'd hit him when she'd told him Friday night that she'd be out of pocket until Sunday night. Before, he wouldn't have said he minded the solitude, but last night he'd felt the loss when he didn't get to talk to her.

Suzie's face brightened and she did a little clap, breaking him from his thoughts. "Yay! That's fantastic news, Wes." She stepped closer and threw her arms around him in a quick, enthusiastic hug before grinning up at him. "I'm so glad it's all coming together for you. What happened to you…" She narrowed her eyes. "Well, let's just say there's a special place in hell for people who purposely try to kill someone's spirit. Brittany's spot has been reserved."

He let out a breath. "I played my own part in that train wreck, but I'm glad that smoking pile of metal is getting smaller and smaller in my rearview mirror."

"Well, I'll be the first in line at your truck," Suzie declared. "What are you thinking concept-wise? May I suggest no shirt?"

He chuckled. "Let it go, Suze. I'm going to make the kids a big part of every step, so it will need to be a consensus. We'll brainstorm this week. I want them to visit the food-truck park, see if they can find a gap in the offerings, see what would make business sense but also be innovative, that kind of thing."

She shoved him in the shoulder. "Well, look at you, all teacher-y and stuff."

The comment rained a little on his happy mood, but he tried not to show it on his face. "Go ahead, make fun."

"No," she said, palms lifted. "I'm not teasing you. I know it wasn't your plan, but it's an oddly good look on you. You were always a good kitchen manager, and so much of that is mentoring and teaching. This isn't that far of a leap. This is good news all around. Plus, the world needs your food. It's cruel to deny them."

"That's very dramatic, but thank you. It feels good to be psyched about something again."

Suzie put her hand to her hip and considered him. "We should go out sometime. Celebrate this return to the world of the living."

He frowned. "You know I can't do the bar scene anymore."

He and Suzie had hung out a lot after hours in culinary school and when he was getting his restaurant ready to go. She was going to be the restaurant's sous chef, so he'd worked with her closely. Brittany had accused Wes of having an affair with Suzie since they spent so much time together and often ended up drinking late into the evening, but he and Suzie had never crossed any line except staying out too late and drinking too much.

Suzie huffed, the air making her bright-pink bangs flutter. "I'm not saying let's go get wasted, Wes. Believe it or not, I've dialed back a lot on that, too. I'm saying let's, you know, go on a date with food and nonalcoholic beverages."

He blinked. "A date?"

"Yes, you know those things that unmarried people do when they are interested in the other person." She gave him a patient look. "I know you don't do much of that since the divorce, but it wouldn't have to be anything serious."

The request caught him completely off guard. Suzie was fun, a talented chef, and attractive in that quirky, do-her-own-thing way. If he hadn't been married back when they'd worked together, they probably would've already hooked up. Now they could. But the thought fell flat for him. "I'm sorry. I'm down for grabbing dinner one night or something, but just as friends. I'm seeing someone."

The words tumbled out before he knew they were happening. He'd meant to give his standard answer. *I don't date*. But that wasn't true anymore, was it? Dating wasn't exactly the right word. He and Rebecca had only agreed to be friends with potential benefits, with no exclusive label or commitment. He didn't even know for sure if Rebecca would want to take it to the level of sleeping together. But this thing with her felt…precious for some reason, something singular that should be protected. He didn't feel any desire to pursue anyone else right now.

Suzie stared at him, eyes wide. "You're *seeing* someone?"

"I... It's new but...yeah."

"Oh my God," she said, teeth flashing in a genuine smile. "That's great, Wes. You really are charging forward finally. Do I know her?"

"Don't think so. She's a lawyer."

She wrinkled her nose. "A lawyer? That's...different."

He laughed. "I'm aware. But she's pretty great."

Her lips kicked up in a lopsided grin. "That's awesome. You deserve to have some fun." She playfully poked him in the chest and gave him a mock stern look. "Just don't let it get too serious, all right?"

"Too serious?"

"Yes, believe me. I'm speaking from a been-there, done-that place. I'm so experienced at the rebound relationship that if I fell over, I'd probably bounce." She made a face. "This is your first dip back into the dating pool. The first ones always feel intense and real and like whoever it may be is everything the last person wasn't. The feelings can come fast, and then you're in too deep by the time you realize you're completely incompatible. That's one reason why I asked you out. I would go in knowing that I'm just a passing phase. No hearts getting broken on either side."

"Wow, that's oh-so-very encouraging, Suze," he said dryly.

She lifted her palms. "I'm just saying. I'm happy you're finally moving forward, but a lawyer sounds very...not Brittany."

His stomach muscles tightened, the words hitting closer than they should. "This isn't about Brittany. And this isn't serious."

Suzie crossed her arms and cocked her head. "All right, I'm just trying to give you a heads-up. I don't want to see you get in a bad situation again. Or worse, getting your heart broken."

"No chance of that," he said, gruffer than he intended.

She flashed him a quick smile. "Good. Now it's time to get out there and wow these people with your French omelets. I'll be in here running the kitchen if you need anything."

Wes let out a breath and gave her a quick shoulder squeeze as he walked past her. "Thanks, Suze."

He tried to shake off the irritation. Suzie was just trying to be a friend, not dump ice water on him. No need to get mad at good intentions. He didn't take for granted that he had such caring friends who'd stuck by him when everything had gone to shit. Most of the people he'd known in his wild, partying days had bailed as soon as he'd ended up in rehab. He was no longer the buzz-worthy, up-and-coming chef who threw great parties.

He was just a divorced alcoholic who'd lost his restaurant. They had no use for him anymore.

But Suzie and Dev had been there the whole way through. They'd been the ones who'd tried to help when they could see him spiraling—not that Wes had let them help. They were the ones who'd visited him in rehab and brought him homemade food so he didn't have to eat the facility's crap menu. And they were the ones who believed he could have a restaurant again and not mess it up.

Even his family hadn't bought into that idea.

Right now, he wasn't sure *he* fully bought into the idea. Knowing he was about to take that leap again, launching a restaurant—even a small-scale one—had an element of blind terror to it.

Sometimes the scariest thing was finally having what you thought you wanted most. Dreams couldn't be touched or marred. There was no failure in dreamland. Reality didn't offer that kind of assurance.

Now there were high stakes. The food truck, the kids, and other people's money were in his hands. The first time, he'd failed himself. That had been horrible enough. But this time he had to worry about so much more. Failing Rebecca. Failing the program. Failing the students.

Wes took a deep breath as the anxiety tried to creep in, and he let the hum of low chatter and the soft lighting in the ballroom soothe him. In rehab, they'd had the one-day-at-a-time mantra hammered into their heads. He would have to lean on it now. Focus on the next task and not gaze too far into the future. He needed to clean a bus. That was it. He could do that.

With Rebecca, he wasn't going to think about it as a relationship or a rebound or anything complicated. They were new to each other. Friends. Acquainting themselves. There was an undeniable attraction that they both wanted to act on. It didn't have to be a big deal.

She was just a woman he liked kissing. A woman he would be working on a project with.

A woman he'd *missed* when he didn't get to talk to her last night.

His stomach sank a little further, and he tripped over a power cord on the way to the omelet station, almost falling.

One thought went through his head as he steadied himself.

*If he had fallen, would he have bounced?*

# chapter

# FIFTEEN

ON GOOD DAYS, REBECCA FELT LIKE A SURVIVOR. ON days like this, she felt like an imposter. The gentle tinkling of silverware against plates and ice cubes against glass grated against her eardrums and made the muscles in her neck tighten. She shouldn't be here. She should be at Bitching Brunch with her friends, telling them how she'd somehow managed to get involved in a food-truck project and how she was spending time with the man she'd once gone up against in court.

Instead, her dad had convinced her to do this speech under the auspices of it being an important way to give back to the community, but she knew it was more about being good for the campaign. This was his dog-and-pony show, and she was the pony. *Giddyup, girlfriend.*

The speaker before her had wrapped up an inspiring talk about her fight against cancer, making everyone break out the tissues to dab their eyes and then rise to their feet in a standing ovation at the end. Rebecca was up next, and her fight-or-flight reflex was so ramped up over what she was going to have to talk about that she worried she'd sprout wings and fly out of the room.

Everyone took their seats again, and her gaze drifted over the audience, finding her father sitting a few tables back from the stage. Every salt-and-pepper hair in place. Suit perfectly ironed. Attention of the guests at the table solidly on him. Even though Rebecca was doing this for him, he hadn't looked her way once since she'd walked to the front of the room. Not that she'd expected him to. Because why would he be checking on her? What would he have to worry about?

Rebecca was as reliable and predictable as the sunrise peeking through the high windows on the side of the ballroom. She'd vowed from a hospital bed many years ago that she would never cause him worry again. She'd stuck to it.

But right now, she felt more like her fifteen-year-old self right before her first running-for-class-secretary speech than the accomplished attorney she'd become.

Her heartbeat thumped in her ears, and her fingernails dug into her palms as the emcee went to the stage to thank the previous speaker and to introduce Rebecca. Her throat felt like she'd swallowed one of the dry pastries on the tables whole. She didn't want to be introduced. She didn't want to tell her story. She wanted to be at brunch with her friends or talking about the food truck with Wes or back at work where she was the confident lawyer doing her thing.

Here she felt too exposed, too...observed. It wasn't the public speaking part. She did that for her job all the time. But this wasn't a courtroom or a divorce mediation. This was a charity brunch full of society's ruling class, and there were reporters here. And gawking people. And she was one of the spectacles. Again.

All because of that documentary on the shooting. She'd thought this part was done. People had short memories and there were always new tragedies, so Long Acre High's prom night had gotten filed away in people's minds after a few years. Not forgotten but no longer a fascination. She didn't think the documentary would be anything but a blip in the news cycle. But the thing hadn't even premiered yet, and there was buzz building, clips leaked. She was that girl again. One of the lucky few. One of the ones who got away.

But she didn't see how that was an accomplishment. She'd been shot in the leg instead of somewhere more deadly. That had been pure dumb luck and Finn throwing himself in front of her to throw off the shooter's aim. And now, because she hadn't turned into a complete disaster, she was an "inspiration."

Such a farce. She had no business inspiring anyone. If these people knew the whole story, they'd run her out of here with pitchforks.

She was an imposter.

Still, here she stood. Because this would help her dad. Because the movers and shakers of Austin were in this room and this was good PR for him. Because she couldn't tell the truth about why she shouldn't be giving speeches like this or why she should be the last person people looked to for inspiration.

So here she was, about to vomit on her shoes.

The emcee was reading her bio. Something about valedictorian and top of her class in law school and successful divorce attorney—all the stuff that she'd spent her life busting her ass to accomplish but that somehow rang hollow in this moment.

*Who the hell cares?*

She clutched her notes in her hand, the cards crinkling under her grip.

"Please welcome Ms. Rebecca Lindt."

The claps and camera clicks were amplified in her head, the claustrophobic feeling growing. Her feet froze in place. Anticipatory glances slid her way because she hadn't moved yet. Her father finally looked at her. His brow wrinkled, and he tilted his head toward the stage as if she needed to be reminded what direction to walk.

She closed her eyes and took a long, deep breath. She could do this. She could get through her speech, answer a few questions, and be done. If she made some sort of scene, it'd be more newsworthy, would bring her more of what she didn't want.

*Pretend it's a courtroom.*

Yes, she could do that. Court was safe. Court was her domain. Where she was in control. Where fear and memories didn't touch her.

She opened her eyes and made her way to the stage, fighting hard to disguise her limp. Everyone in this room knew she'd been injured all those years ago, but she didn't want that pity directed her way. She didn't deserve it. Her heart was still beating. She got to wake up every day and see the sun. So many of her class-mates hadn't gotten that chance. No sympathy should be wasted on her.

The lights on the stage were bright, blinding her view of the audience except for the first row of tables, and she braced her hands on the podium. There was a sheet of paper taped to it, listing the presenter schedule. The top of the page had the slogan for the event.

*Be the Voice That Makes a Difference*

The words landed like stones in her gut. *Make a difference*. What if the difference wasn't a good one? What if you made a difference that ruined everything?

"Hello." The word came out as little more than a choked whisper, and she breathed through the growing panic, trying to find someone to focus on in the front row. *Talk to one person*. That had been a trick she'd learned in speech class in high school. But her gaze caught on a young male face near the stage. One that looked all too familiar as he slouched in his seat. One whose dark eyes seemed to see into her, to dare her. Just like the night she'd been mugged, a rush of dread flooded her. Everything blurred together. Past. Present. Leaving her in some nightmarish space in between.

The boy sneered. *Go ahead, Becca, tell them just how great you are. Lie to these nice people and look like a hero*.

Rebecca's skin went clammy beneath her business suit, and she gripped the podium harder, her knuckles bulging and bloodless. Not him. He wasn't here. He was dead.

*Coward. Coward. Coward*, the boy mouthed, the taunt loud in her ears.

*Not! Real!* She silently screamed the words in her head and blinked rapidly, her vision going liquid. Finally, the tormenting face morphed into one she didn't recognize. One with a different haircut and heavier brows. One with bored eyes instead of accusing ones. Just a teenager attending an event with his parents.

Her ribs loosened a little, allowing her to catch a breath.

"Sorry." She grabbed a glass of water to sip and then

picked up her notecards again. Her hands shook. "My notes were a little out of order. Who knew lawyers could ever be at a loss for words?"

A few polite laughs filtered through the audience, and she tried to focus on what was on the cards in front of her.

"Thank you for the kind welcome." She took another breath in an attempt to force the ugly images from her head and chase the tremble out of her voice.

She could do this.

"In May 2005, I walked into my prom expecting to have a fun night with my date. I had no idea it was the night that would change my entire life...and take so many others."

That was all it took. Any attempt at regaining her composure slipped through her fingers. Pictures pushed at her brain like an angry crowd trying to get in the door, invading and stealing her words. Yearbook images of her classmates, the ones they always used on TV after the shooting, flashed at a rapid pace. Frozen smiling faces of people who would never grow old. Then the sounds joined in. Gunshots. Screaming. Looping scenes of people bleeding on the floor, people who were too still. Trevor's face above her, the chilling sneer, the death sentence in his eyes. Joseph and his gun.

She swayed on her feet, her fingers glued to the podium and her skin rapidly cycling from hot to cold. She closed her eyes, lost for a moment, dizzy, the sounds of the past blending with the present. "I'm sorry, I..."

But right before her knees gave out, a warm hand cupped her elbow with a firm grip, steadying her. Quiet words murmured against her ear. "Easy, lawyer girl. I've got you."

Her brain spun at the familiar voice, trying to put

pieces together and not finding any that fit. Was she dreaming? She leaned into the voice as if it were a lifeline that would pull her out of the abyss of memories or nightmares or whatever the hell this was. "Wes?"

"Yes. It's me. Let's get you off this stage and to a chair." He put his arm around her and she opened her eyes, catching a view of Wes in all black, a stiff chef's hat on his head. He leaned close to the microphone while keeping hold of her. "I'm sorry, folks. Ms. Lindt is recovering from the flu and isn't feeling well this morning. Please enjoy your breakfast. The next speaker will be out shortly."

The crowd rumbled with restless noises—low voices, scraping chairs, clinking silverware—but Rebecca was still fighting the fog in her head and the fact that Wes was somehow here and leading her offstage.

He guided her down a few steps at the side of the stage, and she managed to look over at him, finding his pretty hazel eyes heavy with concern. "What are you doing here?"

"Making omelets for a catering gig."

She frowned, the words not making any sense. "Did I pass out? Am I dreaming?"

He smirked. "So I show up in your dreams? Good to know. But this can't be a dream. Look, I'm fully clothed."

His teasing pushed through the haze in her brain like a strong beam of light, clearing her head a little. "I think I forgot to eat."

"On it. I will feed you whatever you want. Just don't faint on me, okay?"

"Okay." She leaned in to him, letting him take some of her weight as the tremors that had been going through

her body softened. He brought her into a hallway that
seemed to lead to the kitchen, based on the passing
waitstaff, and barked for someone to grab him a chair, a
cold towel, and some orange juice.

A waiter hurried to bring a chair over, and Wes eased
her down into it. Her thoughts were coming back online,
but her stomach rolled and her heart felt like it'd permanently wedged itself in her throat. When another of the
waitstaff brought what Wes had requested, he handed
Rebecca a glass of juice and draped the cool rag around
her neck. He crouched down in front of her, tugging off
his chef's hat and putting his hand on her good knee.
"Drink, Bec. Your blood sugar might be low. You're
white as a sheet."

She took a sip of the juice, the tart liquid cool on her
dry throat, and tried to wash away the remnants of the
anxiety attack. "I'm always white as a sheet. It's called
being a redhead."

He smiled and reached out to tuck a damp lock of
her hair behind her ear. "And she jokes. Does that mean
you're not going to pass out on me?"

"I think—"

"What in God's name?" a booming voice said,
echoing off the walls in the narrow space.

Rebecca winced, and Wesley's hand dropped away
from her face.

"Excuse me, get away from my daughter," her father
said as he strode down the hallway.

Wes's brows lowered, and he glanced in her father's
direction but got to his feet.

"Rebecca, what is going on?" her father said, stopping
a few steps from her, his voice clipped and demanding.

"You don't have the flu. You were just fine when we got here."

Rebecca's fingers curled tightly around her glass of juice, and she forced herself to sit taller in the chair. She didn't need her dad suspecting that she'd freaked out onstage. Lindts didn't run away like that. They powered through. They soldiered on. "I didn't get a chance to eat anything this morning, and I think I must've...locked my knees. I got light-headed and felt like I was going to faint."

Her father frowned deeply, making the wrinkles in his forehead stand out in relief. "Well"—he motioned at Wes—"this man can get you some food, and you can go up and finish after the current speaker."

She glanced at Wes and then back at her father. Her instinct was to say, *Yes. Of course.* That was what her dad was expecting. Rebecca could always be counted on. But the thought of getting back up there and inviting those flashbacks to return had acid rising in the back of her throat. "I can't do the speech today, Dad. I'm sorry. I feel sick to my stomach, and I just... I'll do whatever you need to help with your campaign, but I don't want to do talks about Long Acre. I don't want to keep rehashing it. People already know the story. The documentary will be out soon, and they can get every ugly detail if they want. I don't want to talk about it anymore."

"You can't..." His cheeks turned ruddy. "But that's the reason people book you for these events. They don't want to hear about being a lawyer. They want to hear about what you've overcome. They're inspired by that."

"Then maybe they need to find inspiration somewhere else," she snapped.

He stiffened.

She rarely talked back to her father, but she wasn't in the mood to apologize. He was the one person who should know exactly why this topic was so hard for her. When she'd fallen into a dangerous depression after Long Acre, she'd eventually admitted the truth to him, had told him why she was drowning in guilt, why she couldn't imagine going on with her life. He'd dismissed the very idea back then, telling her she was blaming herself for something that wasn't her fault. He'd taken her to a doctor, had gotten her on an antidepressant, and had encouraged her to keep her mind busy and to throw herself into her studies. The doctor had agreed. Forward motion.

The constant go-go-go of college and law school had kept her head above water with the depression until she'd been able to climb to shore and stop taking the meds. But her father had to know that the guilt had never left her. She'd just locked it away in a dark closet in her mind. But ever since the documentary, the demons had been slipping out. She felt as if she had her back against the door, arms splayed out, doing everything she could to keep them inside, but they were winning. She'd never had flashbacks before this. Depression, yes. Anger, sure. But she'd never had the memories assault her with such visceral force. This was different. She could not keep inviting those demons in by doing these kinds of speeches.

"Rebecca…" her dad said, his eyes holding warning. "I think you're overreacting. If you just take a few minutes to get your head back together and—"

"Sir, excuse me," Wes said, stepping a little closer to Rebecca, "but I think Rebecca needs to get some food and some distance from the crowd. I can take her back to the kitchen and make sure that happens."

Her dad's gaze swept over Wes, taking in his tattooed arms, disheveled hair, and cook's uniform. His lip curled. "I would say that's above and beyond your job description, young man. Just please bring her a plate to our table."

Rebecca pushed herself up from the chair, and Wes automatically put an arm out to her. She felt steadier than she had a minute ago, but that internal shakiness was still there. She braced a hand on Wesley's forearm. "Dad, this is Wes Garrett. He's…a friend. We're working together on a charity project. And I'd rather go eat something in the kitchen. I'm not in the place to socialize right now or get back on that stage. I'm going to be more of a liability to you this morning than an asset."

Her father looked back and forth between the two of them.

"I'll take good care of her, sir," Wes said, his tone easy but an undercurrent of authority there. "I know the head chef. She'll get Rebecca whatever meal she wants. I'm sure everyone back at your table will understand that she's not feeling well and had to go home."

Her father didn't look convinced, and his skin had taken on the mottled tone of anger, but he wasn't going to make a scene. He gave a brief nod. "Rebecca, we'll talk more about this on the way home."

"I'm going to catch a ride with Wes," she said quickly.

Her father's jaw flexed. "Then we'll talk tomorrow at work."

*Fun.* "Sure."

Her dad gave her one last evaluating look and then strode back to his table.

Wes peeked over at her, eyebrows lifted. "Well, he's a barrel of laughs. He does realize you're not sixteen, right?"

She smirked. "I'm not sure. And that was his restrained side. I'm going to get an earful tomorrow about responsibility and honoring commitments and how I let him down."

"Ugh. That almost makes me think my good-for-nothing, always-in-jail father was a blessing. There was no lecturing."

Rebecca sighed as she held on to Wes's arm and let him steer her toward the kitchen. "My dad seems worse than he is. He'll never be warm and fuzzy and he'll always be an insufferable hard-ass, but he's been there for me when I needed him. No one gave him lessons on how to be a single dad to a daughter when my mom bailed, you know?"

"Right." Wes bumped the swinging door open with his foot.

"I try to remember that during times like these when I want to give him the finger and tell him to back the hell off."

They avoided a waiter with a full tray of juice pitchers. "I get it. Family is complicated." Wes led her to an unused corner of the kitchen and found her a chair. "So what happened onstage? Is this really about not eating? You looked…gone. Like you were somewhere else."

Goose bumps chased up her arms, and she gave his hand a squeeze before taking a seat. "You don't want to know where I went."

"Bec—"

"Find me some pastries, chef. I can't deal with any of this on an empty stomach."

*I can't deal with any of this at all.*

# chapter
# SIXTEEN

WES PEEKED OVER AT REBECCA AS HE TURNED INTO the driveway that led to his condo. He'd offered to give her a ride home, but he hadn't told her he had plans for a pit stop.

She seemed lost in thought and had been quiet since leaving the charity brunch, but the second the automatic gates for his complex opened, she blinked and looked his way as if coming out of a daze. "Where are we going?"

"You said you didn't have any other plans for today."

"I said I planned to do laundry, go to the grocery store, and catch up on some paperwork."

He smiled. "See, nothing important."

"Wes…"

"To answer your question. I live here, and I *do* have Sunday plans. And those plans would be way more fun with a partner."

She narrowed her eyes. "That sounds ominous. Or dirty. Or ominously dirty."

His grin went wider. "I love knowing that your mind

went there first. And to be honest, *dirty* isn't a bad word for what I want you for."

Her expression remained stern, but her cheeks colored and something flickered in her eyes. Interest? Temptation? He wasn't sure, but whatever it was, it almost had him derailing his original plan. If Rebecca wanted to go upstairs to his place and get dirty, he was one hundred percent down for that.

But she'd had a rough morning, and despite the easy intimacy they'd created with their late-night phone conversations, this was in person and things between them were still new. He didn't want to ruin it by rushing or even assuming that there would be more than kissing between them. He hadn't touched a woman since his divorce. He would survive waiting a little longer. *Maybe*. *Probably*. Now he just had to convince Rebecca to join in with him on his other dirty plan. Because though she hadn't told him what had really happened onstage today, he had a strong suspicion that what she needed today was a heaping dose of distraction.

He drove around the corner of his building, the last one in the back of the complex, and parked. He hopped out of the truck and jogged around to the other side to let her out. "Come on, lawyer girl. I'll show you what I have in mind."

With a skeptical look, she stepped out of the truck and took his offered hand. Her heels clicked on the sidewalk in her unique, slightly offbeat gait that he was learning to recognize. He now knew it was because of her injury, but it didn't read like a limp to him. Instead she had developed a slower, more deliberate stride that came off as confident, like she was in no hurry to get anywhere and expected people to match her pace instead of the other way around. Plus, it gave her a little dip and sway in her step that he found unbearably sexy.

"Are you leading me out to that ill-fated camping trip you mentioned?" she asked.

He laughed. "Come with me, pretty lady. Let me show you the dark forest behind my condo. Do not be alarmed."

"Not helping, Wesley Garrett."

"I promise, no murderous agenda. Though you might want to murder me when you see what I've got planned." He led her around the corner of the building next to his and swept his arms out to his sides. "Ta-da!"

Rebecca laughed, the light sound carrying on the wind. She let go of his hand and put both of hers on her hips. "Well, it certainly is dirty."

The big, yellow school bus was parked on the empty side of the lot in all its full mud-encrusted, bird-bombed glory.

"Filthy," he agreed. "Which is why we're going to give Adele a bath."

Her attention snapped to him. "Wait, what? Who is this *we* you speak of?"

"You and me and a lot of water and sponges."

"You're kidding, right?"

"The engine work is done, so it's drivable now. I thought I could unveil the project to the kids tomorrow."

"Tomorrow?"

"Yes, and I'm going to hammer home that this will be a lot of work and require a lot of sweat equity, but I want them to be able to see the potential and not focus on how terrible the bus looks right now. These kids are used to getting hand-me-downs and shopping at secondhand stores. We can't hide the fact that this bus isn't new, but I want them to see some of Adele's shine."

Rebecca's expression softened. "I love that you have this mission, but I'm in a business suit." She held her arms out to her sides. "I'm not quite prepared for car wash day."

"Fear not." He held up a finger. "I have clothes you can borrow. You'll be fine."

He'd considered taking her home to give her the chance to change her clothes, but he had a feeling that if he'd brought her there, he wouldn't have been able to coax her outside again. She'd had that look—as though she was ready to hide from the world—when they'd left the hotel.

"Wes…"

"Come on, Bec. I know you don't want to talk about what happened this morning, but I can tell it took something out of you. You've been really quiet and have this haunted look in your eyes. Going home and being alone all day is just going to make whatever's going on in your head worse."

She glanced down.

He held out his hand. "I'm giving you a good reason to be outside on a beautiful sunny day after working nonstop all week, and I'll even throw in full permission to spray me with the hose if I step out of line. How can you resist that?"

She stared at his hand, her bottom lip caught between her teeth. He braced himself for the no, but finally she looked up. "I want that permission even if you don't step out of line."

"Granted."

A hint of a smile touched her lips, and she slipped her hand into his open palm. "Deal."

"Good." He gave her arm a playful tug. "Come on, business suit. I'll show you my humble abode, and we can get naked."

"Hey—"

He chuckled. "In separate rooms. To put on different clothes. What could you have possibly thought I meant?"

She rolled her eyes. "Lead the way, smart-ass."

A little while later, Wes stepped out of his bedroom after changing his clothes and found Rebecca examining the bookshelf in his living room. He didn't keep much in his place. After living with Brittany—who had been obsessed with shabby-chic decorating and had never met a throw pillow, flowered fabric, or ceramic knick-knack she didn't love—Wes had gone minimalist with his condo. Easy to keep clean and calm. His jam-packed bookshelf was the one exception.

Rebecca pulled a book from the shelf and turned when his foot hit the squeaky floorboard by his couch. She smiled his way. "You've got quite an eclectic collection, chef. *My Life in France* by Julia Child?"

"Yes. Don't judge. Julia Child was a badass. Plus, I've always wanted to visit France. That's the cheap way to do it until I can go for real."

"France is amazing," she said wistfully. "I've been once, but it was William Lindt style so I feel like I missed a lot."

"What do you mean?"

"My dad took me along with him for a business trip when I was in college, so it was very fast and education-focused. There was no lingering. I'd like to go again and be able to wander, get a little lost, experience more than the tourist highlights." She flipped through a few pages and then slipped the book back onto the shelf. "You didn't tell me you liked to read."

He shrugged, trying to pull himself out of fantasies of getting lost in Paris with Rebecca. Long walks on narrow streets, eating their way through every delicious meal, drinking local wine late into the evening—no, not drinking wine. He could never have that part of the Paris experience. A pang of loss shot through him. He shifted his stance and smirked, trying to shake the sour thought. "What, I don't seem like the bookish type to you? I feel like I should be insulted."

"Oh, get over yourself," she teased. "I didn't say that. I just didn't know that about you. The guys at work make a point to let everyone know what they're reading like it's a badge of honor…and of course it's always something political or pretentious. And the dates I've been on, men tend to bring it up because they assume I'm going to be hot for a guy who reads."

Wes laughed. "What are these weird circles you run in? In my neighborhood, if you admitted you loved books, you were looked at like you were an alien. And are you *not* hot for guys who read? Because if so, those books are just for decoration."

She gave him a droll look. "They are not. They are too worn and unpretentious to be decorative. You like to read, Wes Garrett. I have found you out. And for the record, you don't need help being hot. It's slightly annoying how"—she flicked her hand in his general direction—"*this* you are."

A smile jumped to his lips as a sharp kick of pleasure moved through him at the playfully perturbed look on her face. "How *this* I am? Someone needs a thesaurus. Check the third shelf."

She gave him a wry look. "So how'd you end up a reader if everyone was looking at you sideways?"

He shrugged. "I didn't start out that way. I was a shitty student, and books weren't exactly a high priority in my family. But when my dad went to prison and my mom was too messed up on drugs to take care of me, my uncle—Marco's dad—adopted me. He was the one who sold me on the idea of books." Wes set the clothes he'd picked out for her on the back of the couch and walked over to stand next to her, examining the shelves. "Ed was a teacher and told me that it didn't matter that I hadn't done well in school yet, that anything I wanted to know was available in books. I could learn from the best teachers in the world that way. Travel anywhere I wanted via the page. Experience things through the eyes of people who'd done anything and everything. Or escape to some fictional world altogether."

Rebecca let out a little sigh. "Ah, books."

"I wasn't all that impressed by the idea at first, to be honest. Then he told me that there was no TV or video games on weeknights at his house so I could either read or do chores." He ran his finger down the spine of one of the first biographies Ed had given him. "I hated chores. Plus, I figured if my uncle and my dad came from the same screwed-up family, yet somehow Uncle Ed had turned out successful and happy instead of a criminal and an addict, there might be something to his logic."

"Sounds like a smart guy."

Wes tucked his hands in his pockets, his lips lifting before he could stop them. "Ed and Carolina are the best. They saved me in so many ways, I can't even count." He took a deep breath. "Which is why I can't stand the fact that I ended up letting them down anyway."

Rebecca turned to him, frowning. "Wes, losing your business as part of a bad divorce isn't a crime."

"Spending a year pickled and ending up in rehab is pretty close," he said. "All that work they did, and I ended up an addict like my parents anyway."

She reached out and gave his shoulder a squeeze. "Stop. You're sober now, teaching kids and forcing a lawyer to scrub down a bus for charity. I don't even wash my own car. You have lots to be proud of."

He laughed, her playful smile breaking through the dark mood that had tried to take over. "Right. I'm working miracles here." He stepped over to the couch and grabbed the T-shirt and workout shorts he'd pulled out for her. "These will be big, but the shorts have a drawstring on them, so you should be able to tighten them. And I have a pair of flip-flops you can use."

"I don't need shoes. I always carry ballet flats in my bag when I wear heels." She took the clothes from him, and a line appeared between her brows. "But shorts? Don't you have sweatpants or something?"

"They're all going to be too long. Plus, it's hot outside."

Her lips rolled inward as she pondered the clothes. "I don't wear shorts except at home. I have pretty extensive scarring on my leg."

He winced inwardly. He hadn't even thought about her leg injury or what scars she might prefer to keep hidden. He'd never seen her in shorts or a skirt, always pants. He should've realized she did that on purpose. "Hey, if you're not comfortable, I'll grab you some pants. Maybe I can find a pair that we can roll up."

She glanced up, indecision in her gaze. "I don't know. It *is* freaking hot out there."

He considered her, seeing the hint of yearning there, the desire to take that leap of faith, but she was scared. He had no idea what she thought he would do if he saw her scars. Stare? Be turned off? Think differently of her? He knew none of those were options, but he hadn't walked in her shoes. He didn't know what kind of reactions she'd gotten in the past.

He took a breath. "Look, I want you to do whatever makes you feel comfortable, but please don't cover up just because I'm here with you. We all have scars, some visible, some not. You've already seen a load of mine."

She nodded. "I know. I just… I guess I like the way you look at me now."

He lifted a brow. "And how's that?"

A small smile appeared. "Like you're always right on the edge of trying to convince me out of my clothes."

He laughed. "That's totally true. That's pretty much a constant state when I'm around you. I'm obviously not doing a good job of masking it."

"Don't," she said. "I like it. I'm not used to someone looking at me like that."

"It's not going to change, Bec. If that's what you're worried about. Your scars don't scare me. They're part of you. And to be honest, I'm really more of an ass man than a leg man anyway. And yours…is top-notch, lawyer girl. Grade A."

She huffed and swatted him with the clothes. "Pig."

He lifted his hands in defense. "Oink?"

She rolled her eyes. "You're ridiculous. But fine, I'll wear the shorts."

"You sure?"

"Yes. You may be a pig, but I don't want to be a chicken." She pressed her lips together in determination. "Now distract me because I'm about to overthink this."

"Oh, we can't have that." He reached out to grip the lapels of her suit jacket and guided her to him. She came willingly and looped her arms loosely around his waist. He liked that things were so easy between them. He couldn't remember the last time he'd felt so comfortable around a woman. So he didn't overanalyze it, and instinct took over. He bent down to kiss her. He'd only intended a quick peck, a reintroduction to this new kissing part of their relationship after all the flirty phone calls. But when his mouth touched hers, fire licked up his spine and all his *hell yes* receptors went off like a string of firecrackers.

All because of the way she responded to him. Rebecca didn't simply accept kisses. She didn't sit back and let him lead. She leaned into it, stated her clear desire to be kissed more thoroughly. And when her lips parted and she made a hungry sound that he'd probably hear in his next erotic dream, he was a goner. His hand shifted to the back of her neck, her skin hot against his palm, and he deepened the kiss, their tongues meeting.

Her hands slid along his chest, her fingertips sending threads of awareness straight downward, and grappled for his shirt like she was going to tear it right off him. He was all for that. He backed her against the bookcase, rattling some of the items on one of the shelves, and aligned his body to hers. Every deprived male cell in his body rushed to the surface, and he had no shot at playing it cool. His cock grew hard and heavy, demanding things it had no right to, while her nails scraped him through his thin T-shirt. All the years of abstinence seemed to coalesce into one pounding fist of need in his gut.

He broke away, panting, and pressed his forehead to hers, trying to rein himself in. "We should probably stop this. Like right now. My bedroom is exceptionally close, and I'm losing my inclination to do the right thing."

"The right thing?" she asked, breathless.

"Yes. Not rushing this. Not talking you into something and then falling on you like an animal. I haven't been with anyone in a very long time. I haven't wanted to." His grip on her neck tightened, his control barely tethered. "But when you kiss me like that, touch me, I can't think of anything other than stripping you down right here, putting my mouth on every inch of you, and then sinking deep inside you and making you scream."

A soft gasp escaped her. "Oh."

He closed his eyes and gave a humorless laugh, her startled response making him feel ridiculous. "And there I go, taking it too far anyway. I'm sorry."

He shifted to pull away, to get some much-needed distance, but she reached out and grabbed the waistband of his shorts, hauling him back close. "Hey."

He lifted his head, meeting her gaze, his blood still pumping hard. "Yeah?"

"Don't apologize for that," she said, voice steady. "For showing me you want me or talking dirty or any of it." She wet her lips. "I'm not saying we should take that step yet either. This is new. We're getting to know each other. But when you say those things and kiss me that way, when you look at me like you are now, I feel…"

"You feel what?" he asked hoarsely.

"*Alive*, Wes. Like every part of me is firing at full speed." She pushed up on her toes and brushed her lips over his. "So please, don't apologize for that. If I don't want to do something, I'll tell you so, and I know you'll respect that. But don't be afraid to be real with me or to say what's in your head. I'm not that easily scandalized. Plus, it's probably in my head, too."

Heat spread through his chest and lower—much, much lower. "Oh yeah, lawyer girl. Tell me what's going on in your head right now."

She smiled innocently. "If I told you that, we'd never get the bus washed."

He made a pained sound and tipped his head back. "You are a very mean lady."

"I am the worst." She stepped away from him and grabbed the clothes he'd lent her.

But as she walked into the bedroom to change, he had a very different opinion running through his mind. She wasn't the worst.

No. In fact, she was turning out to be the very best thing that had happened to him in a long damn time.

Now he had to make sure not to screw it up.

# SEVENTEEN

REBECCA WALKED INTO WES'S LIVING ROOM IN THE borrowed clothes, bracing for the reaction. She knew that Wes would never say anything negative about her scars. He wasn't a dick. But it didn't make her feel any less self-conscious about her naked legs.

After the bad experience in college and years of gawkers in gym locker rooms and swimming pools, she'd developed a bit of a phobia about exposing her legs. She hated the sympathy, the curiosity, the questions—no matter how well intentioned. Not because the scars were so hard to look at. She'd had her knee reconstructed, which had left dark, raised incision marks on her pale skin, and there was a deep puckered scar in her thigh where a bullet had hit her. Her muscles on that side were smaller than the muscles in her other leg, but many people had worse. Her aversion to the scars was less due to how they looked and more because of what they branded her with.

Most people saw them as her mark of survival, but

she saw them as a constant reminder of what she'd done to make Trevor want her dead.

Wes stepped out of his kitchen with two water bottles and smiled when he saw her. No flinch. No gaping. No look of pity. "All ready to get Adele sparkling?"

Rebecca let out a breath she didn't realize had gotten stuck in her throat. He wasn't going to stare. He wasn't going to ask questions. Something tight between her shoulders eased. "I hate to break it to you. I love Adele. But I'm not sure she's capable of sparkling without a new paint job."

Wes shook his head. "Ye of little faith."

"Me of realistic constitution."

He laughed. "Okay, sparkling may be a bit of a stretch. But who needs that? New and perfect is overrated. Adele has character. She's been through a lot and has survived. She is going to be beautiful in her own quirky way."

Rebecca smirked and crossed her arms. "Wesley Garrett, are you sneakily trying to make me feel better about my bared legs?"

He walked over, looking like sin on parade in his thin, white T-shirt and black workout shorts, his tattoos flexing with every swing of his arms. He set the water bottles down and stopped in front of her, taking her hands and lacing his fingers with hers. He held her arms out to her sides and gave her a full up-and-down scan, making her belly flutter with apprehension.

"No, Rebecca. You are not beautiful in a quirky way," he said, his gaze pinning her to the spot. "You are flat-out hot. You need no extra polishing. A lot of sunscreen probably, but no polish."

Her throat tightened at the honesty in his eyes, but

she forced a teasing smile. "Me and sunscreen go way back. We've been BFFs since a traumatizing day in a kiddie pool."

"I'll throw a bottle of it in with the water. Now let's get outside before you distract me with your wicked ways again."

She laughed. "*My* wicked ways?"

"Yes. You're a sorceress. With your business suits and your red hair all pinned up, I was already a mess. But now"—he released one of her hands and twirled her around—"now I get long legs and your Grade A backside to distract me while I try to do charity work. How am I supposed to focus?"

She grinned and poked him in the chest. "Hey, if you're going to objectify me, then I need to be afforded the same right. This shirt of yours? It's coming off, mister. It's way too hot outside for that nonsense."

He grabbed the finger she had pressed to his chest and nipped at the tip with his teeth. "Oh, I'm all for a no-shirts car wash. I assume this applies to you as well."

"Then we'll get arrested."

"No worries. I know a great lawyer. Though she's kind of expensive and, frankly, a little bossy."

She pulled her hand away, laughing. "All right, outside or we'll never get this done."

"And this is a problem, why?"

"Wes!"

"Kidding." He leaned in and kissed her quickly. She loved the little zip of pleasure that went through her at the simple contact. "That's fine. But know that you've just written your own downfall. Me with no shirt? Wet? You know I've been paid for my shirtlessness. You've got no shot at maintaining acceptable behavior in public. You will probably just throw all your clothes at me the minute we're outside."

She gave a droll look. "I will try to contain myself, chef."

He laughed good-naturedly and stepped away. As he strode toward their stuff, he reached behind to tug his shirt over his head. He tossed it aside and then tucked the water bottles in a bag. "Okay, let's do this."

But when he turned back to her, she'd forgotten what she was supposed to be doing. Wes had been joking around with her, but now she saw exactly why someone had thought of him for a Shirtless Chef gig. Long, lean muscle spread across broad shoulders, the tattoos on his arms snaked a little bit onto his shoulders and chest, and his torso was tanned, which meant he'd been without his shirt in public at some point—and it just wasn't fair that she hadn't been present in that public. The man was a sight. And she was staring.

"Rebecca?"

"Huh?"

"I asked if you were ready to go."

"Right." Yes. Of course. They needed to go. There was work to be done. "Sure."

He cocked his head toward the door and she followed him, still gawking and only feeling a little guilty about it. He opened a closet door in the entryway, tossed a bottle of sunscreen in the bag, and then they were on their way.

When they got down to the parking lot, Wes gathered more supplies from his truck and set up everything next to Adele. The sun had risen higher in the sky by then, creating shimmering heat off the blacktop and promising to roast them if they weren't careful. Spring in Texas was turning out to be just a summer preview. Rebecca dug around in the bag and found the sunblock while Wes connected the hose and filled two buckets with sudsy water.

She slathered a good layer on every exposed area, making sure she didn't miss anything. She could get sunburn on long car rides just getting sun through the window, so she didn't mess around. When she finished rubbing some onto her legs, she glanced up and caught Wes watching her. Her first instinct was to think he was examining her scars further, but the look in his eyes held something a lot different. Her neck warmed, and it had nothing to do with the sun.

She straightened and held up the bottle. "Want some?"

"Not yet. But let me know if you see me getting red."

"You mean watch your body very, very closely in the name of safety? I'm on it."

He laughed. "You are such a thoughtful friend."

"Yep." She was thinking thoughts all right.

He strolled over and held out a bucket and the hose. "Which would you like to be in charge of first? Getting things wet or soaping them up?"

Her tongue pressed to the roof of her mouth as images of getting *him* wet and soaping *him* up were the first things that came to mind. She quickly reached for the hose. "Wet."

She needed to turn that thing on herself and cool her damn libido.

He grinned and handed her the hose. "I knew you'd choose offense. I'm going to be soaked in about ten seconds, aren't I?"

"Less." She squeezed the trigger on the hose and shot him with a short burst of water, if for no other reason than to get some space between them so she wouldn't make a fool of herself.

He cursed and jumped back, dropping the bucket and laughing. "You suck, lawyer girl."

She arched a brow and held up the nozzle again. "What was that, chef? I didn't hear you."

He lifted his palms, eyes smiling and droplets of water dripping down his chest. "I said you're wonderful and kind. A queen among women."

"I thought so." She turned toward the bus and dragged the hose closer before letting loose and spraying down Adele.

Wes worked alongside her, soaping the bus with a long-handled contraption that had a sponge on the end and could reach all the way to the roof. Once Rebecca had sprayed everything down, she took on the lower parts with a fat, handheld sponge.

Wes played an old-school rock station on his phone, and they sang along as they worked, in between talking about everything and nothing like they had each night on the phone. How he'd ended up a chef. What kind of law she'd originally wanted to practice. What bands they'd liked when they were growing up. And eventually the conversation devolved into a heated debate about the brilliance (her) or sacrilegiousness (him) of boxed macaroni and cheese. They'd had to end that one in a stalemate.

With all the joking around and friendly conversation, Rebecca had settled herself down and banked the dirty thoughts. Wesley was gorgeous, yes, but she was enjoying his company and the conversation as much as the view. He was easy to be around. She had male friends at work, but all their conversations were laced with unspoken competition and posturing, which could be exhausting. And the friends-with-benefits arrangements she'd had in the past had been a lot more about convenient benefits than actual friendship. Acquaintances with benefits more than anything. She hadn't kept in touch with any of them. But she could see herself forming a real friendship with Wes—with or without the benefits.

But her even-handed view of things didn't last long.

An hour into their project, Wes had moved on to cleaning the wheel wells. Rebecca caught herself watching how his back flexed as he scrubbed at the stubborn dirt, a few droplets of sweat making a journey downward to the place where his shorts sank low and revealed the two indentations on each side of his spine. She wanted to catch the drops of sweat with her tongue and lick each dip in his back.

Which was saying something because she'd never had such an intense urge to lick another person.

But when she managed to drag her eyes upward, she noticed a pink tint on his neck that would quickly turn red in the blast of the Texas sun. "Shit."

Wes turned, peeking back at her. "What's wrong?"

"I've been bad about sunburn watch. You're getting baked. I'll grab the lotion."

She dropped her sponge in the bucket and dried her hands before finding Wes's bag and pulling out the sunblock. She walked it back over and Wes stood, hands dripping with suds. She lifted the bottle, ready to offer it to him, but then had a surge of boldness. "Want me to get it for you? Your hands are wet, and you're not going to be able to reach your back."

His gaze dropped to the bottle, then back to her, some invisible wire of electricity wrapping its way around her most sensitive parts. He wet his lips. "Yeah, sure. Thanks."

Her thighs clenched like he'd just said, *Take me to bed or lose me forever*. But this wasn't *Top Gun*. This was about sunscreen, so she managed to keep her expression smooth. "Turn around."

She would start with his back. Backs were safe. Totally neutral. She could handle that. She squirted the lotion into her hands and stepped behind him. After taking a deep breath, she put her hands on his shoulders, and he flinched beneath her. "Damn, that's cold."

"Sorry," she said softly, only half paying attention because the lotion was cool but his skin was hot and smooth beneath her fingertips. The scent of him—lemon soap, grass, and something uniquely him—hit her hard. And low.

She rolled her lips together and tried to focus. "Does it sting? I hope you're not already burned."

"No," he said, his voice lower than before. "It feels good now."

She added more cream, set the bottle on the ground, and then swept her hands down his back, over the muscles, and dipped her thumbs into those little indentations she'd been admiring, making slow circles. Wes's muscles rippled with tension beneath her touch.

Her mouth was dry, her heartbeat fast. "Turn around."

When he did, his gaze was hooded, his attention heavy on her, but he didn't say a word. He simply leaned over to grab the bottle of lotion and tipped the cream into her hands. She looked down, the eye contact too much, and forced her hands to be steady as he filled them with sunblock again. Every part of her was aware and pulsing in time with her heartbeat now, but when she flattened her hands on the front side of his inked shoulders and dragged the lotion down over his chest, any hope she had of maintaining her cool left her. Every feminine part of her tightened. She kept her face down, knowing she wouldn't be able to hide her thoughts.

Rebecca tracked her hands lower over his abdomen, watching the muscles tense and dip beneath her fingers, but when she got near his waist, he dropped the bottle and his hands gripped her wrists, stilling her. "Stop."

She looked up, finding him with his jaw locked and his hazel eyes stormy. She cleared her throat, trying to find her voice. "Everything okay?"

"No."

She blinked. "No?"

"If you keep doing this, there's going to be no hiding from you or anyone who walks by exactly what this is doing to me."

She glanced down at his shorts and couldn't miss the growing interest. Her throat worked as tingly heat spread all the way to the tips of her fingers and toes. "Oh."

"Right. So maybe I should take it from here before this gets embarrassing." He released her wrists.

Her hands were still on his waist, and she knew she was supposed to move them away. This was venturing into the deep end. They weren't there yet. She needed to back away. Splash around in the shallow end and get used to the water. But instead, all thought spilled out of her head. She gripped his hips harder, leaned forward, and pressed her mouth to the spot between his pecs.

Wes stilled, his body going rigid beneath her kiss.

She kept her lips there, his skin salty and warm, and let her hands travel up his abdomen, exploring. He let out a soft moan. One of desperation. Of barely there restraint.

His response sent bravery bubbling up inside her. She lifted her head. "Wes?"

His face was tipped back toward the sky. "Yeah?"

"You said earlier you were afraid you'd try to talk me into something. You wouldn't have to talk me into anything right now. But I'm tempted to talk you into some things. Tell me not to."

A harsh breath whooshed out of him, and his big hands cupped her jaw as he caught her gaze. "You're asking *me* to talk some sense into *you*? You've got no shot at that. I can't see straight right now. You're all wet and undone, and having your slick hands on me... Bec, all I can think about is taking you inside and stripping you out of these wet clothes and making you feel good. Hell, I'm not even sure I can wait for the walk to the apartment. The driver's seat is starting to look pretty roomy. And the windows are still too dirty to see through."

She laughed at that. "Wesley Garrett, I am not getting naked with you in a dirty school bus."

"I thought we weren't supposed to be getting naked at all. I thought we weren't going to rush," he reminded her.

"You're right. We probably shouldn't rush. But..."

"But?"

"But whose rules are we following?" she asked. "I want you. You want me. We're grown-ups. I know what this is."

"And that is?" he asked carefully.

"Fun, Wes. Just fun between friends. And I want to have fun with you."

"Naked fun," he said, his lips curving.

"Yes, but *not* in a dirty school bus."

He grinned wide. "It was the lack of shirt. I told you."

She looped her arms around his neck. "Nope, it was the books. I've been hot and bothered and completely distracted since. Entire sexual fantasies have been woven. Filthy thoughts have been had."

"Filthy?"

"Does it still count as filthy if it involved soapy water, roaming hands, and a lot of tongue? Things got very, very clean."

"Fuck." He kissed her then, stealing her breath, and then broke away just as roughly. "You're killing me."

"Sorry?"

"Don't be." With that, he grabbed her and lifted her off her feet.

She gasped and wrapped her legs around his waist. "You're going to drop me."

"Not gonna happen." He carried her toward the condo, leaving all their supplies behind. "I swear I didn't bring you here for this."

"I know."

"But damn," he said, holding her tighter, "I'm glad it's now."

She laughed and kissed him. "Me too. Now is awesome."

In fact, *now* was her new favorite thing. This morning she'd melted down onstage and had a flashback, wrestled with an emotional vampire that had sucked every ounce of good feeling out of her. She'd planned to spend the rest of the day burying herself in busywork to block all of it out, to go back to that place where she could hide. But somehow this man had thwarted her plan and had her laughing and turned on only a few hours later.

Everything inside her felt buoyed. As if this morning had tied bricks to her feet and dropped her in the ocean, and Wes had somehow cut the chains loose and not only thrown her a life vest, but plunked her on a speedboat and put the wind in her hair.

She felt…light.

She'd forgotten how that felt.

He'd called her a sorceress, but he was looking pretty damn magical himself. She knew she needed to be careful about having any of those kinds of feelings. She knew that trap. This was how people ended up in her office. They trusted these moments as something more meaningful than they actually were. This was just fun. Attraction and infatuation. Novelty. She couldn't overthink it and mistake it for anything more than that.

So she was turning that analytical switch in her brain off for a little while. She would enjoy this man, this moment, and the fluttery feeling coursing through her. This was what Kincaid had been talking about. Find a guy you like. Be a little wild. Don't make it a big thing. Enjoy the ride.

She'd never done that before with a guy—or in any part of her life, really. Even in her previous experiences with guys, she had stayed grounded and practical. But this thing with Wes could never be mistaken for practical. He was risk wrapped in rebellion and laced with temptation. There was an intensity to her attraction to him that felt dangerous.

*God*. She had a *crush*.

She hadn't had one since Finn, which should probably worry her. But there was no way she was walking away from Wes yet.

This feeling was too good to let go of. Wes was her new drug and, goddammit, she had earned a bender.

"You've got your thinking face on." Wes said as he balanced her and unlocked his door. "What's on that mind of yours, lawyer girl?"

A slow smile touched her lips. "Just you. Lots and lots of you."

"Good. I've always liked being the center of attention."

She laughed. And when he set her down in his bathroom, turned on the shower, and kissed down her neck, her answer was the God's honest truth. This man didn't leave room in her mind for anything else.

That was all she could think about right now.

Not the brunch. Not the future. Not anything at all.

Just Wes.

chapter

# EIGHTEEN

WES WAS HALF CONVINCED HE'D PASSED OUT FROM heat exhaustion and was really lying out in the parking lot having some sort of fever dream. Because he couldn't possibly be in his bathroom kissing down Rebecca's throat, cupping her ass, and about to strip her naked.

They'd agreed not to rush. They'd agreed to be smart. To continue getting to know each other. He wasn't going to be old Wes who did everything on a whim without considering the fallout. But then the lawyer who had once dressed him down with one shrewd, derisive look in court had given him the sexiest, most come-hither gaze he'd ever encountered. *I want you*. And it hadn't been put on. No guile at all.

It had annihilated any good sense he had.

That was one of the things that he couldn't get enough of with Rebecca. She didn't play games like the other women he'd been with. Confident in the courtroom and confident in her decisions. Outside, when she'd put her hands on him, rubbed the lotion into his skin, he'd been in physical pain with the need that had coursed through him. His mind couldn't help imagining her hands sliding lower, dipping into his shorts, taking his cock in her slick hand. His own hands roaming over her body and thumbing the hard points of her nipples beneath that borrowed T-shirt. But he'd forced himself to keep it in check, to not act like some hard-up guy who couldn't control himself.

But when he'd given her a chance to back away, she'd made the move instead. Feeling her lips on his chest had been more erotic than he could've imagined such a simple move being. What it represented had flipped every one of his switches.

She wanted him, and she wasn't afraid to tell him that. No gray areas. No coy games.

Bold and honest.

She wanted to feel good. To have fun.

He wasn't going to let her down.

He lifted his head and pulled the elastic band from her hair, letting it fall loose around her shoulders. The humidity outside had made it curl. He wrapped a lock around his finger and smiled. "You have curls."

She smirked. "Don't tell anyone my secret. I straighten it every morning. I had enough Little Orphan Annie references in kindergarten to last me a lifetime."

He slid his hand over the curve of her ass and pulled her close. "You don't look like Annie. You look like some secret, wild version of the buttoned-up lawyer everyone else knows. I like it."

"There is no wild version of me."

"Liar," he said against her ear, then kissed the hollow behind it, liking the way she shivered against him.

"Kissing some guy on the first night just to see what it was like? A little wild."

She tipped her head back with a sigh.

He slid a hand beneath the wet T-shirt, pushing her bra up and cupping her breast, the feel of all that soft, warm flesh making him go painfully hard. He dragged his thumb over her nipple, and she made a needy sound in the back of her throat that made him lose his words for a second. He licked his lips. "Buying a food truck on a whim to help a charity? Pretty wild, lawyer girl."

She scoffed, but there was no real oomph behind it.

"Getting naked with someone you used to hate on a Sunday afternoon? Definitely wild," he declared. "I think you've just been fooling everyone else with the uptight routine."

She gave a lazy smile, eyes still closed. "Never. I'm the good girl, Wes. The straight-A student. I'm the girl next door."

The mocking in her voice was hard to miss.

"That's what people say, huh?" He pinched her nipple, eliciting a sharp gasp from her. "Well, they're not looking hard enough. Because I felt it when you kissed me that first night. You're all fire, Bec. You've just figured out clever ways to bank it. But you can't hide it from me."

He pulled the T-shirt up and over her head, taking her bra with it, and cursed under his breath as a sharp kick of need almost rocked him onto his heels. Some of her faint freckles had made a path down her chest, a path that he could imagine tracing with his tongue. But what really did him in was the sight of the tight, rosy points of her breasts, announcing just how turned on she was.

"You're so fucking gorgeous I can barely stand it," he said, the words tumbling out of him.

Her eyes blinked open, that deep-blue gaze capturing him. She looked...surprised. He hated that. Hated that being told she was gorgeous was what threw her. Whatever guys she'd had in her life had apparently been idiots who didn't know how to state the obvious.

He tossed the shirt aside and took her wrists, lifting her arms over her head and pinning them to the shower door. "You keep these here for me. I'm gonna need a minute."

Her throat worked and she held his gaze, but when he released her wrists, she turned them to grab the shower door and kept them there. "Wes, the water..."

He pressed his fingers over her lips and smiled. "Patience. A chef likes to savor."

---

*Savor.*

Rebecca was going to implode—just turn into nothing and disappear. No way her body could sustain this level of arousal for any extended period of time. But Wes gave her a look that said he was one hundred percent serious. He wanted her to stand there and let him have his fill.

He reached for the waistband of the shorts she'd borrowed and dragged them down her hips, along with her panties, until they dropped to the floor and she stepped out of them. She had a dart of panic at the thought of being so exposed, but then his hand cupped her breast, and he bent to take it in his mouth.

The wet heat of his tongue grazed across her sensitive flesh and her sex clenched, a soft cry escaping her. The steamy air spilling out of the shower moved over her bare skin, but she was already on fire. Wes sucked and teased, his other hand reaching up to stroke her other breast. Her back arched, and she wondered if it was possible to come just from this. Every nip of his teeth and swipe of his tongue felt like it was between her legs and not just at her breast.

But when he pulled away and looked down her body, the nerves resurfaced like a thousand butterfly wings beating inside her chest.

She took a deep breath. She was no virgin, but for her, sex had always taken a fairly prescribed route. It involved a dark room and sheets and the horizontal position. Being so exposed in the lights of the bathroom had her feeling more than a little vulnerable—and not just because of her scars. But when she caught the look on Wes's face as his focus slid over her, the worry morphed into something else.

Wes looked like a man who'd just been served the most delicious meal of his life. When he'd told her she was gorgeous, she'd at first been taken aback. Men didn't call her that. Pretty, at times. Elegant, once or twice. But nothing more emphatic than that. So when Wes had said it, she'd chalked it up to him making her feel good. But seeing how he was looking at her now, she realized she'd been wrong. His attraction was so visceral she could almost feel the desire in his eyes like a touch.

It made her feel wholly...present. Completely in her skin in a way she'd never felt before with a man. Something tightly knotted unwound inside her. "I think it's exceptionally unfair that I'm the only one naked."

Wes gave her a sly smile and a look full of heat. "Still bossy even with her hands above her head."

"You expected that to change?"

"Nope." He reached for his shorts and pushed them down and off. Rebecca let her gaze travel from the floor upward, taking in the long legs, strong thighs, and then finally the smooth, hard length of him. Her thighs pressed together, the sight of him sending a fresh wave of need through her and reminding her how damn long it'd been since she'd slept with anyone.

Wes took his cock in his hand and gave it an easy stroke as he stepped close again. "Better? All's fair now, Bec?"

"Only if I can use my hands now."

He smiled. "Not yet. I've got places to go." He slid hot palms onto her waist and lowered his knees to the rug. "Things to savor."

Before she could begin to process Wes at her feet, he bent down and pressed a kiss to her bad knee, right over the thickest scar. Her belly flip-flopped, but before she could freak out, he moved up her thigh, kissing over the other ugly places and the smooth ones, and slipped his hand between her legs, stroking over the slick, sensitive skin.

The panic that had been trying to take over evaporated like mist on a hot day. Wes took his time, easing a finger inside her, giving her slow-building pleasure as he kissed his way up. But when he reached the apex of her thighs and dragged his tongue over her clit, all sense of slow-building disappeared. Her head tapped back against the shower door, and she hissed out a breath at the shock of need that zipped through her.

The flat of his tongue rolled over her, and her hands

went to his hair. She couldn't keep them above her any longer, couldn't *not* touch him. He grunted at her grip but didn't back away. He just kept tasting her, his lips and tongue and finger working in a slow, sensual dance, as if he really was savoring her and enjoying the tease.

"Wes…if you keep…I'm gonna…"

He eased back for a minute, pressing a kiss to her inner thigh and then peered up at her, promise in his eyes. "That's the point, gorgeous. We've got all the time in the world. Let me make you feel good. The supply of these is not limited."

"But…" The protest died on her lips as he lifted her bad knee to rest over his shoulder and opened her body to him. He kissed her long and deep right where she ached the most, and her vision blurred as everything sparked like static along her skin.

She closed her eyes and held on to his head as if she were hanging off a cliff and he was all she had to keep from falling. She'd wanted to tell him that if she came now, she wouldn't be able to do that again for a long while. But the words wouldn't form and then the orgasm was washing over her, steamrolling any resistance she could've mustered.

She cried out, her head tapping the shower door, and arched into him, letting herself get swallowed up by all the pleasure. It'd been so long since she'd come by anyone else's touch that she'd forgotten how different it was, how that out-of-control feeling of knowing she was completely at someone else's mercy amplified each sensation. They would give, and she would take. And boy, was Wes giving. He pushed her past the point where she would've stopped herself and called it good, sending her to a more intense, breath-stealing place that had her writhing and cursing and calling his name—all at the same time.

Not until Wes eased her leg back down and she was panting her way through the aftershocks did she realize she was still clutching fistfuls of his hair and had slid halfway down the shower door. She quickly released him and steadied herself. "Wow, that was…"

But Wes didn't let her finish. He stood, his attention hot on her, and cupped her jaw, giving her a crushing kiss.

There was so much in that kiss—need, desire, appreciation, not to mention the illicit flavor of sex—that her body, which had been fully satisfied, revved up again. The heat of his erection pressed against her belly as he kissed her like she'd never been kissed before.

She reached between them and wrapped her hand around him. He moaned into her mouth. "I'm gonna break land speed records if you do that. It's been so long."

The heat of him against her palm and the slick head were enough to have her inner muscles pulsing, her heartbeat relocating to that space between her thighs. "We've got all day, remember?"

He braced his hands on either side of her, his breath rasping against her neck. "Condoms are in my bedroom. I hope to God they're not expired."

"I have some in my purse in the living room. But…" An odd urge hit her as she stroked him, a deep, aching desire to feel him just like this, skin to skin. "It's been over a year since I've been with anyone, and I'm on the pill. Have you been tested?"

"Yes. I'm good, but I can go get—"

She kissed him, swallowing the words and following

her gut. She pulled back and met his eyes. "I'm okay with it if you are."

Something dark and dangerous flared in his gaze. "I've never been more okay with anything ever. This will be slower the next time, I promise. But right now…" He guided her into the steamy space of the shower, the warm water cascading over her skin. "Right now I need you to hold on."

He turned her around and she reached out, automatically grabbing the towel bar fastened to the tile wall. He pressed his body against her back, rubbing all that maleness against her slick skin—rough hair and hard muscle, the thick, hot need of his erection branding her and making the water feel cool in comparison. She nearly purred as she rocked back against him.

He sucked the water off the curve of her neck and then nipped at her ear. "You are the sexiest thing I've ever seen. Spread your legs for me. I need to be inside you."

A hard shudder went through her, and she did as he asked. He wrapped an arm around her waist, keeping her steady as she gripped the bar, and then he was pressing against her entrance, making her stomach flutter and her knuckles go white. When he slid inside, stretching and filling her, she let out a sound of relief, the emptiness finally abating.

He growled against her ear and rocked into her, deep and slower than she'd expected, as if he was still savoring, though she knew he had to be pushing his edge.

"Wes," she whispered, hearing the begging note in her voice over the hard patter of the water.

The arm he had around her slid down, finding her sensitive clit as he sank deep again and picked up a little speed. She tensed, expecting the stimulation to be too much too soon, but the feel of his calloused finger along her tender flesh made an edgy need bloom. She was right there again. She could feel the demand of her body, the pulsing potential. It was just out of reach.

"Please." The word slipped out, unbidden. "I need…"

"What?" he asked hoarsely as he continued pumping into her. "Tell me."

Her hands tightened on the bar. "Fuck me, Wes. I need…fast."

Wes made a sound deep in his throat and his hips rocked faster, thrusting into her while his fingers worked her to the point of being rough.

But that edge was apparently just what she needed because colored dots of light appeared behind her eyes, and an orgasm she didn't think she had in her exploded through her. She cried out, the sound echoing off the tile walls and tightening her throat.

Wes made the sexiest grinding grunts—as if he was mad at her for making him feel so good—and thrust into her fast and deep. Then he went dead still, buried to the hilt, his muscles tensing against her. He made a pained sound and called her Bec and then was moving again, riding out the rest of his pleasure and stretching out hers.

When they finally slowed, sated and spent, he planted his hands next to hers, caging her in. They breathed hard together as they came down from the high, hot water tracking over them like some weird baptism into a new phase in their arrangement.

Wes finally pressed a kiss to her shoulder, eased out of her, and let out a satisfied sigh. "That was worth the wait."

She smiled and turned around to face him. "You've only known me for a couple of weeks."

He touched his forehead to hers, his eyelashes sparkling with water droplets. "No. The whole wait."

"Oh." The years. Something sharp-edged and sweet bloomed inside her chest. "For me, too."

She knew he'd assume she meant the year, but that wasn't the whole truth. Yes, it'd been a year since she'd had sex.

But it'd been her whole life since she'd had anything that felt like *that*.

She could almost hear Kincaid whispering in her ear, *Enjoy it while you can, cupcake*.

*chapter*

# NINETEEN

"I'M GOING TO HAVE TO GET A BIGGER SWEAR JAR. WHEN the kids see the bus, they're going to lose their shit," Wes said gleefully.

"You better add a dollar right now, chef," Rebecca teased, keeping her voice low against the phone and letting her hair curtain her face from the open door of her office. "And I can't wait to see their faces. Hopefully, they won't be offended that it's not totally clean."

He laughed. "We did the best we could."

"We did no such thing. We got it half scrubbed and then spent the afternoon in bed."

"Well, not technically *in bed*."

Her skin flushed at the memory. She'd left Wes's condo late last night on a sated high. After the shower, he'd cooked her a ridiculously delicious pasta dish with random ingredients from his pantry and then they'd attempted to watch a movie on his couch. That'd been a wash. They hadn't been able to keep their hands off each other and had ended up naked on the floor of the living room, even though the bedroom had only been a few steps away. "You know what I mean. We should've been cleaning poor Adele."

"We were up against terrible odds. No reasonable person would've expected us to resist each other. But if it makes you feel better, I got up early this morning and finished the job. Adele is all ready for her debut," Wes declared.

Rebecca's lips curved, her chest filling with fizzy warmth for a different reason. Wes liked to play it cool, but she could tell how much he cared about those kids by all these little things he did. She could picture him at the crack of dawn, scrubbing down that old bus. "Did you wear a shirt?"

He chuckled. "Of course. Didn't want to be randomly attacked by a neighbor."

"Right. Safety first."

"So will you be able to get here this afternoon to see the big reveal? I know Mondays can be crazy," Wes said, his chair squeaking in the background, "so if you need me to postpone it, I can keep it a secret. I don't want to do it without you. You made this whole thing happen."

"I have two new clients on my schedule and one other meeting. I also planned on picking up my canine hero from your brother this afternoon, but Marco said Knight has a minor infection and wants to keep him a few more days."

"Knight? He officially has a name now?"

"Yes, I figured with his black fur and his hero status, it was appropriate. I'm still going to stop by to visit him. Marco said he's allowed to have a few treats now, so I'm bringing him some goodies, but I should be able to get to you around four. I want to be there for the reveal. I'm excited."

"I'm pumped you're going to be able to get here today. Keeping this a secret has been tough. Oh, and remember to email me the last of the paperwork. The school needs it on file if you're going to be working directly with the kids."

"It's already on the way," she said.

"And bring some extra clothes if you want to jump in on the remodeling afterward. I'd bring some of my extras, but if I see you in those again, my mind is going to go to places it shouldn't with children around."

She smirked. "Have you no self-control, man?"

"Nope. Not when it comes to you."

A tingly awareness moved through her, spreading out to the tips of her fingers. "I know the feeling."

"Yeah?"

"Yeah." She looked down at her desk and the big calendar she used to keep her schedule straight. She tracked her fingertip over the spot where she'd marked down the details of the charity brunch. She'd written it in hard, neat handwriting, indenting the paper. Angry writing. No, *scared* writing. She hadn't even realized she'd done that. Everything else was in looping script. She'd been terrified from the start and all through that morning, until Wes had swept in and stolen her away from the whole thing. "And I forgot to say it before I left, but thanks for yesterday."

"Thanks?" he scoffed, his incredulity echoing through the phone. "Rebecca, that's the last thing you need to say to me."

"I just mean for getting my mind off everything after

the debacle at brunch yesterday morning. I was kind of a mess. You are…excellent at distraction."

He was quiet for a moment, and she wondered if she'd said something wrong, but finally he cleared his throat. "I'm happy to distract you anytime, but know that if you ever want to talk about…anything, I'm here. Remember the friend portion of this arrangement. You don't have to pretend that yesterday morning was about skipping breakfast."

Her ribs cinched tight. "Wes—"

"I'm not saying you have to. I just wanted to put it out there. I've worked with these kids long enough that they've taught me a few valuable lessons, and one of them is being able to listen to the hard stuff." His voice had gone quiet, tentative. "So I know we're having fun and keeping things light, but that doesn't mean you can't be real with me. Don't act like everything's cool if it's not."

The truth welled up in her like a tidal wave, ready to bust through the levee and flood out. What would it feel like to tell someone? To tell *all* of it? What had really happened back then, what she'd seen these last few months, the tricks her mind had played on her. But she choked back the urge as quickly as it came. Yeah, that'd be a fun way to annihilate this new thing with Wes in one fell swoop. *Hey there, Guy I Just Slept With, I'm a horrible person, and I might be seeing dead people. What time do you want to hang out tonight?*

She forced an ease into her voice that she didn't feel. "Thanks, Wes. I appreciate that. But it really was just a breakfast malfunction."

He didn't respond for a moment, but when he spoke

again, his tone lacked the ease of earlier. "Okay, but for future reference, my offer stands."

"Noted."

His chair squeaked again, and he let out a breath. "So, see you around four?"

She drew an X over the Sunday square in her calendar, blocking out the brunch and trying to erase it from her mind. "That's the plan."

"Great. See you then."

She hung up the phone and pinched the bridge of her nose, a headache threatening. She didn't want the ugly stuff to seep into this thing with Wes. He was her escape right now. She wanted to park him in a place in her life and put an impenetrable dome over it.

No past. No drama. No ghosts.

A firm knock on her door broke her from her thoughts.

Rebecca looked up, bracing herself for her father and the inevitable lecture about her behavior at the brunch, but her assistant, Marian, was in the open doorway with a grandmotherly smile instead. That smile was a diversionary tactic, though, because there was a shrewd look in her eye—her bat signal to Rebecca. Something was up.

Marian was like the ninja assassin of executive assistants beneath that sensible gray suit, which was why Rebecca had happily taken her on when Marian had come back to the firm after two years of retirement, declaring that being home with her husband all day was going to drive her to drinking. "Morning, Marian. What's going on?"

"Your nine o' clock is running late." She leaned in deeper. "But two police officers just showed up, saying they wanted to talk to you. Do you have any idea what that's about?"

Marian looked ready to defend her and give her an alibi if Rebecca was being accused of something.

Rebecca straightened. "Oh. I… Yes, please send them in. There was…an incident a few weeks ago."

Wrinkles appeared around Marian's mouth as her lips pinched together in concern. "An incident? Is everything okay?"

Rebecca waved a hand, trying to minimize the incident because the last thing she needed was her mugging getting around the office gossip chain and back to her father. "Yes, I'm fine. It wasn't a big deal, but please let them in."

"Of course." Marian slipped out of the doorway, and Rebecca could hear her down the hall. "Right this way, officers. Ms. Lindt is ready for you."

Two cops in plainclothes with badges on their hips walked in, and Rebecca stepped around her desk to greet them and shake hands. The younger Hispanic woman, Detective Flores, was the one who'd called and asked some questions the day after the mugging. The other one, an African American man with graying temples, Detective Montgomery, was in charge of the case.

"Thank you for seeing us, Ms. Lindt," he said, giving her hand a firm shake. "I know you're busy, but we had some new information that we wanted to run by you."

"Of course," Rebecca said, shutting the door behind them and inviting them to take a seat. "Would you like some coffee?"

"No, thank you. We're fully fueled up already, ma'am," he said, sitting in one of the chairs in front of her desk.

Rebecca slipped back into her spot behind her desk,

and Detective Flores set a big, yellow envelope on top of Rebecca's calendar. "We're sorry to interrupt your morning, but we were able to get security footage off one of the cameras from a business a few doors down from where you were attacked. It's a challenging angle and the distance didn't give us sharp photos, so we wanted you to take a look."

"Sure," Rebecca said, her voice steadier than she felt.

She wanted to find out who had done this to her and to Knight, but she also was terrified of thinking about the mugging again and having that trigger something. Her memories felt like a minefield these days. One wrong move and *boom*, the flashbacks and panic would overtake her.

Montgomery opened the envelope and pulled out a few black-and-white photos enlarged to the point of graininess. He turned the first one toward Rebecca. The shot was a front view of her on the sidewalk. She was mid-stride, takeout bag still in her hand, a bland look on her face. But a few steps behind and off to the side there was a hunching figure just out of the pool of light thrown by a street lamp. She couldn't see a face, but the baseball cap was visible. She pointed to him. "That was the other guy, not the one who had the gun. This one ran off when the dog attacked."

"Okay, we figured that. We recovered the hat on the scene," Montgomery said and pulled another picture from the pile and spun it toward her.

Rebecca sucked in a breath, and her heart picked up speed. The other attacker was behind her now, the one in the hoodie. He had the gun pressed to her temple, and her bag was on the ground. Wine from the broken bottle pooled like blood by their feet. Her eyes were squeezed shut. Even without the fine details, just seeing the fear on her face was enough to make her stomach roil. But she tried to focus on the sliver of face between the edge of the hood and where her body blocked him.

Young. White. A strand of dark hair hanging out in full view.

She swallowed past the sudden tightness in her throat. It could be Trevor. If he were still alive. But she knew that wasn't what was making acid burn the back of her throat.

The guy—no, boy—with the gun could easily be Steven. Wes's student. The kid who was excited to make waffle chicken.

"Do you recognize him?" Flores asked, her gaze probably keen enough to catch Rebecca's flinch.

Rebecca knew what would happen if she said yes. She could see the cops rolling up to the after-school program, pulling Steven out of class, singling him out, calling his police officer father. If Steven was the one who'd done this, he needed to be brought in. But on the chance he wasn't, she would cause him all kinds of trouble he hadn't earned. Plus, if the kids found out she was the one who'd called, she'd ruin any chance at building trust with any of them while working on the project.

Steven hadn't shown any kind of recognition when he'd seen her that day in class. He probably wasn't the one. Plus, she'd seen the effect false accusations could have on people. After the Long Acre shooting, so many accusations had been flying around—who had been friends with the shooters, who had known something was up, who had angered them. No fingers had been pointed her way because she'd been lying in a hospital bed. She'd gotten an undeserved free pass. But sometimes it didn't matter if someone had actually done something, anyway. The suspicion alone was enough to ruin lives and relationships.

She needed to show these photos to Wes first. Make sure she wasn't seeing things that weren't there. Wes saw Steven every weekday. He'd be able to pick up subtle differences or similarities she couldn't. She flattened her hands along her desk. "I'm sorry. I can't really see much from this shot."

"You haven't remembered anything else from that night?" Montgomery asked with a frown.

Rebecca shook her head. "I wish I could. I panicked and had tunnel vision. All I could focus on was the dog."

He let out a breath. "All right. If anything else comes back to you, Ms. Lindt, please give us a call. We've had a string of armed robberies in that area, and I want to catch these guys before someone else gets hurt or worse."

Anxiety crawled over her skin like an army of ants. "I understand."

Flores reached for the photos.

"Can I keep these?" Rebecca asked. "Maybe if I keep looking at them, something will click. Plus, I'm seeing the man who intervened this afternoon. I can run these by him for you."

Flores perked up. "You think he saw something? That night, he told us that he ran up too late, that the guys were already running off and he'd been focused on you."

*Focused on her.* Her heart gave a little kick. "It can't hurt to ask him. If anything rings a bell, I'll tell him to call you."

"That'd be great." Flores slid a business card Rebecca's way. "Call us if he has any new information or if anything comes back to you."

"Will do. Thank you." Rebecca stood and led the detectives out, shaking their hands and exchanging the necessary pleasantries, but unease had crept into every cell of her body.

She went back to her desk and stared at the photos, trying to will her brain to see anything she might be missing before she sprung these on Wes. But the minute the guy with the gun started to look more and more like Trevor, she flipped them over and put her head in her hands, her heart racing and her skin breaking out in a sweat.

*No. Enough.*

When she caught her breath again, she picked up her cell phone and did what she should've done months ago.

Taryn answered on the first ring. A clicking keyboard sounded in the background. "Dr. Landry."

"Hey, it's Rebecca."

The clicking stopped. "Hey, girl," Taryn said, a note of concern entering her voice. "What's up? We missed you at Bitching Brunch yesterday."

"I missed y'all too. I had that speech thing."

"Ugh," Taryn said with dread in her voice. "I'm glad the only talks I have to give are academic ones in front of a class or other researchers. I couldn't do the inspirational thing. How'd it go?"

"Fine." Rebecca leaned back in her chair and sighed at her automatic response. "No, that's not true. It was a disaster. I didn't do the speech. I had a panic attack or flashback or something onstage. I thought I saw Trevor in the audience."

"Oh, honey." The genuine empathy in Taryn's voice was like a soft blanket around Rebecca's frazzled nerves. No judgment. No *Let's call for the straitjacket and a handful of pills*. Just understanding and an open ear. "That sucks. I'm sorry. Does that happen often?"

She didn't know if Taryn was asking solely as a friend or as a psychologist, but it didn't matter. Rebecca could use her input either way. "It's a pretty new thing. I think the combination of the documentary and the mugging has stirred up some ghosts. But that's why I was calling. I'm tired of it happening. You still see that therapist friend of yours?"

"Every couple of weeks," she replied.

"Is she taking new patients?"

Taryn didn't hesitate. "I'll text you her number. Even if she isn't, tell her you're a friend of mine and she'll get you in."

"Thanks." Something tight loosened in Rebecca's chest. "That would be great. I hate feeling crazy."

"No problem. And you're not crazy. The effects of trauma are like a chronic illness. They can be managed, but there are going to be flare-ups. I'm a psychologist, and I still get blindsided by stuff sometimes. A few weeks ago, I saw some stupid inspirational quote about sisters on a T-shirt when I was shopping. *Friends come and go, but sisters are forever*. I ended up sobbing in the dressing room like I was at a funeral."

Rebecca's stomach dipped. Taryn had lost her younger sister in the Long Acre shooting. Nia had been on a date with an older boy. Taryn had watched her bleed out. "I'm sorry, Taryn."

"It is what it is. We're all going to get sucker-punched

sometimes. But you're doing the right thing. Seeing someone and talking it out can help."

"I hope so."

"And hey, since we didn't get a chance to catch up yesterday, you want to grab dinner tonight? I'm helping a grad student monitor a study until six, but I'm free after that. Or we can do it another day this week."

Rebecca smiled, the knot of tension between her shoulder blades easing a bit. Sometimes she forgot how nice it was to have her friends back in her life. Women she could call and who would be there without hesitation. "I can't tonight, but later in the week sounds great. Tonight, I have a plans with a dog…and a man."

"A man?" Taryn said, a playful tone returning to her voice. "Like a real live human with a penis?"

Rebecca grinned. "Yes, there is definitely a penis."

Taryn gasped. "Wait. You said that with full authority. You've already verified the presence of this penis, haven't you?"

"I said no such thing. We're only friends."

"Liar. Rebecca Beatrice Lindt, you're going to owe me all the details when we have dinner. Is it the hot C student? Please tell me it is. Kincaid told us she met him, and he was like *whoa* sexy."

Rebecca laughed. "I have no idea what kind of grades he got, but he is a *whoa* sexy chef, so there's that."

"Hell yeah," Taryn announced. "Damn, I'm jealous. Hot *and* will cook for you?"

"Yes. And my middle name is *not* Beatrice."

She sniffed. "Of course it's not. I give random old-lady middle names to people when I want to get their attention. It drives my students crazy."

"Okay, Taryn Mildred Landry. We're on for dinner later in the week."

She laughed. "Deal. And you should send me a photo of this sexy chef so I can drool appropriately. Not his penis, of course. That's for you. Upper half will do."

"Mildred, you trollop," Rebecca teased, putting the proper amount of affront in her voice.

"Hey, Mildred is stuck at a college with overgrown boys who are all too young for her and professors who could apply for Social Security. She needs to live vicariously."

"You send the number of your shrink. I'll send you a pic of my *friend*."

"On it."

Rebecca hung up the phone, and a minute later, Taryn sent the number. In response, Rebecca sent Taryn a completely naked picture of…Knight the dog.

Taryn responded with Bitch.

Rebecca laughed. Nope, Knight's a boy.

> Shut up, Beatrice.
> Smooches, Mildred.

Rebecca tossed her phone to the side, feeling ten times lighter than she had a few minutes earlier. *Action*. That was what had always kept her on track. A problem comes up. Take action and fix it.

She tucked the police photos in her bag, scribbled down the number from Taryn and made a note to call, and then buzzed Marian to send in her first appointment of the day.

*There. Done.* Her dome with Wes would stay intact.

*chapter*
# TWENTY

WES SPREAD THE DOCUMENTS HE'D BEEN WORKING ON all morning across his desk. Permission slips. Rules. Possible business plans. His mind was plugged in and wired, all the possibilities making his blood pump.

This was going to happen. A restaurant.

Sure, it wasn't going to be in the way he'd originally envisioned all those years ago. This wouldn't be some fancy joint that would get a write-up in *Food & Wine* magazine or earn him special snowflake status in the culinary world, but he'd get to enjoy the process of creating a business out of nothing and teaching his students how to do the same. That was something. Maybe everything. He pulled a few more sheets from the printer and laid them on top of one of the stacks.

"Not too much preplanning," he muttered to himself as he sorted things. "The kids need to take ownership in this project with me, make decisions as a team. But after the reveal, maybe we could do a brainstorming session first and then timelines and..."

A light tap on his door had him shutting his mouth and looking up. Rebecca was leaning against the doorjamb, red hair in a curling ponytail and a teasing smile on her face. "Talking to your imaginary friends?"

The sight of her had him inhaling a deep, satisfied breath. She'd made it. And damn, was he going to get that rush of desire every time he saw her now? He'd been attracted to her from the start, but this was different. Now that he knew what lay beneath those clothes, what her lips tasted like, what she sounded like when she lost control, he couldn't keep his blood from heating and his body from moving toward her like a magnet to steel.

He'd been disappointed with their call earlier when she'd clammed up on him and lied about what had happened during her speech. He didn't know exactly what had gone down at the brunch, but he knew it wasn't because she'd skipped breakfast. She'd been somewhere else when he'd reached her onstage. Eyes wide and scared but not seeing what was in front of her. Haunted. He didn't have to guess by what. But she didn't want to talk about it with him yet.

As much as that had stung, he wasn't going to push. Rebecca had been through things that made his childhood look like a trip to Disneyland. He had no idea how she'd managed to get up on that stage to talk about the shooting in the first place. His high school years had been marked with memories of skipping school, bad grades, and then eventually his uncle's well-placed foot in his ass to get him back on track. Rebecca's past was filled with trauma and violence and losses that Wes couldn't fathom.

He didn't blame her for not wanting to talk about it.

They'd only agreed to have a good time together, to be casual friends. He wasn't her boyfriend or confidant. He was a distraction, as she'd said.

So if she wanted a distraction, he would happily distract the hell out of her.

He stepped around the desk and smiled. "My imaginary friends always think my ideas are brilliant." He tucked his hands in his pockets to keep from touching her since the kids would be flooding the hallway any minute. "I'm glad you could make it. I might've exploded if I couldn't tell the group today."

"Crisis averted." She lifted a plastic bag she'd been carrying and held it out to him. "I looked for one of those giant ribbons so we could wrap it around Adele for the kids, but apparently giant bus-size ribbons are not readily available. So I figured this was the next best thing."

Wes took the bag and peeked in. A pile of bright-yellow bandannas was stacked neatly inside.

"I figured we could use them to blindfold the kids when we bring them outside, and then they could use them to keep their hair back while cooking. That seems to be your preferred method."

He looked up and grinned. "That's a great idea. And people will definitely be able to see us coming."

She plucked one out and waved it in front of him. "You're Team School Bus. Of course they're yellow."

"*We* are Team School Bus. You're not getting out of wearing one of these. But thank you." He leaned in for a quick kiss without thinking about it. "I love them."

She looked down. "Wes, I—"

Someone coughed and Wes, still in Rebecca's space, straightened. Steven was a few steps behind Rebecca, hands shoved deep in the pockets of his jeans and his gaze averted. "Uh, sorry, Chef G. I just wanted to check if I could go in the classroom early. I need to look up a recipe in a book you have."

Wes frowned. "Aren't you supposed to be in computer class?"

Rebecca stepped to Wes's side to face Steven, too.

Steven looked warily at Rebecca and then finally met Wes's eyes. "I don't get that programming sh—stuff. I told Ms. Burton I wanted to work on my homework in the library."

"But you want to dig around the cookbook collection," Wes said, his eyes scanning Steven's face, noting the patch of bluish purple near his temple, only partially hidden by his floppy hair.

Steven shrugged, a little sheepish. "I tried something over the weekend and...it didn't go well. Burned something and stunk up the whole house. I wanted to check what I got wrong."

Wes wanted to ask about the bruise but wouldn't do it in front of Rebecca and risk embarrassing Steven. "Room's open. But don't turn on any kitchen equipment."

"Got it," he said with a look of relief. "Thanks."

Rebecca was frowning deeply, watching Steven walk away, when Wes turned to face her.

"You okay?" he asked.

She chewed her lip, still watching the boy disappear down the hall. "You saw that mark on his head?"

Wes sighed. "Yeah, I'll ask him about it later. He'll say he got in a fight."

"You think that's the truth?"

"I think it's possible and hard to prove otherwise if

he sticks to his story. He's had a history of getting in scuffles. But like I told you before, I've met his father and was...unimpressed."

She looked at Wes, a wrinkle between her brows. "Meaning?"

Wes squeezed his temples, weary. "I don't know. At first I thought my aversion to him was from my not-too-positive history with law enforcement. But I think it's more than that, because I've gotten to know a number of cops from working here and they're great. It's mostly a gut feeling with Wes's father, but he reminds me a lot of my biological dad. Like what he's showing us is a well-honed veneer. I think Steven's got a lot going on that he's not telling us."

Rebecca worried the yellow bandanna between her fingers, her gaze sliding back toward the hallway. "You think he's being abused?"

"I don't know," Wes said, able to share information now that Rebecca had gotten approved to be an official volunteer at the program. "I know there's some depression there. A lot of anger and a rebellious streak. I just can't figure out how much of a factor his home life is. A report was made to CPS last year, and nothing came out of the investigation. That doesn't mean nothing's happening, but I'm trying to build up enough trust with him so he'll confide in me. The system can only do so much when it doesn't have complete information."

Rebecca looked at Wes, concern there. "Wes..."

He reached out and squeezed her shoulder. "Come on, let's not talk about this now. If you think too hard about any one of these kids' situations, you'll keep yourself up at night worrying about them. Believe me, I know."

A sad expression crossed her face. "But doesn't that make you feel so helpless?"

"Of course. But it doesn't change the laws or procedures. The best thing we can do is what we're doing," he said, giving her the talk he often had to give himself. "We can be there for them in the time we get with them. Watch. Listen. Be available if they're ready to talk. Set an example. Give them a little fun and respite from whatever they're going through. Help them create some opportunities to better their situation." He took her hand and brought it to his mouth to kiss her knuckles. "That's what you're doing for them by giving them Adele and by being here to help with the project. If I want Steven to open up to me, I have to be patient and build trust."

She frowned. "Did I mention patience is not my favorite virtue?"

He smiled a slow smile. "That's actually one of the things I like best about you. You're all about the action, lawyer girl." He waggled his eyebrows, trying to lighten the mood. "It's come in handy so far. Random kissing the first night I met you. Basically seducing me yesterday after we decided to take things slow. Your lack of patience is paying off in great dividends for me."

She gave him a wry look. "You make me sound like some sex-starved woman with an impulse-control problem."

"Well, if the shoe fits..."

She punched him in the shoulder.

He laughed and grabbed her wrist, pulling her close, closer than he should at work, but the hallway outside his office was deserted. "Good thing I'm just as starved for you. You could've had me that first night if you'd asked. You inspire very loose morals in me."

She bit her lip, her eyes dancing with laughter. "I wanted you that night, too. Even when I thought you were a cheating jackass with an anger problem. Clearly, we're terrible for each other's judgment."

"Awful," he agreed.

"The worst."

"I should probably stop touching you right now because the abandoned closet off the music room is suddenly looking like a mighty fine destination to take you to. No one would hear us with all the racket coming from the room next door."

She pressed her palm over his beating heart and smiled. "No time for making out in the closet. We have to go blow your students' minds with a big, yellow school bus."

Excitement bubbled up in his chest at the thought. "Yes we do. This is going to be such a blast."

The bell rang, and he let go of Rebecca before the halls filled. But when he stepped into his classroom with her, knowing what they were about to announce, it took everything he had not to kiss her in front of everyone. The urge was strong and potent, watching Rebecca stand there, a secret smile on her lips as the kids made their way into the room. It was also dangerous, that swirling sense of rightness within him. Like he was exactly where he was supposed to be at that moment in time. The feeling was downright foreign.

But when they revealed Adele to the class fifteen minutes later, and he saw the looks on the kids' faces as they removed the blindfolds, the emotion surged full and fast. And when a few of his students barreled into him with an enthusiastic group hug, he finally pinpointed what that feeling was. *Happy*.

He'd forgotten what that felt like, and he wasn't sure he'd ever felt it quite like this. Rebecca had given this to him with no strings or ulterior motives. *Here you go, Wes Garrett. Have a piece of your dream and a smart, beautiful woman to share it with.*

It all felt a little too good to be true. He'd learned to be wary of that because the few tastes of it he'd had in his life had been quickly followed by the rug being yanked from under him. But he pushed the worry down for now. Right now, he was here. Right now, he was happy.

When all the kids hurried toward the bus to explore, Wes reached out and grabbed Rebecca's hand, giving it a squeeze.

She smiled his way. "I think they approve."

He wanted to say so much. To tell her how much richer this experience was with her there. To tell her that she had no idea what she'd really given these kids. Given *him*. But all he could manage was, "Thank you."

―⁓―

Rebecca toweled off her wet hair as she padded barefoot to the guest bedroom to get a set of clean sheets. She and Wes had grabbed takeout after finishing up at the school for the day and headed to her place. Wes had been so excited in his boyishly pure way on the way home that the effect had been contagious. So much so that Rebecca hadn't been able to bring herself to show him the police photos yet. She wanted this day to be protected—a perfect, happy memory. So she'd decided to put it out of her mind for the night. Enjoy the moment.

She had. They had barely gotten through dinner before ending up in bed. The buzz of seeing the project get started had been too much and had translated into an insatiable need to touch each other. And even though they'd still been filthy from the hard labor, they hadn't had the patience to get cleaned up first.

The sex had been great. But her sheets were a loss.

She smiled to herself as she took a pile of folded sheets off the shelf in the guest closet. She'd never wanted someone so badly that she hadn't cared about being a sweaty, dirty mess—or *him* being a sweaty, dirty mess. There was something freeing in that, primal. Not just acceptance of imperfection but embracing it, rolling around in it, and not giving a damn about anything but that person and that moment.

Rebecca clutched the sheets to her chest and listened to the old pipes creak in the wall as Wes showered. She hadn't officially invited him to stay the night. They hadn't done that yet, and it felt like a precarious move with the whole friendship thing. But they were both adults. Sharing a bed was just sleeping in the same space. It didn't have to be a *thing*.

She sighed. Maybe it was a thing.

She left the guest bedroom, planning to change the sheets before making any further decisions, but the sound of a knock on her door broke her from her thoughts. She frowned and walked out into the living room, setting the sheets on the back of the couch and making sure her robe was tied. Another hard knock followed, and she glanced at the clock.

It was only eight, so maybe it was a package or something. None of her friends would stop by this late without calling. She headed to the door and peeked through the peephole, finding a familiar face shining in the glow of the porch light.

"Rebecca, open up. I know you're home," her father called out.

She cursed and pressed her head to the door. She'd managed to avoid her father at work today, thereby avoiding any conversation about the brunch. She'd known it was a temporary stay of execution, but not *this* temporary.

There was no use in trying to avoid him, but she needed to get him out of here quickly. She cracked open the door. "Um, hey, Dad. It's a little late —"

He stepped forward, not giving her an option not to back up, and walked in. "It's not late. I just left work. I expected you to still be there, too. I had an event I needed to talk to you about." He glanced at her. "But look at you. You're already in pajamas. Must be nice."

She stiffened and shut the door behind him. "I didn't have anything on my schedule tonight. And after last week's twelve-hour days, I figured I'd earned an early night."

He strode into her living room and turned, arms crossed, not sitting down. "It seems you're all about cutting out early these days. Like doing two words of a speech and leaving."

Her teeth pressed together. "Dad —"

"You left me with a lot of questions to answer on your behalf. The people at the event were quite concerned. And disappointed not to hear your speech."

She sat on the arm of the couch and sighed. "I'm sorry,

Dad. It wasn't my plan to make a fool of myself onstage, and I didn't mean to leave you with cleanup duty. But I was in no condition to socialize afterward. I felt terrible."

"Because you missed breakfast," he said. "By this age, I would think you'd know how to feed yourself before a big event."

"Feed my—Dad, I had a panic attack onstage," she blurted out.

She glanced toward the hallway, but the pipes were still creaking. Wes was still in the shower.

Her father frowned like she'd spoken a language he didn't understand. "A panic attack? You speak in front of people all the time. You're a lawyer, for God's sake."

"I talk about *law*. About cases. About divorce," she said, keeping her voice low. "It's not the same. I can't get up there and talk about Long Acre like that. You, of all people, should get why that's so hard for me. You need to stop scheduling me for these types of events."

"Rebecca."

"It's bullshit for me to go up there and talk about it as if I'm the heroine in this horror story. I wasn't. If it had been a movie, people would've cheered when I got shot. You *know* that. I feel like a hypocrite giving some inspirational speech. I wasn't the heroine. I was a *villain*."

Her father's expression turned thunderous at that. He crossed the room and sat in the chair across from her. He pointed a finger at her, his stare nailing her to the spot. "Rebecca Anne, don't you give me that line of crap. You almost *died* that day. My only child almost bled out in the place where she was supposed to be safe." His expression tightened, a rare flicker of emotion surfacing, but he quickly covered it.

"You have overcome so much. *I* saw you all those months after. I watched you fight all those dark emotions that tried to take you down. You are here because you're a fighter. You have become a strong, successful woman despite all those challenges. If that isn't heroic, I don't know what is."

Rebecca blinked, her chest constricting and her eyes burning. She couldn't remember the last time she'd heard her dad say something so complimentary and with such conviction. "Dad…"

"I haven't forgotten what you told me all those years ago, but you holding on to any blame is ludicrous. Those two boys were disgusting, demented human beings. I don't care what happened between you and that kid. The only ones responsible for those deaths were the two people pulling the triggers and their parents for not seeing what was in front of them." His tone was grave and resolute. "You have zero responsibility for what happened."

She closed her eyes, forcing herself not to cry. She heard his words, but she couldn't accept them. Categorizing people wasn't that easy. Trevor hadn't always been a monster. He'd been on the edge. But you didn't fall over the edge without being pushed.

She'd pushed.

She shook her head. "It's not that cut-and-dried."

"Of course it is. Those kids were ticking time bombs. Why do you think the cornerstone of my campaign is being tough on early criminal offenses? If those boys had been handled differently when they'd committed those first petty crimes the year before—shoplifting, underage drinking, graffiti—that shooting would've never happened. They would've already been locked up or in some juvenile program." He reached out and put his hand over hers, his tone fervent. "If I get elected, we can changes things, Rebecca. I know I'm putting a lot of extra work on you with the campaign, but that's because there's so much riding on it. And I need your voice behind it, reminding people why all of this is so important. Don't you want to make a difference?"

"Of course I do," she said, feeling sick to her stomach. "But…"

"Good. Then you'll talk long and loud and proud. I have another event Saturday after next and have put you down as a speaker. You will show people what you've been through, what you've overcome, and why you're still fighting. All those friends and teachers you lost at Long Acre, they can't speak for themselves. They can't fight anymore. But you can. *You* can be their voice. And then I can make changes happen."

The words were digging into her like painful pinpricks, drawing blood. She could hear the silent message in his words. *You owe them.*

God, did she.

She swallowed past the bile trying to rise in her throat. "Okay," she said quietly.

"Okay?" he asked, catching her gaze.

"Yes, sir."

He nodded. "Good, now—"

"I'm not sure if it's manly to smell like vanilla cupcakes, but that shampoo of yours—" Wes's words cut off, and Rebecca cringed.

She could see her dad's face when he caught sight

of Wes somewhere behind her, saw the souring of his expression.

Rebecca turned around, bracing herself, but it was worse than she'd thought. Wes was standing in the doorway with just a towel around his waist.

"Uh, I'm sorry," Wes said, jutting his thumb to some unknown place behind him. "I was just…"

Her father stood, his jaw clenched. "Rebecca, I didn't realize you had company."

Rebecca took a breath. She was a grown woman. This was awkward, but there was no way she was going to apologize for it. Her father was the one who'd shown up unannounced. "Dad, this is Wesley Garrett. Wes, this is my father, William."

To Wes's credit, he managed to walk into the living room with dignity and shake her father's hand despite his state of undress. "Nice to see you, sir. I didn't realize you were stopping by."

"Obviously." Her father lifted a dark brow. "You're the young man who gave my daughter a ride yesterday."

Wes choked a little and Rebecca closed her eyes, her face heating at her dad's choice of words. *A ride.* He most certainly did. Twice. "Yes, Dad. Wes is…a friend."

"I thought you said he was working on the charity project with you," her father said, sending her a look.

"That too," she said, trying to sound businesslike and like she wasn't at all mortified by the current situation. "He's the culinary instructor at an after-school program for kids. The money's going to fund a food-truck project for his group that will help sustain the program long-term."

"I see," her father said, his eyes back on Wes. "So, Mr. Garrett, do you make a habit of sleeping with women in order to get your program funded?"

Wes stiffened like he'd been pinched.

*"What?"* Rebecca said, horrified. "Oh my God. Dad, you can go now. This is ridiculous. Who I do or do not sleep with is none of your business."

Her father tucked his hands in his pockets, unmoved. "Well, I think it is my business when it's my money this man is swindling you out of."

"Swindling?" Wes said, a thread of anger entering his voice.

Her father looked back and forth between the two of them. "You're taking advantage of my daughter, and I won't stand by and—"

Rebecca threw her hands out to her side. "Enough! Jesus, Dad. I'm thirty-one, not twelve. And I really appreciate that you think I'm so desperate that I'd have to pay someone to sleep with me. That's really nice of you. Now, please, leave."

"Rebecca—" her father said.

She pointed to the door. "Go. Or I'm never doing another campaign thing again. This is over the line. Next time you want to come over for a visit, call first, because, surprise, I have a life."

Her father was red in the face, but he turned and strode toward the door. When he reached it, she thought he'd just storm out, but he turned around. "No, Rebecca, what you have is a distraction. The daughter I know doesn't cut out of work at three on a Monday. She doesn't quit speeches. So I'd suggest if you plan on making partner, you get rid of this."

He stepped out and slammed the door behind him, leaving Rebecca staring slack-jawed after him.

Wes cleared his throat behind her. "Well, that went well. I totally just guaranteed an invite to Thanksgiving dinner. I'll bring the potatoes."

"Ugh." She covered her face with her hands. "I am so exceptionally mortified. I'm sorry. I can't even…"

Warm arms slid around her, and Wes put his chin on top of her head. "For the record, I'd require way more money if someone were to hire me to sleep with them. I'm worth more than a rusted-out bus and some ovens. I'm at least worth a Viking range and a vent hood."

She laughed and leaned back against him. "I'm sorry…for whatever that was."

He turned her in his arms, a lopsided smile on his face. "You have nothing to apologize for. Your dad clearly loves you, but he's got an interesting way of being protective."

"Yeah, threatening my job is really loving."

Wes put a finger under her chin, tilting her face to meet his gaze. "About that. If this whole food-truck remodeling is going to put your bid for partner in jeopardy, please don't feel like you have to keep your obligation to me. I don't want to be that kind of distraction. You know I'd love for you to be there, but not at the expense of your career. Me and the kids can do the remodel. You can have a more advisory role. One that doesn't make you leave work early."

Rebecca stared up him, thankful for the reprieve, but feeling a little numb from her father's threats. Some part of her was panicking. She could be passed over for what she'd been working toward all these years, but she couldn't connect fully to the fear. It was almost like it was happening to someone else. She let out a long breath and looped her arms around Wes's neck. "I don't know what I want right now."

He frowned. "What do you mean?"

"Never mind," she said tiredly. "I don't want to think about work. But I do know one thing I would like."

"What's that?"

"You to stay over."

He lifted his brows. "Yeah?"

She nodded.

"Would it involve *Shark Tank*?"

She laughed, some of the tension leaving her muscles. "It would indeed."

"I'm totally in," he said and kissed her. "Let's break in these clean sheets and heckle some entrepreneurs, lawyer girl."

She headed to her bedroom with him, but no TV ended up being watched.

And when they curled up and fell asleep next to each other late that night, Rebecca forgot to freak out about crossing lines and blurring boundaries.

She'd worry about it all tomorrow.

*chapter*

# TWENTY-ONE

WES TURNED THE CORNER ONTO THE ROAD THAT WOULD get him and his brother to their destination while Marco rambled on about the animal welfare dinner, the changed dates, and the logistical nightmare the event had become. Wes was trying hard to pay attention, but as they rolled closer to where he was taking his brother to lunch, Wes started to sweat a little.

"So the whole thing has sucked up more time than I have to give, and organizing that kind of stuff is just not in my wheelhouse. All that talking, talking, talking. I spend my time dealing with animals who can't speak to me for a reason," Marco said, scraping a hand through his thick hair and making it stand on end, a habit he'd had since he was a kid.

"The event will be fine. They'll have my food to eat, so that will distract them from anything else that isn't perfect." Wes pulled into the small lot next to a redbrick building. "And flatten your hair. You look like you've been electrocuted."

"Yeah but—" Marco's words cut off, his hand stilling on his head. "Wes, what the hell are we doing?"

Wes turned off the engine. "Going to lunch."

"This is Ruby Blue Barbecue."

"I'm well aware," Wes said. "I've heard it's good."

Marco looked his way, dark brows lowered. "What are you doing, man? Torturing yourself?"

Wes's hands flexed on the steering wheel as he steeled himself for what he planned to do. A few steps away stood the restaurant he'd once owned. The building he'd spent nearly every hour in for a year of his life, paying attention to every detail, making big, bold plans. The dream he'd lost.

After the divorce, he couldn't even stand to drive down this road. He'd taken the long way around to avoid it. Then when he'd started the hard drinking, he would find himself sitting on the bench across the street, staring at the restaurant. He'd watch the new owners come and go, hating them, wanting to set a match to the whole place because if he couldn't have it, no one should.

But after a week of working on the food truck with the kids, Wes had woken up this morning with a thought that wouldn't let him go. He'd already made lunch plans with his brother because he'd wanted to break the news of the food-truck project to him face-to-face, to explain to him why this wasn't going to be a road to another downfall. Wes had realized that he needed to do it here.

"I'm okay," Wes said finally. "I want to do this. Maybe to prove it to you. Maybe to prove it to myself. I don't know. But we're going to have lunch here today."

Marco reached out and gripped Wes's shoulder, his gaze serious, searching. "You sure about this, bro? You finally seem to be getting back on your feet. You've been happy lately. I don't want…"

Wes could feel the barely banked fear in his brother's voice, the genuine concern, and it made his ribs tighten. Sometimes Wes felt smothered by his parents' and Marco's constant fretting about him, but in that moment, he saw the truth there. All of it was from a place of love. They'd seen Wes spiral into hell. He'd terrified them, and they didn't want to lose him again.

He patted his brother's hand and smiled. "I'm good, man. Really good, actually. And I want to tell you all about it. In this place."

Marco held his gaze for a moment longer and then nodded. "Then lead the way, brother."

Fifteen minutes later, they were seated inside the high-ceilinged restaurant, a platter of barbecued meats and side dishes in the middle of the table on butcher paper. Wes had expected to feel like he was walking back in time, back into this space where he'd spent so many months, but the new owners had ripped out almost everything he'd put in. The only thing Wes recognized was the placement of the kitchen and a few light fixtures. They'd gone with the full Texas theme, trying for some combination of kitsch and cool, the bread and butter of the Austin market. *We're going to look down home but put enough twists on the standbys so that we can charge gourmet prices.*

Wes tried not to roll his eyes. The food was passable, but the whole vibe was so unoriginal and overdone that it made him gag a little. These owners were clearly from out of town and were trying too hard to look local. Texas was more than barbecue, cowhides, and country music. But that wasn't Wes's problem.

Marco drizzled blueberry barbecue sauce onto a piece of quail. "Why the hell would they put blueberries in a sauce?"

"So they can charge eighteen bucks for a meal," Wes said, slathering a piece of corn bread with honey butter. "It won't last. They butchered this opportunity. There's a better place doing this kind of thing two blocks over."

"So why aren't you freaking out?" Marco asked. "You seem almost *too* chill."

Wes shrugged. "I feel pretty chill." He took a bite of his corn bread and swallowed. "You know how when you break up with someone, people say you need to go date someone else to kind of exorcise the previous relationship? Cleanse the palate?"

"Yeah, I guess," Marco said between bites.

"So, that's why I feel chill. My palate is cleansed. I'm dating someone else now."

Marco frowned. "Wait. Like a woman?"

Wes shook his head. "No. Well, I *am* dating a woman. But that's not what I'm saying. I'm saying I have a new project that's stolen my attention. I feel…over this place now. Like it's officially something that's a part of Past Wes, not Present Wes."

Marco lowered his fork, wary. "A project?"

"Don't get that here-we-go-again face on yet. Just hear me out."

"I'm listening," Marco said flatly.

Wes took a breath and dove in. He explained to Marco about the food truck and how the school played into it. He told him how Rebecca had come up with the idea and how her company had donated the money. He told his brother all of it, down to the concepts the kids were batting around. To his credit, Marco listened without interrupting until Wes was done.

"So," Wes said finally, bracing himself for all his brother's protests and counterpoints. "That's why I asked you to lunch. I wanted to tell you that I'll be in charge of something again and that you don't have to worry about me. I'm in a good headspace about it."

"Wow," Marco said, leaning back in the booth and letting out a breath like he'd been holding one the whole time. "That's... Well, I think it's great if you think you can handle it. I mean, I know cooking is what you love. I just didn't know how you'd be able to do it again in a restaurant setting, all that stress, all the temptation. The late nights. The party culture. But this seems like a way to do it where you get the good parts but not the bad. It's pretty genius actually."

Wes grinned, and the muscles in his neck and shoulders loosened at his brother's blessing. Until that moment, Wes hadn't realized how much he craved that, how much he needed someone in his family to say, *Yeah, we think you're capable of pulling this off.* "I need a voice recorder so I can play back that you called me a genius the next time you tell me I'm a dumb-ass."

Marco snorted. "Don't get cocky."

"And for the record," Wes said. "I think I could handle it either way. I could own a restaurant and resist the temptation. But I think this is going to be a really cool thing. For everyone involved. I'm excited."

"I'm happy for you, man," Marco said, his smile genuine. "And you said you're dating again, too?"

Wes spooned some coleslaw onto his plate. "Yeah, Rebecca."

Marco's eyes went wide. "Wait. Lawyer Rebecca?"

"Yeah, we're not calling it dating exactly because we didn't want the pressure of labeling it. We're friends who are seeing a lot of each other. But I'm feeling like maybe it could be more than that," Wes admitted, saying for the first time what he'd been thinking too often lately. "She's...really great. We've been hanging out or at least talking every night for a few weeks now. She's funny and smart, and I know you've met her a few times, but she's not what you'd expect a serious lawyer to be like."

Marco took a sip of his root beer, eyeing Wes in that way he used to when they were teens and Marco was convinced Wes had stolen something out of his room.

"What?" Wes asked.

He pointed the neck of his root beer toward Wes. "You've got that look in your eye."

Wes paused, fork halfway to his mouth. "What look?"

"That look you used to get when you were talking about opening this restaurant," he said without humor. "It's not a good look."

Wes scowled and set his fork down. "What the hell are you talking about?"

"All I'm saying is don't replace an old addiction with a new one, Wes," Marco said, voice tired. "You know you have a tendency to do that."

The words landed like bricks between them, smashing the former easy mood into dust. Irritation flared in Wes. "Are you kidding me right now?"

"Don't get your hackles up, little brother. I'm just calling it like I see it. You've finally stepped out of the dark place you were in, and now you want to try all the shiny things at once. I get the desire, but it's danger-ous. Get a new restaurant, one. Have an exciting project, two." He counted off on his fingers. "Fall in love with a woman when it's only supposed to be casual, three."

Wes's patience snapped at that. "What the fuck universe are you living in? I'm saying I like her. I didn't say I was proposing and naming our firstborn."

"Good," Marco said. "Don't. The last thing you need is a serious relationship. You're not ready for that. It's like that first day after one of my patients recovers from an illness or injury and feels better. They think they can go at full speed again, but their body isn't one hundred percent yet and they make things worse. Overconfidence is dangerous. You're still recovering."

Wes's teeth ground together.

"I know it may feel like everything is fixed now and in the past, but it doesn't happen that easily," Marco went on. "One bad blow, one thing that leads you to pick up a drink, and you could be back to square one. You could undo it all. Focus on the food truck and your students," he said, going back to his meal. "Baby steps. Don't put yourself in a position to get the rug yanked out from under you again."

Wes took a deep breath, trying to rein in his anger. He'd put his family through hell. He'd made them worry he'd die. He'd laid traumatic worries at their doorsteps. Marco had earned his concerns. It didn't make the lecture easy to accept, though. "I hear what you're saying, but how would I be doing that? Wanting to date someone should be a good sign. A step forward."

"Seeing people, yes, but getting serious about it, no. I've gotten to know Rebecca a little. I've talked with her over these last few weeks when she visits Knight, and I know you. You're both great. But you're from different worlds," he said plainly. "You saved her that night, and there was an attraction. That's it. You need more in common than that."

*That's it*. Was that how Rebecca thought of it? Wes's mind went to the way she'd clammed up about the freak-out at the brunch. About how she called him a fun distraction. About the way her father had looked at him like he was some rodent sniffing around his daughter. Would the man have reacted that way if he'd walked in on her with some suit from the law firm? *Nothing in common. Different worlds.*

"This has 'fling' written all over it," Marco said, breaking Wes from his looping thoughts. "Which is fine. Enjoy yourself. But don't open yourself up to a gut punch, because she'll walk away at some point and get back to her normal life."

Wes pushed his plate aside, his appetite suddenly gone. "Thanks for the vote of confidence, bro."

"I'm not trying to be a dick. But last time I didn't do enough, didn't pay close enough attention, and when I finally realized you were in trouble, it was too late. I promised myself I'd say something if I was ever worried again. So this is me saying it. You have an addictive personality and an impulsive streak. It's part of who you are. Managing that is learning how to recognize when you're getting too deep into something. And I can see it on your face and hear it in your voice when you talk about Rebecca. It's starting. I don't want to be bailing you out of the drunk tank when she ends things."

Wes stared at his brother, wanting to tell him to fuck

off, to throw a punch, but he dug his clenched fist into the ridiculous western-style booth instead, breathing through the urge. Marco didn't understand. Wes knew he had a tendency to get hyperfocused on things. It was what had ruined his marriage in the first place, being obsessed with the restaurant. But Rebecca wasn't a restaurant or booze. He wasn't obsessed with her. He just liked her…a lot.

That was all.

A heavy weight settled on his chest.

He lifted his hand. "Check, please."

# chapter
# TWENTY-TWO

REBECCA WALKED INTO THE AFTER-SCHOOL PROGRAM Thursday afternoon, her cell phone buzzing in her pocket. Email. *Buzz*. Message. *Buzz*. More email. *Buzz*. She pulled it out and turned it off. *Enough*.

After her father's unexpected visit to her house, she'd been pissed but also had heard the wake-up call. Her partnership was going to slip through her fingers if she let the food-truck project and her relationship with Wes distract her too much. She'd worked all her adult life to get that spot. She couldn't stumble and lose it now. So she had taken the week to buckle down and get refocused. In the free time she'd had, she'd squeezed in a few therapy sessions with Taryn's friend. They were still in the opening sessions and Rebecca hadn't shared about the flashbacks yet, but Frieda, the therapist, thought Rebecca's new bout of panic attacks was due to the documentary and her taking on too many things, putting herself under undue stress.

High-pressure job. Campaign assistant. Charity project. New guy.

Frieda had suggested whittling down the list. She wanted Rebecca to pick two areas to focus on and to let go of the others. Rebecca obviously couldn't let go of her job, but she was struggling with the other three. She didn't want to end things with Wes. She felt he eased the stress more than added to it, but she'd accepted that she had to check out of the charity project. Wes had told her she could take a more distant role, but the thought still made her stomach hurt. She'd been looking forward to being hands-on with it, feeling like she was making more of a difference than writing the check.

But she was only one person, and she was tired of feeling on the edge of losing it.

So today, she was going to get dirty and hands-on with the project, get a piece of the experience she'd been looking forward to, but then she was going to have to tell Wes that it was her last day to do that. She needed to be fully present at work.

When she walked into Wes's class and saw him hunched over the table at the front with two of the students, laughing and pointing at something on a list, Rebecca's heart squeezed in her chest. She hadn't seen Wes since the Saturday before, and even though it'd only been a few days, she couldn't help but feel the unmistakable sense that she'd missed him.

That was a dangerous feeling, but she was too mentally exhausted to fight it at the moment.

Wes glanced up from what he was doing, and when he saw her standing there, a wide grin broke out. "Well, if it isn't the one and only Ms. Rebecca Lindt. It's our lucky day."

Some of the students turned her way and smiled, too. Lola called out, "Woo!"

Rebecca curtsied.

Wes left what he was doing up front and strode over, his gait easy, his eyes smiling. He still made her belly flip every time she saw him. Working on this project looked good on him. He'd always been gorgeous, but it was almost as if the project had turned on a light inside him and that energy poured out of him now. He reached her and gave her a chaste kiss on the cheek. "This is a nice surprise. I thought you couldn't get out here this week."

She hiked her purse higher on her shoulder and returned his smile. "I'm sort of playing hooky, but I had a hell of a day in court this morning and needed a break from the office."

"So you figured hard labor in the heat would fit the bill?" he asked skeptically. "You have an interesting way of relaxing, Ms. Lindt."

She laughed. "I know, but the company's good and I finally get to pick up Knight on the way home today. I thought maybe you knew someone who could help me with that."

"I am great with dogs," he said solemnly. "And I own a cool truck that has a lot of room."

"You're hired!"

"Excellent." He took her hand. "So, are you ready to work on the food truck that my evil class is trying to name The Burnt Cheeseball?"

She blinked. "The burnt what?"

"It's exactly what the bus looks like…a burnt cheese-ball," Steven said from his spot at the front table. "Plus, it has a certain ring to it. Very Austin."

"People would remember it," Lola added.

Rebecca shook her head and grinned. "Well, there's that. And it's probably not taken."

"Do not agree with them!" Wes protested dramatically. "Adults are supposed to unite. I need someone on my team."

Xavier walked over and hooked his long arm in Rebecca's. "Nope, we've stolen her. Team Burnt Cheeseball for the win!"

Rebecca looked over her shoulder as Xavier dragged her toward the side door. "Sorry, Chef G."

He narrowed his eyes playfully. "No respect. I get no respect."

An hour and a half later, Rebecca had sweat rolling down her spine as she scrubbed the interior of the bus with a coarse-bristled brush. Pop music drifted in from outside, and Rebecca mindlessly hummed along. Lola and Keisha had created an "Adele Remodeling" soundtrack, which ironically had no Adele songs on it, but the upbeat music had helped the time go by. However, now the late-afternoon sun was beaming through the windows, and even though they'd left two of the windows open—the ones that weren't stuck—the humidity was filling the interior of the bus like swamp fog, making Rebecca's muscles feel sapped.

Most of the class had drifted to projects outside and some were grouped up, brainstorming concepts and business plans. Wes was tinkering with the engine, Keisha playing co-mechanic. Only Steven and Xavier were left with Rebecca inside the bus. At first, that had made her feel a little awkward.

She had eventually shown the police photos to Wes, but he hadn't been able to determine anything. So even though Rebecca had tried to rule out Steven as the potential mugger, that initial suspicion hadn't been totally alleviated. But after a while, the atmosphere inside the bus had relaxed, and the boys had made conversation. Xavier was the chattier of the two. Rebecca had learned a lot about the merits and deficits of the local high school's basketball team. Xavier had been kicked off of it for poor grades, and he thought he could save the team if only he could get his history scores up.

Steven had been quieter, focusing on unscrewing the bench seats one by one, the rusty hardware fighting him. But he'd given Xavier the title of a book that helped break down history into short stories that were easier to remember. Steven had also bounced around ideas with both Xavier and Rebecca about possible menu items for the food truck. Steven played his cards close to the vest, but he lit up when talking about food. Rebecca had seen that look when Wes talked about owning a restaurant. The two were kindred spirits in that way.

"Hey, Ms. Lindt, I think we've earned some snacks." Xavier said. "I'm going to get cleaned up and grab some stuff from the kitchen that I can pass around to everybody."

"Sounds good," she said, swiping her arm across her forehead, trying to keep the sweat from stinging her eyes.

Xavier set his tools down and rumbled down the steps that led outside, rocking the bus as he went. Once he was gone, Steven glanced her way, his expression shifting into an unreadable mask and sweat dripping over the yellowing spot near his temple where the bruise had been last week. But before she could think of anything to say, he went back to focusing on the screws. She frowned, letting her gaze linger on the fading bruise for a moment, the ugly mark only half peeking out from beneath the bandanna he'd tied around his head. But she didn't want to stare, so she returned to her scrubbing.

She figured she should probably be worried being in such close quarters with him because there was a chance he could be the one who had attacked her, but her gut wasn't sending off danger signals. Instead, she had a deep yearning to ask him all the questions hovering on her tongue. *What happened to your head? Are you in trouble? Is someone hurting you? Do you need help?*

She kept the interrogation to herself, though, because she was still a stranger to the kid. He had no reason to trust or confide in her, and she would be leaving the project after today, so no bond was going to develop. There was nothing she could do. Instead, she went for the safe bet of small talk. "I think we're pretty close to wrapping up for the day, if you want to find a stopping point."

"I can stay late if Chef G needs me to. I don't mind," he said, voice gruff.

She glanced over at him. "He'd probably appreciate that on days he can stay late. But I have to go pick up a dog in a little while, and he's going to help me out, so we'll be leaving soon, too."

Steven looked up, a line between his brows. "A dog?"

She watched him carefully, something in his tone making the little hairs on the back of her neck stand up. "Yes. I'm going to foster a dog that was shot in a robbery. I need some help transporting him, though, because he's big and still recovering."

Steven's face turned ghostly pale, and his gaze darted away. His hands fumbled with the wrench as if it were suddenly covered in oil. "Right."

*Oh shit.* Alarm bells went off in her head at Steven's flustered movements, his change in expression. She could see the puzzle pieces falling together in his head, reality dawning.

"You okay?" she asked, her tone careful.

"What?" He stood abruptly, dropping the wrench and almost toppling over the bench he'd been working on. He wiped his hands on his shorts and wouldn't meet her eyes. "I think I need some water. I'm feeling... I'll be right back."

*Shit. Shit. Shit.*

"Steven," she said firmly but not too loudly, the voice she used on people who were nervous on the stand in court. "Wait."

His hands gripped the back of the battered leather seat, his knuckles going bloodless. "Ms. Lindt, I—"

"You know who I am," she said, her tone calm despite her pounding heart.

He looked away. "Well, yeah. Chef G introduced you weeks ago."

"No, you met me on a dark Friday night before then."

Steven sucked in a breath, and what little facade he'd been clinging to dissolved, his face tightening into something pained, frightened. His fingers flexed against the seat. "You know."

Her shoulders sagged with resignation. "I do now."

His head snapped up at that, his eyes widening. "Wait, I—"

She lifted a hand, cutting him off. "Don't."

He deflated, tears springing into his eyes. "Shit. I can't... I'm sorry, Ms. Lindt. I'm so, so sorry. I didn't realize..."

She swallowed hard, keeping her eyes on the boy. "What you did was extremely serious, Steven."

"I know it was. *God.*" He grabbed the top of his skull, squeezing as if trying to block out the thoughts. "Please tell me the dog's going to be okay. I've been... I haven't been able to sleep thinking about it."

She stepped closer to him, trying to create a sense of safety so he'd keep talking, but also making note of the emergency exit door behind her. If he freaked out, she was still far enough away to escape. "The dog is going to be fine. He's been recovering at the vet's office."

Steven's head sagged, and his fingers continued to flex against his skull. "I never meant to shoot the gun. I swear to you. It wasn't supposed to happen like... I needed money, and my friend said it was the easiest way. Use the gun to scare someone and then grab a purse. I didn't even know there was a bullet in the chamber. I never meant... *God.* I never saw the dog coming. I didn't mean..."

"Steven."

His attention snapped up, his frantic gaze jumping to hers. "Please don't tell anyone," he pleaded, his words rapid and panicked. "I'll give you back whatever I took. I never meant to hurt anyone, I swear. I just...I needed money, and I got desperate. I *have* to get out of my house. If I can save enough to move in with my friend..."

"Get out of your house?" she asked, nodding toward his head injury. "If you're in trouble at home, there are services in place to help you. People who can intervene."

That jolted him out of his panic for a moment. His lip curled. "Yeah, right. Services. Not when your old man's a cop."

"Cops aren't above the law."

"Sure they aren't. You know what happened last year when I told the nurse my dad broke my rib? Some nice lady came over, and he sweet-talked her right out the door, telling her about his *troubled son* who'd stolen his motorcycle and had gotten himself hurt driving under the influence. He even showed her pills he said he'd found in my room. Pills, by the way, that were his. He told her he was handling it." Steven's face twisted in angry disgust. "And he did.

"As payment for reporting him, a few days later, he raided my room while I was at school and took everything but a drawer of my clothes and dumped it off at Goodwill. Things I'd bought with my own money. Photos of my mom and other things I'd kept to remember her. My laptop. Even the blankets on my bed. Told me that the only reason I had food to eat and clothes on my back was because of him, and I better keep my mouth shut or I could live on the streets."

All the air left Rebecca's lungs.

Steven's jaw flexed, his eyes shiny even though he was obviously trying to be tough. "The only good thing to come out of that whole situation was that they put me here in this program." His Adam's apple bobbed. "If you tell, that goes away, too. I don't get another shot. They'll throw me in juvenile detention."

Her stomach knotted, the sweat on her skin going clammy. "Steven, I..."

"Please," he begged. "Whatever you want me to do, I'll do. I'll work off the debt. I can do yard work, cut your grass, wash your car, cook your meals. I'm pretty good at fixing things if you need that. Whatever you want. Just *please*, please give me one more chance. I promise I'm not the guy you saw that night. That night scared the shit out of me. I could've killed someone." He wet his lips. "You. I could've killed *you*. And you're this nice person who gave us this bus and who Chef G likes, and I could've messed that all up." Tears escaped now, tracking lines over his dirt-streaked cheeks. "Please tell me there's something I can do."

Rebecca pressed her hand to her breastbone, her brain and her heart in a screaming match. There really was no choice here, right? She *had* to report it. That was the only course of action. She had no idea if all the things Steven was saying were true. He could be putting on a show to get out of it. Armed robbery wasn't some petty crime. He could do it again. Could kill someone the next time.

But the fears wouldn't crystallize in her head. Her black-and-white world had gone hazy gray. Every part of her instincts was telling her that this kid was being honest. That he'd made a huge mistake but wasn't an inherently evil person. He regretted what he'd done. He had a terrible situation at home that had driven him to desperate measures. His father was a cop who authorities were going to be more prone to believe.

She took a deep breath, trying to grab hold of the storm of thoughts swirling in her mind. "How did you get the bruise on your head?"

He looked down and swiped at the escaped tears with the heels of his hands. "I tried that recipe I told Chef G about last week. I was cooking while my dad was sleeping off a night shift because he doesn't like me doing the chef thing. He says it wastes money using all those ingredients and that only a sissy would want to be a chef. But I burned the meal, stunk up the kitchen, and set off the smoke alarm. It woke my dad up. When I tried to explain what had happened, he shoved me and I banged my head on the corner of a cabinet."

"Christ." Rebecca let out a shaky exhale. How the hell was she going to call the cops on this kid and report the robbery? Juvenile detention might be safer than his current home, but it wasn't going to be *good*. If the kid had any shot at making something of himself, being locked up would just make it that much harder. However, she also couldn't stand by and do nothing. If nothing else, she had a duty to report the abuse. She rubbed the spot between her brows.

"Please, Ms. Lindt."

"We have to report your father again, and you have to tell the investigators the truth," she said finally. "If you need a lawyer to help you through that process, to advocate for you, I could help. You should document the incidents that have happened in the past, build up your case. Take a photo of today's bruise. Try to think of anyone who's ever witnessed him treating you abusively or maybe heard him yelling at you so we can get a statement from them. I assure you, your dad won't be able to sweet-talk past me. He may be a cop, but he's not invincible."

Steven blinked, his lips parting. "Wait, you want to *help* me?"

The question fell between them like a heavy stone. She could barely believe she'd made the offer herself. What was she doing? This wasn't her area of expertise or her job. But her answer came more easily than she expected, the rightness of it feeling solid in her gut. "I do. But," she said, eyeing him and using her no-bullshit tone, "I'd need an agreement from you that you will take this chance like the lifeline it is. What you're going through is awful and needs to be fixed, but it *does not* excuse what you did. An animal was injured. You could've killed me or someone else. Whatever happens with your dad, it's not going to be easy. It may involve foster care. But there will be no more breaking laws. No more guns. You *will* give me back everything you stole from me. And when this is all done, you will volunteer somewhere—an animal shelter or food bank, something to give back and make amends."

He nodded, his expression still stunned. "Of course. Anything. I swear."

She stepped closer, her posture formal, and put her hand out. "I am making you a great deal, Steven. I need you to shake on it and keep your word."

He swallowed hard, eyeing her hand, but then he put his hand out, taking hers. He gave it a firm shake. "Yes, ma'am."

"And I'm going to have to report what you told me about your dad."

He winced. "When?"

"Right now. I can call, and they can interview you here."

His eyes went wide. "No. Please. Not here."

"Why? We can keep you safe here and—"

He shook his head. "I don't want anyone here to know. The kids here actually like me, treat me like I'm just another guy. Last time CPS was called, it was humiliating when they came to school. I had to hear all these gross comments about how my dad was probably touching me and stuff. I ended up in so many fistfights over it that I nearly got expelled. I don't want the kids here thinking that stuff about me."

"Steven, they won't—"

"Just give me a few hours. Until seven tonight. My dad's working middle shifts this week. I can get home before he's off work, get my stuff and the money I stashed out of there, and go to my friend's house. I promise I'll tell the social workers anything they want to know, but please not here. I need this place to stay the same."

"I—"

"Hey there, overachievers," Wes said, startling Rebecca as he poked his head into the bus. "Stop working so hard. It's snack time."

Steven quickly dropped Rebecca's hand, and Rebecca forced a smile Wes's way, hoping the thick tension in the air didn't betray her. "Sounds good."

But Wes was far too observant. His gaze met hers, his eyebrows lifting and questions hovering there.

She shook her head slightly, hoping he wouldn't prod. "Lead the way, chef."

Steven sent her one last pleading glance, and she was hit with a bone-deep reminder of that boy so long ago. Not the scary version of Trevor. Not the warped-beyond-repair killer. The boy he'd been before. The lost one. The depressed one. The one who'd trusted her with his vulnerability, only to have Rebecca crush it in her hands.

Her stomach rolled.

Steven was asking for a small reprieve. To give him just a few hours so he could save face in front of the only group he felt a part of. He wanted to have at least one safe space where he was just another kid, someone who was liked, accepted. A place where he was the kid who could cook his butt off and riff on recipes, not the kid who was humiliated on a daily basis by his father and peers at school. Not the criminal.

She had to afford him that. She'd seen what humiliation could do to a person, how it could kill off the good parts inside someone. So she nodded, agreeing against her better judgment to grant him a few hours. His face sagged in relief, his eyes full of gratitude. He turned for the door, sealing the deal. She followed Steven out, trying to keep her expression casual, but her head was tangling with worries and what-ifs, vines knotting around her thoughts.

Wes helped her down the bus's steps and waited until Steven was out of earshot. "Everything okay?"

She cleared her throat. "It's fine."

"Why were you two shaking hands?"

She glanced at Wes, his expression one of curiosity, not suspicion. Now was not the time. "Nothing important. Just telling him what a good job he did in there."

"Oh," Wes said, his smile reappearing. "Great."

Yeah, *great*.

Everything was just *peachy*.

Her stomach sank a little deeper.

What the hell had she just agreed to?

*chapter*

# TWENTY-THREE

"HE'S GONE FROM DOPEY AND PITIFUL TO RESIDENT howler," Marco said, leading Wes and Rebecca to the back of the clinic. "The other dogs let him lead the chorus each night. I can hear him all the way upstairs. So I have to say, I'm glad he's better, but I'm not sad to see him go."

"Oh, fantastic," Rebecca said, a hint of worry beneath her playful tone. "My neighbors are going to love me when I bring home a howler. How am I supposed to make sure he doesn't do that?"

"Read him a bedtime story, and bring him a warm cup of milk," Wes suggested.

"Shut it, chef."

Wes laughed, amused by Rebecca's nervous Nellie routine. She was acting like she was on the way to pick up a baby instead of a dog. "Don't stress, Bec. Knight's used to being wild and free. I'd howl, too, if I were locked up in a cage and had to stare at Marco's ugly mug all day."

Marco flipped him off without breaking stride.

"I'm sure he'll be fine once you give him some room to run around," Wes said, taking her hand and giving it a squeeze. "He just wants his new mommy."

Rebecca shot him a narrow-eyed look. "I'm not his new mommy. This is *temporary*. I am fostering him."

"Uh-huh."

She huffed. "Why does everyone do that when I point that fact out?"

"Because you're secretly a softie. And a softie's kryptonite is sweet, fluffy, sad-eyed animals."

She rolled her eyes. "Marco, tell him that people foster pets all the time and are able to let them go when they find a permanent home."

Marco glanced back. "Of course they do."

"See?" she said petulantly.

Wes bent his head close to Rebecca's ear. "Yes, but my brother doesn't know you like I know you. I've seen sides of you he hasn't. Very *private* sides."

She pursed her lips and flicked her hand in Marco's direction, her cheeks darkening. "Hush. Your brother is *right there*."

Wes chuckled under his breath. He'd been talking about seeing the side she'd shown with the kids this afternoon. But he loved that the mere hint of something sexual could send her mind into that place and make her flushed and flustered.

Since his talk with Marco the week before, Wes had backed away from Rebecca a little bit, had given her some space—both to give her a chance to focus on her work and to give him a chance to prove to himself that he wasn't obsessed like Marco had accused.

He and Rebecca had seen each other once over the weekend and they'd talked on the phone a few times, but he'd dialed down the intensity. Nothing catastrophic had happened. He was a big boy. He could handle it just being a fling. He'd accept it when it was time to move on from each other. He had come to terms with the situation.

At least he thought he had.

But seeing her with his students today had stirred up more than he'd expected. The way she took the kids seriously and talked to them like adults, the genuine kindness she showed them, the easy laugh she rewarded them with when they were goofing off to get her attention. All of it had made him think things he shouldn't. *Feel* things he shouldn't.

And he was beginning to forget *why* he shouldn't feel them.

"Here he is," Marco said, breaking Wes from his ruminating.

A forlorn howl started up, ringing through the kennel and riling up the other animals.

Rebecca burst into a laugh, her hand going to her mouth. "Oh my God, that is the saddest, most obnoxious sound I've ever heard. He sounds so heartbroken."

"He's quite dramatic," Marco said with an affectionate smirk.

"Aww, don't cry, Knight," Wes announced. "Your new mom is here!"

"Stop." Rebecca smacked Wes's arm, earning a lifted brow from his brother. A brow that seemed to say, *So you're still doing this?*

Wes gave him a back-off look.

Rebecca crouched next to the kennel, oblivious to the

silent argument between the brothers. "Hey there, cutie pie. You ready to go home? Huh? You ready?"

Wes bit his lip at the baby-talk tone Rebecca used and tried not to laugh. He would've bet money she wasn't capable of such behavior, but the tough lawyer dissolved into a pile of mushy words at the sight of the happy dog.

Knight, who'd graduated out of the head cone, got to his feet, his tail banging against the side of the kennel, and went from howling to whining and snuffling.

"He's made a great recovery and can do all the normal things," Marco reported. "But his body is still recuperating from all that healing work, so he'll probably tire out quickly. Don't let him get too confident."

Marco gave Wes a pointed look.

Wes sniffed. "I think he's ready to take on the world."

Marco reached down and unhooked the latch on the door. But before he could loop the leash over Knight's head, the dog barreled out of the kennel and launched himself at Rebecca. His big paws landed on her shoulders, and he knocked her right onto her butt, licking her face like she was made of bacon.

Wes jumped forward to help, but Rebecca was hugging the dog and laughing while trying to turn her head and avoid the slobbery onslaught.

Marco managed to get the collar and leash on and tugged Knight back. "Calm down, boy. Sit. *Sit.*"

Knight eventually yielded but didn't look happy about it, and the high-pitched whining started again.

Wes squatted down and ruffled the fur on Knight's fluffy head. "Yeah, man, you got to slow it down. Woo her a little first. Buy her dinner before you try to kiss her. I recommend Indian food. And fancy cheese."

Knight barked.

Rebecca laughed. "Try Italian. That's his favorite. He pilfered garlic bread from me the night we met."

Knight panted and bumped Rebecca's knee with his snout. She sighed and petted him as she looked to Wes. "I'm so done, aren't I?"

Wes smiled, warmth sliding through him. "Absolute toast, lawyer girl."

Or maybe that was just Wes.

—⁓—

Rebecca collapsed onto a stool at her kitchen counter and glanced at the clock—half past seven. She'd called Child Protective Services a little earlier while she was walking Knight and couldn't help wondering if the authorities had headed to Steven's place yet. Her nerves were brittle, but she tried to shove the thoughts to the back of her mind because she'd done all she could for now. The proper channels had been notified.

At least about the abuse. She hadn't said a word about the robbery.

She let out a sigh, mentally exhausted and physically drained, her muscles sapped from the bus scrubbing, a harrowing walk with Knight, and a too-hot shower to wash off all the grime. But Wes had no idea what was going on yet, so she tried to keep her tone light. "Well, if nothing else, I'm going to be able to eat extra dessert now. Knight's going to be like having a gym membership."

Wes smirked from his spot in front of her stove and slid her a bottle of water. His hair was still a little damp from the shower he'd grabbed while she'd walked Knight, and he looked downright edible. She hated that she'd had to keep something from him, but his obligation to report had no gray area. If she was ever pressed for why she waited hours to report, she could claim attorney-client privilege since she'd offered to represent Steven and there wasn't an urgent threat of substantial bodily harm. Steven was going home to an empty house. No immediate threat. But Wes was Steven's teacher. He would've had to report any kind of abuse immediately, no fine print. She couldn't have told him before the seven o'clock deadline. And now she just needed a break from it all.

"And that's Knight in recovery mode," Wes said. "Imagine how long he's going to want to walk when he's fully healed up."

"I'm trying not to think about that." She opened the bottle and took a grateful gulp of water. "He *hates* the leash. Kept trying to back out of it and shake it off. But I've got news for him. I've watched *The Dog Whisperer*. I'm prepared to show him who's boss. And if nothing else, I can outlast him for now. He's snoring in his kennel."

Wes flipped a kitchen towel over his shoulder and grinned. "Strays aren't used to taking orders from anyone. Just ask Ed and Carolina. I don't know why they didn't ship me off to military school within the first few weeks of when I arrived at their place. But smart strays also know a good gig when we see one. I have no doubt Knight will shape up and give in once he realizes how sweet he's got it now." He dipped a wooden spoon into the sauce he was making. "Here, taste this. I didn't have the ingredients to do a proper spaghetti sauce, but I doctored up your jarred one."

She leaned forward, blowing on the steaming sauce

and then tasting it. The spicy, garlicky flavor made her stomach rumble for more. "Damn. That's good. You definitely have a gift. I eat that sauce at least once a week, and it tastes nothing like that. What's that smoky flavor?"

"You had some bacon in the freezer. I chopped up a few pieces and sautéed them with the onion and garlic before dumping the sauce in."

"Of course you did, because you're a genius."

"Obviously." He cocked his head to the side. "Want me to open a bottle of wine? That chianti you have will go good with the sauce."

A glass of wine sounded amazing after the day she'd had, but she frowned. "No, that's okay."

He gave her a skeptical look. "That wasn't very convincing, Ms. Lindt."

She shrugged. "I feel weird drinking in front of you."

His grip tightened on the spoon. "It doesn't bother me, Bec."

She eyed him. "You sure?"

"Yes, I…" His lips flattened into a line, and he set his spoon down. "No, that's not entirely true." He looked at her like he was trying to find the right words. "Truth is, I miss wine. Not in the jonesing-for-oblivion kind of way. Wine was never my drink of choice when things were bad. But I miss how it tastes with food, how it can enhance a meal, the experience of sharing it with friends. So it's not that it bothers me to see someone else drink, it just pisses me off that I was stupid enough to put myself in the position to never be able to have it again."

The honesty in his words hit her in the gut. She could tell it cost him something to admit all that. She got up and stepped around the bar. She wasn't sure how he'd react, but he let her wrap her arms around his waist. "I'm sorry. It's not about stupidity, but I'm sorry that you had to lose another thing."

He set his chin atop her head and hugged her back. "Thanks. In the grand scheme of things, it's a small price to pay in exchange for not being a complete degenerate. I get better stuff in return. No hangovers. A steady job. A beautiful woman to cook for and do unspeakable things to. There really is no contest."

She leaned back and smiled up at him. "Oh, we're moving into unspeakable now, huh? Maybe I should skip the wine and drink a Red Bull."

"Good thinking."

She pushed up on her toes and touched her lips to his, happy to be distracted from the stressful day for a few moments. But they weren't good at keeping things at a peck. Wes cupped her jaw, she parted her lips, and he kissed her until her insides steamed like the sauce bubbling behind him. She slid her hands up his chest and let herself get lost for a moment. God, the things the man could do with his mouth.

When he finally released her, he stared down at her, something tender in his eyes. "If I haven't said it enough already, thank you for making this project happen with the kids and for jumping in to help. I haven't had happy days like this in years."

Pleasure diffused through her, the simple words making her belly dip. "Wes…"

"I'm serious," he said softly, his thumb tracing over her cheekbone. "I've been trying to be cool about it because I don't want to freak you out, but everything about this afternoon felt…perfect. Working on the bus, seeing the kids so jazzed, and you...there with me, looking messy and cute and into it all. This summer is going to be a blast."

Her throat tightened, the words seeping into a guilty place and making her heart beat fast.

"I loved every part of it," he continued. "And it wouldn't have been anywhere near what it was if you hadn't been there to share it with me."

She searched for her voice. "I enjoyed it, too."

And that was the truth. Her conversation with Steven had dominated her thoughts, but the afternoon with the kids had felt oddly natural. Working with the group. Being with Wes. Having a project she cared about.

She hated like hell that she was going to have to let it go.

"I wanted to talk to you about something." He gave her a tentative smile, as if sensing he was treading into waters they could both drown in.

"Okay," she said carefully.

"You've told me from the beginning I'm not your type."

"I—"

He pressed his fingers over her lips. "I *know* I'm not. It's okay. I also know that I have a truckload of baggage I'm dragging behind me." He lowered his hand. "I'm starting over in my life and have all the trappings that come along with climbing up from the bottom again. On paper, I'm high-risk. But today I couldn't stop myself from thinking it anyway."

She eyed him warily. "Thinking what?"

He pushed a lock of her hair behind her ear. "That maybe we're capable of more than distracting each other."

Her blood rushed loud in her ears. "What are you saying?"

His gaze traced over her face. "I'm saying that I like being here and cooking you dinner. I liked helping you pick up your new dog. I like that tonight we'll hang out and share a meal and get naked and all the stuff in between." He lifted a shoulder. "I guess I'm saying that I'd like to make this more official. A relationship. The commitment thing. Which, frankly, is kind of terrifying to say out loud because I swore I would never have one of those again. But…there it is. This feels different. *You* feel different."

Her heart was *thump-thump-thumping*. He was saying things that prodded at that long lost romantic teen she used to be, that girl who believed in fate and finding "the one" and happily-ever-afters. Wes was offering himself without caveats. Taking a risk he'd decided he wouldn't take again. Telling her she was *worth* that risk.

But she couldn't let herself fully revel in it or taste the sweetness of it. With this type of declaration came pressure, obligation. Not to mess it up. Not to damage things on Wes's first try out of the gate after his disastrous marriage. And she couldn't help hearing that voice in her head telling her she *wasn't* worth that bet.

*She* was the high-risk one here. Her therapist was advising her to drop commitments, not add them. Plus, she'd worked in divorce law long enough to know that the number one relationship killer was dishonesty. Right now, she was keeping so many things from him, trying to protect this precious new connection, that she hadn't even given him a chance to know the real person. She'd shown him the idealized version because this thing with him existed in a temporary, fantasy-like space for her. So she'd shown him the woman who took off work on a whim and who helped animals and children. The woman who surprised him with a food truck and gave to charity. The woman who seemed to have it all together.

When he'd seen a glimpse of the real Rebecca at the brunch speech—the Rebecca with demons from the past, the one with a tense relationship with her father, the one who couldn't get a speech out without seeing ghosts—she'd shut him out. Put on the everything's-fine mask. Lied. Because the truth was scary and ugly. He didn't know it, but he wasn't seeing the real Rebecca. He was seeing who she wished she was but could never really be.

"Wes, I—"

He pressed a kiss to her lips. "Don't say anything now. I know this is fast, and we said we weren't going to label things. I'm not putting any pressure on you. I just felt it was important to be honest with you."

*Honesty.* At least one of them had gotten the hang of that.

"So think about it," Wes said. "I wasn't telling you to get an answer out of you. We can eat our dinner and enjoy our night. Just know that the desire to make this a more official situation does exist on my end if you're interested. Okay?"

She nodded, her breath catching in her throat. "Okay."

He smiled and released her. "Good. Now let's eat because you're going to need all your strength for what I plan to do to you tonight."

She managed to return his smile, but she didn't know how she was going to eat a single bite.

*chapter*

# TWENTY-FOUR

WES KISSED REBECCA, WALKING HER BACK TOWARD the bedroom after they'd finished dinner, wanting nothing more than to fall into bed with her and show her exactly how he was feeling. But even though Rebecca was kissing him back and responding, he sensed something was off. She'd been quiet during dinner and distracted. At first, he'd thought it was because he'd dumped the let's-try-a-relationship bomb on her with no warning. He'd been on the other side of that kind of conversation in the past. That had usually been the point where he'd pull the rip cord on whoever it was. *Nice knowing you, thanks, buh-bye now.*

He'd braced for that from Rebecca, had wondered if he'd messed the whole thing up by being so honest. But he'd seen the change in her expression at his words, the yearning there. That had offered salve for the worries. Maybe she wasn't totally ready yet, but at least some part of her wanted a relationship with him, too. So he'd decided to chalk up her quiet mood to their long day.

But now that off feeling was poking at him again. When Rebecca leaned back against her bedroom door and slid her hands up his chest, he could feel the tremble in her hands. He stopped kissing her and eased back, gazing down at her. "Hey."

She gave him a small smile. "Hey."

He pushed her hair away from her face. "What's going on?"

Her brows lifted. "Uh, I'm making out with Wesley Garrett, last I checked."

He examined her expression. Normally, when they kissed, it was like a combustion engine. Instant explosive desire, her leading as much as he did. Right now, he felt like she was only half there, going through the motions, and there was worry hovering in her eyes. "Bec, talk to me."

She let out a breath and sagged against the door, her head tipping back. "I'm sorry. I thought I could block it out. I didn't want to say anything because I didn't want to ruin tonight."

He frowned. "Say anything about what?"

She closed her eyes and pinched the bridge of her nose. "I had to call and report Steven's dad."

Her answer took a second for him to process. "Wait, what?"

She sighed and looked at him, weariness there. "Come on, let's sit down for a minute."

She opened her bedroom door and took his hand, leading him to her bed. Unlike the first night he'd been in here, nothing was out of place. The bed was made, the bedside books stacked neatly, the floor clear except for a stuffed rooster toy she'd bought for Knight. He walked past the spot where she'd jumped into his arms and panicked. That had been weeks ago, but it already seemed like those were two different people, just a movie he'd seen about strangers. So much had changed in such a short span of time.

Rebecca guided him to sit next to her and rubbed her hands on her thighs, as if bracing herself for what she had to say.

"Bec, talk to me. Is Steven okay?"

"Not yet, but I hope he will be," she said with an expelled breath. "Earlier today, you did walk in on a conversation when you stepped into the bus. Steven and I had a pretty serious talk. Some... A lot of things came out. Your instinct was right." She looked over at him, tense lines around her mouth. "His father is abusive. The asshole's managed to avoid getting in trouble because he uses his respected status as a cop to make Steven look like the problem."

Wes's stomach clenched.

"The bruise on Steven's head was because he got in trouble for setting off the smoke alarms with that burned recipe. His father shoved him, and Steven hit his head on the cabinet. But he's had worse. A broken rib. And when he reported it, his father gave away or trashed all of Steven's things, including sentimental items like pictures of his mom, as punishment and threatened him."

Anger surged in Wes, making his teeth clench. "That *fucking* piece of shit. I *knew* he was slimy." His fists curled. "God, poor Steven. He lost his mom and gets stuck with that man."

"I know," Rebecca said, shaking her head. "Steven wants out, but he's been terrified to report anything else. He doesn't trust the system anymore."

"Hell, who could blame him?" Wes said, hot all over with anger. "But you reported it, right? It has to be reported."

"Yes. While I was on my walk."

Wes let out a breath. "Why didn't you tell me? We have a procedure at the program. I have contacts at CPS. I could've handled it as soon as he told you."

She looked down. "That's why I haven't been able to focus tonight. Steven asked me to wait, to give him a few hours head start so he could get what little stuff he had left and go to a friend's house. He didn't want CPS coming to the program. He said kids at his school made some awful comments to him the last time this happened, which ended up in a lot of fistfights. He wanted to be out of the house when the report was made. He doesn't trust that anything's going to change. If this report falls through like the other one, he'll probably try to run away."

Wes pinched his temples, his thoughts whirling. "We can't let him run away."

"I know. I don't think he will yet. I told him to give me a chance to help." She wet her lips. "But I couldn't tell you because I knew you wouldn't have a choice but to report immediately. I wanted to give him that time."

Wes felt hot all over, his anger still simmering but not at Rebecca. Whether it was the right decision to delay or not, her intentions had been good. She was trying to protect Steven and also protect Wes at the same time. He reached out and gave her knee a squeeze. "Thank you for telling me. I'm glad Steven opened up to you. We'll get him some help."

"I hope so." Rebecca looked up from under her

lashes, her gaze wary. "But that's not all. Steven was the guy."

Wes blinked, the words not making sense. "The guy?"

Rebecca rubbed her lips together. "The mugger. The one with the gun. He admitted it to me today. That's how we got into the other conversation. I saw the look on his face when I mentioned I was helping a dog who'd been shot."

Reality crashed into Wes at that, sirens going off in his head. Steven was the mugger. Steven, the kid he'd grown close to, had robbed Rebecca at gunpoint. He turned to fully face her. "He—"

"And I'm not telling the police."

Wes's thoughts rammed into one another like an interstate pileup. "Hold up, *what*?"

Her eyes pleaded with him. "I'm not reporting it. I can't do that to him, Wes. If I tell, he's done. Any shot he has of getting out of his current situation, of going to college or culinary school or whatever goal he has will be gone. I can't help him with his dad and then turn around and push him into juvenile detention. Or jail."

"I get that," Wes said, trying to process it all. "But, Rebecca, he had a *gun*. He shot a dog. He could've shot *you*. That's a really big line to cross. Teaching him that he gets a do-over is... I don't know if that's the best thing."

She slipped her hands into his, her gaze earnest. "I know. Believe me. My father is running on a tough-on-crime platform, so I've heard all the reasons why second chances can be bad ideas. I know Steven crossed a huge line. An epically dangerous one. But in your gut, do you think he's a *violent* kid? Or is he a kid in a terrible situation who made a really bad decision?"

"Bec, you know I care about Steven, but…"

"One thing can change the whole trajectory of a life. One. Thing. I've seen it happen. Imagine if when you were going through your bad time you'd have hit someone with your car while you were drinking."

He winced. He had, in fact, gotten a DUI. But no one had been hurt and no one else had been in the car, so he'd gotten off with a misdemeanor. But it could've easily gone the other way. He still woke up in a sweat sometimes thinking about all the could've beens. He could've *killed someone*. "I'd be in jail."

"Exactly. In jail. Not living your life, helping kids. Not contributing to the world. Not…" She squeezed his hand. "Being this amazing person."

His chest tightened.

"Knight is going to be okay," she said. "I wasn't hurt. Giving Steven one more chance to take the right turn instead of the wrong one could make all the difference for him. I believe he's a good kid who wants to do the right thing. I think that night terrified him. He knows it was a mistake and wants to do better, to be more than that. In fact, if he works really hard, I think he could one day be as wonderful as his mentor."

Wes closed his eyes. The unadulterated belief in her voice undid him. Just unraveled every damn logical argument he had. "I don't deserve to be looked up to like that. He better become more than a recovering alcoholic who let his dream slip through his fingers."

Rebecca reached up and gripped the front of his shirt, getting his attention. "Hey, none of that. Hopefully he'll have an easier path, but he'd be beyond lucky to be like you. You don't see how fantastic you are. You're

a talented chef, Wes. But with those kids, you're...
magic." She pressed her palm to his chest, the gentle
heat stirring something tender and bone deep in him.
"You're doing exactly what you were put on this earth
to do, and the world is better for it."

The back of his throat was burning, her words seeping
into him and waking up places that had long gone dark.
He wanted to refute her compliments, to cast them off
as being kind or trying to give him a boost. But Rebecca
wasn't a bullshitter, and he could see it in her face. She
meant every word of it. When she looked at him, that
was who she saw. A good man. A teacher. Someone his
students could look up to. And of all the things people
had said to him in his life, he wasn't sure he'd ever felt
their impact quite as much.

On top of that, today, she'd put his student first. A
boy who had terrified her with a gun and put her through
a traumatizing robbery. Wes had managed not to go
down the same criminal path as his parents because of
people like her. Ed and Carolina had looked at him and
seen the potential, the good. They'd given him another
chance when he hadn't done anything to earn it. Now
Rebecca was affording Steven the same.

In that moment, a terrifying, rattle-him-to-the-marrow
realization hit him. He wasn't obsessed with Rebecca.
He was falling *in love* with this woman.

For real.

For keeps.

A tight fear gripped him. He thought he knew what
falling for someone felt like, but he'd never felt this
particular type of feeling for Brittany. He'd been drawn
to her wildness and the excitement. He'd labeled that

"falling in love," but it hadn't felt like this. This was picturing the start of a new life and watching it grow with someone else, wondering how much richer this connection could become with time, seeing the future roll out ahead. It was also like stepping off the side of a cliff, not knowing if there was water to land in below — your stomach jumping into your throat and your eyes blind to the outcome.

Falling for Rebecca had *not* been the plan. He wasn't sure what to do with that particular feeling. She hadn't even said yes to a dating relationship yet. She might never. He was falling for someone who had straight up told him she didn't believe in the gamble of long-term relationships and marriage.

Wes swallowed hard, trying to choke back the panic that wanted to erupt. "Thank you for being there for Steven. You're an incredible woman, Rebecca." He grabbed her wrist and tugged her closer, needing to shut down his brain and not overthink this. "And now I'm going to kiss you, so you better tell me to stop if you want to keep talking."

She smiled a smile that reached right into him and twisted every part of him. "No more talking. I'm all yours."

-------~~~-------

Rebecca's brain was whirling, her thoughts and emotions all over the place, but she accepted the invitation for oblivion that Wes was offering. No more thinking. No more worrying. Right now, there was just this.

She let Wes guide her closer, and she straddled his lap as he took her face in his hands and kissed her. His mouth was gentle at first, sweet, but when she slid her hands into his hair, his lips parted on a groan and all semblance of tenderness drained out of them both.

She needed to get lost, and he was going to take her there. His tongue tangled with hers, and his big hands gripped her waist, holding her against him as they kissed and kissed. Soon, she found her hips rocking into him, the feel of his erection growing hard against her deliciously erotic.

He grunted at the slow, dragging contact. "You're gonna kill me, lawyer girl."

"Not the plan," she said but lost her train of thought when he pressed his teeth into her collarbone and then licked the stinging spot.

His hand shifted to her breast, cupping her through her T-shirt and sending tendrils of tight desire snaking downward. "Does this position hurt your leg? Being on top?"

She shivered as his thumb grazed over her nipple. "I'm not even aware I have legs right now."

He laughed and tugged off her shirt, tossing it aside, and then went to work unhooking her bra with one hand. "I want you just like this then. I want to look up and see all of you while I make you come."

She grinned down at him as she climbed off him to shuck her pants and underwear. "So sure of yourself. Who says you can make me do that?"

His lips curled into a devilish smirk as he undressed and then stretched out on the bed. "You worried? Maybe I should take out an insurance policy."

"And how would one do that?"

He reached out and grabbed her waist, lifting her onto the bed to straddle him. But before she could sink down onto him, he slid down the mattress and positioned his head between her thighs, putting his mouth right where she was aching the most. The tip of his tongue grazed her cleft, and she gasped.

"Hold on to the headboard, lawyer girl," he said wickedly. "This is my version of insurance. Satisfaction guaranteed."

"Wes…" She'd never been in this position with a lover. The lamps burning bright and her scarred thigh pressed right next to Wes's head, but before self-consciousness could overtake her, Wesley gripped her thighs with gentle hands and put his mouth fully on her.

Every muscle in her body tensed as sensation rocketed through her and the sharp heat of pleasure rushed through her like a drug. Her hands grabbed hold of the headboard. "Oh God."

Wes hummed in response, which only made more nerve endings light up, and she closed her eyes. A hard shudder of sensation went through her as Wes schooled her on exactly what he thought of her joke about not having an orgasm. Every stroke felt like worship, every touch like sweet fire. The man knew how to savor a woman. And if she had any doubt about if he was enjoying this, it was answered when she glanced back, taking in the view of his naked body spread out on the bed.

His muscles were flexing, his hips rocking ever so slightly, and his erection long and thick and proud. Her tongue pressed to the roof of her mouth at the sight. She'd never wanted to touch someone so badly, to make him feel as good as he was making her feel. But Wes didn't let her get distracted by the view for long. He sucked her clit between his lips, teasing it with his tongue, and before she could even process all that sensation, a shocking orgasm zipped through her. Like a rip cord being pulled.

She cried out, surprised by the suddenness of it, and her back arched with the tight, tense pulses of her orgasm. Her fingers gripped the bed tight as she rode the throes of pleasure, feeling every bit of Wes's tongue, lips, and stubble against her skin. The man was feasting on her, and she was happy to be the meal.

When the intensity eased, she took a deep breath and panted her way down from the high, her knuckles still gripping the headboard like she was hanging off a cliff. Wes shifted beneath her, leaving her straddling his chest. When she opened her eyes, she found his hungry gaze on her, his lips slick and smiling. "Insurance is fun."

"Who knew?" She smiled. "I'm thinking of opening my own policy."

"Yeah?"

She shimmied down his body but didn't stop where he probably expected her to. Instead, she kneeled between his legs and took him in her hand. "Yeah."

Heat flared in Wes's eyes, and the tip of his tongue pressed into his lip. "This wasn't a tit-for-tat agreement, lawyer girl. You don't owe me anything in return."

"This has nothing to do with tits, chef. Focus." She ran her thumb along the head of his cock, spreading the drop of fluid there and feeling a kick low and deep in her own body.

Wes grunted. "Oh, don't worry. You have my complete and utter focus. Bombs could rain down on the house right now, and I wouldn't notice."

"Well, let's hope for no bombs." Then she lowered her head and took him in her mouth.

The sound he made almost did her in, the utter primal pleasure in it, but the feel of him was even better. She was inexperienced in this art. Her sex life had been pretty straightforward in the past, the encounters so short-lived that she'd never gotten much opportunity to explore beyond basic missionary sex in the dark. But Wes had always stirred new urges in her. She'd wanted to lick every part of him from the beginning. Now she would lick *the* part of him that would get him to make those sexy, masculine sounds.

She dragged her hands along his thighs as she caressed him with her tongue, tasting the salty maleness of him and loving the way his thigh muscles flexed beneath her fingers, like it was taking everything he had not to utterly lose it. She wanted to keep making him feel that way. Knowing she could explore and tease him felt freeing. He made her feel so comfortable that this felt like an open invitation to just…enjoy and play and savor.

She traced her fingertips up his inner thigh and cupped him while she took him to the back of her throat. He made a choked sound, and his big hand planted on the back of her head, gripping her hair. He didn't put any pressure, but she felt the need in the grip. He was riding his edge.

So she eased back and took her time, playing a little more and getting herself worked up in the process. Her own desire was pumping through her again as if there'd been no orgasm at all. She shifted, pressing her thighs together tightly, trying to give herself a little relief.

But Wes's grip tightened. "Can't. Bec. Too good. I want you. On top. Let me feel you."

The broken commands made her blood run hot.

She eased her mouth off him and looked up. His gaze collided with hers, and the impact of how he was looking at her almost knocked her backward. Never had she seen such naked desire directed toward her. It felt raw and real and like a drug.

He reached out for her, capturing her wrist and guiding her upward to sit astride him. When she smiled down at him, his hands moved to her waist, his thumbs tracing over her hip bones. "You are the most beautiful woman I've ever seen."

"I think you're out of your head right now, but thank you."

He didn't smile. "I'm out of my head over *you*."

And then he guided her lips down to his and filled her both with his body and his words.

*I'm out of my head over you.*

She closed her eyes and let herself free fall into the moment.

But a while after they'd made love, when she was curled up in the crook of Wes's arm, the words drifted back to her and poked at the dozing monster inside her, the one that she'd tried to hush earlier in the kitchen, the one that breathed the hot, horrible truth down her neck. *I'm out of my head over you.*

As Wes gently stroked her scalp with lazy fingertips, a desolate sadness welled up in her, making her want to cry. She couldn't ignore the facts anymore. This was getting too serious, too real, too dangerous for them both. Part of her wanted to shut down her mind and just get absorbed in how she felt when she was with Wes, to tumble into the way he was looking at her and forget about everything she was dealing with, forget about the

consequences. Pretend that fairy tales existed and people
were meant to be and that a month of knowing each
other wasn't too short when it was destiny.

But those were little-girl dreams. Fantasies she'd
believed when she was too naive to know better.

In the real world, a mother could leave her daughter
without looking back, the best friend you thought was
your prince could fall in love with someone else, and the
places you thought were safe and true could become a
tragic news story.

So even though this felt like the fantasy, the thing
she'd hoped for, she knew it couldn't be trusted. This
was real life with two real people who had real issues.
There would be consequences.

Wes was coming off a terrible time in his life, a
time of instability and drama and danger. Before that,
he'd been married to a woman who acted first, thought
second. A girl with few boundaries and a wild streak.
Rebecca represented the opposite to him, a sanctu-
ary from everything that had torn his life apart. Calm,
steady, lawyer girl.

But she was anything but that. She was selling him
and everyone else around her a bill of goods. She was the
staid mountain that had swirling magma just beneath the
surface, ready to crack and explode, a disaster waiting
to happen. She could feel it in every near miss. The
mugging. The meltdown during the speech. The tense
moments with Steven today.

She didn't have it all together. She couldn't let Wes
get deeper into the quagmire with her. He'd be too
far from shore by the time he realized they were both
drowning. She'd seen the look on his face, heard his

words. *I'm out of my head over you*. He was sinking already. As much as she wished she could give him what he was asking for—a relationship, a commitment, their whole stack of poker chips placed squarely on their future—she couldn't.

She would mess it up. And if she let him get in too deep with her, she'd mess him up, too. Just like she had with Trevor. She'd been selfish then, too. She'd made it about her.

What she felt. What she was going through. What she needed.

So even though the thought of starting something real with Wes made her ache down to her very cells with want, she couldn't go down that road. Wes had hungry demons in his past as well. If she took this too far, let feelings develop into something more rooted and then hurt him, she'd be leading him back to all those temptations.

Or, maybe he would beat her to the punch. If she opened her heart and really let herself feel those emotions again like she had when she was young—that yearning for love and commitment and romance—and then Wes walked away because he got bored or realized she was just a rebound phase or too screwed up to deal with, she wasn't sure she'd recover.

Wes could be her kill shot.

A normal guy walking away was one thing. But Wes had cut deep tracks into her life already, and it'd only been a month. She couldn't imagine how entrenched she'd become if she let it go on much longer. He would not be a man easily gotten over.

When they'd started this thing, she'd thought he'd be an ideal choice to keep things light with. She'd expected a smooth-talking guy, the good-looking chef who knew how to have a good time. That was what she'd signed up for. But she hadn't expected all the other sides to him. The mentor who had endless patience for troubled kids. The friend who held her after a panic attack and didn't interrogate her about it. And the man who hadn't been scared to tell her how he was feeling about what was going on between them.

He was slipping right past all those guards and gates she'd had in place.

So the offer he'd made tonight left her with no choice. She was going to have to say goodbye. End this before they both got burned up in the blaze of it.

"I can feel you thinking, lawyer girl," Wes said softly, the words drifting into the darkness of the bedroom. "What's on your mind?"

She swallowed past the knot in her throat. "Nothing. I'm just lying here."

*Lying to you.*

Wes shifted a little beneath her, dragging her cheek along his chest. Only then did she realize her face was wet. His muscles tensed beneath her. "Bec, are you crying?"

She squeezed her eyes shut and tried to herd her emotions back into the corral. "I'm fine. My eyes are watering."

Wes grunted and slipped from beneath her, leaving her on the edge of the pillow. He reached over, turned on the lamp, and then propped himself up on his elbow to look down at her. Whatever he saw on her face had his expression falling. "Hey, you are. What's the matter?"

She turned her head and swiped at her disobedient tears. "Sometimes people cry after sex. It's a thing."

"It's not *your* thing, though," he said, pushing her hair away from her face. "Tell me what's going on."

"Please..." she said, a plea in her voice. *Not now.* She didn't want to do this now. She wanted a few more moments before she had to let it all go.

Wes let out a breath. "I scared you."

She closed her eyes, her skin somehow hot and clammy all at once.

"That's it, isn't it?" he asked. "I said too much tonight, and I freaked you out. I shouldn't have said—"

She shook her head. "You can say what you want."

"Not if you're not ready to hear it. Goddammit. I should've waited. I got all caught up, and I should've—"

"It wouldn't have mattered," she whispered, the words like glass in her throat.

"What?"

She opened her eyes to look at him, finding that handsome face looking confused, concerned, caring. She hated herself in that moment. Hated that she'd done this to them both, that she'd let it get to this point. "That's the thing."

"What is?"

She met his eyes, more tears slipping silently from hers. "I'm never going to be able to hear it. There will never be a right time."

Wes stared at her as if the words hadn't registered, but then his eyebrows lowered like storm clouds over the sun. "Oh."

"This thing with us, I can't... This wasn't supposed to be like..." The words weren't coming out in any kind of logical way. She couldn't make them cooperate. "With you. I'll never..."

Something chilled in his expression, a hardness sliding in place. "You'll never want a relationship with me," he said flatly. "Did I translate that right?"

*Yes. No. It's not like that.* "Wes…"

He pushed up to a full sit and reached for his shirt, which was at the end of the bed. "No, it's fine. I'm not that slow. I think I got it. I told you I wanted more. You have no interest in that. Message heard."

"Wes," she repeated.

But he shook his head. "Don't. I get it, Rebecca. I was just supposed to be a *distraction*. I was supposed to be *fun*. I changed the game tonight without permission. My mistake. The lawyer just wanted a fling."

She sat up, pulling the covers up to cover herself, her heart pounding hard. "Please, don't leave like this. It's not you—"

He scoffed and gave her a derisive look. "Please don't do that. Don't do the *It's not you, it's me* speech. You've told me from the start that I'm not your type. You told me you didn't want anything serious. I'm clearly a bad listener."

Everything inside her was folding in on itself, collapsing as Wes climbed out of the bed to pull on his pants. She'd known this had to happen, but she didn't want it to happen like this. "Wes, you know this never would've worked. I'm your rebound. And I'm—"

"Ha! Fantastic. Now you're fucking psychoanalyzing me, too? You and my brother should open a practice. Poor, addictive Wes is on the rebound or getting addicted to a girl or setting himself up for another failure." He zipped up his pants with enough force to risk injury. "But no one seems to realize that I'm a grown-ass man.

Yeah, I screwed up. Big time. I'm the first to admit that. But I also have been through enough now to know my own goddamned mind. I know what I feel. And unlike you, I trust those feelings."

He held his arms out to his sides. "So yes, this has been quick. Yes, I haven't been in a healthy relationship probably ever, but that's how I know what's special when I see it now. This—how I feel, how things have been between us—is not normal. It's been abnormal in the best possible way. Which is why I was willing to take the risk and tell you that tonight. Because I didn't want to let it slip through my fingers."

Tears were flowing freely down her cheeks now, and she hugged her knees to her chest.

"And you may not want a relationship with me," he said, his voice bouncing off the walls, "but I'll be damned if you try to tell me this was just physical for you. Because that's bullshit. You know this was good. You know this was different."

*Was*. The past tense rang in her head. *Was*. They were now a *was*.

She wanted to agree, to tell him he was right, but all she could say was, "I'm sorry."

He stared at her and then shook his head. "Right. You're sorry. Me too." He walked over to the dresser to grab his phone and keys. "Thanks for the food truck, Rebecca. I guess I at least got paid for my services, even if I had to take off more than my shirt."

She stiffened like he'd slapped her. But before she could respond, he was out the door.

*Gone*.

Like so many other people she'd loved in her life.

She listened for the slam of the door and then, wrapped in her sheet, barely made it to the living room to lock up. She curled in the fetal position on her couch and let the tears have their way. Knight trotted over from his spot by the door and laid his head on her thigh, whimpering, which only made her cry harder. When she stroked his fur, he jumped onto the couch and curled up next to her as if to tell her she wasn't alone. But she was. Again. Always.

At least it was now and not one year, five years, ten years into something with Wes where she wouldn't be able to recover. At least this pain was familiar.

She'd gotten good at goodbyes.

# chapter
# TWENTY-FIVE

WES LEANED ON HIS ELBOWS AT THE BAR, WATCHING the light catch the facets of the crystal lowball glass and the amber liquid inside. He'd ordered the most expensive whiskey on the menu and could smell the smoky scent even over the food scents in the bar. His knuckles were bloodless against the glass and had been that way for the last twenty minutes.

"Something wrong with your drink, sugar?" the female bartender asked as she grabbed a few bills from the vacated spot two stools over.

Wes didn't look up. "No, it's fine."

"All right," she said brightly. "Well, you let me know when you need a refill, or if you need me to pry it from your hands and dump it down the sink."

He lifted his head at that. "What?"

She shrugged and nodded toward his grip on the glass. "I've seen this argument before. If you need me to help you win it, I can."

He gritted his teeth. "I don't need any help."

"No worries." She tapped the top of the bar. "Give 'em hell."

Then she was off to the other side of the bar where a raucous group of women were keeping her busy.

Wes stared down at his glass again. This was exactly why Rebecca couldn't say yes to something with him. Because his first instinct when he'd left her house had been to come here, like muscle memory. *Get your heart handed to you, drink until numb, repeat.*

But he hadn't taken a sip yet.

He'd imagined the taste of it on his tongue, had felt the smooth burn of it on the back of his throat. He could almost feel that beginning tingle of his limbs getting numb.

But then he'd pictured his parents. Marco. Dev and Suzie. The kids in his class. He imagined their faces and how they'd react if Wes ended up drinking again. He forced himself to remember what that life had been like, what misery had filled his days when he was drunk. He imagined the bus sitting empty and abandoned and never becoming a restaurant. The kids in his class talking about what they could've had.

That had kept the drink in its place.

He could hear the emergency broadcasting system blaring in his head. *This is a test.*

A test to determine if Marco and Rebecca had been right. Had this thing with Rebecca only been a rebound, a new obsession to distract him? The ache in his chest felt like it was more than that. He'd blown it by rushing things with Rebecca, but maybe it'd been an impossible road to begin with.

He'd told Rebecca he knew his own mind, but then

he'd acted like she didn't know hers. She'd told him from the start that she didn't want a relationship, that her job and her parents' divorce had soured her on marriage or anything long-term. She'd told him and he'd ignored that, so whose fault was it, really?

He was the one who'd let himself believe that because his perspective had changed, he could change hers, too. That wasn't fair.

But at the same time, he couldn't help feeling like he'd missed something. He hadn't read all her signals *that* wrong. He wasn't that dense. Rebecca had been swept up by this whole thing, too. He'd caught her watching him sometimes with a look that had taken the air right out of him. Tonight, she'd told him he was an amazing person and magic with the kids. She'd said it with complete sincerity, with…love, and then they'd fallen into bed like they couldn't get enough of each other. No part of him believed that she'd said those things just to pay lip service to him or that she'd slept with him just for the hell of it. But something had spooked her, and she'd shut down.

He'd come here thinking that she'd sent him away because she didn't think he was good enough for her. He was the recovering alcoholic. He was the former delinquent. He was the one with the shot credit and lost restaurant. But the longer he sat here, the more that didn't ring true.

*I'm never going to be able to hear it.*

When she'd said those words, he'd been so taken aback by the whole situation that he'd immediately taken it personally, but what if it wasn't about him? What if she meant that in *all* situations?

*I'm never going to be able to hear it.*

*I'm never going to be able to hear it.*

*I'm never going to be able to believe that someone loves me.*

The second he ran those altered words through his head, something clicked inside him. That was it. He knew those words like they were written on his heart. He'd felt that when he'd first gotten to Carolina and Ed's place. Wes hadn't trusted their kindness, their love, their acceptance of him. He'd expected them to leave or send him away, like everyone else.

Rebecca hadn't been left without parents, but her mother had abandoned her and her father's version of love was barbed and merit based. She'd had a life in high school, and her friends and teachers had been ripped away from her in the most tragic way possible. Good things were temporary in her life. Love was always followed by loss.

*I'm never going to be able to hear it.*

She'd created the loss this time. He couldn't hurt her if she sent him away. He couldn't leave her behind if she pushed him out the door first.

Wes let go of the glass and put his head in his hands. *This is a test.*

Rebecca had given him one whether she'd realized it or not, and he'd failed with flying colors, making it all about him and his ego. *Nice one, Garrett.*

Wes lifted his hand and motioned the bartender over.

"What can I get you, hon?" she asked.

Wes handed her the glass and a twenty-dollar tip. "The whiskey's down for the count."

She smirked. "I never had any doubt. In my

experience, anyone who makes it past the first five minutes is who I'm putting my money on." She dumped his drink in the sink. "I guess I'll be seeing you."

Wes slid off the stool and smiled. "No, you won't."

She lifted the empty glass in salute, and Wes headed out the door. He had somewhere to be, but the minute he stepped outside into the humid night air, his phone buzzed against his hip.

The ringing was shrill in the calm quiet of the evening, cutting through the gentle hum of the streetlights and the passing cars. His hope spiked. Maybe Rebecca had come to the same conclusion he had, but when he pulled the phone from his pocket, it showed *unknown number*.

He stepped away from the bar and hit the button to answer it. "Hello."

"Is this Wesley Garrett?" said a clipped male voice.

"Yes."

"This is Officer Mullins. I'm sorry to bother you so late, but we have a situation that we need your help with."

"A situation?" Wes asked, confused. "I'm sorry. I don't understand. What is this about?"

"Do you know a Steven Gregoire?"

Wes stilled, the words chasing out the last remnants of confusion and making his heart pound. "Yes, he's a student of mine at an after-school program."

"He's in trouble. He's asking for you," the officer explained. "We need to send a car to your house so we can get you to him. The situation is serious."

"Wait, what's going on with him?" Wes asked, worry surging. "And I'm not at home."

"Where are you? It's very important that—"

"I'm out."

"Address," the cop said, all business.

"But what is this—"

"Address, Mr. Garrett. Please. Time is a factor here."

Wes turned to find a number on the building and gave the bar's address.

"Has he been arrested or something?" Wes asked.

"Not yet."

Wes rubbed a hand over the back of his head. "Not yet? What does that mean?"

"The situation is in progress. We're sending a car, and the officers will brief you with what we need from you. Steven is negotiating with us, and he won't do anything until he can talk to you and his lawyer."

"Negotiating?" Wes pinched the bridge of his nose, his mind racing. "His lawyer?"

"Mr. Garrett, your student is holed up in his home threatening to shoot himself. We've done everything we can, but he won't budge until he talks to one of you," the officer said grimly. "We need your help."

Wes's stomach plummeted. "Steven's threatening *suicide*? Jesus Christ. Is he saying why?"

The cop cleared his throat. "Because we're trying to take him in. Earlier tonight, he shot his father."

The view of the building wavered in Wes's vision, but he forced out a response. "I'll be ready when you get here."

The cop car rolled up a few minutes later with flashing lights. A short, broad female cop got out of a passenger side and greeted Wes only long enough to tell him her name was Officer Clement and to verify he was Wesley Garrett. She pulled open the back door. "Please, sir, we need to get you to the scene."

"Of course." Wes tucked his phone in his pocket and hustled into the car, but when he slid into the backseat, he found he wasn't alone.

Rebecca was already there, face pale and eyes red and puffy from crying. "Wes."

The car door slammed behind him, and he turned to her, confused. "Bec. What are you doing here?"

"He asked for me, too," she said, her voice rasping. "I'm...his lawyer."

"Shit." Wes laced his hands behind his head. "This is bad."

Rebecca peered past his shoulder, no doubt seeing the flashing beer sign in the window of the bar before the car rolled forward. She glanced back to him, her features sagging into heartbreak. "Wes, this is a bar. Did you? Are you...?"

"I didn't drink. I was pondering."

She closed her eyes and shook her head. "I'm sorry."

"Hey." He tapped her knee. "Things you don't have to apologize for. My demon. Not yours. But I won. I'm stone-cold sober right now and completely focused on Steven."

Her eyes brimmed with tears, and she lowered her voice so only he could hear. "Wes, this is my fault. I let him *go home*. I *waited*. He shot his dad."

Wes curled his fingers into his palms and took a breath, trying to beat back his own panic. "Those are things we are not going to think about right now, and this is not your fault. We have no idea what happened. All we know is Steven is in danger and may not make it out if we don't help. We have to focus on that right now. Steven needs that."

"Right." She nodded and met his gaze, fear there, but a resolute look coming over her face. "I can do that."

"Okay." He reached out and took her hand and was relieved when she curled her fingers around his. "Can you give us any more information, officers, so that we know what we're walking into?"

The male officer flipped on the siren, even though traffic was nonexistent at this hour, and sped toward the side of town near the youth center. Officer Clement turned and briefed them from the passenger seat.

"Shots were fired late this evening, according to neighbors. When medics arrived, the father had made it onto the porch but had lost a lot of blood from a bullet wound. They rushed him to the ER, and all we know is that he's in surgery. When we tried to go inside, his son, Steven, pointed the gun at his own head and threatened to pull the trigger if we came any further. Our top negotiator has been talking with him, but he wanted to see his lawyer, who he said was you, Ms. Lindt, and his cooking teacher, you, Mr. Garrett. Normally, we don't bring civilians into these situations, but we plan to keep you well away from the danger. We just want you two to talk to him by phone and let him know that you are nearby and willing to listen. We need you to convince him to put the gun down and come out."

"So you can arrest him," Rebecca said, her tone hard.

The male officer glanced at them in the rearview mirror. "Yes. He shot his father."

"Has he said *why* he did it?" she asked.

Wes peeked over at her, finding no sign of the panic he'd seen in her eyes a few minutes ago. She was all business, looking more pissed now than anything else.

Only the hard grip she had on his hand gave him any clue how tense she was beneath all that.

"He said he was scared that his father was going to kill him. But there are no signs of that from what we can tell. His father is a respected police officer, and Steven seems to have a history of problems."

"His father is abusing him," Wes interjected. "Rebecca had to file a CPS report today."

Officer Clement's mouth pressed into a grim line. "At this point, I'm less concerned with the why. I just want the kid to put the gun down and talk to us. We can sort out the rest later."

Rebecca sniffed derisively and sent a look Wes's way. He nodded. Message clear. No one was on Steven's side right now except the two of them. They couldn't mess this up. They needed to get Steven safely out of there so that he could have a chance to tell his side.

Wes gave her hand a squeeze.

They pulled into a middle-class neighborhood with rows of houses that all looked the same. A line of cop cars had cordoned off an area, all their lights flashing. A spotlight was trained on the front door of what Wes presumed was Steven's house. Further out, Wes could see the bright lights of news cameras.

The cops parked behind the main line of vehicles and turned to them. "We're going to walk to that van over there. We'll set up the call from there. Just do everything we say, and we can get this ended with no one else getting hurt, okay?"

"Okay," Wes agreed, but he had no intention of feeding Steven lines from whatever script the cops had. If Steven wanted to talk to him, Wes would talk to him—or just listen, if that was what Steven needed. Whatever it took to get the kid out of that house in one piece.

Wes and Rebecca were led out of the car, a good distance from the house and under the cover of darkness. Rebecca held on to Wes's hand, and he caught the tremor there.

He leaned over, the officers a few steps ahead. "You okay to do this?"

She wet her lips. "I hope so. I'm talking myself out of a freak-out. I don't want to mess this up, but all of this is a little too familiar. It could go sideways for me."

Wes's stomach flipped over. *Shit*. He hadn't even thought of that. This situation was stressful enough, but police, guns, news cameras... All kinds of reminders that could make Rebecca think of Long Acre. "Talk to me. Maybe I can help."

She rolled her lips inward and then nodded, as if making an agreement with herself. "I don't always have control over how these things affect me. Like at the speech. Or the night of the mugging." Her gaze went to the ground, her posture stuff. "My head's all messed up, Wes. Sometimes, too often lately, I...see things, and past and reality can get mixed up in my brain. Like seeing ghosts and losing a sense of what's real and what's not."

She was talking so softly that he barely heard the words, but they hit him squarely in the gut. She was seeing things. Past things. Scary things. He wanted to take her in his arms and chase those ghosts off for her, sweep her away from this situation that could trigger all that pain for her. "Bec..."

She gave him a sharp look. "You have to promise that

if you see me start to lose it, you will take over. I don't want to make this worse for Steven. I'm…a liability right now."

He stopped walking for a moment, halting her with his grip on her hand. "Look at me." When she did, he continued. "You are *not* a liability. Now or ever. To anyone. Steven is going to feel better knowing we're both here for him. If you panic, I have your back. If I notice you acting strangely, I've got you covered."

"Thank you," she said, rubbing her forehead with a shaky hand. "I hate feeling weak like this. I hate feeling *broken*."

Wes shook his head, amazed she'd even go there. "Lawyer girl, you're the toughest person I've ever met. However this goes, you're not weak or broken. You've got completely understandable challenges. Just keep reminding yourself that this is not Long Acre, that you are safe, and I am here to back you up. Focus on Steven. We are going to talk that kid out of there. You are not going to let him down. I know you. This is not going to end in tragedy."

Rebecca pulled her shoulders back and nodded, some of the spark coming back into her eyes. "No, it's not."

God, he hoped that was the truth.

# TWENTY-SIX

THIS IS NOT GOING TO END IN TRAGEDY.

Rebecca hoped with all she had that it was the truth. Every part of her nervous system wanted to trigger the alarms. She could feel the monsters lurking behind every corner. Fight or flight was beating through her with knee-weakening force. But she had to focus on the *fight* portion of that. Not the flight.

She kept repeating the facts in her head, trying to ground herself in the present. This was *not* Long Acre. Steven was a kid who didn't want to die or hurt anyone else. She knew that in her gut. That boy who'd begged her not to tell about the mugging had plans to do something with his life. He was doing this because he was terrified. Reacting. Something had gone very wrong, and he'd gotten himself into this position.

He didn't want to die. He wanted help. He wanted to talk. That was why he'd called for Wes and Rebecca. She needed to hold on to those facts. She would not let this kid down by dissolving into a flashback or panic episode.

Plus, she had to keep her head clear because Steven needed an advocate, a protector. If the cops thought they were going to toss him away without investigating what had gone down today, they had another think coming. Steven now had a lawyer on his side. A damn good one. And she would use every resource she had to make sure that he would be treated fairly.

She and Wes climbed into the back of the police van, and another cop briefed them on the procedure. They were to keep Steven calm. Tell him everything was going to be okay. Talk him into putting the gun down and coming outside. Not offer to go to him. To make false promises if need be. Anything to keep him from hurting himself or someone else.

A little black-and-white TV showed a picture of Steven's front door. Everything looked so still and quiet, no sign of the ring of cops just out of the camera's view. Just a house. But inside was a scared kid, one who'd suffered God knows what behind those doors. One who didn't trust people not to do him wrong—especially cops. But he'd called for her and Wes.

Rebecca was not going to make him false promises, and she was not going to trick him. She was going to show him that some people were worth trusting.

Wes took the phone first after the cop talked to Steven and told them what was going on. Wes sat on the floor of the van, his hand clasping the back of his head as he greeted Steven. Despite the tension on his face, in every tight line of his body, Wes's voice was clear and calm when he spoke. Like he was simply telling Steven what they were going to do in class today.

"Hey, man, it's Chef G. I'm here to talk about whatever you want."

Rebecca couldn't hear Steven's end of the conversation, but she watched it play out on Wes's face. The line between his eyebrows, the anguished crinkle around his eyes. Steven's pain was Wes's pain in that moment, the teacher absorbing the emotions of the student.

"I don't blame you, Steven. I know what it's like to be scared at home, to tiptoe around minefields. To feel like no one is on your side and that things will always be this bad. I've been there. But this isn't the answer. Things *can* get better."

Rebecca sank to the floor across from Wes and reached out to press her hand to his knee, to offer whatever support she could.

"Did I ever tell you my dad was in jail?" Wes asked. "He got locked up when I was a teenager, and I had to move in with my aunt and uncle who I barely knew. I thought it was the end of the world. My dad was out of the picture. My mom had a drug problem and couldn't deal with me. I didn't know what I was going to do. I didn't fit in anywhere. Didn't know how to act like a normal human being without fighting or getting in trouble. Didn't know there were other options for someone like me. You're way further along than I was at your age. I see you at the program. You're a good kid. Smart. And talented in the kitchen. You've got a future."

Wes shook his head at whatever Steven said.

"Yes you can, Steven," Wes insisted. "You haven't ruined everything. But you will if you don't put the gun down and stop all this. You can have another chance. The gun takes away that chance."

When Steven responded, it apparently wasn't what Wes wanted to hear. He gave Rebecca a heartbreaking look.

She took a breath and put out her hand for the phone. Wes mouthed, *Are you sure?*

She nodded.

"Steven, I want you to talk to Ms. Lindt. She can explain what I'm talking about."

Wes handed Rebecca the phone, and she took it with a shaking hand. "Steven."

"Ms. Lindt." The hoarse voice was broken with tears. "I'm so sorry. This wasn't… I didn't plan. I was only going to come home and pack, and he came home early and caught… I thought he was going to kill me." He sobbed for a moment, his breath coming out in choked bursts. "I don't know what to do. They're never going to believe me."

"Steven," she said, surprised to hear the calm in her voice. "Take a breath and listen to me, okay? I'm here for you. If you shot your father because you feared for your life, we will make sure everyone knows that. I am not going to let anyone steamroll over you because your father's a cop or because you're young. I *believe* you. I know you didn't want to hurt anyone, and I know you don't want to hurt yourself."

There was a rustling sound on the line as he moved around. "Maybe that's for the best, though. If I just end it. What the hell am I going to do now? Even if I don't get thrown in jail for good, who would want to take in a kid who shot someone? I don't have anyone. I have nothing. What's the point?"

"The point is," she said, his anguished tone cutting into her like tiny shards of ice, "that you aren't alone.

You have people in your life who care whether you're here or not. You're Chef G's star student. Who else is he going to geek out with over old recipes?"

Steven sniffled.

"And think about your friends in the class. Lola will be pissed, Steven. *Pissed*. Xavier and Keisha will be gutted. And when we open The Burnt Cheeseball and are the first food truck in town to be run by teenagers, you're going to miss out. Your food will not be on the menu. Your talent will die with you. And I know that I don't know you that well yet, but I've lost a lot of people in my life." She glanced at the cops who were listening in on headsets and turned her face away, trying to block them out and just talk one-on-one.

"I was a Long Acre High survivor. I saw friends and classmates lose their lives before they could even figure out who they were supposed to be in this world, before they ever got a chance. I don't want your friends to go through that. And *I* don't want to lose someone else. Please don't make me lose you, too."

She could hear him crying softly now. "But they're going to take it all away from me. I know what they're saying to you. You're just telling me what I want to hear. They're going to put me in jail. This is all a trick."

She swallowed hard. "Do you think I would lie to you, Steven?"

"I don't know, but I know you're surrounded by cops. I know they're hearing everything we say. I know you'll probably tell me anything to get me out."

She took a deep breath and glanced at Wes. "If I come in there and look you in the face and tell you all this with no one else there, will you believe me?"

Two cops were staring at her. One started shaking his head, and the other was waving her hands, calling Rebecca off.

"Yes," Steven said. "Please. I need... Yes. Just you. No cops."

Wes was looking at her with wide eyes.

"Okay, give me a minute, and let me see what I can do," she said quickly, her mind already working. "I just need you to promise that if I come in there, you will not hurt me or yourself."

"I wouldn't hurt you. I swear," Steven said fervently.

"I know," she said with a nod. "I believe you."

Rebecca handed the phone back to the cop.

Wes leaned forward, his head already shaking. "Bec, you can't do this."

"He's not going to hurt me," she said, her voice oddly steady.

"You don't know that for sure. He's on the edge," Wes protested. "I don't think he'll hurt you on purpose, but he could still hurt himself. And what if..." He lowered his voice to a whisper. "What if it triggers stuff for you? I won't be there to help."

She wiped her sweaty palms on her jeans, her heart pounding. "I can handle this. I don't blame him for not believing me. I know if I look him in the face and tell him what I can do for him, he'll listen."

"Ma'am," the male officer said, "we can't let you go in there. He's not stable. It's too dangerous."

Rebecca stood. "I'll relieve the department of any liability, sign whatever you need me to. This kid is terrified and needs a friendly face. He's not going to hurt me. And he's not going to come out until he believes that he has a chance not to get locked up in jail. I know I can give him that chance, and he'll see that truth on my face. It's the best shot we have. I will go in acting as his lawyer."

Wes got to his feet next to her. "Bec…"

The two cops looked at each other. Rebecca could tell they didn't like it, but that they were out of options. The next steps would involve more force and had a much higher likelihood of someone getting hurt. The female officer sighed. "He could take her as a hostage."

Wes frowned, worry etched into every inch of his handsome face. "Bec…"

She took Wes's hands in hers and squeezed them. "I can do this. He's not going to hurt me. You know that. You know him."

Wes let out a harsh breath. "He didn't mean for the Knight thing to happen either."

A ripple of unease went through her at that, but she shook her head. This wasn't like that. She had to trust her gut on this one. "I'll be okay. I wouldn't go in if I thought he'd hurt me."

Wes cupped her face in his palm, and the concern in his eyes knocked her off-balance for a moment, but finally he nodded. "Go help him, but then come back safe to me." He pinned her with a look. "There's a conversation we need to have. I've got things to say. Don't even try to get out of it by getting yourself shot."

She smirked. "That'd be one hell of an avoidance tactic."

"Yes," he said seriously. "Don't do that."

"Right." On impulse, she leaned forward and kissed his cheek. "It's a date."

He let out a long sigh.

Ten minutes later, they'd put Rebecca in a bulletproof vest and led her to the end of the sidewalk. That was as far as Steven said he wanted the cops to go. Rebecca stared along the broken pavement, her heart pounding so hard her breastbone hurt. The squad car lights flashing along the front of the house, the sound of voices around her, the tension like a fog in the air, all of it was trying to flip those dangerous switches inside her, the ones that would steal her away from this moment and drag her backward, make her useless. She couldn't let that happen.

*Focus.*

She inhaled deeply, taking in the scent of the magnolia tree nearby, and forced herself to notice all the things that anchored her to this moment. She needed to stay here. Fully present. Steven needed her strength. He needed her *here*.

She made her way up to the house and gently knocked on the door with two quick raps, something she'd warned Steven she'd do. The door lock clicked, and he called out that she should count to ten and then come in. She said the numbers aloud, and then with a surprisingly steady hand, she grabbed the knob, opened the door to the darkened interior, and stepped inside.

The coppery smell of blood hit her hard in the darkness, the familiarity almost knocking her over. A shock went through her like she'd run face-first into a wall. That smell permeated her nightmares. Scenes flashed through her mind—images of pooled blood beneath bodies, her own blood spreading beneath her leg, Finn bleeding on top of her. Bile rose in her throat, and she squeezed her eyes shut as the memories banged at the doors in her mind.

"Ms. Lindt?"

The small, trembly voice was like a flaming dart in the darkness, cutting through some of the visions trying to trample her. She swallowed back the burn in her throat. "Yes. It's me."

Steven flicked on a lamp. "Please don't be scared. I swear I won't hurt you."

She forced her eyes his way, tried to breathe through the panic, and as her pupils adjusted to the sudden light, she spotted Steven sitting in a back corner of the living room. He'd positioned a recliner between him and the two windows that flanked the television. Heavy curtains were drawn over the windows, but the edges were lit with the flashing blue and red of the police lights. The small, shadeless lamp he'd turned on had a dusty bulb and a yellow glow. His hair was soaked with sweat, his lips crusted with dried blood, and a dark bruise marred his cheekbone.

All those lanky limbs of his were pulled tightly to him, knees to chest, arms wrapped around them. Like a small child who was hiding from the boogeyman. She wanted to rush over, make sure he was okay, comfort him in some way. But the shiny black of the gun hanging loosely in one of his hands loomed large, freezing her to her spot.

She licked her dry lips, dragging her gaze from the gun to focus on the kid. On his eyes. She'd seen remorseless eyes, empty, cold gazes. Steven's were brimming with emotion.

She lifted her palm as if trying to calm a startled

animal. "I know you're not going to hurt me. That's why I'm here, even though the cops don't want me to be."

"I don't want to hurt anybody," he whispered, looking down.

"I believe you. I'm going to come closer, okay?" she said carefully. "I need you to promise me you won't move the gun. I have a phobia about them, and I can't promise I won't freak out on you if you move it around."

He glanced up at that, guilt there, and nodded. "I won't."

She approached him with painstaking steps, and when she was within about three feet of him, she lowered herself to the floor. Her eyes wanted to zero in on the gun, but she knew if she did, she'd lose her grip on staying in the moment.

"I don't want to go to jail," he said as if to himself.

"I know, honey." She settled onto the cold tile floor as best she could. She lifted her phone. "I'm going to tell the police I'm in here and okay." She spoke into the phone and then told them she needed a minute. She put it on mute. "Okay, they can't hear us right now. Tell me what happened. Just you and me talking. I'm not wired, and I don't have to tell because I'm your lawyer."

Steven shook his head, tears tracking down his cheeks. "I shot him."

"I know, but what happened?"

He wiped a hand down his face. "He was so…angry. He came home early and caught me packing. I should've played it off, but I was just…over it. I told him I wasn't coming back, and no one was going to make me because he was an abusive asshole and that he was going to lose his job. It was such a dumb thing to say. He knew I'd reported him again when I said that. He lost his shit. Told me at least if he was going to get reported, he should make it count. He punched me and knocked me down. I was dizzy, but I managed to get to my feet. He was coming for me again. I thought he was going to kill me."

His voice caught there, and he had to take several breaths before continuing.

"I ran to the kitchen, and when I saw he'd left his gun on the counter after he'd gotten home, I grabbed it and racked the slide. I didn't want to shoot him. I just wanted him to feel what it was like to be that scared. I told him to back up, to leave me alone. But he charged and grabbed for the gun. It went off, or I pulled the trigger. I don't even know. It was all so fast." His words stuck in his throat at that. "Is he… Did he…"

Rebecca took a steadying breath. "I don't know. Last I heard, he was in surgery."

Steven pressed his palm over his eyes, crying. "I don't want him to die. I just wanted him to leave me alone."

"I know," she said, trying to keep a soothing tone. "I know that's what you want. And I can help you with that, but in order for me to do that, I need you around. We can build a case, Steven. You were abused. You felt threatened. It was self-defense. Your father will probably survive, and the charge will be less. There are a lot of things working in your favor. But suicide is the worst answer. That way, he wins."

Steven lowered his hand and looked down at the gun in his right hand, a dark look in his eyes. "He always wins anyway, so what's the point?"

She shook her head. "The point is he's never met me

before. I take personal issue with the bad guys winning, and I'm not afraid of bullies. I can't promise you a certain outcome, but I can promise you that I will give everything I have to fight for you. And it's not just me. I have loads of lawyer friends who can help us out. Plus, Chef G will have your back. He's seen the bruises. He's been worried about you for a long time but didn't have enough evidence to report. You have people in your corner rooting for you."

She reached out to touch him, but he jolted, the gun automatically going to his temple.

"Don't," he warned.

She heaved in a breath and lifted her palm in surrender, a head-to-toe tremor working its way through her. "Please. I wasn't trying to take the gun. I wouldn't do that. Please point it down again. You're scaring me."

Guilt flickered in his gaze, and he held her stare for a long moment, but then he slowly lowered the gun.

Her phone buzzed. The line had dropped, and Wes's name lit up her screen. "I need to answer that. It's Wes checking on us, okay?"

Steven nodded. She hit the speakerphone button.

"Tell me you're both okay," Wes said. "The police line dropped."

"We're okay," she said.

"I don't think I can go out there, Chef G," Steven hiccuped. "It's too late. I've done too much."

Rebecca's heart had lodged in her throat, and she could barely breathe after the swift move with the gun, but she managed to maintain her outward composure. "It's not too late, Steven. You're only sixteen. We all make mistakes."

He scoffed. "Sure. I'm sure lots of teenagers commit crimes and possible murder and come back from that."

"You *can* come back from this," Wes said, his voice crackling on the line.

But Steven wasn't listening. They were losing him. He was getting knotted up in his own tangled thoughts.

Rebecca swallowed past the tension in her throat but didn't look away from Steven. *I'm sure lots of teenagers come back from that.* She forced herself to ignore the open line on the phone and did the only thing she could think to do to get Steven's attention. "What if I told you that when I was sixteen I did something that helped lead to many people's deaths?"

Steven's attention jerked her way, his brows low. "What?"

Her throat wanted to close up, but she pushed past the automatic roadblock. She needed to say what she'd only ever said to her father. "I've only told one other person this, but once upon a time, I was friends with one of the Long Acre shooters. Secret friends, but friends. And one day, to save my own image, I humiliated him in a way that I know he never came back from, a way that helped turn him toward the choice he made the night he killed so many of my classmates."

Steven's lips parted.

"I've lived every day knowing that I did this horrible thing," she said, her chest tight with anxiety. "No, I couldn't be put in jail for it, but I've been where you are. After it happened, I didn't want to go on. Ending my life seemed like the only option. But when I took a bottle of pills to make that happen, my dad caught me. And I promise you, my first thought when I got to the hospital was, *Please don't let me die*. I changed my mind the instant I realized I might not make it. That gun"—she nodded at the weapon in his hand—"isn't going to give you that option. It's so fast, so final, you won't get the chance to take it back."

He looked down, his shoulders shaking with his soft crying.

"I'm not going to pretend that I'm past what happened back then, that I'm not still eaten up by guilt. I am. Every day," she said. "But I'm not sorry that my dad caught me with the pills. I cherish every day of my life because I know how easily it could've been taken away, first by the shooting, then by my own hand. And I'm trying in my own way to make up for the bad decisions I made back when I was in high school. You can do that, too. Use your life for something good. You can have another chance. Have this be a beginning instead of an ending."

Steven lifted his head. His eyes were puffy from the tears, but a glimmer of yearning was there.

That was all she needed. Hope. A sign that he wanted to live. She nodded at the gun. "Please put the gun down, Steven. *I need you to trust me*. We can walk out together. And yes, they're going to take you to the police station. I can't prevent that. But know that I'll be there, too. We'll start working tonight on how to get you out and get the truth told."

He held her gaze, his Adam's apple bobbing. She could see the wheels turning in his head, the options being weighed, but finally his shoulders sagged. "I'm scared."

"I know. That's okay."

He shifted, lifting the gun, its barrel flashing in her

vision, but before she could freak out, he leaned forward and placed the gun on the floor in front of her.

The tight knot of fear inside her released, letting her take a full breath. Ignoring the gun, she stood and put out her hand. "Come on. Let's get you out of here. I know a certain chef who's going to be happy to see you."

Steven took her hand, his fingers clammy and cold against hers, and got to his feet on wobbly legs, tears dripping off his cheeks. Even though he was taller than she was, he looked small in that living room, hunched and young and on the verge of collapse. She wanted to hug him, tell him it was going to be okay, that the worst was over, but he didn't need platitudes right now. He needed water, medical care, and a place where he could be safe. She could get him the first two right now. The third she vowed to make happen, no matter what it took. She put her arm around him, picked up her phone, and led him out.

Steven lifted his hands above his head as he stepped through the front door, which looked to take all of the energy he had left. A rush of people came forward. The officers took him from her, cuffing him, and leading him away. She told him it was going to be okay, and he gave her a resigned nod of understanding. *I'm trusting you.*

When they guided him toward a police cruiser, Wes ran to her and threw his arms around her. Even though she knew he—and who knows who else—had heard her confession, she couldn't find the energy to stress about that right now. She just let herself be enveloped by the embrace.

"Thank God. When the line went silent…" He kissed the top of her head and squeezed her tighter. "I think that was the longest few minutes of my life. Are you okay?"

She returned the hug, leaning into the strength of him, adrenaline crashing. "I'm okay."

"Yeah?"

She pressed her cheek to his chest, all the things she'd said inside opening up like Pandora's box. He knew. People knew. "I'm not sure I'm okay."

Then she started crying and didn't stop for a long damn time.

# TWENTY-SEVEN

REBECCA SAT IN THE WAITING AREA OF THE POLICE station Friday morning exhausted from having been up all night and hollowed out emotionally. She'd talked to Steven briefly and had wanted to make sure everything was being handled correctly, but now she could barely see straight. The realities of the night were settling into the cracks inside her, making them splinter more, breaking through the mental glue and tape and staples she'd used over the years to keep it all together. Every part of her was screaming silently.

Wes walked in with a to-go tray of two steaming cups of coffee from the shop down the street and a paper bag. He handed her one of the coffees. "They didn't have any breakfast sandwiches, but I got a few donuts. And sorry it took so long. I had to come in through a back door. A cop getting shot by his kid is big news, so the press is out there in full force. I also heard someone in the coffee shop mention that a Long Acre survivor was involved."

"Shit." Dread settled deeper as she accepted the coffee. "This is going to blow up. I don't want to be part of the news."

"Not something we can control, unfortunately." Wes sat next to her and sent her a sidelong glance. "But that's all they know about you right now. No one else heard the other stuff."

"What?"

He stirred his coffee. "I didn't know if you knew. What you told Steven. It was just me on the line. I didn't have it on speaker because I couldn't hear anything with all the racket outside."

She looked down. "Oh."

"So that, uh, information is safe with me."

The words hung heavy between them. He'd heard so much. How she'd hurt Trevor. Her suicide attempt. All of the ugly things she never wanted anyone to know. Before she'd gone into Steven's house, Wes had said she owed him a conversation, but she doubted he still wanted that now. He was probably thanking his lucky stars she'd ended things last night. Who'd want to sign up for that kind of train wreck?

"Any word on when you can see Steven again?" he asked, blessedly changing the subject.

She cleared her throat. "I think I'm done for now. He needed to get some rest, so I told them to let him sleep. I also called a lawyer friend because I'm trained in this kind of law, but I've never practiced it. I'd feel better working with someone experienced. He said he's willing to help."

"That's good." Wes tapped his fingers against the paper coffee cup. "If you're free to go, I can give you a ride home. One of the cops drove me to my car. It's parked out back."

She peeked over at him. The last time they'd been alone together, she'd sent him out of her house and straight to a bar. He didn't owe her any kindness. But she needed to get out of this place, wash the night off, and get some rest. "That would be—"

The door at the front of the station swung open and banged against the wall, cutting her words off and drawing both her and Wes's attention.

Her father burst into the lobby with a scowl on his face and his tie askew.

*Oh, shit.*

"Sir, can I help you?" the officer at the front desk asked.

But her dad's eyes were already scanning the area, his mission clear. His gaze landed on her and Wes, and his face reddened. "No, I've found who I was looking for, thank you."

"Incoming," Wes said under his breath.

Her father straightened his tie with brute force and strode over to her with that purposeful, command-the-room way he had. Like a king in his court, no matter where he went. He stopped in front of Rebecca, an examining gaze sweeping over her. "The news reports said you're okay."

"I'm okay," she said, too tired to put any emotion into it.

"Good," he said gruffly, betraying that maybe part of him had been truly worried. But that quickly shifted into his angry voice. "I can't believe—What were you *thinking*, Rebecca? That piece of shit *shot* someone. He had a *gun*. And you just *walk in*?"

"Dad, don't talk about Steven like that," she said,

frustration entering her voice. "It's a long story. And I can't do this right now."

"Sir, Rebecca has been up—" Wes started.

"The hell you can't listen," her father said, cutting Wes off like he wasn't there. "You don't make a man answer a middle-of-the-night phone call from the police about his only child and then tell him you don't have time to talk."

She pinched the bridge of her nose and tried to channel some semblance of energy to face her dad's fury. He'd been worried. She could appreciate that. "I'm sorry, Dad. I didn't mean to scare you."

"You did scare me. And you're still scaring me. Because I heard some other things from my contact at the news station that you better tell me real fast aren't true." He sent Wes a look that could strip the paint off the walls. "Will you excuse us so I can talk to my daughter?"

Rebecca's hand shot out and dug into Wes's thigh. "No, he will not. Wes is staying."

Her father's jaw clenched, and he dragged a chair over to sit and face them. "Fine. He can hear this too then. Might as well since it also concerns him."

Rebecca's stomach rolled. "Dad, I think we should save whatever talk you're about to give me for some other time somewhere else. I'm exhausted, and you're clearly angry. We should—"

"Your name is all over the news, Rebecca," he said, ignoring her request.

"I'm aware," she said curtly.

"At first it was the heroic story of local lawyer and Long Acre survivor Rebecca Lindt bravely going in to save a teen from a suicide attempt," he said, his words stark and angry. "Then the truth came out."

"That is the truth, sir," Wes said calmly, clearly not intimidated by her father's blustering. "Rebecca did save Steven. You would've been proud. She was tremendously brave."

"Do not tell me what I should be proud of or what my daughter is," her father said, sending Wes a hateful look. "The news is now reporting that my daughter, a lawyer in *my* firm, has agreed to represent a delinquent who *shot a police officer*. You better tell me this is bad reporting, Rebecca. I need to hear that right now. Say it."

Rebecca sat up taller in her chair, too exhausted and emotionally empty to give a flying fuck about her father's temper tantrum. "That's the truth. Steven was being abused. He shot in self-defense. I'm taking his case."

"You *are not*. I don't care what this man's put in your head. He's got his own record, so I can't say I'm surprised he'd swindle you," her father said, eyeing Wes with disgust. "But I am not having my firm involved with this case. A cop killer."

"Steven's dad is going to make it. This won't be a murder trial," she said, her anger bubbling hot.

"That's just dumb luck," her father said, flicking a dismissive hand. "We know what his intention was. Do you know how this reflects on my campaign?"

"Are you kidding me right now?" she said, whisper-yelling so the cops at the desk wouldn't get a show. "This is a kid's life, Dad. I know this boy. I've worked with him in Wes's program. The charity project—"

"Is a goddamned farce," her father finished. "You've been used by this man. If I had known my money was going to some program that funded kids like this—delinquents, dangerous criminals—I would've never allowed it. My name and my firm *will not* be tied to that. I'm pulling the funding today."

Wes tensed next to her.

"*What?*" Rebecca said, forgetting to keep her voice down. "You can't do that."

"I can, and I will. You weren't seeing straight when you allocated the money. You were charmed out of it," her father said, his tone hard.

"Oh my God, stop it," she said, pressing her fingers to her temples where a headache was knifing through her brain. "I'm a grown woman. Wes didn't trick me out of anything. If you know nothing else about me, you know that I'm smart. A guy with a cute smile and a few clever lines isn't going to turn me into some empty-headed idiot who hands over her bank card. Wes has never asked for anything. He didn't *want* the money. He wanted to raise it on his own with the kids. I had to convince him to take it for the program. The whole thing was *my* idea. And it's a good idea and a great program."

"The funding is done," her father said, dismissing her argument. "And you're going to drop this case. Right now."

Rage zipped up her spine like a line of firecrackers. "You're out of your mind."

"Rebecca," he warned.

"You can take the program funding," she said, the words like bullets. "I can't control that, but you can't make me drop a case. That's my call."

Her father's face went even redder. "If you take it, I will let you go from the firm. No partnership and no job."

An icy chill splashed over her, like she had tumbled backward and landed in cold water. *No partnership*. No job. All her work to get to where she was at the firm *gone*. She breathed through the rush of panic and put a firm picture of Steven's anguished face in her mind, his desperate need for help when he'd put that gun to his head. "Then I'll start my own firm."

Her father pointed a finger at her. "Don't play poker with me, young lady. I will not sacrifice the reputation of my firm and this campaign so that you can take on some pet project for your boyfriend."

Her fists clenched. "Are you hearing yourself right now? This is not poker or some game. I will *walk*. You know I can. You've always pushed me to be the best. Well, mission accomplished. I have the money, the reputation, and the skills to do this on my own. You can't force me to give in."

"I don't want to, Rebecca, but I *can*. And I will do it if you force my hand, because it's what's best for you. You are flushing everything you've worked for down the toilet right now for *nothing*," he said, his tone deadly. "I knew early on that you had a piece of your mother's impulsiveness in you, a part of her reckless personality. I did everything I could to train it out of you, but some things are rooted deep. I will not stand by and let you ruin everything like she did. You will not destroy all that you've worked for, *all you have,* for a whim. For some tattooed punk who can't give you anything but a broken heart and an empty bank account down the line. By the time your mother realized her mistake, her exciting boyfriend had dumped her with nothing to her name. She had to crawl to me for help."

A hard jolt went through Rebecca. "What?"

*She came back?*

"She wanted it all back. Her life with me. The stability. The money. You. But it was too late. There is no coming back from mistakes like that. I gave her money and told her to leave us be. But if she had controlled that impulsive urge when she met Mr. Excitement, she'd have her family now, a good life. I will not let you turn out like her."

Rebecca's eyes swam with tears, and Wes grabbed her hand. She didn't know if she was devastated, angry, or both. "She came back? How could you keep that from me? She was *my mother*."

"I did it for your own good. And I'll do that again if you don't come to your senses on this case. I don't want to do this. I'm asking that you don't put me in this position."

A loud buzzing had started up in her ears. *I don't want to do this*. He'd been making threats. She'd thought he only meant the loss of her job, but something about the way he'd said it made cold dread go through her. "What position?"

He gave her a grim look. "If you don't drop this case, you're going to force me to go to the press with an explanation of why you have such a bleeding heart for a young criminal."

Rebecca choked, the floor feeling like it was tilting beneath her feet. "Dad...you..."

He reached out and put a hand on her knee, his gaze earnest. "Despite what you may think right now, this is the last thing I want to do. I love you. Everything I have done your whole life is because I love you and want what's best for you. I don't want to hurt you. But you're not seeing reason. You're going to mess up your life."

"You wouldn't do that to me," she said, the words spilling out. "Just to save your campaign. You wouldn't."

"No, I wouldn't. Not for the campaign. I would do it to save *you*. All you have to do is drop the case and cut your ties with this program. Then no one else ever has to know. The press will go away. You can go back to your normal life. A life you seemed to be happy with not that long ago. If you get your head clear and sit down and think about it, you'll see how obvious the decision is. This is not a hill worth dying on. Some other lawyer will take this kid's case and do fine."

The words were a cyclone in her head, the emotions muddying up her thoughts. *He can't. He can't. He can't.* Panic pushed at her frayed composure, threatening to overtake. "I—"

"She'll consider it and get back to you," Wes interjected.

She turned her head sharply, and the room spun a little.

Wes gave her a pointed look. "Rebecca has been up all night and under a tremendous amount of stress. This is not a good time to be making decisions. Nothing is going to happen with the case for a little while. You both need to take a break from this conversation and talk in a day or two. Right now, emotions are running too high."

Her father harrumphed. "So you can get ahold of her and rally her to your side?"

Wes's teeth clenched, and he turned to look at her father. "Your daughter broke things off with me yesterday, so the magical spell I put on her has apparently worn off. I must not have put enough eye of newt in the cauldron," he said, the words barbed. "But your daughter is exhausted and has been through hell in the last twelve hours. You are making it worse. So maybe save the blackmail for after she's gotten some sleep and a little food in her."

Her father stood like someone had poked him with a cattle prod. "Blackmail—"

But Wes wasn't getting interrupted again. He got to his feet, using the three inches of height he had over her dad to full effect. "And you, Mr. Lindt, also need to step away from this because my guess is you really do love your daughter. But you're about to set fire to that relationship and burn it to the ground. I don't think that's what either of you wants. So whatever your agenda is, whatever reasons you're giving yourself for giving her this ultimatum, maybe think about if that's worth losing your only kid over."

Her father's face went full red, but his attention jumped to her.

Rebecca stood and held her ground despite everything imploding inside her. "Wes's right. I've got to get out of here."

"Rebecca—"

Rebecca reached for Wes's hand, needing something to anchor her. He took it and gave hers a squeeze, a simple reassurance that made her feel less alone. She didn't know where she and Wes stood at this point relationship-wise, but in that moment he was exactly what she needed—a friend.

She gave her dad one last look, and she and Wes walked toward the back of the station, escaping it all.

For now.

But she knew it was only temporary. She couldn't run

far and fast enough. The past had dogged her all her life, breathing down her neck, nipping at her heels. She'd worked hard to stay one step ahead.

Now, she'd finally stumbled.

The monster had finally caught up, and it was out for blood.

# chapter
# TWENTY-EIGHT

WES PULLED INTO REBECCA'S DRIVEWAY, THE ROCK music station on low and Rebecca's quiet breathing playing soundtrack. When they'd gotten into the car, she'd looked shell-shocked. Her skin was waxen, her eyes bloodshot, and her expression blank. She'd started to explain or apologize or something about the way her father had acted, but Wes had told her to rest. They could talk about everything later.

She'd given him a grateful look and laid her head back against the seat, closing her eyes. Two stoplights later, she was sleeping.

Wes turned off the engine and climbed out of the truck. When he opened her side, he gave her shoulder a gentle shake, but she didn't open her eyes. She'd fallen into that deep sleep a body demanded when it'd been kept up for too long under intense stress. He didn't want to jolt her out of sleep, so he took her keys from her purse and headed up to the house to unlock the door and thanked the universe that she hadn't set her alarm. He let Knight out into the backyard so the dog could relieve himself and not disturb Rebecca with a happy welcome. Then, once Wes got back to the truck, he slipped his arms beneath her and carried her inside.

She stirred a little at the movement and nestled her cheek into his shoulder, taking a deeper breath and releasing a small contented sigh as if she liked that spot against his body, as if it settled her. He knew she was sleeping and her reaction was an unconscious thing, but it kicked up a dust storm of yearning in him. He wanted her there against him. He didn't want to give that up. He wished he could rewind time and go back to yesterday and have a do-over.

Wes carried her to her bedroom, set her on the unmade bed, and slipped off her shoes. When he was pulling the sheet over her, her eyes fluttered open. "Wes?"

"Yeah, lawyer girl," he said quietly. "It's me. I'm just getting you to bed. You need some rest."

"You're always trying to get me in bed," she said sleepily.

He smiled, that little glimmer of the Rebecca he knew giving him some comfort that the last twenty-four hours hadn't completely crushed her. "This time it's only for rest."

She mumbled something else, but he couldn't understand it. Within seconds, she was fast asleep again. Knight wandered in and, after giving Wes a sniff, jumped up on the bed with Rebecca like he'd always slept there. He curled up next to her and put his chin on her hip.

"You gonna keep an eye on her, big guy?"

Knight licked his chops and gave Wes a look that

seemed to say, *As if I'd do anything else. She's my person. This is my new gig.*

Wes gave the dog a head scratch and gave Rebecca one last long look. Then he left the bedroom, closing the door a little behind him but leaving a crack in case Knight wanted to go back in his kennel. Wes knew the proper thing to do would be to leave, to lock the house and tuck her key under the mat or something, but then he imagined Rebecca waking up and all the shit she'd had to deal with in the last twenty-four hours descending upon her like a hurricane.

He would rather be here in case she needed anything. Plus, he'd been up for over twenty-four hours and probably was not safe to drive. If she wanted him to leave, she could tell him that when she woke up. For now, he trudged over to her couch, grabbed a blanket off the back of it, and stretched out to grab some sleep.

When his eyes opened, Wes thought he'd just been out for a few minutes, but the room was dark and the scent of vanilla was filling his nose. He blinked a few times to clear his head and then rolled over, finding Rebecca sitting in the nearby armchair, her hair damp and her body wrapped in a robe, a mug clasped in her hands. The whole room smelled like her freshly showered scent.

He pushed himself up to a sit, trying to clear the cobwebs. "Hey."

"Hey."

He scrubbed his hands over his face. "I'm sorry. I must've crashed hard. What time is it?"

"Just past nine," she said, her voice quiet. She set the mug of whatever she'd been drinking on the side table. "I'm sorry. I had to let Knight out. I didn't mean to wake you."

"Just wanted to stare at me while I slept like a creepy kid in a horror movie?"

Her lips twitched at the corner. "Yeah. I'm weird like that."

He ran a hand over his hair, trying to tame his bedhead. "I hope you don't mind that I crashed here. I was worried I was too tired to drive."

She tucked her legs beneath her and grabbed another mug off the side table. She held fresh coffee out to him. "It's decaf."

He took the mug from her and took a long sip. "Thanks."

"And I'm glad you stayed. Not just because you shouldn't be on the road," she said. "I still owe you a conversation. I was sitting here trying to think of how to go about that."

He warmed his hands on the mug. "Bec, you don't owe me anything."

"That's not true." She reached down and grabbed the remote control from somewhere beneath her. She clicked the TV on but left it on mute. "What happened last night is all over the news already. I'm not going to have much time to figure this all out, but thank you for getting me out of the police station this morning. My dad... I was blindsided."

Wes pushed the blanket off and glanced at the news on the screen. *Police officer shot by son, stable condition* was the headline along the bottom of the screen. "Anyone would be. That was...insane. Your dad is intense."

"I'm sorry for all the things he said to you," she said,

her voice catching. "And I'm sorry about losing funding for the program."

He looked back at her.

Tears shined in her eyes. "You're going to lose a restaurant again. And the kids are going to lose—"

He set his coffee down and got up, crossing the room in two strides and then crouching in front of her. "Hey, none of that, okay? I'll survive. The kids will survive. It's not over, just…delayed."

"But they were so excited," she said miserably. *"You* were so excited."

"We were, but we can get there again. We at least know what our goal is now. We can fund-raise, find investors, whatever it takes. And I'm going to put my own money I've been saving into the project, too. I'd been planning that anyway. We'll still get a food truck built. It will just take a little longer."

A pang of loss went through him at the thought of the project slipping through their fingers, but unlike the first time, that didn't feel like the end of the world. The kids in his program were scrappy. *He* was scrappy. They would figure it out, and it would get done somehow. Even if it took years. He would make sure it happened.

"I don't want to mess things up for you," Rebecca said, pain in her voice. "Please don't let this derail you. You've come so far, and if…"

He reached out and brushed her hair away from her face. "Hey, I'm solid."

"You were at a bar last night."

"I was," he agreed. "I ordered a drink and didn't take one sip. And, believe me, if I managed not to take a drink last night, I promise you I can handle this."

"But you were there," she said as if that explained everything. "Why?"

"Because going there was like muscle memory," he said with a sigh. "I was upset and hurting. I'd lost something important to me, something I hadn't even realized I wanted." He looked at her. "I'd lost *you* right as I realized I was falling in love. I didn't know if I could take that sober."

He hadn't meant for the words to come out quite that honest, but once they passed his lips, he felt something release in his chest, a tightness easing. Regardless of how she felt about him, it felt good to get those words out.

Her gaze jumped to his, a startled look there. "Wes…"

"I'm okay, Bec," he said gently. "I'm not saying that to make you feel guilty or expecting you to say something back to me. You told me what this thing between us was supposed to be up front. I'm the one who changed the rules of the game on you. I'm just telling you that I'm not a man on the edge anymore. Last night was a test. I passed. I was hurting, but I didn't want that drink. I was already walking out when the police called. So, you're not going to mess things up for me. Break my heart, yeah, but I'll deal. That's part of life. I can trust myself to handle that now. You gave me that gift. You forced that face-off with temptation, and I won."

She stared at him and then shifted out of the chair and slid down to sit next to him on the floor. "Only you could spin me acting like a lunatic into me doing you a favor. What is wrong with you, Wesley Garrett?"

"Many things, I'm sure." He scooted over, giving her room, and forced himself not to put his arm around her. He looked over in the flickering light of the TV.

Rebecca was staring at the screen with a tense expression, lips pressed into a line, hands clasping a throw pillow like a life raft. "I never wanted to hurt you. I... You have to know that this has been more than a fling for me, too. We both changed the rules. But I don't even know why you're still here after what you heard."

"Bec..."

"My father will tell everyone. If I don't give in to him, he'll stick to his word. He doesn't make idle threats."

Wes watched her carefully, treading lightly. "Tell them what exactly?"

She pulled the pillow closer to her, her fingers working the piping around the edge. "That I'm a hypocrite and a liar. That I'm a horrible person."

He frowned. "Bec—"

"Don't." Her eyes were red-rimmed, but no tears had fallen yet. She looked down at the pillow again. "Just let me get it out. You've heard enough. You might as well hear all of it." She rolled her lips inward, her expression taking on a faraway quality. "In high school, I was... intense. Like I told you, all my focus was on getting the top grades and making my transcript for college look stellar. Achievement equaled love in my house, so I ended up craving it like an addict. I needed the A's. I needed to be editor of the paper. I needed to be student council president. The last one was the hardest because I wasn't naturally outgoing or beautiful, which made a popularity contest a challenge."

Wes wanted to refute the not-beautiful part but he kept his mouth shut, sensing he would spook her and keep her from telling him more.

She ran her teeth over her lip and picked at a

loose thread on the pillow. "All the pressure I put on myself took its toll. I started flipping out over minor things—a B on a test or getting a reporter position instead of editor on the paper. The little failures sent me into a pretty dangerous depression. An angry one. My dad finally noticed, and my doctor sent me to a therapy group for teens. I was willing to go but didn't want anyone to know, so I attended one in the next town over."

Wes propped his elbow on the cushion of the chair, leaning his head on his hand, listening.

"Trevor Lockwood was there," she said, a hollowness in her voice.

"Trevor, one of the shooters."

She glanced his way briefly and nodded. "Yeah. He'd threatened suicide a few months before. So he was in the group for depression, too. He was the only other kid from my high school, and I didn't know much about him except that he'd transferred into Long Acre High sophomore year, had that stoner vibe, and took remedial classes. We ran in completely different crowds at school. But the therapy was kind of ridiculous. The head therapist talked to us like we were kindergartners, and she used all these woo-woo, new age techniques. So even though Trevor and I weren't friends at school, we ended up talking a lot after group and bonding over how lame we thought the whole thing was."

A shiver of foreboding went through Wes. "You became friends."

Her gaze went back to the loose string. "It was a weird thing, that bond we developed. The friendship existed in an alternate universe, at least in my mind. A secret society kind of thing. At school, we didn't acknowledge each other. It was like an unspoken agreement."

"Understandable. Therapy is private."

Her fingers dug into the pillow. "Then I messed it all up."

Wes could see the tension roll through her, stiffening her posture. "What do you mean?"

Her throat worked as she swallowed. "One night after group, I'd had a really rough week and was feeling all this pressure. I got this urge to just...not be me for a little while. To feel what it was like to not give a damn. To be free of all of it." She shook her head as if admonishing her former self. "So I asked Trevor if he wanted to go somewhere, do something, anything.

"He said we could go out to the lake and get high, but I wasn't going to do any kind of drug that would stay in my system. So he bought some liquor with a fake ID and shoplifted some snacks from a convenience store. Of course, I didn't go in with him because I wasn't willing to take the fall for it." She blew out a breath. "Which makes me sound like a selfish bitch."

"Or a smart, law-abiding girl."

She frowned. "But I wasn't that night. I was going to drink that liquor and eat that food. I just wanted someone else to take all the risk on my behalf. It wasn't fair. But he did it without thinking twice, even though I knew he would be facing big consequences if he'd gotten in trouble again. He just...did it. Maybe I didn't believe he would."

Wes's unease grew. Once upon a time, he'd been a lot like Trevor. And he knew exactly why a kid would take that risk. A pretty girl who wanted to spend some time alone with you was a great motivator.

"We drove out to the lake after that," she said, her voice soft, lost in the memory. "We both got tipsy—not wasted, but enough that it felt illicit, which was what I'd been after. All the pressure had stirred this surge of rebellion in me, and it felt exciting and powerful to push back against it for a little while. To give everyone the middle finger. But then I took it too far."

Wes stayed quiet, letting her go at whatever pace she needed.

She glanced over at him as if gauging his reaction but then looked away again. "I kissed him. Not because I was so into him, but because it felt dangerous and impulsive. My dad had drilled into me. Don't drink. Don't be alone with boys. Don't put yourself in compromising positions. I'd always listened. But now there I was, alone at the lake, buzzed, with this edgy boy who I wasn't supposed to be friends with, and I wanted to push back on all those rules. So I kissed him."

Wes ran a hand over the back of his head. "I'm guessing it was well received."

A despondent look crossed her face. "That was heady, too. That someone wanted me like that. I could feel how into it he was, how excited. That was new and thrilling to me. The wanting. The physical stuff. I'd been pining for my best guy friend for years by that point with no luck, so it felt good to be on the other end of all that desire." She tucked her hair behind her ears in an almost little-girl way, like she was back in that teenager's shoes. "But when it started to go further than I was ready for and began to feel a little too good, I put a halt to things. Stopped everything cold." She sighed. "Part of me wishes I could say he was aggressive about it or pressured me to keep going, so I could tell you he was always a villain. But he didn't. He was completely cool about it—stopped and apologized, made a joke about outdoor sex being a bad idea anyway. And he took me home."

Wes absorbed all of that, imagining the scene, the simple act of teenagers getting wrapped up in hormones and alcohol and new experiences. Almost everyone had a story like that. But this was no ordinary experience in a life. That boy Rebecca had kissed would become a mass murderer. How could a kid who'd been a gentleman with a girl take such a sharp turn? Had something happened in between? A bad year. A family trauma. "How long before the shooting did all this happen?"

"Weeks," she said softly.

Wes's stomach flipped over. "*Weeks?*"

Her eyes glistened again. "After that night, I came back to my senses, realized how stupid I'd acted, how close I'd gotten to doing something really reckless. Plus, I was embarrassed. I skipped the next few weeks of therapy group to avoid him. I continued to pretend I didn't know him at school, though I'd noticed him trying to catch my eye a few times. I basically shut him out completely. But then one day after lunch, when I was passing out flyers for a student council event, he stopped me." She swiped at her eyes. "He asked me to prom in front of a group of people, including Finn, my friend I had a crush on. People were looking at me, whispering. I panicked. Trevor was not someone I could be associated with at school."

Wes knew what was coming, but he stayed quiet, letting her get it out.

"I said…" Tears fell down her face and her fingers

squeezed the pillow. "I said, 'Who are you again?' and laughed." Her voice snagged on the word. "I *laughed* at him, Wes. Humiliated him in front of all those people. And I saw the look on his face. I saw that glimmer of decency and hope die in his eyes, saw how it hardened over. I killed something in him in that moment."

Wes's heart broke at the anguish in her voice. "Rebecca…"

She shook her head, tears flowing freely now. "That's why I can't get up and do those speeches my dad always wants me to do. Why I can't stop seeing Trevor every-where. Why you should run away from me far and fast." She looked at him. "Because I'm not a Long Acre survi-vor. I was an *instigator*. I was a linchpin. If I hadn't…"

Wes watched her crumble, her hurt ripping him in two. "Oh, baby. No, that's not…"

But she wasn't listening. She'd begun to sob, her shoulders shaking, so he gathered her into his arms and hugged her, letting her cry against his shoulder. He rubbed her back and pressed his lips to the crown of her head and held her, his mind lost in a spin.

Wes had his own experiences with guilt, but how the hell could any one person hold on to something this heavy for all this time and not completely lose it? Rebecca was carrying around the responsibility for so many people's deaths, for a national tragedy.

Most people wouldn't have given it another thought if they'd done what she'd done. She'd acted like a snotty teenager in a weak moment. Who hadn't? But of course Rebecca hadn't forgiven her sixteen-year-old immatu-rity. She'd been raised to be perfect, to always do the right thing. Her father didn't believe in second chances.

She'd made one mistake and believed she'd lit the fuse to the bomb.

"I'm sorry I pretended to be someone else," she said into his shirt. "I'm not who you think I am. I'm a horrible person. And soon everyone else is going to know it, too."

"Hush," he said, smoothing her hair. "You think this changes who I think you are?"

"Of course it does."

He shifted and tipped her face up to him, but she wouldn't look at him. "You're not a horrible person. A horrible person wouldn't have given that incident a second thought, would've never entertained any blame."

Tears sparkled on her lashes. "Wes, what I did…"

"Was what a million other teenagers do every day," he finished. "They turn down dates. They get rejected. They get embarrassed. They try to save face in front of friends. They get crushes. They get their hearts broken. They tease and get teased. They sometimes make bad decisions because they're young and inexperienced. Because they're *kids*. They get scared out of their minds because life is overwhelming and weird and hard to figure out when you're so new at it." He wiped away one of her tears with his knuckle.

"If you want to play the blame game, where would it end? How about placing blame on your dad for putting so much pressure on you to be perfect and helping create the depression that sent you to that group? Or how about your mom for leaving? Or your crush for not dating you? Because then no Trevor kiss would've happened. Or what about the guy who sold the liquor to Trevor and helped start what happened at the lake? Or the group counselor for being ineffective? Or Trevor's and the other shooter's parents for not knowing their kids had access to guns? Or whoever provided guns to those kids in the first place?"

She stared at him, eyes bloodshot.

"You're a lawyer," he said. "You know how a story can be twisted to make anyone look like the villain. Look at what Steven's facing right now. We know he's not a bad person because we know the background and we know he's young. So were you. You were one very small piece in a tapestry of Trevor's life. In that one moment, you didn't create a murderer, Bec. Trevor was deeply troubled to do what he did. There were a million points in his life that coalesced to create that tragic night. *He*, ultimately, made that decision. He made a plan with the other kid. He killed people in cold blood. That is not your fault. You can't hold on to that blame. It's not yours to carry around."

Tears dripped onto the pillow, and she looked down.

"Rebecca," he said, reaching out to cup her face. "You are the most big-hearted person I've ever met. You bought me my dream when I'd lost it. You gave a group of kids who have next to nothing an amazing opportunity to do something great. You gave a kid who mugged you at gunpoint a second chance because you believed in him. Who else would do that? You are…a spectacular, loving, beautiful human being. Hell," he said, "you made a guy who'd sworn off relationships forever fall head over heels for you. If that isn't working miracles, I don't know what is."

Rebecca closed her eyes.

"You see, Bec, you've got it all wrong. You didn't

pretend to be someone else around me. You gave me the best gift. You let yourself be who you really are with me. Underneath all this hurt and trauma, all the pressure and expectations, this is you. I got to meet that girl, and I'm so damn lucky for it."

She opened her eyes and stared at him, something tender and fragile moving across her features. Something he'd been longing to see. A sliver of hope. A crack in the door.

He cleared his throat. "Frankly, what's unfair is that you showed me who you are and then expected me *not* to fall for you. Really, it was an impossible bar to set for me. I have an addictive personality, you know."

A tiny smile peeked out at that, a little twitch of the lips. "I've heard that rumor about you."

"I've also been told I'm cute. And smart. And highly insightful. You should listen to me."

"You are." She reached for his hand and let out a long sigh, laying her head against his shoulder. "You may also be impossible not to love back."

The words were simple and to the point, but they cut right through him and stole his air for a moment. "Hold up, *you love me back?*"

She lifted her head from his shoulder and gave him a *well, duh* look. "I'm a complete mess over you, Wes. That's not the point."

His chest filled with something big and powerful, a hot, sweet rush. "Oh, no, I think that's a big damn point, lawyer girl. In fact, I think that is *the* point of all the points. It's like the Grand Master of points. Like the point all the other points aspire to be."

"Wes, you're not getting it," she said, some fire

coming back into her tone. "Why the hell would you want to be with me after everything I've just told you? After everything you've seen? I'm a disaster right now. I'm in therapy for panic attacks and flashbacks. I'm about to lose my job because there's no way I'm dropping Steven's case, and my dad's going to go to the press. My life is about to *explode*."

He shifted so he could face her fully and put his hand on her shoulder. "Bec, you're the one who's not getting it. I want to be with you *because* you're the woman who's going to let her life explode to help a kid who needs it. And you're not a mess. You're a human who's been through some tough shit. We both have things we're working on. I'm not exactly without my own baggage. I will always be a recovering alcoholic. I'm rebuilding my life because I *did* lose my job and a lot of other things. I don't want to be with you because I want some neat and perfect life, lawyer girl. I just want *you*. All the parts of you—scars, life explosions, misguided love of boxed macaroni and cheese… I'm all in."

"You…" Rebecca stared at him for a long moment, a confused expression on her face, and then fresh tears slipped down her cheeks. The fight seemed to go out of her, and she touched her forehead to his. "Wes."

He ran a hand over the back of her head and closed his eyes. "Bec."

They stayed that way for a few seconds, her breath easing into a slower, calmer rhythm, but Wes's whole body stayed tense, his words and confessions and offer floating between them unmoored.

Finally, her voice broke the silence. "You lie. You're never going to let go of the mac-and-cheese thing."

The breath he'd been holding whooshed out of him. He lifted his head and cupped her face, erasing her tears with his thumbs as something rusty unlocked inside him. She wasn't going to run away. He swallowed past the emotion lodged in his throat. "Okay, you're right. The cheese is powdered. That's just unnatural and uncalled for."

A tear-choked laugh tumbled out of her, and he inhaled that sound like it was a drug.

"But all the rest is truth, Bec," he said softly. "I know you think relationships are a bad bet, but taking a gamble has two sides to it. Sometimes you push all your chips in, and...you win."

"And you think we're going to win?"

"I don't know," he said honestly. "But what I do know is that I don't want to walk away without finding out. The biggest risk isn't the risk of failing. It's the risk of letting what could turn out to be the love of your life slip through your fingers because you were too scared to take a chance. I'd rather have a failure than a regret."

Her lips curved at that. "You're a pretty smart guy, Wes Garrett."

He shrugged. "Meh, I'm a C student at best."

She burst into a laugh at that, her hand flying to her mouth when she snorted.

He smirked. "What? Something I said?"

She shook her head, eyes smiling. "Nothing. And you're an A-plus. Don't let anyone tell you any different."

He dragged her into his lap and kissed her.

When he pulled back, she pushed his hair away from his eyes and looked at him with a bewildered expression. "How the hell did I manage to fall for you in a month?"

The words filled him up inside, made his chest

expand. "Well, first of all, I'm spectacular in bed, so there's that."

She gave him a droll look.

"And I cooked and fed you delicious food, so it really couldn't be helped. Also, I've heard a rumor that you can be impulsive."

She grinned, the effect like sunshine after so much grief. "Maybe I am."

"Maybe that's okay." He waggled his eyebrows. "Wanna go to Vegas?"

She poked a finger to his chest. "Slow your roll, chef. First, we have a kid to free from jail. Then we'll talk."

"That, lawyer girl, is a deal." Wes pressed his lips to hers, savoring the privilege of being able to do that again, of having her here in his arms. "So do you know what you're going to do about your dad?"

Her shoulders lifted with a deep breath, her expression sobering. "Yes. The only thing I can do."

"What's that?"

She lifted her gaze to his. "I have to tell my story first."

# chapter
# TWENTY-NINE

TARYN ADJUSTED HER DARK-RIMMED GLASSES WHILE fiddling with the settings on the small voice recorder she had in her hand. Rebecca sat across from her at a table in the university's psychology building Monday afternoon and tried not to jump out of her skin. Outside in the hallway, student voices chattered in a dull drone as they changed classes. Rebecca rubbed her damp palms on her jeans.

Taryn looked up, concern heavy in her brown eyes. "You sure you want to do this, Bec?"

Rebecca inhaled deeply and nodded. "Yeah. I need to. And if it helps your research, all the better."

Taryn spent part of her time teaching forensic psychology at the university, but most of her day was spent researching the criminal mind—the young, developing criminal mind, in particular. Rebecca couldn't imagine wanting to poke around in those dark places, but she understood Taryn's drive to get answers. After her younger sister was killed in the Long Acre shooting,

Taryn had vowed to figure out ways to prevent those kinds of tragedies from happening, to come up with ways to identify troubled kids before they jumped from troubled to deadly.

Rebecca wasn't sure those kinds of whys or hows could be pinpointed, but she was going to give Taryn all the information that she had. Maybe her experience with Trevor could offer some insight and help in some way. Regardless, Rebecca would rather tell her close friend about what had happened between her and Trevor than tell a reporter who would sensationalize everything. The information would get out either way, but at least Rebecca could put it into the most useful hands first.

Taryn pushed her headband back, keeping her cloud of tight, black curls away from her face, and sent Rebecca a tilted smile as she set the recorder between them. "All right. I've delayed enough. We should be good to go. Is it okay to admit that I'm trembling?"

Rebecca cocked her head to the side. "That's supposed to be my job, doc."

Taryn rubbed her lips together, smoothing her bright-pink lip gloss. "I know, but this is a first for me. I've never interviewed a friend about Long Acre. This feels more intense."

Rebecca's chest squeezed tight. "Honey, if you don't feel up to this, please don't do it on my behalf. Believe me, I know how important it can be to keep those closets locked. If you're not ready to—"

Taryn shook her head, something resolute coming into her eyes. "Oh no, don't you go giving me a pass, lady. That's not why I'm telling you."

Rebecca sighed and ran her fingers over her ponytail,

a nervous habit from childhood that seemed to reappear at times like these. "Maybe I'm trying to give myself a pass. I'm afraid that when I'm done with this, you're going to hate me."

Taryn gave her a pointed look. "Don't even go there, Bec. I know you. Nothing you're going to say is going to make me hate you. And, trust me, we all have things about that night that we wish we could take back. I know I do."

Rebecca looked up, catching the tightening of Taryn's expression, the grip of something sharp overtaking her friend—pain, grief, *guilt*? But the moment was gone as quickly as it had appeared.

"We're doing this interview," Taryn said resolutely, not giving Rebecca the chance to ask what had put that anguished look on her face. "That's not in question. I'm just letting you know that I'm probably not going to be one hundred percent put together about it. I reserve the right not to react like a proper impassive researcher."

"You absolutely have that right." Rebecca reached out and put her palm up on the table between them. "And who in the hell is one hundred percent put together anyway? Maybe if I'm fifty percent and you're fifty percent, we'll make it to the other side of this thing."

Taryn put her hand in Rebecca's, her smooth brown skin warm against Rebecca's cold fingers. "We've got this. We will do the interview. I will take notes. We will cry. And then afterward, we're going to dinner to get a big-ass margarita with our puffy eyes and sloppy mascara while you tell me all about that new boyfriend of yours."

Rebecca smiled. "It's a deal."

Taryn sat back in her chair, took a breath that lifted her

shoulders, and hit the record button on the device. "Okay, Rebecca, tell me about when you first met Trevor…"

—⁓—

Rebecca headed down the hallway toward her office Tuesday morning, vaguely hungover from too many margaritas with Taryn and feeling like a stranger in a strange land. The phones were ringing and keyboards clicking as normal. The muted steps of expensive shoes on thick office carpet played bass. And the scent of slightly stale coffee filled the air. It was the same world she'd visited as a kid when she'd stopped in to see her dad. The same world she entered almost every weekday of her adult life. The law firm that would one day be part hers. But now that wouldn't be so, and she was an intruder in a home that used to be her own.

She hadn't made any announcements yet, and her father hadn't returned her calls, but the decision was already made. She was officially representing Steven. She'd told her father in one of the messages she'd left him that she was going to tell her secret. Then, she'd done it yesterday, telling Taryn every part of her short-lived connection with Trevor. No going back now.

Marian's desk was empty when Rebecca passed. That was a small relief. Rebecca didn't quite know how to break the news to her assistant yet. Ideally, she'd take Marian with her, but wherever Rebecca set up shop, she wasn't going to be able to offer Marian all the perks and benefits she got here at a big firm.

Rebecca grabbed a few empty boxes from near the copy machine and headed into her office, prepared to call all of her current clients and then pack up her office. She stepped inside, her vision blocked by the armful of boxes, and headed in the general direction of her desk.

"Rebecca."

She let out a startled yelp and dropped the boxes, the cardboard tumbling to the floor in an avalanche.

Rebecca put a hand to her chest when she saw where the voice had come from. "Jesus, Dad, you scared me. What are you doing in here?"

Her father was standing near her window, his hands tucked in his pockets, a joyless expression on his face. "The doorman called me when you arrived. I wasn't sure you were coming back."

She pulled her shoulders back, fighting to keep a calm, civil attitude. "I have personal items to pack up. Plus, I need to call all of my current clients and transfer their cases to the other attorneys."

Her father stepped forward and gave her an evaluating look. "I'm not going to prevent you from taking your current clients with you, Rebecca. If they want to follow you, that's their choice."

She bent over and restacked the boxes, needing to do something with her hands. "That's okay. I can wrap up the cases that are in the final stages, but afterward, I'm getting out of the divorce business."

"You're—" Her father scoffed. "Right. Of course you are. Who cares that you've spent all these years building your expertise in that area? Seeing the reality of relationships every day would put a damper on your new romance. Can't let that happen. Don't want to mess with the fantasy he's feeding you."

She straightened and crossed her arms, her hackles

going up. "Enough. What exactly is your problem with Wes? You don't even know him."

"I know enough," he said. "I did my research. I know he's divorced and that you represented his wife, that he cheated on her. That he threw a tantrum in court."

"The tantrum was justified, and he didn't cheat."

"Right. I'm sure that's what he told you. I also know he has a DUI, a stint in rehab, and a juvenile record. His parents are career criminals, and he declared bankruptcy after the divorce," her father said, rattling off his list like he was proud of it. "And I've been around long enough to know that a smart, successful, wealthy attorney who's still single in her thirties is a prime target for someone like him."

Rebecca's fingernails dug into her arms. "Right. We're ripe for the picking, us thirty-one-year-old spinsters. We just want our princes to come and save us from it all."

"That's not—"

"Yes it is," she said. "You say I'm smart, but you must not believe that. You must think I'm some desperate, pitiful thing who can be tricked because she's so needy for some male attention. Come on, Dad, are you listening to yourself?"

"Smart people can be stupid when it comes to relationships," he barked. "Believe me, I know. I married your mother."

"I am not being stupid," Rebecca said, her voice carrying across the room and ricocheting off the wall of windows. "I'm not desperate for attention. Getting a guy in bed is really not that hard."

He cringed.

"I don't *need* a man. I wasn't looking for one. But I met Wes, and yeah, on paper, all that stuff in his past looks awful. But that paper doesn't list all the other things. Like how he's overcome a terrible childhood and has a loving adopted family now. Or how he came out of addiction and has rebuilt a new career at the school, helping kids who are struggling. You don't know that when I was being mugged, he ran up to intervene, to help a stranger, with no hesitation even though it put him in danger. He is a *good* man. He is going to be part of my life. And if you don't want to be anymore because of that, then I guess that's your choice. But know that it's not mine. You are creating this rift. Not me."

"I want what's best for you. I want *the* best for you," he said, some of the edge leaving his tone, earnestness replacing it.

"No," she said, a pang of sadness moving through her. "You want what you *think* is best for me. Those are two different things. Like keeping Mom out of my life. I'm sure you thought that was best, but it left me *without a mother*. Maybe she wasn't the greatest—yes, she made bad choices—but she was the only one I had. If you hadn't sent her away, maybe I would've had someone to call when I needed a woman's advice. Maybe I wouldn't have felt so alone all the time or like I was someone who was easy to abandon."

Her father's Adam's apple bobbed, something pained moving over his features. "Rebecca…"

"I know you've done what you thought was best for me in my life. I know you love me. And you did give me so much. I love working in law. I love that you taught me to be independent and tough and driven." She put her hand to her chest. "So much of who I am is because I had you in my corner. Mom left. Even if she wanted to come back, she left in the first place. You stayed. You did the hard stuff," she said, the words spilling out of her like hot tears. "But that doesn't mean there weren't holes and gaps. It doesn't mean you always did the best thing. It doesn't mean that you're not seeing things through warped glass.

"Right now, you are *not* doing what's best for me," she said emphatically. "You are about to cut me off from the only family I have. You are about to take away my father. Simply because I love someone and want to see how that goes and because I want to take a case that means something to me. You are about to *lose* me, Dad." Her voice caught in her throat, and she had to take a breath. "Is that all I'm worth? The cost of being right?"

Her father's eyes were locked on her, and to her astonishment, they began to shine in the fluorescent lights of her office. He pulled his hand from his pocket and swiped a hand down his face as if trying to erase what he'd revealed. "Rebecca, I don't want to lose you. You're my daughter. You're what gets me up in the morning. You have been since the day you were born."

Rebecca's chest tightened, and the inside of her nose burned.

"But this… It's so hard to watch," he said, eyes going liquid again. "You have this path that will lead you to so much, a partnership, a stable career. This firm is supposed to be yours one day. You have a legacy that you've earned. I don't want you to throw it away for a man. Or for some punk kid who needs to be in jail."

Rebecca took a deep breath and stepped forward. She

reached out and took her dad's hands in hers, giving them a squeeze. "Dad, I hear what you're saying. I know you're worried about me. But you have to let me mess up. I don't think I'm making a mistake on either of these decisions, but if I am, so what? You've raised me to be tough enough to handle the falls. And I know we are on different sides of the fence on the issue with Steven's case, but that's okay.

"Tell the press we have different political views on that matter. Tell them whatever you want. I've already told the truth about what happened with Trevor to a friend who's going to use it in her research, so it's not a secret anymore. But you've got to let me do my own thing. You have to let me try. And hey," she said, lightening her tone, "if I fail, think of all the I told you so's you'll get to throw my way. It will be like hitting the fatherly lottery."

He scoffed at that, but a hint of a smile touched the corners of his lips.

"Please don't make this an ultimatum, Dad," she said softly as she let go of his hands. "We don't always agree because you raised me to be headstrong. Don't punish me for being like you."

He lifted his eyes at that and let out a sigh, rubbing the lines on his forehead. "Someone taught you how to argue a point."

She arched a brow. "Uh-huh. Wonder who that could be."

"I still think you're making a mistake."

She could hear the shift in his tone, the white flag. She gave him a little smile. "Noted."

"And I can't have the firm associated with that kid's case," he said gruffly. "My campaign…"

"I know. That's okay. I think striking out on my own may be good for both of us. Give us some breathing room." She gave his shoulder a squeeze. "Maybe give us a chance to practice a father-daughter relationship instead of a boss-employee one."

He smirked. "I guess that wouldn't be terrible, even though I do love being the boss. Being your dad is better."

Something tight and tangled loosened inside her chest. "So you're firing me?"

He inhaled a long breath and adjusted the knot on his tie. "Yes. I am."

She grinned, and though she hadn't done it in years, she put her arms around him for a hug. He still smelled like the same woodsy cologne she'd grown up with, and that made her want to cry. "Thanks, Dad."

He settled his arms around her and patted her back in that awkward way he had. "I love you. And I'm sorry that I never told you about your mom. I was trying to protect you. She would've left again. I didn't think either of us could handle it twice."

She closed her eyes. That was one thing she at least knew for sure. Her dad was difficult and bossy and set in his opinion, but she never doubted that he loved her and wanted to keep her safe. She'd seen his face when he'd walked into the hospital room after the Long Acre shooting. That grief-stricken look that said he was being ripped apart on the inside. The tearful relief when he realized she was going to be okay. That was not something easily forgotten. Underneath all the other stuff, that was what mattered.

He released her from the hug and gave her a stern look. "*Do not* go and get married behind my back. You get a dangerous look in your eye when you talk about this man of yours."

Rebecca laughed. Wes *was* dangerous. In all the very best ways. "I'll be sure to send you a ticket to Vegas. We're leaving next week."

"*Rebecca Anne Lindt.*"

She gave him an evil grin and lifted her palms. "Kidding, Dad. Kidding. I'm in no rush."

No rush at all.

She was going to savor every moment because for the first time in longer than she could remember, she felt free.

Free of her secret. Free of her father's expectations. But most of all, free of herself and the protective fence she'd put around her life.

Maybe she'd finally gotten there.

Maybe she'd reached the good part.

# epilogue

## SIX MONTHS LATER

Wes washed the raw egg off his hands and reached into the cooler to find more butter. He'd put his favorite old-school rock playlist on low and was singing along to Autograph's "Turn Up the Radio," making the guitar sounds with his mouth and tapping his fingers on the fridge door to the drumbeat. His birth parents hadn't left him with much, but they had introduced him to his favorite era of music.

There was something about rock music and cooking that paired well. Finding notes that went together was like finding flavors that complemented each other. Being bold and loud with creations but still fine-tuning the nuances that made the dish sing. Not being afraid to take risks. Fighting hard not to be a one-hit wonder.

Making a comeback when it was time.

He found the butter and grabbed a serrano pepper to add to the Southwestern Croque Monsieur. When he closed the cooler, he was still singing along and playing air drums with the stick of butter and the pepper. He turned toward the griddle and almost dropped everything when he saw Rebecca standing in the doorway of the school bus grinning at him.

"Damn, lawyer girl. You scared me. I thought you said you were meeting up with Taryn tonight." He took a few strides to cross the small kitchen space inside the school bus and leaned down to kiss her.

"My spidey senses are finely tuned to alert me when there is delicious food to be had," she said, wrapping her arms around his waist. "Taryn and I finished up early. She's decided to use my information for her research but keep it all anonymous since my dad decided not to go public with anything. I told her I was okay if she released it, but she said the media attention would be distracting and unhelpful."

Wes eyed her. "How do you feel about that?"

She shrugged. "I had come to terms with my connection to Trevor being out there, but I know the media would just sensationalize it. It could hurt the firm, and I don't want it to affect the kids whose cases I'm handling. So I can't say I'm unhappy about it not going public. But I'm glad I finally told the story and that Taryn can use it for something more important than a news story for people to gawk at. That matters."

"It definitely does. And now you get to be home and leave that behind and eat my food."

Somewhere in the yard, Knight barked.

Rebecca laughed. "He heard the word 'food.' But yeah, when you told me you might do some recipe testing, I rushed here. I didn't want to leave you with only a dog as a taste taster. They have notoriously untrustworthy palates."

"True. They do lick their own butts."

"Right. So I am here to save you from that horror."

He grinned. "So thoughtful and self-sacrificing."

She nodded sagely. "Yes. You are very lucky I arrived in time."

The simple words swept through him and filled him up inside. Rebecca had no idea how true that was. Yes, he was lucky to have her here tonight, but it was so much more than that. He thought back to that lonely night walking down the street after the Shirtless Chef party, how empty and angry he'd felt, how lost. He couldn't predict now where that road would've led him if he hadn't stumbled upon Rebecca that night, but he had a good idea it would've been nowhere good.

"You must be hungry. You didn't even change clothes yet." Her hair was piled into a messy bun atop her head, something she liked to do after she got home from work where she had to be all buttoned-up and lawyerly, but she hadn't changed out of her pinstriped suit yet. The whole effect just made her look powerful and hot, which he didn't realize he had a thing for until he'd started dating Rebecca. He tugged on her jacket lapels and brought her in for a kiss.

"Mmm," she said, smiling as he released her from the kiss. "I didn't want to risk missing anything."

"Well, you're just in time. I was about to test out Steven's idea for a Southwestern Croque Monsieur. We tried it in class today, but I want to make sure that if we put it on the menu, we can turn it out for customers quickly with this equipment."

A look of affectionate warmth crossed her face. "He's coming up with new ideas a lot lately. I guess he's settling in with his aunt?"

"Seems to be." Steven had been cleared of charges, thanks to Rebecca, and Steven's father had lost custody. But it'd been a transition for Steven to move in with an aunt he barely knew who lived in the Austin hills, far from his old neighborhood. But his aunt and her husband had been welcoming and had done everything they could to ease the transition, even letting Steven continue to attend the after-school program despite it being a half-hour drive from their neighborhood. "I think they've worked the growing pains out. He's not used to having people who actually care where he's going and what time he'll be back. But he's been in a great mood the last two weeks. He also may have developed a crush on Lola. He's been trying to cook things he knows she'll like and then getting all red-faced and awkward when she compliments his food."

"Uh-oh." Rebecca laughed. "Warning: drama ahead."

"I don't know," he said with a shrug. "I think Lola's into it. She watches him when he's not looking with this little smile on her face. It's really kind of sweet."

"Aww, you're such a softie. I bet that one day they'll make a beautiful restaurant together," Rebecca said, slipping past him into the truck and shutting the door behind her so Knight didn't sneak in. She snagged a pinch of shredded Monterey Jack off the cutting board and popped it in her mouth. "So, guess what I got today."

"Sexier? Because I think that actually happened. That suit is doing things to my imagination that could shame the paint off this bus," he said, giving her a slow up-and-down look. "You should undo another button on that shirt. It's hot in here. Wouldn't want you to faint."

She smirked and playfully undid her top button, letting her white blouse gape open enough for him to see the edges of her lacy bra. "Better?"

The front of his jeans got a little tighter. "Much."

"But that's not what I'm talking about."

He turned off the flattop griddle, his skin now truly overheated. "What did you get?"

She reached behind her and pulled something from the waistband of her slacks. She held up an envelope and grinned. "Permission for Adele to park her pretty yellow butt at the food-truck park, three spots over from Dev."

Wes's mouth fell open. "Really? Like, no more paperwork? No more red tape? They told me—"

"They were giving us the runaround is what they were doing, so I *may* have called in a small favor from my dad. He knew the guy who was dragging his feet on the permits and did his thing. We can roll Adele out for her debut next month, which should give the class enough time to wrap up all the finishing touches, finalize the menu, and get it out of my backyard."

"You're serious," he said.

"I am."

Wes crossed the small space, a rush of excitement going through him, and picked her up off her feet. "It's really happening."

"It's so happening!" she announced, laughing as he spun her around and nearly knocked everything off the narrow counters.

He gave her a hard kiss and sat her on top of the bare prep table, parking himself between her knees. "The kids are going to be so excited."

"Yes. The kids," she said, tracing her fingertips down his chest and sending hot tendrils of desire curling through his body. "It's totally about the kids."

He chuckled. "Okay, maybe I'm a little excited about it."

She arched a brow and sent a pointed look downward, tucking a finger in his waistband and tugging. "Well, you're excited about something, chef."

He braced his hands on either side of her and crowded her against the darkened windows. "Oh, that has nothing to do with the truck. That has everything to do with my very beautiful, very unbuttoned lawyer girl spread out on my prep table. I'm suddenly not so motivated to do recipe testing."

She looped her arms around his neck, her blue eyes wicked. "Maybe I'm suddenly not so hungry."

"A shame." He kissed down the curve of her neck, his hand sliding along her thigh. "Guess we'll have to find something better to do to work up an appetite."

"We can't do this here," she said, tilting her head back to give him better access to her neck. "Anyone could see us. And I'm pretty sure it would be a health code violation."

He chuckled against her skin and blindly reached out to find the light switch. The bus went dark except for the moonlight spilling through the narrow, horizontal windows. "Now, no one can see us."

"Wes," she gasped.

"Hold on, lawyer girl. We're about to christen Adele."

—⁓—

Rebecca's heart was thumping hard in her chest and her blood pumping hot as Wes guided her legs around his waist and then lifted her off the table. Her rational side said they should go in the house. There was a perfectly good bed, couch, or living room floor to violate. But when Wes carried her to the back of the bus where they'd had enough room to set up a VIP table with two bench bus seats flanking it, a sharp thrill went through her.

Wes set her atop the table and pulled off his T-shirt, leaving him in just the black bandanna that held back his hair, his tattoos, and a pair of worn jeans. Her libido gave a sharp kick, and she licked her lips. "Maybe we should rethink this Shirtless Chef thing. We'll make millions."

Wes gave her a rougish smile. "Ready to share me already?"

"No, you're right," she said with a nod. "No sharing. There'd be blood."

He braced a hand beside her on the table and unbuttoned her slacks with the other. "I have to say, this slightly violent side of you makes me a little hard."

She reached down and slid her hand over the front of his jeans, the stiff length of him hot against her palm. "Feels like more than a little."

"Well, my woman is about to be stripped naked and wearing only moonlight and a smile soon, so what else would you expect?"

She smiled as he tugged her slacks and panties down her legs. *My woman*. Once upon a time, that probably would've raised her feminist hackles. She didn't belong to anyone. But with Wes, it pushed all her buttons because she'd finally figured out what people really meant when they said things like that. From the outside looking in, she'd never gotten it. Now she did. She was his, and he was hers because they chose to entrust their hearts to each other. A bold and scary choice, but one that gave her fear no longer.

She'd never felt more right about any decision in her life.

Wes pushed her jacket off her shoulders and then she unbuttoned her blouse, letting it and her bra fall to the floor. He gave her a ravenous look that made a hot shiver run over her skin.

He cupped her breast and ran a roughened thumb over her nipple, making desire curl low and liquid in her belly. Then he was lowering himself to his knees, kissing each part of her along the way. Mouth, neck, breast... His tongue tasting every inch of her. Sternum, belly, hip... Wet, stirring kisses that left flames burning in their wake. The slope of her pelvis, her inner thigh...

Her fingers curled around the edge of the steel table, need pulsing hard at the center of her. "Wes..."

"Patience. This is a multicourse meal." The tip of his tongue tasted the inside of her knee and then trailed upward, making her muscles clench and her back arch. "I want to enjoy every bite of it."

He was going to kill her. Just make her melt like cheese on a griddle and slide right onto the floor. But when she looked down at him and saw the strong lines of his face in the moonlight, the intent look in his eyes, she knew he was torturing himself as well. The chef knew how to savor, how to build up for the main course so that every morsel provided the ultimate satisfaction. He wasn't going to let either of them go hungry.

She lay back on the table, not trusting her muscles to hold her up, and he teased her for a little longer with his tongue, with his skilled fingers, with his dirty words. But when she cried out his name, the begging note cracking in her voice, he finally relented. He kissed the center of her, dragging his tongue over her clit one last time and then slipped his fingers out of her.

He stood, his gaze devouring her as he undid his jeans and shoved them down. The fact that he didn't kick them off just made her burn hotter. He was desperate now too. Hungry.

He took himself in his hand and gave his cock a stroke as he stepped between her legs, dragging all her attention to the filthy, toe-curling display. She reached out and put her hand over his, following his movements for a moment, her fingers getting slick with his arousal.

Wes grunted under his breath and took her hand in his, bringing it to his mouth and kissing her knuckles. "Keep that up, and this will be done quickly."

She smiled and leaned back on her elbows. "I have trouble keeping my hands off you."

He tucked his hands behind her knees and moved closer, rubbing the head of his erection against her and setting off every needy nerve ending inside her. "I know the feeling. I guess addiction isn't always a bad thing."

"Not this time."

Wes pushed inside her, filling that empty, aching space in her body and all the formerly empty spaces in her heart. The connection electrified every sensitive inch of her, and her head tipped back in pleasure. Wes was done with the teasing, his hips pumping deep and steady.

"Touch yourself," he said, the words thick with need. "I want to see my girl take what she needs."

In her former life, those words would've made her freeze up. Sex had always been such a clandestine affair in the dark. A balance of hiding her scars and trying not to overthink things. Now, no fear entered her system. With Wes, she always felt beautiful and sexy. No performance, no smoke and mirrors, no covers to hide beneath. Just her. Naked and free. In every way possible.

She slipped her hand between them and touched herself where she liked. Wes made a pained sound. "I'm never going to be able to look at this table again without picturing this. We're going to have to sell the bus, or I'll get nothing done."

She laughed, though the sound came out choked and twined with a sound of pleasure. "Worth it."

"So worth it." He picked up the speed of his thrusts, his chest damp and glistening with exertion, and she forgot how to respond to any kind of conversation.

She closed her eyes and tilted her head back. The feel of him inside her, her slippery fingers, and him watching her were too much. Her body was racing past any kind of control. "Wes…"

"*Bec.*" Her name was a plea, and she felt herself go over, crying out and arching on the steel table, the metal warm beneath her. Wes followed quickly behind, burying deep as he came, and gripping her legs like he would fall apart.

A satisfied moan rocked through the interior of the bus as they both floated back down to earth. Wes braced himself on his elbows, poised above her and breathing hard. "The bus is going to need a good, hard cleaning."

Rebecca grinned up at him. "Butt prints on a table are definitely a health code violation."

He laughed, the thunderous sound filling her up from the inside. "Yep. Don't care right now, though."

"Me neither. This was just what I needed. *You*."

He peered down at her, and the look that came across his face nearly broke her in two. He kissed her forehead. "You are the best part of my day, Bec. I'm so glad you're home."

She closed her eyes and let the words melt into her. *Home*.

All her life that word had been barbed. Home was the place she'd almost run away from when her mom had left. Home was the empty hallways when her dad worked late. Home was Long Acre where she'd lost so many people and so much of herself.

Home had never felt like this. Like the right key sliding into the matching lock.

Like forever.

Finally, she was exactly where she was supposed to be.

She reached up and cupped his jaw. "I love you, Wes Garrett."

He kissed her again. "I love you back, Mrs. Garrett."

A tingly ripple of contentment went through Rebecca at the sound of that. No one knew to call her that yet, no one knew what they'd done on their seemingly spontaneous trip to Paris last weekend. "Think we should tell everyone yet?"

Wes smiled down at her, his handsome face so

familiar to her now but no less breath-stealing. Dimples appeared beneath his scruff. "We're going to freak everyone out."

"You look super worried about that," she said drolly.

He eased away from her and pulled up his jeans. "I'm not. I'm not worried what anyone thinks but you and me. I've never been so sure of a decision in my life."

She sat up and then let him drag her into his lap in the booth seat. She laid her head on his shoulder. "Me neither."

And that was the truth. She'd spent her life following the rules, doing what was proper, what was expected. Her one act of rebellion early on had cost her so much that she'd been terrified to ever stray off script again. But now she realized that the best parts of life were outside the lines, scribbled in the margins, in the parts without facts and rules and closing arguments. There, it was just feelings and intuition and knowing down to your bones that you'd found the person you wanted to be with forever.

So when she'd walked into that Paris church with Wes and promised him a lifetime, she'd never felt so reckless or so very sure of something in all her life.

Soon, they would tell everyone and make it official here. They'd plan a proper party to celebrate and invite family and friends.

But for now, forever was just for them.

*Here's a sneak peek at Roni Loren's next unforgettable book!*

# The One You Fight For

Shaw Miller made his coffee order at the counter of the bustling shop and dug a few bills from his wallet. He could feel the gaze and smile of the cashier on him as he plucked out the money, but he chose not to look up. He would need at least two cups of coffee and a different personality before he was in the mood for small talk.

The pretty redhead took the money and kept her gaze on him. "Hey, have we met before? I don't think I've seen you in here, but you look familiar for some reason."

He glanced up briefly and tried to appear nonchalant, even though the words sent his gut twisting into a knot. "I don't think so. But I've been told I have one of those faces."

"Maybe so. Or maybe I was just wishing I'd met you before." She gave him a sly grin.

The flirtation bounced off him like hail against a windshield. He shoved two bucks in the tip jar. "Where do I wait for my coffee?"

Her smile faltered a bit at his flat tone, but she cocked

her head to the right. "Over there. Chris will set you right up. And here—" She slid a loyalty card across the counter. "Next time we'll be even faster because we'll already know your order."

He pocketed the card and mentally scratched this coffee shop off his list of places to frequent. "Thanks."

"Anytime, darling."

*As long as anytime is never.*

With his coffee in hand, Shaw hurried out of the mocha-scented shop and into the cool morning. *You look familiar.* His long strides ate up the sidewalk as he headed to work, and he couldn't help checking over his shoulder to see if anyone was following—an old habit he couldn't seem to break.

Rivers, Shaw's best friend and the one who'd coaxed him back to this town, would tell him that he was overreacting. Rivers had assured him that his fears about returning to Austin were overblown. Shaw had changed his name, his look, and had cut the traceable ties to his old life as much as anyone could in the world of the internet. He'd covered all the bases. But the woman at the coffee shop had, for a moment, looked at him like she'd recognized him for real, and that had sent ice through his veins.

Shaw *wanted* to dismiss it as his own paranoia. It wouldn't be the first time that he'd thought someone was looking at him askance, only to be reading too much into it. Last night at the bar, he'd even had a brief snap of fear that the sexy singer who'd lost her shoe had looked at him with some hint of familiarity at first. But based on the fact that "James with a z" had been about to ask him to coffee, he knew he'd been wrong on that one. Of course, that hadn't meant he could accept her invitation—as much as he'd been tempted by it—but it did prove he was prone to thinking the worst.

Being stalked by the press for so many years made him see motives in everyone and feel like he was constantly under surveillance. But this time at the coffee shop, he'd seen real recognition in the woman's eyes. She just hadn't placed him. That was what had made the cold hand of fear grip his chest. Maybe later on today, her brain would click, and she'd realize who she'd been talking to. Maybe not. Either way, he wasn't going back to that coffee shop.

When he unlocked the back door of the soon-to-be-open Gym Xtreme, the steamy, chlorine-scented air hit him in the face like dragon breath. He grimaced and finished the rest of his coffee before tossing the cup in a trash can in the hallway. As Shaw entered the main part of the gym, his footsteps echoed in the cavernous warehouse space like he was in some horror movie, but fear was the last thing he felt when he stopped and looked around.

Sunlight streamed in from the skylights he and Rivers had gotten installed, but the main lights weren't on. Dust motes danced in the air, and the reflection off the pools painted blue patterns on the far wall. Despite the stuffy atmosphere and too-warm temperature, the tension in Shaw's shoulders eased. He closed his eyes and took a deep breath. A quiet gym was like entering his own version of church. It was the only place where his mind went still.

A clink of metal sounded to his left, and Shaw craned his neck that way. Rivers was balancing on a ladder as he adjusted something on a set of still rings in the gymnastic area, his blond hair slicked back from either sweat or a dip in the pool.

"How'd it go at the permits office?" Rivers asked, not looking away from his task but apparently hearing Shaw's footsteps. "I hope it's more fun than the DMV."

Shaw snorted as he walked over. "It made the DMV look like a rave, but we're all squared away. I's dotted, t's crossed, ridiculous fees paid."

"Great."

Shaw pulled his shirt away from his chest, the material starting to cling. "What happened to the AC? It feels like the inside of a gym sock and smells like a swim meet in here. Are you trying to save money on the electric bill?"

Rivers sniffed. "No, I'm not choosing this misery. The system froze up. I already had a guy out to look at it. He said to turn off the units for a few hours so they can thaw and to consider adding another one to cover this much square footage. He said once we have people in here, it will only get hotter quicker, and in the summer, we'll be completely screwed."

"Fantastic. More expenses," Shaw groused. The gym was bleeding money, and Shaw was having a hard time finding ways to stanch the wound. He'd helped Rivers plan this project down to the penny, but the old building had issues they hadn't been expecting, the equipment had been pricier to build than the original estimates, and the insurance was through the roof. If they didn't have a stellar opening month, they were going to drown before they ever made their first lap around the pool.

"I know. It sucks." Rivers glanced down at him. "But it is what it is. We can't have people passing out from the heat."

"At this rate, we're not going to have people at all because we're never going to open."

"It'll all work out." Rivers smiled, unperturbed, which tended to be a natural state for him—hence the reason Shaw was in charge of the business finances. Rivers returned to checking the still rings, yanking on them. "The smell is because I got all the pools treated again. The chemical balance was off. Now they're clean and ready to catch all the people who will fall off our badass challenges."

Shaw smirked and stepped under the rings. "I'm not sure I would market them that way. *Come to the gym that is sure to crush your spirits!*"

Rivers snorted. "Breaking spirits to rebuild them, Shaw." Rivers put a hand to his chest, a dramatic look on his face. "We're doing spiritual work here. The people need us."

"Yeah, okay, Reverend McGowan." Shaw eyed the other side of the high-ceilinged space that they'd converted into what would hopefully become Austin's premier extreme gym—a place for people who wanted to train and test themselves on ultimate athletic challenges. The side he and Rivers were on had more traditional exercise equipment and weights, along with a full setup for gymnastics. Equipment to get people ready for the harder stuff. Those things were vital, but the other side was hopefully where the money would be made. There were crazy-hard obstacles that tested strength and balance to the extreme—a huge curved wall to run up, rock climbing apparatus with nearly impossible angles, rolling cylinders to run over, ropes to swing on, various riffs on monkey bars to test upper body strength, and two deep swimming pools and a few foam pits that would catch people if they fell off the obstacles.

He and Rivers had come up with the idea after drinking too much beer one night and watching too many episodes of *Ninja Warrior Challenge* when Rivers had come into town to visit him. Shaw had thought his best friend was joking. They'd had crazy conversations like that before when they'd been college roommates. Rivers was an inventor by nature and a big talker. But then a month later, Rivers had shown up on Shaw's doorstep in Chicago with a stack of paperwork. Rivers had leased out the warehouse in Austin, quit his engineering job, and had developed a business plan—a plan that included Shaw moving back to the town he'd sworn he'd never return to and running the gym with him.

Shaw had refused. His life plan was to lie low and to never do anything that would have the press ever sniffing his way again. So what if he was miserable and unable to find decent work because of the reputation that followed him around like a plague? But when Rivers had laid out the plan—Shaw changing his legal name, the business being listed under Rivers even though they'd split the profits, and Shaw getting to handle the business's finances while also being a trainer—Shaw hadn't been able to walk away.

Besides the much-needed job, his friend had been offering him a taste of freedom he wasn't sure he deserved but that sounded like a dream. A fresh start. A job that would let him be in an environment he loved. His best friend—hell, his only friend—living down the street instead of across the country. The only sticking point was that it was in Austin, just down the road from the place of his nightmares, where everything in his world had been ripped away and burned to ashes. Where he wasn't just hated and feared in a general sense, but in very, very specific and personal sense.

He deserved that hate.

Shaw had come anyway, even when he knew it would be temporary. Everything in his life was. Putting down roots anywhere had always invoked trouble. He'd lost the right to roots. Secretly, Shaw had vowed to give time to this project for a year. He'd take some business classes to finish up the degree he'd had to abandon all those years ago and work as a trainer at the gym. He'd help Rivers get the business off the ground, build himself a little nest egg, buy a houseboat, and then leave Rivers to run the gym. He hadn't told Rivers that he wasn't planning on staying permanently, but he'd cross that bridge when necessary.

The close call in the coffee shop today had only confirmed the necessity of that plan. It'd probably been a false alarm this time, but it wouldn't be every time. He just hoped that he could actually make it the full year. The clock was already ticking. Someone would eventually recognize him. Someone would call the press. The cycle would start over.

"We're still on track to open next week?" Shaw asked, examining his friend's work on the rings.

"Yep." Rivers climbed down from the ladder and wiped his damp face with his T-shirt. "Well, open to the public at least. I signed us up for a charity event tomorrow morning."

"A what?"

"You're coming. Don't try to get out of it. If we get a

lot of interest, I may open for a sneak preview this week and give a few tours. I don't want to lose good leads if we get them. The event looks very Austin quirky, so I have a feeling it will get some press, which we desperately need."

"A charity event with *press?*" Shaw's stomach sank. "No way. You know I can't be anywhere near a goddamned camera."

Rivers made a dismissive sound. "You won't be. I've already thought this through. It's a Halloween run, costumes encouraged. We'll make sure you have a good one. You'll just be there to participate and give out flyers for the gym. As far as anyone knows, Lucas Shaw is just a trainer here. They have no reason to pay attention to you."

Shaw let out a breath, the name Lucas still sounding weird in his ear. He'd chosen to keep the Shaw part of his real name, Shaw Miller, because if he or Rivers slipped up and used the name Shaw, there would be an easy explanation. But getting used to an entirely new first name was going to take a while.

"I hate the idea of any press being involved," he groused.

"I know. But this is too good an opportunity to pass up," Rivers said.

Shaw couldn't deny that fact, and he did trust Rivers not to purposely expose him to anything that would blow his cover. He should be relieved that Rivers had handled things and created a great promotional opportunity, but the thought of charities and press still made him itchy. "Fine."

"Excellent." Rivers gripped his shoulder. "And don't worry, man. I told you I was willing to be the face of this thing, and I meant it. I'm not going to expose you to any of that. Plus, I have such a pretty face."

Shaw grunted.

"But if we want this business to be successful," his friend explained, "we have to jump on opportunities like this, get people excited and spreading the word. There needs to be some sizzle and pop."

Shaw gave him a droll look. "Sizzle and pop?"

"Yes. Don't make fun of my very technical marketing terms." Rivers nodded toward the equipment. "Now get up on these rings and tell me if they're going to break and kill someone."

Shaw smirked. "Nice. I've been demoted to guinea pig now?"

Rivers stepped back with an unrepentant grin. "Oink oink."

Shaw pulled his T-shirt over his head and tossed it at Rivers's face. "Guinea pigs don't oink, dumbass."

Rivers caught the T-shirt before it hit him and flipped it over his shoulder. He folded his arms and waited. "Show me what you've got, big man."

Shaw shook his head and dug a rubber band out of his pocket to pull his hair back. He didn't have any chalk for his hands or ring grips, and cargo shorts weren't ideal for flexibility, but he was just testing the things out, not doing a routine. He did a few quick shoulder and back stretches to make sure he was loose enough before reaching up. Rivers had set the rings lower than Olympic height so Shaw was able to jump up and grab them without assistance.

The rings felt achingly familiar in his hands as he hung from them, the scattered thoughts of the morning settling into singular focus as he adjusted his grip and made sure the whole apparatus wasn't going to fall apart on him. Once he felt confident the rings would support him, he lifted his weight, his arms working to keep the rings as still as possible, and raised himself up until his hips were even with the rings and his arms were taut. After a few seconds, he exhaled and spread his arms out to form a T with his body, an Iron Cross.

The strength and focus required to keep his body and the rings steady in that pose were like the rush of a drug, every part of him working toward the same goal. Shaw's muscles quivered with the effort, and he lifted himself again, tilting forward and swinging his legs behind and upward to invert the cross. He glued his gaze to a spot on the floor and tried to hold the upside-down position for as many seconds as his body would allow him. *One, two, three…*

"Damn," Rivers said. "It kills me a little that we can't market you. *Former Olympic-level gymnast will personally train you on feats of strength!* A photo of this alone would sell a shit-ton of memberships. Hell, I could probably fill up our rosters with all my single friends—gay or straight. We could oil you up and let them pay to ogle."

That made Shaw choke, and it broke his concentration. His muscles gave up the good fight, and he swung down out of the inversion. He dropped to his feet on the mat beneath with a muted thump, out of breath, his muscles burning from the effort. "Stop flirting, McGowan."

Rivers smirked and tossed Shaw's shirt back at him. "As if you'd be so lucky. You're not my type."

Shaw caught the T-shirt and tugged it back on with a grin, not insulted in the least. "Too straight, huh?"

"Straight?" Rivers crossed his arms and lifted a brow. "Oh, you actually still have an orientation? I thought yours was *monk.*"

Shaw's mouth flattened. "The rings work. We won't kill anyone."

He tried to move past his friend, but Rivers put a hand on his arm, halting him. "Come on, don't be like that. I'm not trying to be an asshole."

"You're not doing a very good job of it," Shaw grumbled.

Rivers didn't relent. "I'm just trying to wake you up a little. You've been here for months, and I have yet to see you do anything but go to the apartment, classes, and back here. Every time I ask you to come out with me and my friends, you have an excuse."

Shaw had, in fact, gone to a bar last night, but Rivers wouldn't count it even if Shaw told him. He'd gone in because he really wanted a drink, and the place was dark with loud music. Not a place to socialize. A Johnny Cash *I Drink Alone* kind of place. But somehow he'd ended up outside with a pretty woman, treading into way too dangerous waters.

The liquor had loosened his good sense, and he'd found himself drawn to the woman who'd sung her guts out and then run off stage, and not for the obvious reasons. The woman was a knockout with her cloud of dark curls, her black-rimmed glasses, and a pink blouse that had exposed just a hint of smooth brown skin at the open collar. She was all curves and quirky sophistication. Rivers would say *nerdy hot*. But Shaw didn't think her kind of *hot* needed any kind of qualifier.

But despite all that, the thing that had drawn him to her was the way she'd sung on stage. She hadn't opened her eyes the whole time, but once she'd gotten started, it was like she'd opened a vein and let it bleed onto the floor in front of them. Her voice hadn't been classically pretty. It'd been powerful and raw, with sandpaper rubbing the high notes. He'd felt each word of her song like she'd shoved the music directly into his chest, sending some sort of adrenaline straight into his system. He'd been sweating a little by the end. So when she'd stumbled by him, he couldn't stop himself from reaching out. He'd wanted to help her, but more than that, he wanted to know why she was running.

But he should've minded his own business. In those brief moments outside the bar, she'd nudged a part of him he'd thought he'd long cut the wires to—that part that said he should smile at her, flirt, and get her story. The part that said he could want the normal things a man could want.

What a fucking lie that was.

"I don't do clubs," he said to Rivers, shutting down the memory of last night, of him walking away from her like some coward who couldn't even manage to tell her good night.

"Fine, go to a movie then. A bar. Whatever. You don't need to do the monk thing anymore. I get why you shut yourself off from the social scene, but this is a big town. You have a new name. You don't look like the guy from the news stories anymore. Go out, have fun, take a roll in someone's bed."

"Riv," Shaw warned.

His friend raised his palms. "All I'm saying is don't rule out a simple hookup. It's unhealthy not to get laid at least every now and then." He gave Shaw an up-and-down look. "I don't know if it's wise to test out that use-it-or-lose it theory, you know? What if you actually *can* lose it?"

Shaw's fingers curled into his palms. "I'm going to make some calls to price out adding another AC unit."

"Shaw."

Shaw ignored him and kept walking. *Use it or lose it*. Right. Like his damn dick was going to fall off if he didn't have sex. Ridiculous.

The thought sent a shudder through him anyway. He tried to shake off his irritation as he made his way to the office. Rivers meant well. The guy thought he was helping, but these types of discussions were off the table. Rivers didn't get it.

Shaw had tried that road and had ended up getting serious with someone. The one woman he'd dated after the Long Acre shooting had acted as his confidant, had gotten him to open up about all the shit he was going through. Then, when things didn't work out between them, she'd sold her information to the press.

*An unnamed source close to the shooter's brother, former Olympic hopeful Shaw Miller, says he's drinking too much, angry, and a loner. Studies show that mental health issues run in families. Joseph Miller, the master-mind behind the Long Acre shooting, was reportedly suffering from…*

After reading the article, Shaw had thrown his laptop against the wall. He hadn't read a news story about himself or touched another woman since.

Sex was amazing. He missed it at an almost primal level. But no matter how good it could be, it wasn't worth risking feeling that exposed again, that…violated.

Rivers didn't get it. He couldn't.

No one could know what it felt like to be stripped down and no longer seen as an actual person but only as a news headline, a sensational sound bite to be sold and collectively hated. To be shamed. A name to be thrown around the dinner table and judged.

*Mass murderer's brother.*

*Fallen Olympic hopeful.*

*Shaw Miller* was now just a name on endless web pages. A cautionary tale. A common enemy.

He didn't get to meet a pretty woman at a bar and ask her out. He didn't get to want the things normal people wanted. That life had been stolen the day his brother had ended all those others.

*COMING JANUARY 2019*

# acknowledgments

I love having the chance to tell the stories of the Long Acre characters, so I want to thank the people who make it possible for me to do that.

To my family, for putting up with writer insanity—because there's a lot of that going on around here. I love you guys.

To my editor, Cat Clyne, for her insight, enthusiasm, and all those smiley faces in my edits. Thank you for loving these characters as much as I do.

To my agent, Sara Megibow, for her unwavering support, encouragement, and expertise. I'm glad I have you in my corner.

To the entire Sourcebooks team for championing these books, giving them beautiful covers, and for being so great to work with.

And as always, to my readers. I couldn't do this without you. Thank you for continuing to read my books. You keep reading, and I'll keep working hard to give you the best stories that I can. Deal?